WILD INSTINCT

ALSO BY T. JEFFERSON PARKER

Laguna Heat
Little Saigon
Pacific Beat
Summer of Fear
The Triggerman's Dance
Where Serpents Lie
The Blue Hour
Red Light
Silent Joe
Black Water
Cold Pursuit
California Girl
The Fallen
Storm Runners
L.A. Outlaws

The Renegades
Iron River
The Border Lords
The Jaguar
The Famous and the Dead
Full Measure
Crazy Blood
The Room of White Fire
Swift Vengeance
The Last Good Guy
Then She Vanished
A Thousand Steps
The Rescue
Desperation Reef

WILD INSTINCT

A NOVEL

T. JEFFERSON PARKER

MINOTAUR
BOOKS
NEW YORK

This is a work of fiction. All of the characters, organizations, and events portrayed in this novel are either products of the author's imagination or are used fictitiously.

First published in the United States by Minotaur Books, an imprint of St. Martin's Publishing Group

EU Representative: Macmillan Publishers Ireland Ltd, 1st Floor, The Liffey Trust Centre, 117–126 Sheriff Street Upper, Dublin 1, DO1 YC43

WILD INSTINCT. Copyright © 2025 by T. Jefferson Parker. All rights reserved. Printed in the United States of America. For information, address St. Martin's Publishing Group, 120 Broadway, New York, NY 10271.

www.minotaurbooks.com

Designed by Omar Chapa

Library of Congress Cataloging-in-Publication Data

Names: Parker, T. Jefferson author
Title: Wild instinct : a novel / T. Jefferson Parker.
Description: First edition. | New York : Minotaur Books, 2025. |
Identifiers: LCCN 2025019333 | ISBN 9781250907912 hardcover | ISBN 9781250907929 ebook
Subjects: LCGFT: Fiction | Detective and mystery fiction | Novels
Classification: LCC PS3566.A6863 W55 2025 | DDC 813/.54—dc23/ eng/20250604
LC record available at https://lccn.loc.gov/2025019333

The publisher of this book does not authorize the use or reproduction of any part of this book in any manner for the purpose of training artificial intelligence technologies or systems. The publisher of this book expressly reserves this book from the Text and Data Mining exception in accordance with Article 4(3) of the European Union Digital Single Market Directive 2019/790.

Our books may be purchased in bulk for specialty retail/wholesale, literacy, corporate/premium, educational, and subscription box use. Please contact MacmillanSpecialMarkets@macmillan.com.

First Edition: 2025

10 9 8 7 6 5 4 3 2 1

For the Acjacheme people, among the ancients of California

We will be known forever by the tracks we leave.

—*Dakota proverb*

WILD INSTINCT

1

This cat is a big male.

Mountain lion, *Puma concolor*.

He's old and weather-bleached, with a scarred face and a chewed ear, and shoulder muscles shifting like saddlebags under a thick beige pelt. Tan eyes. He pads along with slouching confidence. Swaying, like he's had a couple.

This security video is surreal, and by now, almost a week old: The cat saunters northbound on the Coast Highway sidewalk in Laguna Beach, window-shopping, maybe, or checking his look in the storefront glass. He considers Diane's Leather Boutique, the Hair Affair, Pacific Vibrations Surf Shop, from which a guy in a black hoodie and red Jams steps out, sees the mountain lion not six feet away, scrambles back inside, and slams the door behind him.

The cat moves up Coast Highway and off camera.

Here in the Orange County Sheriff's Department headquarters, Detective Lew Gale studies the video. He's a brawny man, half

Acjacheme Indian, with a face like carved mahogany and unexpected gray eyes.

He looks away from the video and considers his boss, Undersheriff Elke Meyer.

Her radio is tuned to the helicopter deputies now trying to find a cat that has killed and partially eaten a man in Caspers Wilderness Park, near Laguna. This, just hours ago.

Gale, an experienced hunter, knows if they haven't found the mountain lion by now, they probably won't.

"I saw this video online in the *Laguna News* last week," he says to Meyer. "He's old."

"Too old to be our man-eater?" she asks. "Don't the old ones do that kind of thing?"

"No," says Gale. "The lion that killed the biker in Caspers Park twenty-one years ago was a young cat."

"Well, as of two hours ago, we've got another man-killer in Caspers Park," says Meyer. "What is it with that place? A public park in Orange County, California? Two killings, and that terrible mauling of the little girl? Wilderness, no kidding."

Caspers Park and its nearby Santa Ana Mountains are where Gale as a boy used to hunt and hike with his father and sister. He was born in San Juan Capistrano, a mission town not far from the wilderness, and grew up there.

"It's good lion country," says Gale. "Hills with big boulders and thick underbrush. Lots of deer. It's a lot like the New Mexico country where I tracked man-killers."

"Why can't our helicopter guys find him? They've got good scopes."

"Elke, the choppers just scare the cat. He'll hunker until dark, then go about his business."

The radio voices are loud, and crackling with static.

"Pete, we're circling the campground again. In case he's sticking near his kill. What's your ten-twenty? Over."

"Southeastern tip of Caspers, Connor, near the private property line

and Roberts Road. The cover is thick down there. Unless he comes out and stands on a rock to see what our commotion is about, we won't find him. Over."

"Elke, where's Gale? Over."

"He's on his way with Mike Carpenter and a dog. Over."

"Rough country for man and dog. Over and out."

Meyer goes to the radio and turns the volume down. Sits, gives Gale a worried look.

"This Laguna vid was shot six days ago," says Meyer. "Twelve and a half miles away from where the hikers found the body this morning. So, if this is our bad boy, he had time enough to get from Caspers Park to Laguna Beach, and back to the park again."

"Easy," says Gale. "They range for miles and they move all night."

Gale, in his days as an Orange County helicopter deputy, has flown over the rough country surrounding Caspers Park scores of times.

Now he looks out the third-floor window on this October Friday morning and sees not the drab concrete complex of the Sheriff's Department headquarters in Santa Ana. Closing his eyes, he imagines the route that a mountain lion might take from Caspers Park to Coast Highway in Laguna Beach, and back again. He pictures the eastern expanse of chaparral that funnels down to a sycamore-studded gap leading directly into the Laguna backcountry hills, and eventually to Aliso Creek Beach, which abuts Coast Highway south of the city. A stealthy lion could follow the dense greenbelt north toward town and suddenly find itself on the Coast Highway sidewalk, watching those big, shiny things roaring by.

There's also the Laguna Coast Wilderness Park, where Lew Gale hiked and camped as a boy as well, twenty thousand acres of uninhabited hills and canyons that could offer an ambitious—and very lucky—cat access to Coast Highway.

"A lion can cover ten, twelve miles a day," says Gale. "The old ones, not so much."

"The Laguna one sure did. I'll bet this is him."

"We don't want to kill the wrong cat, Elke."

"Then find the right one, Lew. If it's not this Laguna cat, it's going to be obvious. From the video. I know you have the skill set for this kind of work."

Meaning his tracking years in New Mexico and his sniper months in Afghanistan. Both of which led him to a spot on the Orange County Sheriff's SWAT team's Predator Tracking Unit.

It's a part-time gig that occasionally gets him outdoors and into some interesting action, such as this. The predator tracking unit nets him a monthly "special assignment enhancement" of $175.57, in addition to his sergeant-detective salary.

"Public Affairs will post about PTU tracking this man-killer," says Meyer. "I told Daniela Mendez that she'll have to wait to make her homicide debut with you. Your new partner. I think she'll be a good one."

"I think so, too."

"How long do you think it will take to find this homicidal lion?"

"Two, three days."

"Well, October is a good month for sleeping under the stars. Be careful."

Gale turns off the radio and Meyer gives him an it's-about-time look. "The buzz is the lion victim is Bennet Tarlow," he says.

"The buzz is true, Lew. The third, that is. Bennet Evans Tarlow the Third."

"Oh, boy."

Great-great-grandson of the Tarlow Company founder Willard Evans Tarlow, Gale knows. Who built the family fortune on a vast Spanish land grant dating back to the eighteenth century. Two hundred thousand acres of SoCal mountains, meadows, and a generous slice of the coast. The Tarlow Company has developed residential, resort, and commercial properties in ten states and Puerto Rico, and, until just a few hours ago, Tarlow III was the handsome face of the organization. He was a fixture in the *Los Angeles Times*, *The Orange County Register*, *Laguna Weekly*, and on the PBS show *Inside OC*. A political donor, a titan of charity, and a bastion of the Orange County Diocese of the Catholic Church. Never married. Rarely photographed or filmed without a beautiful woman nearby.

During his lean patrol years, Gale did off-duty security work for Tarlow and liked the man.

Bennet Tarlow. Killed and eaten by a mountain lion, on land his family donated to the county for a park, Lew Gale thinks.

What a goddamned way to go.

Adding Bennet Tarlow's death to his long list of things that make no earthly sense.

Let that one cook, Gale thinks.

But it's going to blow up.

"Want to see him?" asks Elke Meyer.

The coroner's assistant, a young Asian woman, wheels Bennet Tarlow III from the cooler vault, pulls off a white sheet specked with blood, and sets it on a stainless-steel table.

"This is a very brutal one," she says.

The room is cold and smells of alcohol, but now, in the slipstream of the removed sheet, Gale smells the meaty human insides of mankind.

Tarlow's tattered body and clothes are stuck tight with oak leaves, mountain lions often hiding their kills.

His face is half-gone and his scalp and forehead are badly lacerated, but his teeth and skull are intact.

So Lew Gale recognizes approximately half of him.

Tarlow's shirt and blue jeans are torn away. His ribs are extant but his chest and stomach gape, raggedly asunder. No heart or lungs, Gale sees, no liver or kidneys. No innards. All of them presumably eaten or left on the ground. Blood and tan oak leaves are stuck to his pants and boots.

A reeking mess.

In all his years in law enforcement, and his months of combat in Afghanistan, Gale has never seen a human killed as food.

He remembers having coffee with Tarlow and a lady friend, bodyguarding him at a prizefight in Las Vegas. Another Fury-Wilder rematch. The woman was a redheaded beauty—Laguna Beach by way of Fort Worth, he remembers—suddenly ashamed of himself for picturing her in front of her companion, the painfully butchered and half-devoured Bennet Tarlow.

The woman had a funny name. Norris something.

"When is the autopsy?" he asks.

"Later today," says the assistant. "The sheriff knows the media will blow up when we identify him."

"It's blowing up already," says Undersheriff Meyer. "People don't like the idea of being killed and eaten in a county park."

2

At the kill site, Gale, Predator Tracking Unit K9 handler Mike Carpenter, and Mike's burly German shepherd, Knight, cross the plastic crime scene barriers under the watchful eyes of two uniformed deputies.

The men shrug off their backpacks and set their rifles across them. Knight stands leashed amid the oak leaves and acorns, whimpering and trembling, riveted by Mike's pack. Here the ground is shaded by the big oaks that grow just east of the Ortega Flats campground.

Two sheriff's SUVs preside from the dirt road nearby, lights flashing. From a camp clearing, a den of uniformed Cub Scouts and two supervising adults watch from atop a picnic table. Knight, taut on his lead, sizes them up for just a moment, then turns his quivering black nose to his handler's backpack again.

One of the deputies leads them down a narrow game trail that wends through the shade of the oaks and to a patch of acorn-strewn dirt roughly ten feet square enclosed in yellow tape. The black, oily dirt appears wet.

Knight surges for the black patch but young Carpenter yanks back hard and cusses him.

Gale kneels just outside the tape, where a dusty shaft of sunlight slants through the trees and touches the earth in front of him.

He sees that the dirt and leaves and acorns aren't black at all, but deep, drying red. Notes the pale scraps of gut and bone and sinew. And the intestinal fragments oddly purple now in the sun.

Carpenter orders Knight to sit down and stay, then pulls open a locking evidence bag from his backpack and gives Knight a whiff. Knight tries to take the red shop rag dampened with mountain lion pee bought on a hunting website, but Carpenter is ready for this, and he whips the bag up and away.

"Stay," he says, easing the still-opened bag down for the dog to smell. Knight's hackles flare, and his body trembles like a tree in the wind. Carpenter slaps the bag gently to Knight's black snout, then seals it and puts it back in his pack.

Unleashes Knight, who bounds into the oak grove.

"Hunt 'em up, boy," says Carpenter.

Knight works meticulously, quartering the meadow ground, nosing the hills of boulders sprouting dense manzanita and sage, and the matilija poppies blooming their last in the mid-October warmth.

Carpenter uses neither a whistle nor voice commands, animal tracking being a stealthy pursuit. Knight stops and looks back to his handler often.

Gale, who as a boy hunted quail and doves and sometimes deer not far from here, feels strange with the ponderous sniper's rifle now in his hands instead of the trim 20-gauge bird gun his dad gave him for Christmas one year. The rifle is a Barrett MK 22, weighing just over fifteen pounds, with a range of two thousand yards. Gale had killed a fellow sniper at 1,275 yards in Sangin Valley, Afghanistan, as a Marine private, age nineteen. His target was ninety-two years old, according to his grandson, a Taliban informer.

Gale's fifth, confirmed.

He stops for a moment, takes a slug of water from a canteen on his belt, listens to the far-off cars on Ortega Highway, watches a FedEx cargo jet easing down toward Orange County's John Wayne Airport. He notes how little this land has changed since he was a boy, although the humans have stepped up their invasion by air, land, and sea. Just north of here, thousands of trucks on a dozen freeways daily belch to and from the ports of Long Beach and Los Angeles, the busiest in the country. Tonight, he'll see satellites gliding through the stars.

He trades out his canteen for his Zeiss binoculars and scans the ridgelines of the hills, alert to the boulders into which the big cats blend when waiting for deer. The binoculars collapse a thousand yards into an optically pure circle in which a fence lizard basks on a south-facing rock.

The day cools into late afternoon as Gale, Carpenter, and the dog climb in elevation.

Nearing the base of the Santa Ana Mountains, Knight alerts in a thicket of toyon and lemonade berry, goes into that slinky, butt-down German shepherd crawl, and slowly follows a game trail into the darkening bushes.

Carpenter gives Lew Gale a respectful nod. Gale is his senior, and his skills as a department SWAT marksman and a Marine sniper put him first in line to shoot, on the very real chance that the lion has taken cover in the brush, curious, as most mountain lions are, or even considering an ambush of Knight, an easy kill.

Reversing his SWAT cap for an unimpeded view, Gale follows the dog into the thicket, hunches his shoulders through the high brush, hugging the Barrett to his chest. He thinks of patrol in Sangin, minus the constant, low-grade fear of being shot by a sniper from so far away he'd be dead without hearing the shot.

Which was how he'd killed nine men.

The copse opens into an arroyo lined with sycamores, their white branches heavy with yellow and brown leaves the size of dinner plates.

Gale listens to the crunch of his boots on them. Within his Acjacheme/Juaneño blood, he retains an ancestral talent for quietly stalking game here in these wooded hills.

The arroyo widens into a large meadow that rises gently into the Santa Anas of Cleveland National Forest.

No cat.

Knight turns and looks hopefully at Gale, who raises both hands palms-up and shakes his head, letting the sling have his rifle for the moment. Knight continues, his urgency gone but his movements still optimistic.

The meadow climbs toward the mountain but as Knight disappears over a rise and Gale makes its summit, he sees that the valley below is larger and deeper than he'd expected, and heavily wooded with oaks and sycamores and the pine.

White hoop buildings are tucked beneath the trees, dozens of them, and the strong, skunky smell of cannabis hangs in the cooling air.

No movement there, that Gale can see.

"Not again," says Carpenter, coming up just behind him. "Some of these shitheads keep guard dogs. Pit bulls and other good killers, you know?"

So he blows three sharp notes on his Acme Medium Thunderer. Knight reverses direction and strains uphill, tongue flapping.

Rifles slung and handguns drawn, Gale and Carpenter put twenty feet between each other and start down into the dense woods, the stink of weed, and the eerie buzz of insects.

Some of the hoop buildings have been slashed into long shreds of opaque plastic that hang limp in the breeze. Making a statement, Gale thinks.

He sees a man dead on his back near the entrance of the third grow house. Hands bound. Eyes wide. A bullet hole in his forehead. Flies all over him. He looks to be Laotian, known for their slave labor on these illegal marijuana farms, which are owned and run not by Laotians at all, but by competing American gangs and Mexican cartels.

Toeing their way through the grow, Gale and Carpenter find big canisters of fertilizer and pesticide. Hundreds of yards of PVC irrigation pipes, and electrical cable for water and power to be bootlegged in from distant landowners and public utility lines. Plastic cisterns. Hoses everywhere. Propane bottles slung into the brush. Bales of chicken wire and plastic sheets to protect young plants. Trash and more trash: small mountains of black plastic bags torn open and emptied by animals, the flies buzzing in the cans, crows watching from the trees.

In spite of the dank stink of the marijuana, there's not much weed left. The processed and pressed bales are too valuable to leave behind. The floors of the cleaning and packing tents are sticky with cannabis scraps and oil. Everywhere are mounds of useless stalks and stems too risky to burn.

Then, another Laotian man apparently executed near a cache of new irrigation valves, timers, spaghetti drip line, and emitters. And another, gunned down while trying to run into the woods, now slumped between plastic canisters of fertilizer, still holding a baseball bat in one hand.

"When?" asks Carpenter.

"Two nights? No vultures yet."

"Seems right."

"These cannabis pirates are bad people," says Gale.

"Savages," says Carpenter. "It started with the cartels."

Gale ponders this for a moment. The "savages" remark unintentionally pricks his Native Acjacheme spirit, the Acjacheme known as trusting people, even of the conquering Spanish. Back in those days, there were occasional Indian threats of violence against the soldiers,

Gale knows, but what were spindly Indian arrows used to kill birds and rabbits against the booming blunderbusses of conquerors?

Gale's mother, Sally, is one of the kindest, most deeply accepting people he knows.

His proudly Spanish father, Edward Gallego, has a temper that follows no racial nor cultural lines.

At age eighteen, the year his father left home, Luis Gallego changed his name to Lew Gale.

"The Laotians are poor and peaceful," he says. "So they get ripped off badly."

"I'd rather not be poor and peaceful, if this is what it gets you," notes Carpenter.

Another jet leans into John Wayne Airport from above. Knight sleeps under an oak, in a slant of sunlight.

Lew Gale sits on a boulder down by the shaded creek, calls the crime in to Dispatch on his satellite phone.

Fifteen minutes later, he sees a sheriff's helicopter lowering to the massacre site. Then another.

3

Late that night, long after Carpenter has brushed the burrs and stickers from Knight's thick coat, and retired to his tent, Gale looks up at the stars and thinks about Bennet Tarlow. He seems to Gale to have been the perfect man: an upright, bipedal omnivore; intelligent; capable; hardworking; a prosperous survivor—and maker of necessary things. Homes and resorts. So, if there's free will, how could Tarlow have possibly let himself be eaten in a park by a mountain lion? But if life is fated—authored by God or many gods or even just anonymously—what coldly detached architect had led Tarlow to the claws and fangs?

And Gale thinks of the old cat, out in this national forest doing the same thing that he's doing—bedding down on a cool October night. Maybe thinking about Tarlow, too. Or more specifically, the taste of man, which was the cat's first, most likely. Funny to eat a live human being without even a whisper of shame in you. "Funny" clearly not the right word. Neither is "shame." The question in Lew Gale's practical, law-enforcement mind is: Will he do it again?

A more pressing question in his human heart right now is: Who killed the Laotian men?

He thinks of Marilyn, his ex-wife, a bright young woman with tastes for the finer things far more developed and refined than his. A mismatch of ambitions and satisfactions. Not of attractions.

Just before sleep, Gale drifts into his darkest place, as he does most nights. Feels it gathering up his body and his mind, drawing him into a slow orbit. He looks down on the stark tan desert of Sangin Valley, the startling green poppy fields quivering with red blooms, the boulder-strewn Sangin River, the village with its dusty shops, the humble mosque, the school and the boys, only the boys, scurrying in and out. He sees the men he killed, some of them in bloodied traditional dresses and turbans and sandals, some in the somber gray-and-white tunics of the Taliban, some in baggy Western trousers, head wraps, and combat boots. Always bearded, their faces sun-darkened and deeply wrinkled, some with their eyes open, their expressions fierce and noble and resigned.

Tonight, as always, the last face Lew Gale sees is that of an old man, whom Gale had first noticed on a village patrol in the Sangin open-air market. He was buying vegetables. He looked directly at Gale. He had a fierce face, framed by a full white beard, and Gale guessed by his well-worn, white, high-top Cheetah sneakers that he must have walked some distance in them. Cheetahs were popular with the Taliban—and many Afghans who were not Taliban—for comfort and durability on the rocky roads and trails, and the fact that many Cheetahs were accented black, green, and red—colors of the Afghan flag. His gait and motions were slow and deliberate, befitting a man so old. Lieutenant Papini said that Cheetah Man was Taliban through and through, a local fucking hero, of course, a reputed sniper with at least ten Russian kills, and five British, and almost certainly one kill ten days ago—Private Chilcote—down by the abandoned village near the river.

The next evening, after clearing it with his sergeant, Gale sent up a surveillance drone to shadow Cheetah Man from a home behind a bakery, where smoke and men's voices billowed from the security screen door. Gale watched the drone's video on his satellite phone. When the old man was far ahead of him, Gale sent the drone back to the FOB and followed him on foot along a ridgeline, watching him through the powerful scope of his sniper rifle.

Five kilometers later, Cheetah Man disappeared into a dilapidated farmhouse far back from the trail. No screens on the windows, no door in the frame. The house was part of a small village that had been occupied by the British, and abandoned by them two years prior. The wind-blasted mud structures were roofless, the palm trees shrouded by brown fronds.

In the failing light, the old man walked briskly through the doorway and came out a few minutes later with a duffel over one shoulder and a rifle slung across the other. He disappeared into a mud-brick granary with a torn steel roof that overlooked a forking trail. Gale had circled this part of the trail and village on his drone printouts just last week, where Chilcote had been killed by an invisible sniper ten days prior. *A village building?* Gale had written in his impeccably neat hand. *Rooftop but few roofs. Granary has elevation.* A 3rd Battalion, 5th Marines fire squad had searched the village and found no one, no footprints, no evidence of a sniper having nested there.

The sun set and the cold crept up from the ground and Gale looked around for a place to call home. He was alone. He had a canteen of water, a couple of MREs, a survival blanket, and nineteen years of life in him. His basic training sergeant had quickly seen young Gale's rifle skills and put Gale on a sniper's track.

He spent two hot days and two cold nights alternately watching from and dozing in a smooth, body-sized divot in a rocky hill seven hundred yards from the village. His teeth chattered but the blanket seemed to help. As a boy, Gale liked hunting by himself for birds and rabbits and deer, but now, hunting alone for men made him feel edgy and exposed.

No one came or went from the dead village, or from the granary where the old man had gone. Through his rifle scope Gale saw the shooting slots chiseled through the thick mud walls. Three of them, all on the second story, all with different views of the trail. They were small rectangles, just big enough for a sniper to get his gun and the top half of his face through. They made for a tough shot, though he had once made one like it.

Gale got his look when the old man emerged from the granary just after first light on morning three, his rifle slung over one shoulder, his white, black, green, and red high-top Cheetahs happily bright in the advancing desert light.

The old man collapsed in a puff of dust and didn't move.

Lew Gale's heart was thumping hard and he felt the adrenaline coursing through him but his hands were sound and his fingers steady.

Five minutes later, in the growing light, Gale looked down at Cheetah Man's craggy but somehow benign face, his flat black eyes, the blood that had jumped from his chest into his snow-white beard.

The gun slung from his shoulder had fallen loose beside him and Gale was astonished to see that it was an old shotgun, not a sniper's rifle, not a rifle of any kind. Seeing the old man emerge from the farmhouse in the half-light with a gun, Gale had observed and presumed and assumed and failed to identify.

He took pictures on his phone.

Inside the granary he smelled the opium, noted the black-tarred hookah pipe, the plastic bottles of water, the scraps of food and paper wrappers already attracting mice. There was a mattress on the floor, heaped with dirty blankets and oddly festive pillows with purple and white piping, certainly handmade in Sangin.

Upstairs, Gale sat on a wooden chair and put his face to the sniper's slots, one at a time, following the trail on which Private Chilcote died until it disappeared down toward the river. Up here the smell of opium smoke was stronger.

What we have here, thought Gale, is an old man with a bird gun stopping off for a few days of R & R.

Later, back in Sangin, Gale showed one of his pictures to a boy—a helpful occasional translator and village busybody. The boy told Gale that the dead man was Amardad, which meant "one who is immortal."

"Why kill him?" asked the boy. "Amardad hunted birds, not men."

Gale looked away.

Felt like time had stopped. The boy was young and slender and had straight black hair that fell almost to his eyebrows like a pageboy's.

"It was a mistake," Gale said. "In the dark I didn't see he had a shotgun that shoots only a few yards. Not a rifle for killing men."

"The man you wanted was Amardad's brother, Ali," said the boy. "He was the best sniper in Sangin. They look very alike, their wives got confused. He killed many Russians and British, then the British killed him. With a drone. Three months before you Americans got here."

"Then who shot Private Chilcote on the trail by the abandoned village last week?" asked Gale.

The boy looked at Gale with a puzzled expression. "Anyone. Everyone. Not me! So can I come with you to America when you go?"

"We don't do that."

We don't bring back the people who helped us.

Gale's heart seemed to cough up some shameful, insipid stone, which caught in his throat and hurt violently.

4

In the early-morning light, Knight yips his lion alert on a narrow game trail that leads into the mountains. The big German shepherd snorts and shuffles, nose in the air, tail and hips low.

Gale, his stomach sloshing with an energy drink and protein bars, clomps along behind the dog, rifle in his hands and pack snug to his back.

They cover some ground now, Knight's thick coat lifting and shifting, Gale falling into an easy rhythm behind the dog.

Knight veers suddenly off trail and zigzags through a swale with spring-fed cottonwoods and damp, calf-high grass. A quarter mile of this, and he stops and looks to Gale as if for advice. Then sneezes and drives his snout deep into the grass and sets a straight course down the middle of the little meadow, which leads him back to higher ground and the game trail.

He stops again and looks at Gale, snorts and yipes in frustration, then puts his wet nose to the air and continues along more slowly now, body relaxed and urgency gone.

"He was hot on a cat until the grass," says Carpenter.

"You'd think the dew would hold the scent," says Gale. He remembers with his dad and their springer spaniel, Ernie, working the little springs and creeks not far from here for quail.

But less than half a mile farther uphill, snorting his way through the mountain boulders, Knight alerts again and his body changes: muzzle up, hocks bent, hips low.

This is cat country, Gale thinks: the precarious piles of boulders, the dense growths of rabbit brush and manzanita growing between them. In the ten years he hunted these Santa Anas as an adolescent and young man, he saw only two mountain lions. Both of them tawny and still as the rocks, observing him from above in landscapes like this.

Knight leads his men up the base of the mountain in long switchbacks, ascending higher and higher.

Gale and Carpenter traipse along behind him, Gale feeling the elevation in his legs, and the weight of his heavy Barrett in his arms. The late-morning sun is warm. He lifts his SWAT cap and wipes his forehead on the sleeve of his flannel. Forty-three is the new sixty, he thinks. Just add an IED and bourbon.

Onward and upward.

Even as a boy, Gale disliked heights.

He tries to keep his eyes up and at the same time navigate the rocks and the spaces between them. His foot slips into a small crevasse and his ankle turns. He feels incompetent, mutters a curse, and looks back at Carpenter, climbing steadily toward him. Sees Knight out in front, scrambling up a boulder, front nails scratching, hind legs straining, Gale wondering at the animal's fearlessness.

Elke Meyer on his phone, her voice clear. He remembers when there was no reception out here.

"How's our mountain lion of interest?" she asks.

He tells her they haven't seen the cat, but are getting close.

"We identified the victim as Bennet Tarlow yesterday," says the undersheriff. "Sheriff himself did the press conference. The Coast Highway video went viral, of course. They're calling him the Killer Cat."

Gale feels a blip of anger.

"We can't kill the wrong cat," he says.

Or man.

"Lew, get it through your head that the old mountain lion on Coast Highway is probably our Killer Cat. The chances are overwhelmingly good. The corridors line up between Laguna and where you are right now. That's what the Fish and Wildlife scientists say."

A pause.

"Maria Brown from the *Times* wants to talk to you when this is over and the Killer Cat is no longer eating people. I told her I'd inquire."

"Have Carpenter talk to her."

"She wants *you*, Lew. Got herself a Pulitzer for that, as you know."

"I'll do my job, Elke, but I'm not talking to her again."

"I know, I know, and I don't blame you. But Lew, you could put us in a good light. Sheriff Kersey wants good light. Up for reelection soon. He asked me to make sure that you're clear on that."

"Let someone else take the shot, Elke."

And clicks off.

They plod up the mountain with slow switchbacks through afternoon heat, stopping often to water Knight and themselves.

Knight alerts near a stand of toyon, red berries bright in the sun. The big dog heaves himself along a slender trail, then lurches into a tight chute between the boulders and disappears.

Ambush predator, thinks Gale. Ambush territory. They jump you from behind, crush your neck in unbelievably powerful jaws while their front claws clamp your shoulders and their rear claws rake open your back.

Gale again reverses his sheriff's cap and ducks in after him, gun pointed down. Knight turns a corner, and by the time Gale rounds it, all he sees is the dog's thick dark tail vanishing behind a rounded granite boulder the size and shape of a VW bug.

Gale follows Knight into a swale terminating at a stone rampart too vertical and tightly packed to climb without carabiners, ropes, and pitons.

Knight looks at Gale and whines, coat bristling, then takes off along the rocky base.

Gale catches up with him at a big rock, flat as a tabletop, on which the dog stands, looking up.

A mountain lion sits gazing high above them, framed by a V in distant rocks the same mottled tan as he is.

Gale can see the far-off dome of its head and little spikes of ears. If he hadn't been looking for a lion, he wouldn't have seen it. It could be looking at him. Known for their curiosity, Gale thinks.

Not to mention guile and stealth.

He swings down the monopod shooting brace, extends the leg to full length, and plants its foot firmly in the earth. Then raises the Barrett slowly to his shoulder. Knight watches him. The heavy gun balances perfectly on the brace, and Gale sets the distance for a thousand yards.

In the pure optics he sees the cat's face as if it's fifty feet away. The breeze moves a tuft of his chest hair. Killer Cat, no doubt. Gale sees the scarred face, the tan eyes, the tip-chewed right ear of the cat as on the security camera in Laguna Beach, taken a week ago.

He's disappointed that he'll have to kill this old cat.

He admires its boldness, endurance, and fortitude.

Admires how he padded from the Santa Ana Mountains to Pacific Vibrations Surf Shop on Coast Highway, and a week later back to the mountains behind Laguna to kill and eat the multimillionaire land developer Bennet Tarlow. Then dodged two professional hunters and an experienced tracking dog for nearly twenty-four hours and ten miles of the rough backcountry in which he was probably born.

Gale offs the safety, and the vibration shivers the scope out of focus for a split second, and when it resolves, the cat is gone.

Finger on the trigger, Gale scopes the rocks in a widening circle but no lion. Waits motionless and hears Carpenter crunching through the brush behind him.

"He's up there, Carp. The big chewed-up one from Coast Highway."

"Killer Cat. I will be damned. But I'm not surprised."

"He was in that V above the boulders. Looking right at me."

Carpenter swings up his Weatherby and peers through the scope. "What's the best way around this mountain?"

"Knight can figure it out."

Three hours later they've circumnavigated and climbed the mountain. Gale stands before the V where Killer Cat had been, the wind in his face.

Knight stares at Carpenter wild-eyed with scent, but he holds his handler's commands to sit down and stay. He pants loudly, tongue lolling off the left side of his jaw, his flanks studded with sage pods and brambles, tail twitching.

"Hunt 'em up, boy! Hunt 'em up!"

Less than an hour later, weary Knight has lost the scent.

They hunt past dark and set up camp in a stand of digger pine. Gale looks forward to his bourbon again.

It's Elke Meyer on the satellite phone.

"How's my favorite lion-tracking detective?"

"I got a good look at him. Knight tracked him twelve miles from the kill site. It's the big cat from Coast Highway in Laguna."

"Did you shoot?"

"I offed the safety and he vanished."

"How far out?"

"A thousand yards."

"Wow."

"Not much wind. It would have been a long but clean shot."

"I'm glad you didn't kill him, Lew."

Gale can't imagine why.

"Lew, um, the autopsy on Tarlow finished up just a couple of hours ago. He died from gunshot. Two bullets in the back of his head. Killer Cat chewed him but didn't kill him. Tarlow had bled to death before the cat found him. Say nothing about this. So, get back to the kill site first thing in the morning and figure out who did this. Daniela Mendez—your new partner—will meet you. *Do not* tell anyone what I've just told you. Including Carpenter. That comes from Kersey, direct. A car registered to Tarlow was found parked in a campsite in Caspers—not far from where they found his body. It's in impound now."

5

Early morning at the Caspers kill site. Frost on the grass and lilacs under a pale blue sky.

Lew Gale hands Detective Sergeant Daniela Mendez a to-go coffee cup with a heat sleeve.

This is their first job as official partners, Mendez having aced her "homicide school" courses over the months and gotten assigned to Gale just last week. They've only talked a few times since then—coffee in the county courthouse cafeteria—which is how Gale knew to put half-and-half in hers.

Gale agreed to her as a potential partner because of her reputation for hard work, and for captaining the OC Sheriff's pistol team. He liked that because, in his experience, deputies good with guns seemed calmer and more peaceable on duty, though he knew this might not actually be true. He also liked the idea of her as his partner because she struck him as solitary, like himself.

Mendez comes from the Special Investigations Bureau—Vice/

Human Trafficking. At thirty-eight, she's a single mother, hard-faced, dark-haired, and gym-fit.

She wears black jeans, an OCSD windbreaker over a work shirt—hiding the gun on her back—and black athletic shoes.

Gale touches his paper cup to hers.

"Two bullets," she says. Her voice is crisp. "Still inside his skull. Our luck."

"I want to see the kill site again," he says.

"If that's even what it is," says Daniela.

"Exactly," says Gale. "A big cat can easily drag a man around."

"And so could another man."

In the fortysomething hours since Gale was first here, the patch of blood-darkened soil and oak leaves hasn't changed much. A few red ants, and two yellowjackets buzzing low but not wanting to land.

The crime scene barriers and tape are gone and there's a faint trail of trampled leaves in the direction of the campground. Crime scene looky-loos, Gale thinks, coming and going.

Mendez hunkers beside the bloody ground, balanced on the balls of her feet to keep her pants clean.

"When I first saw the pictures of this, I didn't think it looked like enough blood," she says. "A gallon and a half for a man Tarlow's size? That's three milk cartons. The coroner says he bled to death. I don't think he died here."

"No," says Lew Gale. "What caliber were the bullets?"

"Twenty-two. Mushroomed out and still inside him."

"That's a close-up execution load," says Gale. "Quiet and it does big damage, bouncing around like that."

"They didn't see the entry wounds at first because his scalp was torn up so bad."

"Shot from behind?"

"Yes," says Mendez. "Near the center of his head."

They sit side by side on a cold concrete bench of a long, stained picnic table oddly positioned here, well away from the nearest campground.

Mendez briefly checks her phone, then brushes away the acorns and sets her laptop down in front of them. Finds the coroner's report and cues up a video clip of Bennet Tarlow's body on an examination table.

Gale can almost smell the formaldehyde and the bleachy stink of the autopsy room. Always hated those places.

The drastic Y cuts have already been sawn from Tarlow's armpits to his sternum, and converged into one, straight down his middle toward where his navel no longer was. Ribs rudely splayed, revealing all.

Mendez lets Gale move forward at his own pace, the autopsy progressing through its painstaking stages, the body parts photographed, removed, and weighed, beginning at the top of the chest cavity by the masked coroner himself, Dr. Jerry Bachstein.

"Time of death?" asks Gale.

"The evening before the hikers found him," says Mendez. "Plus or minus eight hours. The lion pretty much destroyed whatever forensic evidence Tarlow's body might have held. Except the bullets."

"Drugs or alcohol in his system?"

"The serology was iffy," says Mendez. "Because the blood was in short supply and contaminated. A blood thinner and blood pressure meds, probably. Jerry couldn't say much about his heart because it was mostly gone. Ditto his liver, one kidney, and both lungs."

"Any DNA that wasn't Tarlow's?"

"They're still running random samples. Jerry says low chance of anything but the cat's. He apologized. He's trying."

"Stains? Fibers? Anything trace?"

"Bits of oak leaves and lilac. Soil. His watch, wallet, and car keys were still in his pants. A small Swiss Army knife. A pendant around his neck. All at the lab. No phone, unfortunately."

"A pendant the cat didn't tear off?" asks Gale.

"An owl," says Mendez. "Silver, on a stainless chain. Here."

"An owl in flight," says Gale. "Native Americans almost always saw them as messengers of death."

Mendez finds a close-up of the pendant, a two-inch owl, wings spread, roundheaded. Both owl and chain clotted with blood.

Gale nods, scrolls through the next stills: blood and guts and the remains of a man.

"Let's go find the rest of Bennet Tarlow's earthly blood," he says. "I worked for him a few times, years ago."

"Moonlighting to pay the bills?"

"Yeah. He was a nice guy."

"Somebody disagrees."

Circling outward from the alleged kill site, they find blood—lots of it—less than a hundred yards away, in the bed of a seasonal creek nearly hidden by a big oak tree.

Vultures hop and squabble in the sandy, brush-tangled wash. Yellowjackets flicker and chew the clots and clods. The blood looks to Gale as if it could have been poured, spreading out in a neat, round pool. In a way it was, he thinks: a gallon, maybe more, pouring from the holes in Tarlow's pressurized skull, his heart pounding away in confusion, his thoughts in ruins, as he stared into the night sky, unable to do anything but tremble. Private First Class Battaglia died that way on Gale's drenched lap in Sangin, a fellow sniper caught by an Afghan sniper.

Lying in the bloody tableaux, like a clue dropped by the Patron Saint of Detectives, is a black camera with a long white lens connected to a folded aluminum tripod.

"You always this lucky?" asks Mendez.

"I just make it look easy."

They photograph and shoot video of the crime scene, then Daniela Mendez calls in the CSI unit.

"So how did Tarlow get from here to the bogus kill site?" she asks. "By Killer Cat or Killer Human?"

They follow a trail lightly specked with dried blood, but trampled by something large and heavy.

The CSI van rolls toward them through the trees.

In a small dirt clearing Gale sees a body-width imprint framed by enormous lion prints, which point to the now discredited location where Bennet Tarlow was once believed to have lost his life.

Back at the updated kill site, triangulating with the slope of the streambed and the dense cover along it, and assuming a right-side ejection port that most semis have, Gale and Mendez estimate which direction the gun was pointed when the bullet hit Tarlow from behind. And where the fired casing might land.

He remembers from his hunting days that semiautomatic guns often threw the empties farther than he'd think. Just like fallen birds were often farther away in the field than where they seemed to land. Which never fooled the dogs' noses.

Gale sees a brassy flash in the green and finds a spent .22 casing in it. No wonder the shooter didn't find it, he thinks. Maybe he didn't even try. Maybe, of course, he wasn't a he.

Of course there might be another.

"Nice work, Detective," says Mendez. "But I'll call your bet."

She holds up a stick with another .22 casing wobbling lazily on top. A small smile on her hard face.

Gale smiles back. She shoots the casing with her phone, then picks it up with a small, clear plastic bag.

Nearby, they find two sets of footprints coming through the wash from the direction of Cottonwood Creek Campground, where their plain-wrap Sheriff's Department Explorers are parked. But only one set leading back, with the longer stride of a large man, running.

Mendez shoots those, too, then they follow.

The sandy soil is too loose to capture anything but general, nonspecific prints, but their locations and distances apart indicate to Gale two adult Homo sapiens walking pretty much side by side. Familiar with each other. Not one with a gun to the other's head. Tarlow's recovered and blood-drenched wallet contained credit cards and $140 in cash. Friends? A lover? A Tarlow Company associate?

"These prints want to say they knew each other," says Mendez. "Doing what out here, after dark?"

"Oh boy," says Gale, his standard response to questions he can't answer, or doesn't want to.

"That's what my son says when he's not going to answer me."

At the campground they talk to everyone, but none of them were here the night of the murder. One of them confesses that he and his two girls—both visible in a clearing, trying to get a kite to fly—had gone to the crime scene yesterday and looked at the blood. But they hadn't touched anything or crossed through the tape, though others had.

"Anybody suspicious?" asks Mendez.

"No one," says Dad. "Just campers and bike riders and runners."

"Anyone with a camera with a big white lens?"

"No cameras, just smartphones."

Gale watches the girls sprint across the little meadow, squealing, one of them trailing a kite with the face of Taylor Swift on it, but Taylor just bounces along the ground and won't take off.

From the other side of the clearing a man watches the girls, too, a dark figure almost hidden in the trees.

"Daniela."

They walk the meadow's perimeter, Gale alternatingly watching the kite girls and keeping tabs on the man in the trees. The girls finally get Taylor airborne and when Gale looks back to the man, he's gone.

"Looked like he was wrapped in a blanket," says Mendez. "Tall."

Gale finds the spot where the man was standing and follows him through cottonwoods. The path is well-worn and wider than a game trail. The cottonwoods are still in leaf, and rods of sunlight illuminate the dew on the damp ground.

Blanket Man watches them from amid the white trunks as Gale approaches and waves.

The man is wrapped in a black blanket, and, Gale sees, camo combat boots not unlike his own in Sangin. Blanket Man's hair is long and dark, his face lined, and his beard and mustache gray. Six five, Gale guesses.

"Sheriffs," says Blanket Man. "You're not gonna clear us out, are you? We got nowhere to go."

"No. I'm Gale and she's Mendez. We'd like to talk if you have a minute."

"I believe I do."

"And you are?" asks Gale.

"Bingham. I go by one name. I'm honorary head of security here."

The man stares at Gale, who knows the look. "You serve?"

"One MEF out of Pendleton."

"Don't mess with MEF," says Gale.

"No, sir, don't. You?"

"Three-five. Sangin, Afghanistan."

"Ouch." Bingham nods with some respect, Gale sees, then turns in to the trees. Gale and Mendez follow.

6

The encampment is deep within the cottonwood forest.

Gale smells fire before he sees the freestanding tents, tarp lean-tos roped to the trees, shacks of plywood scraps and blankets and more tarps—blue, white, gray, and green—and others too old and sun-bleached to be much of any color at all. There's a small beaten pickup truck with a bug screen improvised over the bed. And a camper shell with no truck to cling to, lying in a neat clearing on which Gale sees broom marks.

Some of the ragged people stare at them, some wave, most of them ignore the detectives. Twenty or thirty by Gale's estimate. A dog approaches, tail wagging. A tabby cat preens in a patch of sunlight.

Gale notes the smoldering campfires in improvised, rock-ringed pits. And propane stoves and heaters under precarious roofs made of plastic kiddie pools perhaps scrounged from visitors to the campground. And the shopping carts, some of them heavy steel. God knows how they got them here through the wilderness.

Bingham walks between them, heading north toward the far end of the encampment. He smells strongly of a deodorant that Gale used in seventh grade at El Toro Elementary School. His black blanket sprouts holes and his jeans are stained and torn at the knees. Hair to his shoulders, lank and dirty.

"I didn't see or hear anything unusual that night," Bingham says.

"A twenty-two pistol makes a sharp, kind of popping sound," says Mendez. "A rifle a longer swoosh, higher pitched."

"I know."

"Were you here the whole time?" Gale asks.

"I used the campground bathroom once."

"Is that what you were doing just now, in the meadow? Heading for the bathroom?" asks Mendez.

"Yeah. I go when there's no people."

Bingham stops and reaches inside the blanket, shows the deputies a triangular shard of white hand soap and a green toothbrush.

"I wash in the sink, but the water's just a cold dribble."

"Where were you living before this?" asks Gale.

"Mendocino, in the woods. Before that, Oregon. Before that, Iraq."

"Doing what after the Marines?" asks Mendez.

"Herb. Got a little weird so I came to Laguna to see a friend. Ended up here."

Gale smells the sweet stink of pot smoke in the air, and Bingham cuts him a glance. A white-haired woman in a yellow housedress sits in a camp chair outside a red tent. A black pit bull at her feet. She looks over at Gale.

"Three shot dead at a grow a few miles away," says Gale. "Just a few days ago. Laotians, we think."

Bingham nods. "Out here it's LA bangers run by the Mexican Mafia versus white Riverside County guys. Back-and-forth raiding and killing. The Laotians team up with the Riverside guys. Work like slaves for about nothing. Get their passports taken away. Get ripped off and raped. The law runs them out but they come back a half mile away. Different grow, same mess. You people can't hardly do anything. Nobody can."

"I know some of those women," says Mendez. "Most of them are trusting. All of them are desperate. The men and boys, too."

"Be more ugly until the feds legalize it and the prices come down. Stoners aren't going to pay dispensary prices with rent high and gas at six bucks a gallon. Until then, *mucho dinero* in the illegal grass biz."

The woman in the yellow dress stands and stretches. Takes a hit on the pipe and ducks inside the red tent.

"Did you know any of those people at the grow massacre?" asks Gale.

"No, sir," says Bingham. "Not my world anymore. I'm just going to live here in peace until you throw us out. Enjoy your investigation. The skinny redhead dude in the gray lean-to does not like to be bothered. There are guns and knives but most of these people aren't prone to using them. Decent folks, most of them. Bad luck. I'm going to try for that bathroom again."

Gale and Mendez work the encampment back south toward the meadow, leapfrogging each other, quizzing the tent, lean-to, vehicle dwellers.

Every few interviews, they stop to compare notes. Neither come up with any leads. Most of the homeless have heard of a murder not far from them, a few nights back, a developer of some kind, a rich man.

"I think the gun was too far away to be heard," says Mendez.

"And the trees, muffling the sound," says Gale.

"I'm seeing and smelling plenty of dope. Plenty of needles. Filthy clothes and people. A lot of them are probably zonked-out pretty early. I'm surprised we haven't been ordered to close this place down."

"That judge won't let us."

"Wish he could see this," says Mendez.

"I've seen worse."

In a lean-to at the southern tip of the encampment, Gale introduces himself to Vito Pesco, a stocky, clean-shaven man with a florid face and thinning, shiny hair combed straight back. Gale guesses him to be forty, but he's missing some bottom teeth and his face is deeply creased and he looks north of fifty.

Inside the white-tarped lean-to, Gale notes the cot with its bedding neatly made up, a small wooden picnic table, and a bench on which boxes of canned goods sit. Pesco has lots of ravioli, spaghetti, tomatoes, asparagus, and beets.

He's sitting in a blue, low-slung canvas beach chair, a blue cooler on his left, and a vacant matching beach chair beyond that.

He wears shorts and flip-flops, and a black windbreaker against the fall chill. His legs are thick and suntanned.

"Have a seat," he says, and Gale settles into the blue canvas chair. "There's beer in the cooler."

"No, thanks. Too early."

"Well, it's five o'clock somewhere."

"Were you here the Thursday Tarlow was killed, late afternoon or evening?" asks Gale.

"I haven't left here in over a month," says Pesco. "Friends and family bring me food and beer, clothes, and stuff. Where'd it happen exactly?"

"Down in that stand of sycamores by the dry creek bed. It was a twenty-two-caliber gun. Two shots. You might have heard them from here."

"I play music CDs a lot after dark. There's radios, too. It's not loud but I didn't hear a shot. But I did see something strange around eight that night. I had to use the bathroom there at the campground. Dark out here, so I used a flashlight. I was washing up in the sink and I heard vehicles coming into the campground. Doors opening and closing. Not unusual, really, but there's not a lot of people coming and going that late. Then voices, men's voices, kind of low. Sounded friendly, or like they knew each other. I could hear their footsteps on the gravel. They went past the bathrooms and down the trail. When I finished up, I saw the two cars that had just come in. I'm a car guy. Used to be, anyway. I walked over and checked out a shiny new Suburban High Country. Dealer plates still taped to the window. That's the SUV I'd have if I could afford it. Big enough to sleep in. Pretty good mileage for something that big. The other vehicle was an old white van. A rusty Econoline, not a family van. Had a Bear Cave sticker on the bumper. That's a biker bar in Huntington Beach. Then I hit the trail and turned on my flashlight and cut back through the meadow for, well, home."

Pesco takes a beer from the cooler and cracks it open.

"You're sure it was two male voices?" asks Gale.

"Yeah, I'm sure. I was listening hard, hoping they weren't headed into the restrooms."

Gale watches a plump red-shouldered hawk perched in a tree, tugging off shreds of something in its talons and swallowing them down.

"Got to admit, Detective, I never thought I'd call a place like this home. I had my own restaurant in Santa Ana for two years. Pesco's. I had a decent apartment on Bristol, not far from your headquarters. I had a girlfriend and she had a daughter. We all got along just fine. But I hit the needle and shot up all the money and lost my girl and closed the place. Ann-Marie filed a complaint against me for molesting Analiese, got a restraining order but the DA didn't file. Lack of evidence."

Gale looks at Pesco in profile, just a cooler away, sizing up the man's story. Guilty men rarely confess a crime, but child molestation is in a class of its own when it comes to denial.

Pesco seems to read Gale's mind.

He turns and looks at the detective with clear, pale blue eyes. "I never touched the girl in any way like that. I really liked her. She told the cops that. It was a vengeance thing. I hit the streets in Tucson, then came back to Santa Ana, then came here. I honestly for the life of me don't know what's next."

Gale's bullshit monitor sounds only a soft alarm. He's somewhat trusting—for a cop. And in his twenty years since choosing that path, he's only been wrong a few times.

"Any convictions?"

"Drunk in public is all. I was always real careful with the H. And lucky."

Pesco takes a long draw of beer. "I kind of like it here."

"What color was the Suburban?" asks Gale.

"Midnight blue. I had to see that interior so I used the flashlight. Jet-black leather, perforated. So good looking. Didn't check out the van because it was old."

"Did you try to open the Suburban door?"

"Absolutely not."

"Look at the plates?"

"No, I didn't. The van's neither."

"Did you hear or see the men out there on the trail ahead of you?"

"No," says Pesco. "It was dark and that trail splits and splits again. Goes forever. What did you think when it turned out the mountain lion didn't kill the guy?"

Gale thinks about this. "I was happy we didn't have to shoot him."

"What if it gets a taste for humans?"

"Well, Mr. Pesco, that could be a real problem."

"Bears can."

"I've heard it said."

Gale watches Mendez approaching, checking her phone while she walks, then sliding it back into her rear pocket. She looks at him, her hard face without expression, palms up as if she's had enough of this place.

7

Bennet Tarlow's new midnight blue Suburban sits in the sheriff's impound yard in Santa Ana.

It's already drawn a light coating of dust, which reflects dully off the darkened glass of the windshield.

Mendez stands with her hands on her hips, parsing the big blue beast.

Gale stands aside and lets the impound deputy unlock the driver's-side door.

"All yours, Detectives. They've dusted for prints, used luminol for blood and body fluids. Shot pictures and video. This vehicle was just put into service last week, so it's pretty clean. They took a leather briefcase off the passenger seat for processing. Left everything else like you see it. Kind of a mess."

Gale circles the Suburban clockwise. Notes the road dirt on its tires and the heavy blanket of fine dust accumulated on the liftgate window. He notes the High Country model designation on the rear liftgate and the subtle dark blue glitter of its body, subdued by the dust.

Wonders why Tarlow and his companion would come in separate cars to the same place, park near each other, walk side by side from the campsite to the trail, then down into the brushy creek wash where Tarlow was shot in the head and left in the sand to bleed to death.

Gale takes from his jeans pocket a leather-bound notepad, made by a distant nephew of his in San Juan Capistrano, and writes his speculations regarding the separate vehicles used to transport Tarlow to his execution. Wonders if a third party was waiting for them. Possibly. But no third set of footprints in the creek bed. Though a third person might have taken a different exit route from the dying Tarlow. Might have used the wash, but obscured the prints with a leafy tree branch, or even a broom or blanket or garment—an old Native trick that might have been applied by his Acjacheme/Juaneño ancestors on his mother's side. He's seen the Taliban do that in the Sangin Valley sand, using the opium poppy stalks uprooted after harvest. Specifically, the old man going to and from the long-abandoned village house, from which he fetched his shotgun, whom Gale later assassinated as the sniper he was not.

Third party in dark? he neatly writes. *Cover tracks w/ flashlight or cell phone like Pesco?*

Unlikely, he thinks.

Camera, big lens, tripod. Why?

Gale opens the door and retractable steps drop into place, and he climbs into the driver's seat. Mendez takes the passenger side and they close the doors.

The new-car smell is strong. The black leather looks top-grade. White fingerprint dust marks the dark dash, the computer screen, the black leather steering wheel and shifter, the turn signals, and window controls. The chrome and brushed aluminum accents have been dusted with black.

The console stowage and dashboard glove box have been left open, and their contents appear to be stuffed haphazardly back into place.

"No *Good Housekeeping* seal of approval," says Mendez.

"Sure smells good, though."

"I do love a new car. What do you drive, Lew?"

"An old 4Runner that won't give up. You?"

"A red Corvette to make me feel young. It's the only expensive thing I've ever bought myself."

Gale nods. "I'll bet you're worth it, Daniela."

"I'm convincing myself of that."

Mendez runs the beam of her laser pointer over pale smudges of luminol on the floor mats, in which blood, body fluids, and secretions glow blue in infrared light, but Gale sees no such glow.

"I'm drawing a blank on why Tarlow and his companion took two vehicles to the same destination," he says. "It suggests that Econoline Man knew he'd ride out alone."

"Yes, planned," says Mendez. "Not impulse. I can't see a third person out there. Two voices heard by Pesco, right? You made sure to confirm that?"

"He said two."

"Well, then I agree with you," says Mendez. "Tarlow's buddy knew he'd need his van. But why not shoot him from the front, or through an ear, wipe down the gun, and put it in Tarlow's hand? Pretty easy way to throw us off."

"Because this way it's a statement," says Gale. "A warning. Maybe punishment."

"Sure," says Mendez. "A guy with that much money and power. You know he's made enemies. Probably a lot of them. And Tarlow was a social creature. I've seen him in the society pages for years—those glossy Orange County magazines. A bachelor. Nice looking. Always with a woman or two. Or three. Plenty of jealous husbands around."

"Maybe jealous girlfriends of Tarlow's, too," says Gale, again remembering Tarlow's companion at the Las Vegas heavyweight fight that night. Norris.

Gale checks the compartment of the door beside him, running his phone light down into the black recesses.

Then turns down the sun visor and slides open the vanity mirror and light. More black fingerprint dust on the mirror.

Checks the eyeglasses bin, which opens at his touch. Empty, except for a scrap of heavy paper, folded in half, with a faint black line running near the torn top. Gale wonders if the CSIs overlooked it. Would be easy, he thinks, tucked up near the roof by the interior lights that shine in your eyes.

He fingers out and unfolds the scrap. Roughly the shape of Virginia, he sees—a flat bottom with a torn, hilly top. Heavy white stock that's been quickly or sloppily torn out.

The numbers are written in a neat, forward-slanting, draftsman-like hand that reminds Gale of his own, and of his father's. Ten digits, spaced and hyphenated like phone numbers.

He holds it out for Mendez to see.

She looks up from the messily repacked glove compartment.

A beat of silence between them, both detectives trying to figure this.

Gale names the number *Tarlow Suburban* in his contacts, then dials.

His call goes to voicemail:

"Hi, it's Patti. Leave a message and a callback number please."

To Gale, Patti sounds assured and pleasant. Professional. Thirty-something? Hard to tell age from voice.

He leaves his name and work number, which will lead Patti to his own voicemail greeting, which is brief and makes no mention of the Orange County Sheriff's Department.

He calls Glen Osaka in the crime lab to see if they found a personal calendar/planner in his leather briefcase from the Suburban. No dice, says the Cybercrimes technician.

"And no phone, I take it."

"No, Detective, no magic bullet like that."

"CSIs will be bringing you a camera we found here at the kill site," says Gale.

"How'd we miss it the first time through?"

"Wrong site. Either the cat or the killer moved him. I want to know what's on it."

"I'll hustle it through."

Gale rings off and hears the low buzz of Mendez's phone. She opens her door and turns her back to him.

"You know you're not supposed to—"

Gale catches a few words: "I'm not coming home . . . tonight . . . maybe . . . don't worry, Mom."

Then silence as the call ends.

Mendez slams the door shut, turning to Gale. "Sorry."

"Don't be."

"Jesse. Everything's fine. His girlfriend leads him around sometimes."

"Eighteen, I think you said?"

She nods. Stares at her phone like it will get Jesse back on.

"Senior at Tustin High," she says. "All work experience this semester, with only two classes—auto shop and gaming. Twenty hours a week at Bowl Me Over in Santa Ana. Started out bussing dishes two years ago and he's up to assistant manager now. Of the kitchen, not the whole alley. Inward and quiet, but basically a good kid. No, a great kid. Never knew his late father but don't get me started on him. Tell me to shut up, Lew."

"Shut up, Daniela."

A look in her hard eyes, half a smile.

Now Lew Gale's phone throbs, and *Tarlow Suburban* appears above the number.

"Hello, Patti," he says.

"How can I help you?"

"My partner and I are investigating the murder of Bennet Tarlow. He had your number in his SUV and that's where I'm calling from. Can you talk?"

"Are you a private detective or law enforcement?"

"Orange County Sheriff's deputy."

She pauses. "I'd rather not talk by phone. I can meet you in half an hour."

She gives Gale her office address on Coast Highway in Newport Beach and hangs up.

8

Patti DiMeo is a Realtor with Lido Estates in Newport Beach. Her office is in Lido Marina Village, part of a row of quaint shops looking out on Newport Bay. Good views of the yachts at anchor and those moving slowly along Lido Channel. Some of the vessels look huge. The midafternoon sunlight seems to part for them.

Gale looks out at all this. To his mind, Newport Beach is still true to its roots: white, wealthy, conservative, and proud. Its favorite son is John Wayne. In many ways Newport is the opposite of Gale's birth town of San Juan Capistrano, seventeen miles southeast, near Caspers Wilderness Park.

Patti is abundantly blond, blue-eyed, slender, and suntanned. A black knit suit, a white blouse, and a pearl-and-emerald choker. Gale guesses midthirties and sees no wedding ring. She's square-jawed, with a pretty smile, and, to Gale, intelligent-looking hands.

He scans the Lido Estates listings on one wall. A few of the homes for sale look small, slightly Cape Cod–ish, with white picket fences and little green lawns. Some look to have been built in the

1950s and 1960s. Some are extravagant contemporaries of stone and glass. The lots are small and the homes look crowded together. The cheapest one Gale sees is listed for $6.5 million; the most expensive is $27.5 million.

First, some small talk about the south Orange County real estate market, which Patti says is trending up again as the holidays approach. Corona del Mar and the Irvine Coast are quite hot right now. Lots of value down on the peninsula if you don't mind the traffic. The beach is what you're really buying.

"When did you last see Mr. Tarlow?" Gale asks.

"The week before they . . . found him. The Tarlow Company hosted an invite-only preview for a handful of the top OC Realtors. I got the call for Lido Estates. Tarlow was introducing Wildcoast—their proposed development outside of San Juan Capistrano, near Caspers Park. We Realtors were one of his focus groups. Tarlow Company showed artist renderings and videos of other developments from, well, across half the globe, actually."

"Must have been an impressive show," says Mendez.

"It really was," says DiMeo. "Wildcoast isn't a traditional development at all. It's designed to be chartered as a full civic entity—a city. Five square miles. That's half the size of the city of Laguna Beach. Single-family homes, condos, and apartments. Affordable housing. Not token affordable, but one-*quarter* of all the units, built into the pricing by Tarlow Company and the city of Wildcoast. Schools, churches, two synagogues, two mosques. Two shopping centers, anchored by upscale retailers. A downtown Main Street made of solar-generating cobblestones. With city hall, a monster library, two public pools, shopping and dining with high-ratio pedestrian circulation. An equestrian center and trails into the beautiful mountains near Caspers Park. A small airstrip for private craft only. Every single rooftop—residential and commercial—made with solar tiles. A small wind farm tucked back in the foothills. Parks and big public gardens where people can grow flowers and food to eat. They're calling them 'victory gardens.' Isn't that all, just, well, the coolest?"

"I know a little about it," says Gale. "The local governments and environmentalists aren't happy. The Natives, even less so."

His mother, for example, one of the official spokespersons for the Acjacheme nation of San Juan Capistrano, isn't exactly happy about a small utopian city built on land that once belonged to her ancestors. A nation that remains unrecognized by the Bureau of Indian Affairs, on technical grounds. Thus, no sovereign land and mineral rights, no federal aid, no casinos.

"Oh, lots of people are livid," says Patti DiMeo. "A small group of protestors picket outside the Tarlow building every afternoon, then the Newport cops run them out or arrest them. Natives. Non-Native locals. Everybody wants to hold on to what they have. Not build a new city! Keep the demand high and the supply small and the prices up. To them, Wildcoast's a NIMBY but not like homeless shelters or halfway houses or fulfillment centers. They're talking about something that, when you learn about it, sounds more like paradise. Beautiful architecture in a beautiful setting. Tarlow Company has a reputation for high-end excellence. They're outdoing themselves on this one."

"When do they propose to break ground?" Gale asks.

"This was all just concept. They say construction will begin in two, maybe three years. Which seems early to me. You wouldn't believe the design reviews, regulations, permits. Federal, state, county, city. Imagine the financing. I think five years is more realistic."

"Sounds like you'd love to sell some homes out there when Wildcoast is up and running," says Mendez.

"I'd love to *have* one. Either way, I'll be first in line."

She nods and looks out the window.

"Had you met Bennet before this preview?" asks Gale.

"No."

"Did you give him your personal number?"

"I did. He asked for it."

"Did you write it down for him?"

"Yes."

"Why not just text it to him?"

"We were talking about how intrusive phones have become and he made a joke about doing things the old-fashioned way. So I got my Montblanc out of my clutch and wrote the number near the bottom of the complimentary Tarlow Company notepad in the swag bag. Tore it off and gave it to him and asked him if that was old-fashioned enough."

With a slender, intelligent finger, Patti DiMeo wipes a tear away from one eye. Then the other.

"Is it true that he was partially eaten by the Killer Cat?"

"Yes, I'm afraid so," says Gale.

"But the animal didn't kill him?"

"Some other animal did," says Mendez. "He died of gunshot wounds."

DiMeo stares out the window and Gale sees the shine of her cheeks in the sunlight. Wipes them again.

"Such a nice guy. A famous man and all that, but you know, he was just easy to talk to and not full of himself. No arrogance, or even pride. Humble, almost. I thought, smooth-talking dude. Thought of Indira Gandhi's famous, 'Don't be humble, you're not that great.' But I believed him. He was aware of himself but not impressed by himself. I was so tickled to tear off that number and give it to him. I remember both of us thinking it was kind of funny."

"What did you talk about?"

"Well, Wildcoast and more Wildcoast. After the formal presentation and all the Q and A, Mr. Tarlow came up to me on the deck of the Tarlow Company building. It's fifteen stories up, in Newport

Center. Views of the entire universe. That black ocean heaving away, out there. We yapped about where we grew up and school and sports, and about big families, which I come from. He seemed almost regretful, being an only child."

"How old are you?" asks Mendez. "And where did you grow up?"

"Thirty-five and Newport Beach."

"Married?"

"Never."

"Did Mr. Tarlow tell you why he wanted your personal number?" asks Mendez.

"At first I thought, wow, Bennet Tarlow wants to talk to *me* about a job. But he didn't want to call at work, leave his name with a receptionist or voicemail. He gave me a raised-eyebrow kind of look and I gave him one back. We were both aware of what asking for a personal phone number implies."

A young man comes through the office door and hands a folder to DiMeo without looking at either detective. He closes the door behind him and the room goes quiet.

Gale watches her set the folder on the desk in front of her and stare down at it, sighing.

"Something unusual happened last week," she says. "Three days after the Wildcoast concept focus and two days before Mr. Tarlow died. A staffer from Kevin Elder's office made a morning appointment to discuss properties for sale here on Lido. Elder is the Seventh District Orange County supervisor, as I'm sure you know. This man identified himself as Grant Hudson. Young guy, a navy suit and a white straw fedora. I assumed he was scouting real estate possibilities for his boss, because it's not likely that a thirtysomething man on the county payroll would be looking to buy a home for himself in Newport Beach. Of course I didn't ask. He was interested in four bedrooms and two baths, something with 'some character,' he said. I invited him to look at the pictures on the wall there, and he did.

He didn't spend much time on any of them. I figured he was deep into sticker shock. He sat back down across from me and asked a few questions about schools and boat slip leases. He was interested in joining a yacht club. Then, right out of the blue, he said he saw me out on the Tarlow Company building deck, talking with Bennet Tarlow at the Wildcoast concept preview, and asked what we had talked about. I told him we talked about Wildcoast—what else would we have talked about? He said he saw me write something on a notepad and tear off the bottom and hand it to 'Bennet Tarlow III.' He assumed it was my personal line and asked me if Mr. Tarlow had called. I told him no and asked him to leave my office. Said I'd introduce him to another agent if he was even remotely interested in buying a home through us."

Gale sees the embarrassed blush on Patti DiMeo's face.

"That was more than rude," says Mendez.

"It was really weird."

"What did he do?"

"Put on his hat and walked out."

"And Bennet Tarlow called, didn't he?" asks Mendez.

"Yes. The morning of the day he was killed. He asked me for coffee the next day at nine, my choice where. We were set for the Moulin in Laguna. At first, when he didn't show, I thought he'd stood me up. Not surprised. Look, I know I should have called the police but I was just too blown away to think straight. Still am. But I'll come in and make statements or depositions or whatever it is you detectives do. I'm sick to death about this and I'll do what I can to help you, and put Bennet Tarlow's killer on death row. Maybe I shouldn't say that. I'm supposed to be a liberal Californian but I'm not. I believe in the death penalty."

"This interview is enough for now," says Gale. "Thank you."

She wipes the corner of one eye with a balled fist. "I've got a four o'clock."

"Yes, thank you, Ms. DiMeo," says Mendez. "We'll put his ass on death row for you. Or hers. Done deal."

Sitting in his small office in the Orange County Building, Grant Hudson says his conversation with Patti DiMeo in her office was pretty dull.

"Kind of a bimbo I'd say."

Admits he asked her about writing something on a complimentary Tarlow Company notepad they all got in their swag bags. And tearing a strip off the bottom of the pad and handing it to one of the most powerful men in the United States.

"I thought that was more than a little interesting."

"Why did you want to talk to her about it?" asks Mendez.

"Wouldn't you? The Tarlow Company's Wildcoast lies smack-dab within the Seventh District. Kevin Elder—my boss and esteemed supervisor—has his concerns with a megalopic development paving over five square miles of pretty much pristine, *genuine* wilderness. Will this multibillion-dollar profit center truly serve the citizens of Orange County? So I thought I'd confront Ms. DiMeo about giving Tarlow her personal phone number. I assumed that's what it was. Maybe Bennet Tarlow confided something to her that he has not confided to us. He was incommunicative with government at all levels. And famously popular with the ladies, so . . ."

"I can tell you're truly devastated by his murder," says Mendez.

Hudson shrugs. "I feel bad for him. Sure. A life cut that short. I'll bet he called her, didn't he?"

"Not that we know," says Gale.

"Can a cop perjure himself?"

"Only in court," says Gale. "Not to a midlevel government cockroach like you."

"Oh, that stings, but not that much! I've got a five o'clock if you don't mind."

"Where were you on the evening and night that Bennet Tarlow was murdered in Caspers Wilderness Park?" asks Mendez.

Grant Hudson leans forward, taps the desktop computer keyboard, raises his eyes to the monitor, and slides his mouse. "Aha! Dinner at the Grove with the boss and a Tesla factory relocation team. Food was fantastic. Sorry you guys didn't get an invite."

"No Tarlow there, I take it," says Daniela. "Maybe heading out after an early cocktail."

Hudson shakes his head. Gale's been to the Grove Club just once, as the guest of *his* boss, Sheriff Kersey, and Bennet Tarlow. It's where Gale and Tarlow first met, and what led to Gale moonlighting as security for the developer. Insiders call it the Grove, never the Grove Club. The Grove is a late 1800s mission-era hacienda main house, repurchased, restored, and converted to a private club by the secretive Paladin Society—conservative businessmen and women, politicians and right-wing Hollywood movers and celebrities.

As Gale got to know Tarlow through his bodyguarding, he began to see him as an affable libertine not fully synchronized with the Grove at all.

"Where do they want to build the factory?" asks Gale.

"Oh, come on, kids! I can't tell you that. Somewhere in the great County of Orange."

"Help us with your alibi," says Mendez. "Two names from your alleged night at the Grove."

Hudson pushes back with open hands. "I'm not going to sic you mutts on my friends. You want that, charge me with something and take me downtown."

"We asked you a simple question," says Mendez. "So why won't you answer?"

"You are wasting my time. And yours."

"You called Bennet Tarlow one of the most powerful man in the United States," says Gale. "Do you know anyone who would want him dead?"

Hudson scoots rearward in his wheeled chair, locking his hands beside his head. "Not a one."

"Do you think Tarlow was honest?" asks Gale.

"I think the powerful play by different rules than you and me."

"What about his politics?" asks Mendez.

"Weird enough, a liberal," says Hudson, pedaling back to his desk. "He always played superior to us. Suspicious of government overreach. Big on personal rights."

"Abortion, LGBTQ rights?"

"Sure."

"What about environmentalists, the EPA, Department of the Interior?"

Hudson gives Mendez a look, then Gale. "Lots of disagreement over Wildcoast. Years of it. Some of it hot."

"Tarlow doesn't sound like Grove material," says Gale.

"My dear policeman," says Hudson. "Everything in this country begins with money and power. Even the Grove."

"Some names would be nice," says Gale.

"Nope. No specific individuals that I know. I'm being honest here. Talk to Tarlow's people if you want names."

"You called him 'famously popular with the ladies,'" says Mendez.

"So?"

"Does that reputation follow him into places like the Grove?" she asks.

"It was never a secret."

"Did Tarlow have an interest in men, in that way?" Mendez asks.

"Not that I know. Kind of doubt it though, with all his female company."

"Yeah," says Gale. "Mr. Hudson, what kind of car do you drive?"

Hudson taps his fingers on the desktop. "A Lexus."

"Do you have a second vehicle?"

"Got a vintage Bronco I take off-road now and then."

"Know anyone who drives an older Econoline? White?"

Hudson shakes his head and stands. "Look, I didn't like Bennet Tarlow III. But I *really* don't like that he got shot dead. I can't help you with his enemies. I'm not in a position to know. But any Grove bartender might point you in the right direction, if you can get yourselves in."

"It's called a badge," says Gale.

"Grove security is tough."

He knows two fellow OCSD deputies who freelance as Grove security.

"Ask for John Velasquez," says Hudson. "You can use my name if you make it that far, but I'm not sure what it will get you. He's there most of the time. Sorry, now, but you need to go."

"Can you pave our way into the Grove as guests?" asks Mendez, with a look to Gale.

"Only members can do that," says Hudson.

"How many times have they turned down your application?" asks Mendez.

"Once. I'm fattening up the bio before I try again."

"You'll get in someday," says Mendez. "People like you always fail up."

Back in his Explorer, Gale's phone rings.

"Owls in a tree," says Glen Osaka. "An adult and two fluffy owlets. Twenty-six exposures taken at ten o'clock in Caspers Park, the night Tarlow was killed. The mom looks pissed. Next most recent were taken two months ago in Tahiti—a whole lot of exotic birds and a woman with red hair and a pretty smile. The camera's a digital, so easy to open up and loaded with information. I googled Tarlow and sure enough, one of his hobbies is bird photography. He's had pictures in the *Audubon* magazine over the years, some in *National Geographic*, too."

"Can you send me the owls?"

"I've never seen such big ones. Even the owlets. Bigger than our great horned owls, by a lot. Weird face. On their way, Gale."

"Any prints on the camera gear that aren't Tarlow's?"

"Not a one."

"Thank you, Glen. You're more than good."

Gale looks at the owl pictures, all twenty-six of them.

It's a weird-looking owl alright, regal and powerful and haunted. Lit brightly against the darkness, a phantom.

9

At the bottom of blue tile steps leading to the front door of the Grove, Gale's fellow sheriff's deputy—fingers laced at his beltline, dressed in a navy suit, white shirt, and red tie—notes Gale and Mendez with a curt but respectful nod.

"Detectives," he says. "What a nice surprise."

"Thought we'd ask around about Bennet Tarlow," says Gale.

"This is the right place."

"But what we'd really like is a drink in that bar."

"Of course. The mood around here has been subdued since what happened."

The young deputy nods again and the detectives set out on the long steep rise of steps. Before them stands the former hacienda manor house, now the Grove Club, bathed in the outdoor mission-bell lamps, its interior alive behind white curtains. Two elderly men in tuxedos descend from above, escorting two much younger women in evening wear.

Standing at the immense front door, a second OCSD deputy, gray buzz cut and a mustache, and dressed almost exactly like the first, gives Gale and Mendez a stony look and pulls on the wrought-iron handle.

"Thank you, Sergeant," says Mendez. "You look sharp in that suit."

"Shucks, Dani."

Gale leads them into a dark brassy bar just off the balconied, two-floor dining room. Black leather booths with privacy curtains along two walls. Another wall is a floor-to-ceiling triptych oil painting of Mission San Juan Capistrano, beautifully lit: the mission proper in the center panel, flanked by a pastoral scene of Indians at labor in an abundant cornfield, and a third panel table depicting Father Junípero Serra pouring water over the head of a full-grown man on his knees in the mission baptistry.

Two television screens are discretely hung over the busy bar, high enough up that the drinkers have to crane their necks a bit to watch.

Gale notes that CBS Channel 2 out of LA is showing Sheriff Kersey's press conference, and he's just now stating the cause of death of the celebrity businessman Bennet Tarlow III.

Two young patrons move down for them and the detectives squeeze in. There are three bartenders—a sleek, silver-haired man; a beefy, bald Black guy; and a pretty Vietnamese woman—all in black slacks, white shirts, black bow ties, and red vests.

With an assessing look, the sleek one sets coasters in front of them and takes their orders.

Gale holds out his badge wallet and the barman peers at the shield, then at its owner. Mendez next.

"What can I do for you, Deputies?"

"John Velasquez?"

A nod.

"Grant Hudson says he was here the night that Bennet Tarlow died," says Gale. "He said you might talk to us."

The bartender gives Gale a flat look. He's thin-faced and elegant as a snake, thinks Gale.

Takes their drink orders, then goes through a swinging door near the mirrored shelves of liquor. Gale figures he's getting permission to either talk to them or ask them to leave. He's back in five minutes with a bourbon on the rocks for Gale and a beer for Mendez.

"Hudson was here," says John Velasquez. "With his boss, the Supervisor Kevin Elder, and two Tesla guys, one of whom picked up the tab. They had drinks and dinner, and stayed late. Ten, ten-thirty."

"Seen them here before?" asks Mendez.

"First time Tesla."

"Do Hudson and Elder come here often?"

"Oh yeah. Usually guests of the Tarlow Company. Elder is Seventh District supervisor. The Tarlow Company is a big donor. I'll be back."

The detectives drink.

"Excuse me," says Mendez, working her phone with both hands. "Just have to message Jesse."

Gale takes another sip of bourbon, tastes that wonderful power and promise. He listens to the tap-tap of Daniela's thumbs. Which reminds him of Patti DiMeo's fingers. Which remind him of Tarlow's companion for fight night in Las Vegas, Norris something, the Laguna Beach by way of Fort Worth redhead. Beautiful, intelligent young women.

Hudson has "bimbo" Patti wrong, he thinks. Norris had a soft laugh but a sharp tongue. Of course, they can't help but remind him of his ex-wife, Marilyn, a blond beauty he'd met in high school in San Juan Capistrano. Danced exotically with grace and resentful aggression, and was proud of her IQ. Wanted more. Now, five years gone to Las Vegas, an actual showgirl.

"Sorry," says Mendez.

Who reminds him not at all of Marilyn, who back then didn't want children anyway. And certainly not later, not with a ruined, post-traumatic Marine with a taste for liquor and no desire to talk about what he'd been through in Sangin. It half amazes him now that they lasted as long as they did. They haven't talked since. When the phone doesn't ring, it's Marilyn.

"No, it's good, Daniela."

Velasquez sets down two more drinks. "On us."

Gale asks him about the last time he saw Bennet Tarlow.

"The week before he was killed," says Velasquez. "He had dinner in one of the booths. He preferred the bar to the dining room. Two men with him. Kevin Elder and Kyle McNab of PacWest Mining."

"Who picked up the check?" asks Mendez.

"McNab. He was pissed off about something. Elder trying to smooth him over. Don't ask me what."

"Is McNab a regular?"

"I've seen him half a dozen times in the last year. Never, before that."

"So, what's cooking with the Tarlow Company and PacWest Mining?" asks Mendez.

Velasquez shrugs. "The Tarlow Company works decades ahead, on three continents. Makes my head spin, all the things they build. I just get bits and pieces of it in here."

He moves down the line, takes an order from two well-dressed women, midforties, fresh in from Santa Fe, Gale guesses. Lots of suede and turquoise, alert to each other but more alert to the people at the bar.

A few minutes later, the bartender is back.

"Had you seen Bennet Tarlow with any new players recently, except the Tesla guys?" asks Gale.

"New faces, always," says Velasquez.

"Any of them surprise you? Unusual or out of place?" asks Mendez.

"The USC Engineering Club. Very Bennet to bring them in, wine and dine them, let them pick his brain, give them career advice. Starstruck kids."

"How did Bennet Tarlow II and III get along?" asks Gale.

Velasquez gives him a sharp look. "Not for me to guess. I hear rumors but I don't see them together here. Not often."

"Let's have a rumor or two," says Mendez.

Velasquez goes down the bar to welcome a young tech titan and his wife, Oscar and Nora Samuelson. Gale sees them often on the PBS *Inside OC* weeknight show. The Samuelson Foundation is a sponsor. Oscar wears a brown, Italian-cut suit and a narrow green tie; Nora a sleek green suit that compliments her short red hair.

The bartender leans in for some direct conversation. Laughter and a comment from Nora, then more laughter. Gale puts them in their late thirties, Daniela's age. The glow of prosperity is upon them. He watches her size them up with her hard dark eyes.

Velasquez makes and serves the power couple their drinks. Gale wonders what he makes in tips for a night. A smiling man, arms wide, comes up on Oscar from behind, claps his hand on Oscar's shoulder. Gale recognizes him as the owner of the much-maligned Los Angeles Angels, formerly the Anaheim Angels.

Then the bartender is back.

"Okay, the basic plot is, Tarlow III loved the homes he built and doesn't cut corners," Velasquez says. "But his father prefers the office towers and warehouses—the monsters, the 'fulfillment centers'—out in the Inland Empire. Most of which—again, rumors—Bennet Tarlow II lowballs on cost and highballs on rents. The Tarlow Company owns those towers and commercial centers outright. But the homes that III loved to build, Tarlow Company does not own. They get sold, right? Home ownership. American dream. So, it was Commercial Hardball II versus Softy Home Builder III. These are rumors a bartender picks up, but from what I overhear in my bar, they're right on. I hope I've helped you. I hope you find whoever shot Bennet. I liked him. He was one of the good guys. It's about to get busy in here. So excuse me, the man who gave the greatest player in the history of baseball to his crosstown rivals needs another drink."

"Just a couple of long shots," says Gale.

"Fire away."

"A white Econoline van. Older and beat up. Rust on the body, down low along the wheel wells."

Velasquez parts his hands and shakes his head. "Won't find anything like that in our lot."

Gale shows Patti DiMeo's picture on the Lido Estates web page. Another headshake.

"One more round, and the bill," Gale says. "And thank you."

"Coffee here," says Mendez.

Velasquez gives her a minor smile, raps his knuckles gently on the bar top, and moves away.

Mendez gives Gale a look. "Well," she says. "End of day one, partner. We *should* be having a drink. Meet at Tarlow's home tomorrow morning? I've got some family things later."

"Me, too."

She raises her eyebrows hopefully.

"Tarlow has a cottage in Laguna and a mansion in Newport," says Gale. "Gets most of his mail in Laguna, so we'll start there. We have to know where he left from, bound for Caspers that night. To meet up with his companion in the white van. Or, maybe following him."

"Walk backwards, starting at the crime scene," says Mendez. "Just like they taught us in homicide school. Maybe we'll find a helpful neighbor. Or find his calendar."

"That would be nice," says Gale.

"It's probably on his phone," she says.

"In the bottom of Irvine Lake or the Pacific."

10

An hour later, Gale steps into his San Juan Capistrano adobe home. It's on an alley off Los Rios Street, in the historic district, not far from the mission.

The Amtrak Surfliner roars northbound, a few hundred feet from his front door.

The adobe was built not long after President Lincoln had claimed Mission San Juan Capistrano from Mexico and returned it to the grateful Spanish friars. It was they who had recruited the local Indians to build and worship in it. His mother's family had lived in this place for five generations, descending from the Acjacheme who originally built it under the Spanish. Her Native blood is Gale's half.

While the train thunders past, windows rattle, dishes clink in the cabinets, and the roof timbers creak.

His mother sits on one end of the couch in the lamplight, a basket in progress on her lap.

"So late, Lew."

"Tarlow."

"It's awful. But good you didn't have to shoot that lion."

"I never really wanted to."

"No. We take so many orders. Still."

He pours three fingers of bourbon and takes the glass to his room, where he hangs his paddle holster and gun on the door. Heads to the kitchen and opens the refrigerator. Microwaves a big bowl of chicken tortilla soup and eats it standing up at the counter. The counter tiles are Mexican and well made, over a hundred years old, cobalt blue with red filigree near the edges and one small yellow quail in each middle.

"How do you like Daniela after one day?"

"She's good, Mom. She'll be a good homicide detective."

"Single, you said?"

"You know I did, Mom. A divorced single mom, like you."

"Your papa called today. The principal offered him a raise so he wouldn't retire."

"Well, the school district gets its money's worth out of him."

"He doesn't want to retire anyway. He just doesn't want them to forget that he can."

That's Dad, thinks Gale: getting his way by threatening to leave. Then leaving anyway.

He rinses his dishes, fetches his own in-progress basket from the spare bedroom and sits at the opposite end of the blue couch. Sets his bourbon on the lampstand, turns on the light, and sets the basket on his lap.

His basket is a classic Acjacheme made up of black geometric designs—oddly Grecian—staggered within a circle of thick, tightly wound straw, mostly undyed. Many days from now he'll finish it with a circle of rust red, bordered by interlocking rectangles of thin black. His mother taught him the pattern when he was ten and showed some interest.

It was much harder than making the bows and arrows his grandfather taught him to build. It took him ten years and twelve baskets to get one balanced and symmetrical. Quit for the war but picked it up when he came home. What he liked about weaving was how you could go slow and get it right, and let your mind wander while you worked. You could listen to music and hum along. You could think about sports and, later, girls. Even early on, he'd enjoyed the doing just as much as the ending. This will be his forty-third, one for each year of his life.

Now he takes a sip of bourbon and looks down at his project.

I'm a basket case.

A former bow-and-arrow maker, now a basket maker.

A former man.

Jesus help me.

Chinigchinich—god of the Acjacheme—help me.

He wonders how a mega-builder like Bennet Tarlow III spent his evenings. Wonders why he and his companion took two vehicles to Caspers that night. Wonders what the old, beat-up, rusty Econoline said about its driver. And about Tarlow, too.

Also wonders if Mendez made it home okay, and how she spends her evenings. A day like today—face-to-face with murder—can take it out of you. Especially if you've got a hard-assed attitude to keep up.

He takes the leather notebook from his hip pocket and reviews his notes on this first day in his revised investigation into the death of Tarlow. Notes that Daniela Mendez is smart and has a hard but handsome face. The general drift he's gotten from the department deputies is that she's not a woman who takes things lightly.

Later in bed he takes up a time-aged manuscript given to him by his great-grandmother.

Blood & Heart was written in Spanish by a mission-educated twenty-one-year-old Acjacheme named Luis Verdad in 1815, passed down and nearly forgotten through the decades, and this English version was translated by Gale's great-grandmother.

Luis Verdad is the name given to him by Father Serra, erasing his Native name, which Verdad states in his introduction was "Oso Nada" or "Bear Swims."

The manuscript is 135 pages, translated from Verdad's original handwritten Spanish. It's the oldest piece of Juaneño Mission Indian writing extant. There's a carbon copy behind glass in the Mission San Juan Capistrano museum store, and $15.99 paperbacks for sale, with a colorful cover of a boy with a primitive bow walking along a beach.

Lew Gale has read these pages countless times, a lifelong companion on his way into his dreams.

He likes the aged pages better than the slick museum paperback because they feel as if Luis Verdad has touched them himself.

Blood & Heart is the story about Luis at age twenty, a respected hunter and warrior, tracking a mountain lion that has carried away his young sister, Magdalena. The huge cat snatched her from the garden outside the Verdad family's newly built adobe house near the mission grounds, and Luis fears she is dead but he wants to find her "remnants" so they can cremate her and send her to heaven in the Acjacheme way.

And he wants to kill the lion. The lion has done this three times before, dragged people off—right there in the village not far from the mission's walls—and Verdad promises his mother and father that he will end this evil.

Luis Verdad sets out with his friend and fellow hunter Bernardo Rio. They each have their best bows, twenty good arrows with fire-hardened foreshafts and obsidian tips, and stone arrow straighteners. Also, for his tracking skills and optimistic attitude, they have Luis's hunting companion, Water Dog.

Verdad says in the introduction of *Blood & Heart* that the older men are afraid of this lion because of its size and lack of fear and its taste for human blood. He's now taken four Acjacheme, and there are rumors of Cahuilla and Luiseño victims as well. Lions can travel miles in a single day. Some say this cat has killed and eaten dozens, and others say scores. Some elders and medicine men believe that the lion lives in "a cavern of light in an underground sea," which is a resting place for spirits on their way to the afterlife. And, if Luis doesn't find Magdalena's body, that means she's been taken to the cavern. According to Verdad, the elders openly admit to being more terrified by this lion than by the much larger and much more numerous grizzly bears that routinely kill Natives, traders, and pirates, though often avoid people and the mission grounds.

Even after his many readings over nearly four decades, Gale isn't sure whether this account is fact or fable, or how much of which. He keeps changing his mind. In his introduction, Verdad says his tale is factual, just as his given name means "true." His grandmother and mother have both told him that it is true, but the detective hears mythmaking here. Which he enjoys almost as much as the stories' glimpses of Acjacheme life in the days of the Spanish padres, and is part of the reason he's read it so many times.

As he reads, Gale hears Luis's voice, a young man speaking Juaneño-accented Spanish:

We killed and ate rabbits and birds along our way. There was water in the creek and it was hot in summer. Bernardo built nooses from oak shoots and tried to trap turkey at night as we sleep. Turkeys are bigger than quail but quail blood is sweeter. Water Dog tries to catch tadpoles in the ponds and when we are at the ocean he hunts fish and crabs in the tidepools.

We have been hunting for two days. We've seen three bears and two large rattlesnakes, but no lions. We followed the blood trail until it ran out, but I was able to find the trail again using footprints and trampled brush and twigs broken off. It looks as if the lion is carrying something large, by the way the grass and earth are smoothly beaten down. This saddens my heart because it might lead us to Magdalena.

I believed we would find her by now, or maybe only what of her is left, but no. Is this cause for sorrow or for hope?

I have named the big lion El Diablo, after the devil in Father Serra's Bible. Fear and superstition keep the men of my tribe from joining this hunt. Bernardo and I have fear and superstition too but we want Magdalena to go to what the Franciscans call heaven. This we call afterlife. Bernardo and I have the hearts of the warrior-priests we both wish to become someday.

This morning Water Dog found the remains of a deer buried under oak leaves. This is how the lions behave. I do not know if it was our lion or another. I was happy the deer wasn't Magdalena, but the longer we search for her and for the lion, the more I must accept that she is dead.

Gale drifts off, again wondering about his centuries-old relation to Luis Verdad and his sister, Magdalena. And if the lion that carried her away was a long-ago ancestor of the cat that buried Bennet Tarlow under the leaves not at all far from Mission San Juan Capistrano.

Connections, coincidence, conspiracy, Gale thinks.

Fragments, and fragments of fragments.

Killer Cat, lions, Marilyn, Sangin, the old man and the blast and after.

Luis Verdad and Bennet Tarlow III.

His dreams.

11

Late, free from the Grove, Daniela opens her front door about the same time Gale does.

Her old Tustin house is on C Street, a cramped, century-old two-bedroom two-bath Craftsman bungalow into which she and Jesse barely fit. Square wooden columns support the roof over the front porch. Jacaranda trees tower over the little house, and in spring the fallen blossoms carpet the lawns and sidewalks and half of the street.

Mendez can tell by the lights being on that Jesse—to her surprise after his call today—is home. Even from here in the tiny living room she can see his closed bedroom door, and the mute flicker of his gaming monitor along the floor.

She knocks on the door her usual three times, then pushes it open.

Jesse turns to her in the LED-spangled dark, his face covered by opaque goggles that make him look like an otherworldly praying mantis. His gaming keyboard is actually two keyboards, one on his left and the other on his right. They're littered with tiny red, purple, and chartreuse light-emitting diodes, some pulsing, some still. The monitor displays the usual bloody sword decapitations, axe dismemberments, and machine gun slaughters that so fascinate him. He's playing against people all over the world, people he's never met.

"Sorry I called you at work," he says.

"Sorry I barked at you. It was my first day with this new partner."

"Yeah, you said. Catch a good case?" he asks, a fan of TV cop shows.

"The developer who everybody thought was killed by the mountain lion."

"Weird story. Shot in the head, I heard on X."

He takes off the goggles, revealing his trim, handsome face, his mother's intense brown eyes, his seemingly perfect balance between boyhood and manhood. Shiny black hair. A ghost of a mustache. His arms and legs skinny but muscled. He lifts weights in PE.

"I thought you were with Lulu tonight."

"She went out instead."

"Homework done?"

"Just about to get started."

It's almost midnight, and Daniela is used to her son's late nights. She fought him for years over this, then gave in, mainly because he gets up with the sun almost every morning, energized. Ready for school, work, homework, Lulu, gaming, gaming, gaming. Hard for her to believe he gets by on so little sleep. No drugs involved, no whacky supplements or diet. She watches for those things while covertly tracking him through his phone, with her TeenShield app. Twenty-nine bucks a month to know exactly what he's up to, when, where, and with whom. She can even activate his video and audio, sent to her own phone live, with real-time Google locators.

She's deeply ashamed of herself for this, but Daniela is ruled by fear.

She's seen a lot.

Still, she dreads the idea of Jesse discovering her spying.

"Something to eat?" she asks.

"I'm good."

He dons the mantis mask and returns to his world.

Daniela heats leftover enchiladas, take-out from last night. Eats them standing up in the small kitchen, rinses the dishes.

In the privacy of her room, she calls Father Malone as she often does late at night.

"Dear Daniela."

"Bless me, Tim," she says softly.

"Jesus loves you and forgives your sins."

"My first day as a homicide detective."

"How did it go?"

She sits on the bed. "It's Bennet Tarlow."

"A sad horror."

"Interesting man. He built homes. Thousands of them."

"I have parishioners who live in them."

"I left five years in Vice to take this assignment. From Vice to Homicide. I don't know if that's moving up in the world or down."

"You have always burned for justice, Daniela. The Lord marked your heart for it."

"I feel foul around the dead," Mendez says. "I keep seeing the body, and what the lion did to it. To him."

"You were cleansed when you were baptized. You are human, but you are God's daughter. And when He looks on you He sees you are good. His work is good."

She thinks about this. Hears Tim Malone's soft breathing.

"I love you, Father," she says.

"I love you, Dani. How is the beloved son?"

"I don't know. I honestly do not know."

"Bring him back to the Church. It will put Jesus back in his heart."

"I'll try."

Father Tim tells her about meeting with the cardinal today, as part of Tim's quest to be named a bishop.

To Daniela this journey seems to be a lifetime project that weighs heavily on Father Malone's good and generous soul. He broods on his conversations with his superiors, scrutinizes the innuendo and cryptic asides, parses inflections, ponders true meanings.

She hurts at the hurt in his heart.

Later she showers, puts on her sleep shirt, and props up the pillows in bed.

Gets about three more pages of Luis Alberto Urrea's *The Devil's Highway* and is lost to exhaustion, but not before she affirms how good her life is, compared with so many other people. People on the run from criminals, drugs, poverty, and violence at every turn. Persecuted for who they are.

The people she has sworn to protect and serve.

Her people, not that long ago.

She starts her nightly prayer to the Virgin Mary and falls asleep before amen.

12

Bennet Tarlow III's Laguna Beach cottage is on Wave Street, overlooking Shaws Cove.

Gale notes the small front yard, the white picket fence, the lawn, the orange tree in its middle. Birds-of-paradise blooming in beds, geranium and succulents in colorful Mexican pots. It's early, and Gale hears the warning peeps of house wrens in the awnings.

"Nice view," says Mendez. "I'm surprised a billionaire doesn't have a grander place."

"That'll be Newport."

He works on a pair of latex gloves, steps onto the porch, and picks the lock, an older, well-worn model that welcomes the tension tool and opens easily.

Mendez gloves up and collects the *Times* from the front patio pavers and yesterday's mail from a box shaped and painted like a killer whale.

A small foyer with a rounded arch, a short entryway into the high-ceilinged living room. White plaster walls, dark wood floors, a floor-to-ceiling window framing the gnarled rocks and the surging blue water of Shaws Cove. Built-in bookshelves comfortably stocked with hardcovers, big art books in stands.

What catches Gale's eye are the big framed photographs of birds hanging on the white walls. Many of the birds are exotic, to Gale at least. Magnificent feathers, intense faces, many of them caught in flight. He recognizes a band-tailed pigeon, handsome and common in the mountains near San Juan Capistrano.

All signed by Bennet Tarlow.

"Really likes his birds," says Mendez. "Exotics. I don't recognize any of them. Those owls Osaka sent were haunting. The way the owlets are almost as big as mom. Stuffed into that rickety nest. Those gigantic fuzzy heads. Yellow eyes."

"Yeah, like mountain lions with wings," says Gale, thinking Luis Verdad might say that.

There are classic Laguna plein air paintings on the walls, handsomely framed. Some photographic portraits and family pictures, too.

Gale slips his phone from his pocket and dials Tarlow's cell number.

No ringtone, nothing.

Gale imagines this room on the afternoon and evening before Tarlow's death. A Thursday.

Tarlow had worked in his office until 5:45 P.M. that evening, according to Bennet Tarlow II, his father, during Gale's brief phone call, in which Tarlow II had refused to set up a meeting until later.

"I'm processing," he said.

According to him, his son had ducked into his dad's top-floor suite to say he was leaving. This was usual for him, Tarlow II said.

Even though they were talking over the phone, Gale heard the sudden choke in Tarlow II's voice when he said he was glad he didn't know this was the last time he'd see his son alive.

"*Don't know what I'd have done with that information,*" he said. Added that after work, Ben often went to Muldoon's, walking distance from the company building.

"*I hope you kill this fuck,*" he told Gale.

Gale asked if he could have his son's calendar on hand for their interview the next day, but Tarlow II said his son took it home from work at night. His son never let his secretaries keep his physical calendar. He kept it to himself.

"*He was private and disorganized,*" Tarlow II said. "*He mostly worked from home. Felt more creative there than in a high-rise office with distracting, million-dollar views in four directions.*"

Gale had asked for Tarlow's cell number and Tarlow II complied. Gale had thanked him, then rang off and called Muldoon's and, after being passed along to three people, been told that Bennet Tarlow III had not been there on his last night.

Now, standing in Tarlow's Laguna kitchen, Gale wonders if the man had eaten here the evening he was murdered.

The refrigerator is practically bare, just bottled olives and salsas, some coffee creamer. A still-sealed wheel of Gouda. Some greens, wilted. Carton of orange juice, unopened. Dishwasher with exactly one plate, a knife, a fork, and a spoon in it. A builder's economy, thinks Gale. Measure twice and cut once. There's a Trader Joe's chicken cacciatore box and an empty tub of gelato in the under-sink wastebasket.

Mendez hovers, watching Gale work. "Wish I could read your mind," she says.

"Probably put you to sleep. I'm just trying to figure out if he was here that evening."

"The neighbors," she says.

"Let them wake up. We'll check his home office, find his calendar and his phone."

"Yeah, I feel lucky, too," says Mendez.

Tarlow's home office is a cool, east-facing room looking out on the small backyard. A privacy row of Italian cypress, a large birdbath with a statue of St. Francis of Assisi in it, the fountain turned off.

The recessed ceiling lights are strong and Gale places himself in the rolling task chair, pretending he owns the place. As if he knows where everything is. Becoming the vic. Scans the desktop for Tarlow's phone.

Plenty of room but nothing doing. The desk before him spans the better part of two converging walls. Mahogany, he sees, no dust. Plenty spacious enough for a large monitor, a printer/scanner, a desktop computer, neat stacks of papers, pictures in frames, reference books propped along the two walls.

But the heart of the room are two drafting tables in the middle, exactly centered on a deep red Persian carpet. Acjacheme Gale—an admirer of rugs, baskets, and bowls—sees that the rug is very old and valuable.

Mendez hits the switch and the overhead lights flood the tables. Gale hears her approaching the drafting tables.

"We just stubbed our toes on Tarlow's calendar," says Gale, smiling to himself at their easy luck.

"And a miniature model of Wildcoast," says Mendez.

Gale looks down at Tarlow's At-A-Glance monthly planner, sitting on the desk, to his right, in plain sight, as if the man had left it there for him.

It's open to October.

October 4:

Concept Preview/realtors/7–10/dinner

October 6:

Four days before his murder, Tarlow has a noon with Kyle McNab of PacWest Mining. Based on John Velasquez's memory, this was Tarlow's second meeting with McNab inside a week, thinks Gale.

October 11:

The morning after his death, Tarlow has a Friday nine A.M. with *Patti D/Moulin!!* cafe in Laguna.

Gale notes Tarlow's neat draftsman's printing, and in the exclamation marks, feels the man's giddy optimism.

Circles back.

October 1:

Norris/noon/Newport house

No exclamations.

But there she is, Gale thinks. Norris, from the championship heavyweight fight in Las Vegas three years back—the woman who had been easing in and out of Gale's thoughts since Tarlow was identified as the apparent victim of a mountain lion attack.

October 7:

Dad lunch 1/Rothschild's

Classy place, Gale thinks.

October 8:

Elder/office

Next comes the money shot—Thursday, October 10—the day of his death:

Hair/Ong/4

Vern/6/Newport

Gale surmises that Bennet Tarlow got his wavy blond hair cut the day he was murdered by someone he very likely trusted. Jimmy Ong was a well-known hair stylist with a swank salon in Newport Center.

But it looks like "Vern" might well have been with Tarlow for at least part of the night he died. Vern, whom Gale doesn't know and badly wants to.

He searches the calendar back through September, finding a September 27 entry that hadn't caught his attention the first time through. There he is again, clear as day:

September 27:

Vern/Muldoon's/10

"Wildcoast is really something," says Mendez. "It reminds me of Stepford but I don't know why."

But Gale says nothing, lost in Bennet Tarlow's last days.

He scans ahead through October, hoping for something to catch his eye, but nothing pops.

Back to September, he sees nothing unusual or repetitious.

Gale thinks how odd it is to compare a person's plans before and after their life is over. How similar they are. Some identical. Rights and rituals. Friends and lovers. Why is that odd, though? Because of the grim irony that Tarlow had made every one of these entries in his own neat hand, and probably consulted this calendar pretty much every morning, watching his future line up to greet him day by day and week by week? Then a detour, accompanied by someone Tarlow trusted. At night. A very big owl photographed in a tree. Twenty-six exposures, then a sudden surprise.

Too sudden for fear, bitterness, or regret.

The same surprise he had sprung on nine men in Afghanistan, utterly unaware of their pasts or futures.

He rises and uses his phone to shoot all twelve months of the calendar's year.

Standing beside Daniela now, he looks down on the brightly lit drafting table, which holds not drawings at all, but a miniaturized model of Wildcoast, complete with tiny adobe homes, handsome beam-and-stone retail buildings, and a city hall promenade and parking lot shaded by solar panels framed by drought-tolerant cacti and succulents. Beyond are groves of oranges and avocados. The streets are pale gray; the green street signs look hand-painted.

Gale is struck by the craftsmanship, the construction of this thing. The patience that went into it.

"All built by Tarlow's own hand, I assume," says Mendez. "Think of all the hours. I'm surprised he did his drafting and model building at home. Isn't that what a high-rise office is for? All that good natural light?"

From a heavy black notebook chained to the model table, Gale reads the introductory text, lets his eyes roam the model town. Notes the wood-and-glass civic center on Main, the dozens of cul-de-sacs in the rolling hills studded with adobe houses, the fashionable Craftsman homes, the pale blue community pools, the solar-tile roofing on the industrial buildings, the big greenbelts left to native plants and grasses and trees—all faithfully created by hand, Gale thinks.

I build bows and arrows by hand, Gale thinks. Baskets. Bennet Tarlow builds a miniature city by hand. And is getting ready to build the real thing . . .

There's even a centerpiece lake in a very large public park, marked by a pin in its center, which the heavy notebook tells him will be filled with on-site natural groundwater.

"Okay, Lew," says Mendez. "It's time for the Thursday calendar reveal."

"A haircut and a guy named Vern," he says.

An almost pitying look brushes Mendez's hard, trim face. "Nothing with one of his hotties?"

"Unless her name is Vern," Gale says.

"Vern sounds like a guy who drives an old white Econoline," says Mendez.

A beat of silence.

"Some things you don't put on your calendar," says Gale. "You're looking so forward to it, you don't need to write it down. You've done it before. You wouldn't forget."

Tarlow's computer comes to life when Gale hits the space bar. He's surprised that a developer of multibillion projects is lax enough to leave his home computer asleep and password unprotected.

He reads Bennet Tarlow's latest emails; calls up his printer history—nothing catches his interest; then scrolls down through Tarlow's Google favorites: National Weather Service; *Los Angeles Times* and *New York Times*; Amazon; United Bank Swiss; Wells Fargo; Orangecounty.gov; California.gov; his district's house representative; both California senators.

He shuts down the computer and peripherals, then loads them

into his white take-home Explorer, bound for the OCSD property room.

The blinds in Tarlow's master bedroom are open, and Gale looks out at the orange trees and the empty birdbaths and seed feeders and the bright hummingbird stations without sugar water. A few hummingbirds cruise the empty feeders. Two doves and a towhee peck the ground for spillage; finches on the spent seed feeders look annoyed.

Bennet Tarlow and his birds, thinks Gale.

Here in the bedroom, there's a musty, sheets-might-need-to-be-washed scent. The bed is unmade and appears to have hosted a fitful sleeper. Or two?

Gale dials Tarlow's cell number again but gets the same silence.

The en suite bath, open through a wide barn door, exhales the light of pale green tile inside.

Gale turns on the lights.

The detectives stand in the cool room, just looking.

Gale notes the nightstands on either side of the king bed: a clock on one, lamps and books on both, no cell phone.

He really wants the damned cell phone.

But he's pretty sure the killer took it, because the killer is in that phone. Somewhere in all those bits and bytes, he's in there. And he knows it.

There's a robe thrown over a leather armchair and Gale checks the two deep, empty pockets.

He takes pictures. Macro shots, just to give him the general shape of things he might need to know later.

Mendez, too, video.

The high but narrow cedar dresser is dusty. Gale wonders why a billionaire doesn't have a cleaning service.

No pictures on the dresser. Gale opens the drawers, top to bottom: socks top, underpants next, T-shirts, then sweaters.

The built-in closets have the suits, dress shirts, trousers, jeans, neckties, belts, outerwear, boots, and shoes. It seems like a modest enough wardrobe for a rich and single young man who likes the ladies.

The bathroom suite has dark blue tile walls with tropical birds in reds and yellows and greens. A big shower with nozzles at both ends and a black bath towel slung over the sliding door.

There's a dated oak countertop and twin sinks.

Mendez opens the four under-sink cabinets one at a time, says nothing.

Gale smells the familiar, high-pitched scent of Irish Spring soap and notes the bar in the dish. His dad used it when Gale was a boy, probably still does. Gale wonders why a billionaire doesn't have upscale soap. Hell, he thinks: Maybe he just likes Irish Spring.

One neighbor saw Tarlow getting into his new Suburban the last morning of his life, around seven. She was walking her dog. No, she'd never seen an old white Econoline van in Tarlow's driveway or on the street by his house. *This is just horrible. Do you have the suspect yet?*

Another neighbor says he'd only seen Tarlow a few times since moving here, six months ago. The morning they met, Tarlow was out in his front yard in an Adirondack chair, reading a real paper newspaper, not his phone. Last time? *Couldn't say.* White Econoline? *Nope.*

A third neighbor would see Tarlow coming and going now and then, early mornings and evenings. Not on the evening in question. No white Econoline van. This neighbor had thrown a Fourth of July party two years ago and "the developer" had come and stayed just long enough to watch the fireworks show off Main Beach. Tarlow was with a pretty redhead in a white dress and a white floppy hat. *Didn't introduce us.*

Norris strikes again?

Gale still can't remember her last name, if he ever knew it to begin with.

Maybe in the emails, he hopes.

"Let's get our loot to the lab," says Mendez. "Then we can ransack Tarlow's Newport Beach palace."

13

Mendez is right about the Newport Beach palace.

It's a two-story contemporary extravaganza of rock, steel, and glass, overlooking Corona del Mar State Beach. Nothing like the Laguna cottage, Gale notes. A wall of Italian cypress trees, trimmed flat on their tops, surround it on three sides. Gale has gotten the code from Bennet Tarlow's father.

He parks in the porte cochere, leaving room for Mendez. Steps out of the vehicle and sees how different the grounds are here, compared with Tarlow's Laguna cottage: cactus and succulents and decorative reeds, a rectangular pit of aqua-colored glass globes.

He waits for Mendez, who is still in her black Explorer, looking down at her phone, thumbs moving.

Inside, this home looks less lived-in than the cottage. Neat and minimal living room. Hard angles. Gray, black, and white. No clutter, few accent pieces or works of art. Sunlight floods in. It's already warm in here, and Gale wonders idly what the air conditioner must cost to run in the summer.

He calls Tarlow again. Nothing. Gale knows the damned phone is deep in a lake or the ocean or maybe smashed to tiny pieces being picked over by the seagulls in a landfill.

Hope is cruel, he thinks. Desire for something you know you will never have.

The dining room has a large glass tabletop supported by wooden caissons. No dust on the table. Three candlesticks in crystal holders, never lit. Twelve black enamel chairs.

The kitchen is sleek and modern, with stainless-steel appliances and a black granite island. A black glass-top stove and a black built-in oven beside it.

"Place looks staged," says Mendez. "Like it's for sale."

The black granite counter has four steel-backed barstools along one side and a large, glossy white bag sitting in the middle. There's a red dragon on it. The handles look like bamboo and the bag says:

BAMBOO
CORONA DEL MAR
DINE IN/TAKE OUT/DELIVERY

In smaller print below, Mendez reads the street address, phone number, and email.

A delivery slip lies on the counter beside the bag.

"The last supper," says Mendez, taking up the slip. "Delivery dispatch time, six fourteen P.M. Driver is Amanda. Two number twenty-fives. Medium sake. Sixty-five dollars and seventy-five cents. Paid with a Mastercard, nothing on the tip line."

"Tarlow liked cash," says Gale, remembering the way he palmed the tip money on fight night at Caesars Palace.

Mendez sets the slip back on the counter and photographs it.

Two red place mats lie in front of two stools, but there's a third stool between them with no place mat, as if whoever had last dined here were very large people.

Or maybe, Gale guesses, didn't know each other well enough to sit closely side by side. White plastic chopsticks and their paper wrappers rest on napkins—one neatly folded and the other wadded into a loose ball.

"Choice place for fingerprints," says Mendez. "Black everything. And white plastic chopsticks. The print techs will eat this room alive."

Tarlow the engineer folding neatly, thinks Gale.

White Van, the wadder-upper.

Or maybe Vern.

Or someone else . . .

The detectives contemplate this gust of activity within the still, silent angles of the house.

Gale pulls the wastebasket from under the sink and sets it on the counter, noting four black Styrofoam containers, lids locked, and the emptied soy sauce packets. A metal, half-liter can of sake and a half-pint of cheap bourbon.

Tarlow and White Van, respectively? Gale wonders.

The two downstairs bedrooms have en suite baths, and, like the living and dining rooms, are unbothered by the details of everyday living.

The second-story master suite takes up the whole floor. Plaster walls with oversized windows and skylights to let in even more light, as if the windows might need help. A steel beam ceiling.

Mendez chooses one of three remote controllers from the neatly made bed and opens the skylights and some of the windows.

Hum of motors, a gust of fresh air.

"It's not for sale, is it?" asks Mendez.

"Patti DiMeo would have mentioned that. No signs."

"Why would an award-winning home builder live in such an ugly place?" she asks.

"Kind of a broad question, but maybe he's scourging himself," says Gale.

Mendez gives him a look, her hard face beveled in a slant of sunlight. "Scourging himself for what? His fortune? His cutesy looks? The way his family has usurped Indigenous land and Indians here for, what—a century and a half? Your ancestors among them?"

"My ancestors? Yes," says Gale, remembering his great-grandmother's tales of her mother's long hours of labor at the Mission San Juan Capistrano, sewing the bedsheets slept on by the soldiers in the garrison. Mending their uniforms and emptying the officers' bed pots.

Then off to Mass, morning and evening.

"Maybe he's punishing himself for all his girlfriends," says Gale.

"He doesn't seem the type," says Mendez. "Players aren't wired for regret. Only good people are. In my experience."

"Tarlow didn't act like a player when I worked security for him," Gale says. "He was very attentive to Norris. None of that 'arm candy' posturing."

A skeptical look from Mendez, then a moment of silence in the hot glass cage of a bedroom.

"I didn't mean to pry about your family and your Indian background, Lew. I read that *Los Angeles Times* article about you in Afghanistan. Dark stuff. But you came off as a man on the mend. A man who was paying up."

"Me and my big mouth. I didn't have to say all that to the *Times*."

"Maybe you needed to," says Mendez. "Good things grow with oxygen and light."

"So does cancer."

"Don't let yourself go there."

"Noted."

"How do you pronounce that tribe of yours?"

"Ah-hawsh'amay."

"Again, slower?" she asks, her face intent with concentration.

"Ah-hawsh'amay."

"Ah-hawsh'amay."

Then an awkward silence.

"Let's get ourselves to Bamboo," he says.
"Good. I'm starting to feel lucky."

Bamboo is a glassy, well-lit restaurant on Coast Highway, minimally full with late-lunch customers.

Amanda Cho is at the register, slim, short, and smiling, with red streaks in her long black hair.

Her smile goes away when Mendez tells her why they're here, and they show their badges. She says something in Chinese back into the kitchen, then leads the detectives to an empty table by the window.

"Tea or drink?" she asks.

They decline and Amanda sits. Looking from Gale to Mendez and back, she shakes her head, a cloud of suspicion passing behind her eyes.

Gale takes out his notebook and a pen.

"What you say to us is confidential and protected," says Mendez. "You have nothing to fear."

"Yes, okay," she says. "Mr. Tarlow was kind man and very polite. What happened to him is tragedy. I couldn't believe a mountain lion would do this. I delivered dinner to him the night before he was found in the mountains. I delivered to him once and sometimes twice a week when he was home. I know he was very rich and traveled a lot. Do you have a suspect, or an interesting person?"

"We're close," says Mendez. "Can you tell us the day and time you arrived at Mr. Tarlow's home?"

"Thursday evening, a little after six. Mr. Tarlow buzzed me through the gate and I parked in the porte cochere."

"Were there any vehicles parked there already?"

"Yes, Mr. Tarlow's new blue SUV, and one old white van."

Gale's eardrums do that funny, good-news pulse.

Mendez smiles coolly.

"Describe the van," says Gale.

"Old and big. A commercial van. Like for deliveries. No windows."

"California plates?"

Amanda purses her lips. "I think so."

"Did you see anything unusual or distinguishing about it?" asks Gale.

"No. Just old. I remember all this because I'd seen it there before. Maybe three or four times in the last month or two."

A good heart flutter for Gale.

"Did you see rust on the van?" asks Gale.

"No."

"A sticker on the bumper for the Bear Cave?"

"No. I didn't look at it very hard."

"But you saw it every other week?" asks Mendez.

"Yes, maybe approximately. I always thought it was a funny vehicle to be at Mr. Tarlow's house. So plain, and everything about Mr. Tarlow so perfect."

"Did Tarlow pay you at the door?" asks Mendez. "Or did he invite you in?"

"Always he invited me in."

"Was he alone?" asks Gale.

"No. Jeff was there. The white van was his. When the van was at Mr. Bennet's, so was Jeff."

"Last name?" asks Mendez.

Amanda shakes her head. "I don't know his last name."

"Describe him," says Mendez.

"Big man," says Amanda. "Tall and wide. Muscles. Red hair. Red beard and mustache. Tan eyes. Jeans and Metro Gym T-shirts."

"Tell me about that face," says Gale.

A beat of silence. Amanda looks away, Gale watching her eyes revert to some other place for counsel and, probably, judgment.

"A big face, like the rest of him. He looked as if he owned me and expected to . . . do whatever he want to me. These are feelings I had. He never threatened or touched. He said almost nothing. But he spoke through his eyes. The first time I was there with both men, Mr. Tarlow tipped me fifty dollars. Always fifty. The next time, Jeff gave me seventy-five. And the next also. New scratchy bills, like from a bank."

Gale pictures the big red man looming over petite Amanda, boring into her with his tan cat eyes and pressing the crisp bills into her small pale hand.

"Amanda," says Mendez. "What relationship do you think the men had?"

"I wondered from the first time. Mr. Tarlow? Nice clothes. Always good hair and shaved. A black tuxedo once. But Jeff? Jeans loose and he always pulling them up. Always the black Metro Gym T-shirts. Motorcycle boots scuffed, with those big brass rings."

"How did they act toward each other?" asks Mendez.

Amanda nods. "Like when I was there, I was interrupting something important. They seemed like men getting ready to do something after they ate. There was a feeling of . . . purpose."

"Not friends?"

"No. Different. Maybe like . . . on the same team."

"Who seemed in charge?"

"Mr. Bennet."

"Why didn't you call the police when you learned that Mr. Tarlow was murdered the night you saw him and Jeff?" asks Gale.

She looks away, through one of the Coast Highway windows.

"ICE. And I thought you would contact me. Maybe find the Bamboo bag and the delivery bill."

"We don't care about your legal status, Amanda," says Gale. "We're not even allowed to ask."

A small, slightly embarrassed smile. "Thank you, Detectives."

"Thank you," they both say.

Gale and Mendez sit together in Gale's SUV while he runs a warrants check on Jeff Vern. The Explorer's department computer screen is clear and bright.

Gale makes sure his Warrants Department knows he's on the

Tarlow murder and needs this information soon, like, right now. Wants it sent to Mendez's email also.

A moment later, six *Jeff Vern*s come onscreen, but none of them are Amanda's burly, bearded redhead.

Not close.

Next, Gale receives two *Jeff Verne*s and a *Jeff Vern*—firm nos.

Flips it to *Vern Jeff* and strikes out completely.

Same with *Verne Jeff*.

Vernon Jeff is a strikeout, too, as is *Jeff Vernon*.

Gale and Mendez sit in pissed-off silence. Gale starts the SUV to run the AC and they turn the vents into their faces.

"Thank you," she says.

"I played Little League with a guy named Jeffs," says Gale. "Burt Jeffs. Scrappy guy, third base, big ears."

"You know," says Mendez. "The 's' might be easy for a Chinese immigrant to miss."

Vern Jeffs gets Gale exactly nowhere with Warrants, but he redirects to *Vernon Jeffs*.

A moment later, Mendez gives her screen a hard-faced smile.

Vernon Jeffs is a ringer for the man described by Amanda Cho.

Age fifty.

Six-four, 260 pounds.

Gale's heart thumps like a dryer on tumble.

He's got a DUI from five years back, a school-zone firearms violation from ten years ago, dismissed, and a battery charge that got him six months when he was twenty-one.

Mendez grabs her phone, throws open the door of the Explorer, and slams it shut.

Gale's eyes are still on the computer screen. The California DMV Law Enforcement database says Jeffs owns a fifteen-year-old Ford Econoline. DMV has the VIN but doesn't specify color.

Gale checks the Federal Firearms Registry, then ATF, but neither has firearms registered in his name.

Mendez swings back into the SUV, a small smile on her face. "Amanda says it's him. Absolutely no doubt. She got his face perfectly. Just like the trafficked girls and boys in Vice. They remembered every last detail of the people who sold and raped them."

Gale calls the Costa Mesa Metro Gym on Harbor, gets the day manager, and asks for Vernon Jeffs.

Never heard of him, so Gale calls the other five Metro Gyms in Orange County, but none of the employees have heard of him either.

It's almost two o'clock by now, and Gale and Mendez are both starved, so they go back inside and get a couple of #25s—spicy beef chow mein.

A small flickering light goes on in Gale's racing brain. "The Econoline had a Bear Cave sticker on the bumper, according to Vito Pesco. It's a biker bar. I knew a guy from Sangin who liked the place. Michael Kobila. We drowned ourselves there, on occasion. Mike used a gun to finish the job."

"We took down a pedo there last year," says Mendez. "He was dumb enough to meet our plant there, and the bikers were *that* close to beating him to death. Which I was kind of pulling for. Funny place for Bennet Tarlow III."

Gale checks the Bear Cave hours—one P.M. to two A.M.—then calls on speaker.

"Vern Jeffs there?" he asks.

"Who in the hell are you?"

"Lew Gale. Friend of Michael Kobila."

"Oh, Mikey. Shame. Yeah, Vern's on nights."

"I'll meet you there at nine," says Daniela.

"Good."

Gale has a few hours to kill and knows where to kill them. So does Mendez.

14

As a member of the Acjacheme tribal council, Lew Gale's mother, Sally, runs the monthly Juaneño Nation Market, which falls on this sunny October afternoon on the Capistrano Mission grounds.

He spots her at her usual table, a handsome woman, black-with-gray hair worn long, jeans, and a long-sleeved blouse, red, with a shell-and-glass bead necklace that ends in a white clam half shell.

She rises from her basket-piled table to give her son a hug. She's tall and lithe, sixty.

"You were out early this morning," she says. "Any breaking news on Mr. Tarlow?"

"None, Mom."

"Well, your brother is here and he'll want an update."

"Wish I had one."

"What are you doing here?"

"Have a couple hours off."

Gale follows her gaze to his younger brother, striding across the courtyard in jeans, a tucked-in white shirt, a bead-and-clam necklace like his mom's, and cowboy boots.

They shake hands, crunching hard for a power squeeze—always in competition. Franklin takes his brother by the arm and leads him into the shade of a big pepper tree.

"Do you have a suspect yet?"

"No, Frank."

"Tarlow was desecrating sacred ground with his goddamned Wildcoast," says Frank.

"Someone shot him in the head, brother."

Frank shrugs.

"The Tarlow Company has owned that land for over a hundred years," says Gale.

"You don't own the land," says Frank. "The land owns you. It was ours for thousands of years before Tarlow got here. And that's not all they're doing to us."

Gale says nothing, just waits for his brother to lob another angry but true platitude his way.

"Tesla is courting the Orange County supervisors for a factory! On Acjacheme burial ground east of Wildcoast! Not that you care much about the sacred."

Gale nods, looks into his brother's clear, black eyes. "Hearing anything from the Grizzly Braves?" he asks.

Frank's Grizzly Braves are a band of young Acjacheme men and women—and Indian sympathizers—who hang out at the Outpost bar when they're not picketing the Tarlow Company, bailing each other out of jail, writing letters of hot grievance to newspapers, blogging aggressively online, and attending Frank's Native Studies classes at UC Irvine.

"About who might have put the bullet in him?" asks Frank. "Unfortunately, no. They're learning what I teach them to understand. Tarlow Company as nature killer, Indian hater. Stole our land to exploit it and make money off it. Don't get me going on all that."

"You're always going on that, Frank. It's what you do."

"Was the bullet still in him?"

"I can't be talking about that with you. Why does it matter?"

"Caliber. What caliber?"

Gale lets his vision drift past his younger brother. Frank has been fascinated with evidence and forensics ever since they were boys, watching crime shows on TV. When they were little, Frank was always the attacker. The Indian brave with the bow and arrow. The sheriff with the six-gun. The platoon sergeant in the jungle. Gale has long wondered if Frank's day job might be a little dull.

"How's UCI treating you?"

"Same old. Tenure and sabbaticals. Native Studies never had it so good."

"Cathy?"

"Perfect, as always. Up in LA a lot. The band is off on tour tomorrow, for two months. She's my alibi for the night Tarlow ate it."

Gale says nothing. Four-plus decades of shock talk from his bookish, tightly wound little brother.

"What do you need with an alibi?"

"I'm not one bit sad for him," says Frank. "Whatever the reason, he got what he had coming. The Spanish owe us for approximately a hundred and sixty-five years of genocide, rape, the obliteration of Acjacheme culture, religion, and language. The Tarlow Company is just finishing what the Spanish started. The world is a better place without him. Speaking of worthless Spaniards, have you seen Dad lately?"

Gale shakes his head. "Been a while. Never know when he'll show up."

"I'll never understand why Mom lets him back under her roof."

"She still loves him, bro."

"Never understand that, either."

Gale sits in the shade at his mother's basket table, making occasional small talk with the mission tourists. They're interested in where Sally gets the reeds and branches used to make them.

"We still have some sources back in the valleys," she tells them. "We lost access to a good spring when they built the high school. So sometimes we have to buy supplies."

"They're beautiful," says a pretty mom holding hands with a small boy and girl. "Do you weave, too?" she asks Gale.

"Nothing like she does!"

"Your faces have so much character. May I have a picture?"

Gale has been asked this before by tourists, here in this very place. Takes something out of him.

He agrees and endures, for the sake of . . . what, exactly?

She brings the children up closer to the table and gets out her phone. Lew and his mother join them in front of the baskets, and they all lean in and the woman shoots selfies. Buys a big wheat-colored basket with a splendid geometric web running through it. Gale puts it into a handled burlap bag, sorry to see this beautiful thing fly away, but okay with his mom getting some money. He's never made a basket that good in his life. Nor bows, nor arrows.

The woman and her kids walk off.

"When I see little children, I think of you and Frank," she says. "And your father. He was a good man but not a good husband."

"I know you do, Mom. I thought he was a good dad, until he ditched us."

For Carol, then Isabelle, thinks Gale. A Luiseño and a Cahuilla. "The conquistador," he says.

Gale hasn't gotten over his sense of abandonment by Edward Gallego, the proud Spanish-German American who at eighteen married his mother, seventeen-year-old Sally Jones, a full-blooded Acjacheme Native, right here in this mission. Good Catholics both. Begrudged permission from Sally's parents.

When Edward Gallego left, it felt more like full betrayal. Not just of him, but of his mom and little brother, too. Lew was eighteen. When he heard his mom crying in her room, he wanted to find Dad and pound him. Not likely. Edward was a former Marine boxer, and by the time he left his first family, he was a Capistrano High School history teacher and a wrestling coach.

Later, Sally leads a tour of the cemetery, located on a hill above the mission, housing the bodies of the converts since 1776.
    Lew and Frank traipse up the road in the brewing heat, along with a handful of tourists and fourth graders from Guin Foss Elementary in nearby Tustin, who, like all California public school fourth graders, are studying the missions in history class. The girls look animated and happy, the boys mostly bored. Gale remembers studying this mission in fourth grade and the odd feeling of walking the grounds and taking tests about where you had spent your entire life in a small home just a few hundred feet away, and where your ancestors had been renamed, converted to Christianity, taught to farm, and lost their language and most of their culture. Over half had lost their lives just a few short years after the founding of the mission.
    Spanish diseases and forced labor.
    Confinement, lashings, and poor diet.
    Their names changed, their language forbidden, their culture banished, their religion replaced by a man nailed to a cross.
    Their bodies exhausted and their spirits broken.
    Mother Nature herself, too: the Capistrano Earthquake of 1812, killing forty Acjacheme parishioners at Mass in the mission church their forebearers had built by hand.
    Lew thinks about Daniela's son at Tustin High, the "great kid," inward and high strung, with a manipulative girlfriend, a job at the bowling alley, and a deceased father.
    The boy, living with his single mom deputy, who puts in some long hours for $70,000 a year, working for a county where the average cost of a home is $1.09 million.
    Age thirty-eight, widowed.
    Gale and his brother find shade under a big sycamore tree. Gale listens to his mother's voice, watches the tourists and schoolkids.

Wonders again what it would have been like to have a son or daughter of his own.

Most of the graves here at the mission cemetery are unmarked. The few headstones are crumbling and cracked. Some fallen, others propped up by rocks. Weeds and gopher mounds, the iron fence pickets rusted and askew.

"They took our lives and left us with this," says Frank.

Sally gives a short history of the cemetery, then asks for questions. None.

She makes the rounds of the visitors, holding out a beautiful basket.

Gale hears the tinkle of coins and the sound of cash.

Sally thanks them, and a dollar bill flutters out of the basket in the breeze.

They start back toward the mission, and Frank pulls him aside again. "One of my students posted some pretty harsh things about Tarlow. Said she'd like to burn him at the stake and eat his face. Interesting, considering what actually happened to him. Her name is Geronima Mills. You can find her on most of the socials."

"Interesting," says Gale. "Burn Tarlow at the stake and eat his face."

"She was not at my Thursday night class when Tarlow was killed. And she hasn't been back since. I texted her, no reply. I've sent you her number."

Before leaving the mission, Gale sits in the back of the chapel, then kneels and lets his thoughts out. He hasn't really believed in all this since he was eighteen. Left the home, left the faith. But Sally and Edward had staunchly brought him and his brother up in the Church. The brothers baptized by Father Ordonez right here in the mission baptistry. Never missing a Mass or a Confession.

Sangin shattered the last of his faith and blew away his future, but the voices inside him still murmur to be heard, and Lew Gale brings them here to let them speak.

From his Explorer, parked in the sun with the air conditioner on, Gale calls Geronima Mills, leaves a message about meeting her to talk about Wildcoast developer Bennet Tarlow.

Half an hour later, Gale is back in Laguna, a heavy plastic grocery bag in one hand, opening the gate to Bennet Tarlow's backyard bird sanctuary and walking in.

No food means no birds.

He takes the pet store hummingbird nectar from the bag and fills the empty feeders with red sugar water.

In the small garage Gale finds the wild birdseed inside a galvanized aluminum trash can, fills the pet store bag, and takes it back to the yard.

When he's done with the hanging seed feeders, he tops off the bright yellow birdbath with the hose, then sits in one of two aqua blue Adirondack chairs in the shade of the patio overhang.

And waits, picturing Tarlow doing all this every morning, because he had built up such an avian following here in his sanctuary.

You have to open the bird café or you'll lose your customers.

He pictures those impatient hummingbirds dive-bombing Tarlow like they used to dive-bomb his mom when she opened her bird sanctuary in the morning, trying to get her back inside so they could drink.

And he sees in his mind's eye Tarlow photographing the out-of-habitat great gray owl raising her brood in the sycamore tree near Wildcoast.

Hears the pistol pops.

Flinches in the blue chair.

Pictures Tarlow collapsing.

Tarlow's backyard birds return rapidly.

Half a dozen hummers, their red throats flashing in the sun.

Doves landing clumsily on the seed feeders.

A sleek little phoebe splashing in the bath.

Gale sits an hour, reading his case file, then goes next door, where the friendly neighbor who had entertained Tarlow and possibly Norris something or other at a Fourth of July party is watering his roses.

"Detective," he says, cutting off the hose water. "Have you made an arrest?"

"We're working it hard," says Gale.

"What's in the bags?"

"Birdseed and hummingbird nectar. Can you fill up Bennet's feeders once a day? The side gate is unlocked. There's more seed in the trash can in the garage; keep the lid on tight for the mice. Refrigerate this nectar."

The man gives Gale a yes-sir look and nods.

"You got it."

"Thank you from Tarlow and his birds."

15

Daniela Mendez drives her red Corvette past the gate and onto the driveway of Father Timothy Malone's modest tract home in Orange. The house is fifties ranch style, stucco and rambling, surrounded by a high, dense hedge of white oleander trimmed flat on top. Three navel orange trees, large and potently fragrant, grace the lawn. This nearly hidden, very private property is Father Malone's pride and joy, relief from the rectory of his earlier clerical life.

His voice on the intercom is deep and smooth as the whiskey he drinks.

They embrace, almost formally, then sit in the little dining room, where Father Malone serves Daniela a Bordeaux blend and himself the Quiet Man bourbon.

Daniela smells the fish and potatoes baking in the kitchen. Rosemary sprigs on the salmon.

"How is Jesse?"

"I'm so worried, Tim. The girl, the gaming. His silence. He carries it around with him. It's where he hides."

"Is Lulu a good influence, at times?"

"I suppose. She doesn't drink or do drugs, apparently."

"You've never really liked her. With him, I mean."

"No. I hope I'm not a hypercritical mother."

"I think your judgment is fundamentally sound. It always has been."

A soft throb of doubt in her mind echoes back through Daniela's thirty-eight years.

"I know I baby him too much," she says. "Coddle and protect him. Maybe I turn into a fire-breathing dragon when I see them together."

Daniela takes a sip of the wine. Good as always. Father Malone has always known his way around wine and liquor and fast cars. Sometimes they get in one of Tim's cars, or sometimes they take Daniela's Corvette, and take turns driving high into the local mountains, tearing up the hillsides and blasting through the turns. Adrenaline, fear, joy.

She looks into his eyes, blue and deep-set in a lean, ascetic face. An aquiline nose, a blast of gray-black hair, upright as if windblown. He's thirty years her senior. Timothy Quinn Malone. She still likes looking at that face. It's changed since she was seven. Still beautiful to her.

"And the guilt is so big, Tim," she says. She feels it in her throat right now, a painful lump. "All the lies to give him a father. Leaving him with friends, then daycare when I was young and at work. Or here. Trying to Disneyland mom him on my free weekends. Which I'm going to get less of with this homicide work."

Tim Malone sips from his glass. His bottle sits just off to his right side. Daniela has always thought the Quiet Man was an odd pick for him. Father Timothy Malone, with the piercing tenor in Mass. All that volume, coursing out from his slender body. Of course, privately, his voice is softer.

"Dani, you're raising a strong-willed and intelligent young man. All of your sacrifice and hard work will pay off someday. I'm not an idealist about human nature. But I'm optimistic about what a human being can become. With the Father, the Son, and the Holy Spirit. And a mother like you."

When Tim Malone talks like that to Daniela Mendez, she's twelve again. Overflowing with God. Protected by the Spirit. All through Tim.

"I wish," she says. "I wish it could be different."

A long beat then, another sip of wine, another draw of the Quiet Man.

"There have been many years of wishing for both of us, Dani. This is what God has given us three."

"Less wishing from you than me, Tim. Those years have worn on me. Because I can't change them. And neither can you."

"No," he says.

"Back then, Tim, I thought you could do anything."

"I? Not quite."

"Have I apologized enough? Too much?"

"You don't have to apologize again, Daniela. I won't apologize to you, either. That is what we decided, a long time ago. I am half responsible for everything that happened. The good and the painful. I am very clear on my sin, far beyond the breaking of my vow. And how I failed you and Jesse."

"Jesse needs you."

"He would destroy me."

Daniela nods but says nothing. This conversation has the same words and the same shape as the hundreds they've had over the last eighteen years. Many of them right here in this oleander-walled tract hideaway, which lies far from the Azusa Church of the Holy Martyr, where Daniela Mendez attended her first Mass at age seven, the age of reason, performed by Father Timothy Malone.

Father Tim excuses himself and comes back a few minutes later bearing plates of oven-poached salmon, baked potatoes, and steamed asparagus with butter.

The same first supper they enjoyed together here, nineteen years ago, her last day as a virgin.

As usual, this supper conversation now turns to news, cars, politics, sports, and parish gossip, in which Daniela still takes an interest, having attended her last Mass in Azusa nineteen years ago, before moving to Orange County, Jesse starting to show in her trim, nineteen-year-old body. She misses some of those people. A lot of those parishioners seemed so old then, but here they are, still ticking, as Tim accounts for them in the soft tenor he has when he's not in the pulpit.

Daniela sees the hint of the whiskey on his lined, ruddy face. He's sixty-eight years old, she thinks. To her he's still more than a man and almost a god.

When the conversation thins, Daniela pushes her plate aside and stands—staring at him, heart pounding—another established piece of this long-standing rite.

Father Tim does likewise.

She goes to him and offers him her cheek to kiss, then they take each other in a long embrace during which Daniela's heart beats even harder and she hugs him with strength and love, all that she has, as she has always done, and will forever.

By the hand she leads him down the hallway and into their room.

Two hours later, Daniela walks into Bowl Me Over in Santa Ana and sees Jesse, bussing tables in the Burgers & More café. He's got on the red Bowl Me Over apron with the big bowling ball knocking laughing pins into the air. He waves and gives her a rare smile, then swiftly masks it with his standard blank scowl.

She goes to the café bar, orders coffee, and waits.

A moment later he's across the counter from her.

"Mom. Like, what do you want?"

She studies his slender face, so much like his father's, his black hair swept back, eyes brown and tender. The nests of pimples in the hollows of his cheeks.

"I'm working tonight," she says. "Just wanted to see you. I'll be home late."

"Any updates on the murder?"

"Sorry."

"I know you can't tell me anything. It's cool."

Jesse looks past her and smiles.

Daniela turns, and Lulu Vega gives her an unsweetened look as she takes the barstool beside her.

"Hi, Daniela. What are you doing here?"

"Visiting my son."

"Me, too!"

Daniela's suspicious eyes lead her to the far side of the café, where four Barrio Dogtown gangsters are settling into a booth. They're gazing hard back at her, a swarm of shaved heads, white singlets, khakis, and ink.

When she turns back to Jesse, he's looking at them, too.

Her first thought: Go over and say hi, badge them, shake things up. Maybe warn them off of Jesse and Lulu. Just let them know a cop is watching.

Second thought, though: Is Lulu Vega affiliated with Barrio Dogtown?

Her third: Don't humiliate Jesse.

"You know them?" she asks Lulu.

"Everybody knows Barrio Dogtown. The fat one is Flaco Benitez. He went to high school with my brother. Came to our house a few times. Mom hated him but Dad thought he was funny."

"Lulu and me are going out after work," says Jesse.

"Lulu and I," says Mendez.

"Not you, Daniela—Jesse and I," says Lulu.

"Clever, Lulu. I get it."

Daniela eats a light dinner for appearances, mad-dogging Barrio Dogtown between her house salad and a small sashimi platter.

Watching her son clearing tables, she feels the familiar avalanche of guilt descending on her. Jesse has never shown suspicion of her. Never inquired about her occasional absences. Never questioned her grand lie, that he was fathered out of wedlock by a U.S. Air Force flight mechanic named Javier Lopez who died before Jesse was born. In the few pictures she has shown him, Lopez is a good-looking, big-smiling man. Six months pregnant and thinking ahead, she had scavenged them from an Azusa estate sale scrapbook that she bought for twenty-five cents.

Her mom and dad made a stoic show of believing her tall tale, Papa having forgiven her sin of the flesh with the holy man, Mama not.

All of which makes moments like now—seeing Jesse torn between a bratty manipulator like Lulu and a seducer like herself—borderline unbearable.

She feels the telltale ache of love in her guts, love of Jesse and his father.

She waves to Jesse, loading his bus cart. Pays up and leaves an exorbitant tip that her son will get a part of, then heads for the Bear Cave.

But first veers off to the Barrio Dogtown bangers, swings open her blazer to reveal her Sheriff's Department shield, and leans over their table.

She rattles off a terse greeting in Spanish, gets four surprised faces, then haughty grins that escalate to laughter.

"You stinking dog fleas leave my son alone," she hisses.

More laughter.

Then curses, following her out.

16

Gale and Mendez sit in his plain-wrap Explorer, casing the Bear Cave from across the street. The bar is part of a strip mall east of the old Huntington Beach downtown. In the streetlights Gale sees some scraggly palms, sagging telephone lines, and an oil pump gnawing patiently in the near dark.

"The pump stinks," says Mendez.

"The smell of money," says Gale.

"Smell of benzene and lung cancer. Nice bikes, though."

Gale counts twelve Harleys, two Indians, and one Kawasaki Ninja parked apart as if segregated. Their chrome and colors ripple in the neon blue of the Bear Cave's sign.

Gale loves motorcycles. He rode with friends after Sangin but didn't want to join a club. Sold his Fat Bob for ten thousand dollars and put that down on the 4Runner.

An older white Econoline is parked away from the bar, in front of Hair Affairs salon, long closed for the day. Through his binoculars, in the faint light from the storefront, Gale can see the body rust through his binoculars and the Bear Cave sticker on the bumper.

"Never thought I'd be so happy to see a beat-up old van," says Gale, entering the license plate numbers on his phone.

"Think it's enough for a search warrant?"

"No, but I'll write it up anyway."

"Jeffs is six-four, two-sixty," says Mendez. "Red hair and beard, as of last week. I guess we won't have any trouble spotting him. Interesting sheet, too. A DUI, six months in county for a bar fight, a dropped rap for carrying a gun within a thousand feet of a school. Trunk of his car. Judge ruled the search was illegal."

"That thousand-feet law is tough," says Gale. "You're going past schools you don't even know are there. *On* school grounds is a different thing."

A beat while Mendez composes her rebuttal.

"I think it's a good law," says Mendez. "I worry about Jesse at school. It gets into my mom head that a bullied kid, or some crazy, is going to bring his birthday gun to school and open up. Lew, Jesse was bullied into a fight, freshman year. Older kid. Jesse whaled on him. Cost them both three days' suspension but it never happened again. The two boys actually became friends."

Gale considers this, wondering if he would have been as good a father as Daniela is a mother. Before the war, he had looked forward to that. But after the war, it was only a distant concept.

Then he was back from Sangin, the hospital weeks, then:

Bourbon, then pain pills, his future shrinking, watching Marilyn's collapse through the haze.

Seems like hundreds of years ago. At forty-three he feels ancient and futureless and unrecognizable.

He watches as three burly bikers crash through the Bear Cave door and move to their choppers. They do look like bears.

"That's a happy ending you don't see every day," says Gale. "The boys becoming friends, I mean. Happened to me, too. Eighth grade.

Some dumb, good-Indian dead-Indian stuff, but it got to me. Charley Webster. We fought and got kicked out for two days. But years later in high school we got to be pretty good friends. Double-dated on grad night at Disneyland."

In the dark cab, Gale feels Daniela's eyes on him.

"Are you sizing up how Indian I look?"

"No. God, sorry. Yes."

"Mom's Indian and Dad has mostly Spanish blood. I'm the Native and the conquistador, rolled into one. That's where I get my crazy good looks."

Mendez thinks of Jesse. A Mexican-American mom and an Irish-American father.

A quick shudder passes through her as she thinks of what happened just hours ago.

The three Harleys make a flatulent exit, passing the oil pump on their way toward the beach. Fog rolls in.

"Ready, partner?" Gale asks.

"Not quite," says Mendez. "How are we going to do this? Get him to talk to us?"

"Just a meet and greet for starters. The key here, Daniela, is not to really worry him."

"Just make him think?"

"Let him cook," says Gale. "And don't name Amanda Cho. Go vague on her."

"Let him cook. I like that. Vamos."

Two bikers at the jammed bar turn and check them out. They look like distance runners, thin bodied, with inked, ropy arms and vests emblazoned with flaming crosses and the words

ONWARD SOLDIERS

The bottom rocker says

HUNTINGTON BEACH

They glance coolly at Gale, but one offers Daniela a beard-framed smile, and they give up their stools near the serving station.

"You look good enough to eat," he says. "Jesus loves you and so do I."

"I'm pure poison," she says with a sharp little smile.

Gale notes the tables and booths, the kitchen behind a brick half wall in back, the hallway to the restrooms, the low roar of the patrons and the music on the jukebox.

He locks looks with one of the bartenders, filling a pitcher from the tap. He's tall and wide. Clean-shaven, with short red hair. He's got the look of menace that Amanda Cho described. Small eyes. Like Vernon Jeffs in his hairy jacket mugs.

The big man sets two full pitchers at the serving station, and a lean woman in a short leather skirt and a sleeveless Bear Cave T-shirt carts them away.

Presumed Jeffs turns to Gale, who shows his star briefly, then slips it away.

"We like cops," he says, leaning close to cut through the din.

"We like bartenders, Mr. Jeffs."

Who gives Gale a so-what look. "What'll it be?"

"Draft Coronas with lime for the lady and me."

He's back a minute later with the beers, limes notched into the rims of the glasses.

"I'm Lew, and this is Daniela," says Gale.

"So cough it up, then."

"We're working the murder of Bennet Tarlow."

"Two little detectives for a big shot like him?"

"You know," says Mendez. "It's the size of the fight in the dog, and all that."

"Cute," says Jeffs. "You serve, Lew?"

"Three-five, Sangin."

Jeffs nods. "Bosnia for me, then Congo."

"Congo?"

"Don't ask."

"Got it," says Gale. "Did you know Bennet Tarlow?"

"No. He came in here a couple times with some friends."

"Ever been to his home in Newport?"

"Never. Wouldn't know it if I saw it."

"Must be some mix-up, then," says Gale. "We've got a witness who said you were at Tarlow's place last Thursday, the evening he died."

"Nice bluff," says Jeffs. "But you don't have a witness. What you have is someone who saw a guy who looks like me. Or maybe has bad eyesight, or hallucinations."

"He described you pretty well," says Mendez.

"I don't know where *he* was, lady, but Thursday evening I was with my wife. Right, Mindy?"

The skinny woman in the black leather skirt sets down two empty pitchers and Jeffs takes a handle in each hand, lowers them into the stainless sink.

"Right what," she says.

"Me and you at home Thursday. Our day off. These cops think I was down in Newport Beach at some rich guy's house."

"Well, hell, Vern—let 'em think what they want."

She gives Gale the once-over, Mendez a dismissive glance.

"The trouble with cops is there's too many of you," she says to Gale. "No one's safe anymore. It's a police state. We were both home Thursday last, watching TV."

"Anything good on?" asks Mendez.

"Piss on you," Mindy says and walks away.

Vern Jeffs shrugs. "I can't remember. Probably *Ozark*, again. Like, it's our fourth time through."

The other bartender yells something at Jeffs.

"Sorry, Deputies, I got a job to do," he says. "You want to talk again, charge me for whatever you think I did. I'll have a lawyer with me."

He's back in five minutes.

"What do you need a lawyer for?" asks Mendez.

"'Cause I know you people think you're tricky. You make shit up. I know that, because I was with my wife on Thursday and I didn't know Tarlow."

"We have a few more questions," says Mendez.

"Arrest me."

"You don't want that," says Gale. "You tell us the truth about that Thursday night, and we'll be happy if it's one big mistake."

"You already know it was a big damned mistake. Fact, I might have to file a complaint against you. Harassment at my workplace. Drinking alcohol while on duty. Harassing my wife."

"Speaking of alcohol," says Gale. "A shot of Maker's Mark?"

Daniela shakes her head.

By now the crowd has thinned out but Jeffs, Mindy, and the second bartender are still hopping.

Jeffs delivers the shot of Maker's, then hustles off to the other side of the horseshoe bar.

A few minutes later he comes back, wiping his hands on a white towel.

"Your van was seen near the murder site the night Tarlow was killed," Mendez says. "The rusty white Econoline, down by Hair Affairs right now. It was parked next to Tarlow's new Suburban. They got it on the Caspers Park campground security camera, plates and all."

Gale thinks the security camera lie is unnecessary and bad. Didn't think to tell Mendez not to, but now wishes he had.

Vern smiles, and his tan, mountain-lion eyes glitter.

"Nice try," he says. "They don't have security cameras out there. I know 'cause me and Mindy and our club camp out at Caspers a lot."

"The security cameras are new, and your van is on the video," says Mendez. "Look, Mr. Jeffs, we think you were with Tarlow before he died. You probably had a perfectly good reason. You probably parted ways long before he was killed. We just want to know why you were there in the first place. Maybe some others were there, too. We need solid intel on Mr. Tarlow to find out who shot him. Can you make a few minutes for us tomorrow morning, downtown sheriff's building in Santa Ana? Real informal. No lawyers. Mindy, too. Just to clear up some details? Give you a chance to sleep on things."

"Better yet," says Gale. "Give us a few more minutes tonight. After your shifts. Coffee's on us."

Jeffs sets another pair of beer pitchers into the big sink. Squeezes a plastic bottle of dish soap, runs the water.

"I got nothing to hide and I'm not talking to you. I wasn't anywhere near Tarlow that night, or any other. Except for here, like I said. I don't believe you got my van on video. That's a bluff. Fuck you. Get out of my bar."

"You and Tarlow walked past the Cottonwood Creek Campground bathrooms the night Tarlow was killed," says Gale. "We have a witness to that. Tarlow died about fifty yards from there, later that night."

"I read about the Laotian weed growers," says Jeffs. "Talk to them. Not a one of them saw me because I wasn't there."

"They're all dead, Mr. Jeffs," says Mendez. "Last chance to do this the easy way."

Jeffs spreads his big hands on the bar counter, towering over the detectives. Leans in.

"Go to hell. Both of you. You can't frame me."

Gale leaves cash and a good tip, checks to make sure Vern and Mindy aren't looking, cups the shot glass in a paper napkin and slips it into his pocket.

Back home, he brushes the shot glass with dragon's blood fingerprint dust—his favorite from his latent fingerprints training.

Three clear prints emerge as the brush lightly passes, one of them a nice, fat, Vern Jeffs's thumb.

Gale smiles, sips his bourbon, shoots close-ups of the prints and sends them to Osaka to check against the utensils used by Tarlow and Jeffs when they had the Chinese dinner in Tarlow's Newport Beach house.

Gale then fills out the warrant request form for Judge Carl Schmidt, based on Vito Pesco's descriptions of the two vehicles in the Cottonwood Creek Campground. One, a new Suburban belonging to Bennet Tarlow III and the other an older Econoline registered to Vernon Jeffs.

Also based on Amanda Cho's claim that she saw Jeffs with Tarlow the evening before his death.

On the .22 bullets in Tarlow's head.

And the .22 casings at the kill site.

Give me that gun, Carl, he thinks. The Honorable Schmidt being the Superior Court's most law-and-order judge.

He's about to send the request form to Judge Schmidt when his phone buzzes.

"Lew Gale."

"This is Geronima Mills, returning your call about Wildcoast. Sorry to call so late but I was having a nightmare and woke up thinking that I owed you a call. Frank's brother. Are you a private or a real detective?"

"Both."

"Clever."

"I'm in charge of the case."

"Do you have a suspect yet?"

"None."

"Are you trying me on for size, based on my openly hateful reels and videos?"

"Exactly."

"Try no further, Mr. Gale. The Tarlow family and company have been squatting on Acjacheme land since 1865, when the queen of Spain signed a land grant over to Mexico, who raped and pillaged a little, then sold the land to Bennet Tarlow's ancestors. Now the Tarlow Company wants to build a city for millionaires there, with no repatriations for the so-called Juaneño Nation, no consideration for our sacred land, culture, religion, or language. For ten thousand years. And certainly no respect for the people themselves. We at Stopwildcoast will do just about anything to keep that hideous thing from ever existing. But. We are not in favor of shooting Bennet Tarlow dead."

"That post of yours about burning him at the stake and eating his face got my attention, Ms. Mills. And the fact that one of your X tags is Killwildcoast."

"We live in an age of stagecraft and performance."

"What do you do in real life?"

"UCI Library. Fifteen bucks an hour."

"Do you own a twenty-two-caliber semiautomatic handgun?"

"I do. Aluminum, and rose colored. Sold to me as a 'chick' gun. Was one used on Tarlow?"

A beat while Gale's brain whirs.

"We don't know," lies Gale. "The lab is working up the firearms and toolmarks."

"But surely you know what caliber."

"Yes, a twenty-two. Do you know Vernon Jeffs?"

"I do not."

"Did you know Bennet Tarlow?"

"I've seen him come and go from his company headquarters in Newport Beach. Lately, in a new blue Suburban. I've never gotten to shake his soft, puffy hand."

"Where were you on the evening he died?"

"Which was?"

Gale fills her in.

"Beats me."

"Get your calendar," says Gale. "Tell me where you were."

Geronima Mills's phone clacks down, and Gale hears the tap of fingers on keys.

"Hmm . . . Mom's house. Here's the number."

"How come you haven't been back to school since the murder?" he asks.

A catch of breath, then: "I've had enough of Frank and the Grizzlies. They roar but they don't act. They're casino chasers. Half of them have little or no Native blood at all."

"Do you?"

"Half Acjacheme. The unrecognized. Like you and Frank."

"So, you've dropped out?"

"Of college, not the world. I'll fight Wildcoast tooth and nail. Like the mountain lion that half ate Tarlow. Good luck finding who killed him."

"Good luck to you, too, Ms. Mills."

"Have you arrested anyone for slaughtering the Laotians?"

Gale's heart sinks every time he thinks of those young men, all in their early twenties, according to Coroner Bachstein.

"Not yet."

"Buy me a drink sometime."

"Why?"

"I want to know who you are."

"Maybe."

Gale hangs up, toasts his laptop with a shot of bourbon, then hits the send button, launching his warrant request to Judge Schmidt.

Showers and gets into bed.

He hears Luis Verdad's Acjacheme-accented Spanish voice in the rattling of the pages:

Bernardo has always smiled at Magdalena and tries to be near her when she is in our lean-to or grinding the acorns on the boulders. Now he is fearful that we will find her.

Water Dog came upon a smell the next day and took off into

the brush. I didn't know if it was a lion, or turkey or quail or the rabbits he loves to chase and eat.

We were farther than we had ever been from the mission. Just over the mountains was the Cahuilla tribe, very fierce ball-and-stick players who my father said hated the Spanish and refused to belong to a mission.

We Juaneños have gone to war with the Cahuilla many times. And with the Luiseños, and the Gabrielinos and even the Chumash from the north.

Wars are generally fought over insults, stolen rabbits, or an old disagreement that has not been resolved.

In a war, each side has thirty to fifty male warriors. A level meadow is chosen for the battle. The two nations face each other from half a kilometer apart, bows and arrows ready. Behind them are thirty to fifty females on each side, who are arrow guardians. They chase after the enemy arrows when they fly in and do not hit a man. Then collect the arrows and give them to the men when they run out.

The arrows are used when the warriors are approximately one hundred steps apart but some of the stronger archers commence before. The arrows are very thin and fast but you can see them coming. But if there are many arrows you can't see them all. Most archers don't try to avoid the arrows because they are too busy shooting their own arrows, or receiving fresh arrows from the arrow guardian women, who sometimes have to pull an arrow from a wounded or dead man.

The war is over when one side retreats. Wounded enemies are sometimes given water and food and medicine, sometimes captured and taken home, sometimes killed with clubs and hatchets, and occasionally beheaded. The heads are kept as trophies and decorations for our vanquech, or sacred enclosures. These temples we build far away from the mission, hidden in dense vegetation because all Acjacheme beliefs, language, dancing, and history are forbidden. Those found in a temple are arrested and taken to the mission jail near the soldiers' barracks, and often whipped.

After a battle, the victorious Indians go back to their hidden vanquech and dance for up to three days, stopping only to eat rabbits and deer and many birds and sometimes lizards and large grasshoppers. The food is not cooked in any way, as they taught us at the mission, but torn by teeth and knives. The blood is swallowed and thanks is given to Chinigchinich, one of our gods. The Spanish have taught us how to cook food but our traditions survive in secret.

The dancers pause only briefly to eat, sleep, lay together, partake of peyote cactus, or bathe in the creeks that are warm in the summer and cold in winter. The dancing is organized and directed by ritual specialists, and has specific steps and motions and rhythms for men and women.

If the Spanish find us dancing, the dancers are beaten, and also taken back to the mission and locked inside for several days. The Franciscan fathers admonish them and preside over the punishments but always forgive us, in the name of Jesus Christ Our Lord, who loves us. Some Juaneños passionately love Father Serra for bringing Jesus to us, but many only pretend. The Franciscans call us neophytes, which means a person new to God. Some of us call the Franciscans *crilsin,* which means invaders, or people not of our world. Others call them *bor'bascala,* or "white pigs." I am glad to read and speak Spanish because most of these Acjacheme words will die when we do, man by woman, word by word. Many people have died here in the mission, of disease and in the big earthquake, and because of the sickness of our hearts when we are denied our way of life and how we eat and how we speak and what we believe and our dancing. The Spanish have taken our spirits and yet they preach love of their Holy Spirit.

Late that day, Water Dog lost his trail and I have trouble finding it on the hills of boulders and the arroyos thick with toyon and manzanita. We see a bear watching us from a green meadow. He is silver and hump-backed and contrasts beautifully with the orange poppies. Soon the trail and all its signs were gone and we were tired. I didn't tell Bernardo but I felt as if I was thousands of kilometers away from Magdalena and would not see her again, even in parts.

That night we ate two hares, which are larger than the rabbits but much tougher and less flavorful.

We slept near a spring on blankets we carry on our backs and in the morning we climbed a steep rise and saw the vultures circling over a distant hill.

We went there without talking and I felt this heaviness in me and Bernardo did, too, and even Water Dog who is always hopeful seemed sad.

And there we found Magdalena's white blouse, torn and bloody and discarded in the brush.

And we smelled what the vultures smelled and we found her in the manzanita.

Osaka calls a minute later.

"No," he says, "I can't match your fingerprint with the Newport house kitchen or dining room."

"Hell, Glen, that thumb is textbook."

"We didn't find *any* prints that weren't Tarlow's. One of my people told me it was the cleanest island counter he's ever seen. Like housekeeping had just been there. Ditto the cooktop area, the sink, the drawer hardware, the dishes in the sink *and* the cabinets."

"What about the plastic chopsticks and the sake can and the bourbon bottle in the trash?"

"Tarlow's on the can but the bourbon bottle was clean."

"So Jeffs wiped it all down."

"Someone did."

Gale punches off and beds down.

Falls asleep fast, sees the Killer Cat, padding down the hallway of his boyhood home.

The cat stops and looks at Sally's closed bedroom door, then comes to Gale's door and sits, tail twitching.

The detective jumps wide-eyed from his bed, lands loudly on the hardwood floor, heart beating hard.

17

"Mr. Gale? My name is Norris Kennedy. I was a friend of Bennet Tarlow. I remember you from a fight in Las Vegas—Fury-Wilder three."

Early morning in San Juan Capistrano, Gale still in bed, sunlight streaming into the little bedroom in the house where he grew up.

It's just hours after being invited to hell by Vernon Jeffs.

And less than an hour since he sent off the search warrant request to the Honorable Carl Schmidt for the home and white Ford Econoline belonging to Vernon Jeffs.

And learned that no prints of Jeffs were found in Tarlow's Newport Beach home.

"When can we meet?" he asks.

"I'm in Laguna. Moulin on Forest?"

Gale and Mendez arrive first and take an outside table far in a corner. The café is busy as always this morning, mostly locals and their dogs, who all seem to know each other, and plenty of well-heeled tourists tucking into their crepes, omelets, and lattes.

Norris Kennedy is much as Gale remembers her, a pretty redhead with one dimple and a measured smile, shapely.

Introductions but no small talk.

"I didn't call sooner because I had no idea who would kill Bennet," Norris says.

"Do you now?"

She gives Gale an assayer's stare, unblinking dark brown eyes boring into him, then Mendez.

"He was one of the most energetic, ambitious, and complex men I've ever known," she says. "I was a city attorney in Las Vegas at the time, specializing in gaming and hospitality, so I've met more than a few people like that. Businessmen, politicians, gangsters, Hollywood. The gamut. I could go on and on about Tarlow but I won't."

The detectives' silence draws her out. "The Tarlow Company is a house divided," she says. "Bennet and his father detested each other. His stepmother took her stepson's side on most things. The big issue was always profit. Bennet, in his father's eyes, was a mediocre builder and a poor businessman. Bennet thought of his dad as a money-grubber and a bore. Then there's the patriarch, the original Bennet Tarlow himself, strong but mostly silent at ninety, presiding over the world from his mansion overlooking Crystal Cove in Newport Beach."

A waiter brings them breakfast. A little dog in a blue vest, pulling on his leash and wagging his tail pleadingly, puts his front paws on Norris Kennedy's bistro chair before his owner yanks him away.

"Sorry, Norris," he says. "You know how he likes you. Jasper, sit!"

"No problem, Bob. He won't get this breakfast!"

"Jasper, *heel.*"

The three begin breakfast in silence, Gale stealing a long look at Norris while she shakes pepper onto her omelet. She's less effusive than he remembered her, more matter-of-fact, and somehow more beguiling.

"What?" she asks Gale.

"Nothing. Just observing."

"That's Robert Clark," she says. "He made the classic surf movie *Laguna to Mavericks*."

"I loved that movie," says Gale, who surfed Crystal Cove ineptly, but successfully hunted nearby lobsters as a boy.

"I did, too," says Mendez.

A silent beat.

"Suspects?" asks Kennedy. "Persons of interest?"

"Yes," says Mendez.

"Who?"

"No," says Mendez.

"I think you should be looking at Ben's projects, especially Wildcoast. There's been resistance within Tarlow Company since the beginning. Resistance from certain county supervisors, support from others. Stiff resistance from Native Californians whose ancestors lived on the land back to ten thousand years ago. Ben was fearful about everything to do with that development. Developers don't build cities from scratch but that's what he was trying to do. I can't tell you how many very intense phone calls he had. Sometimes late at night."

"Names?" asks Gale. "Companies? Organizations?"

"No. He'd always politely excuse himself, go to another room, and close the door. I certainly heard the word 'Wildcoast' several times. Do you have his phone?"

"We think the killer destroyed and dumped it," says Mendez.

Gale looks over at the surfer twins, and their athletic, probably prosperous parents. Exactly the kind of people who want to live in Wildcoast, he thinks. Wonders if they might even qualify to buy a home in one of the "affordable" tracts.

"It's hard to believe that the Tarlow Company could be divided on Wildcoast," he says.

"There's something at stake there that I don't understand," says Norris. "I tried to talk to Bennet about it, straight on. More than once. But I didn't really know what questions to ask. I didn't have a place to begin, other than his constant agitation, and the phone calls he wouldn't let me hear. He deflected. Evaded."

"Which of the Orange County supervisors are opposed to Wildcoast?"

"Kevin Elder, Seventh District, is *concerned*. That's where Wildcoast would be."

"Grant Hudson's boss and idol," says Mendez.

"Grant is insufferable," says Norris. "Ben could hardly be in the same room with him. Kevin, on the other hand, is a decent man. Liberal and left, for an Orange County pol. Like Bennet. Environmentally aware, like Bennet. A single guy, enjoying it. Like Bennet. Tell him hello from me."

"Do you know Vernon Jeffs?" asks Gale.

"Never heard that name," says Norris Kennedy. "Your interesting person?"

"Big guy," says Gale. "Bodybuilder. Tends bar, up in Huntington."

"Doesn't sound like Tarlow material," she says.

Another silent bump, then:

"I do think Bennet was killed over something in his work," says Norris. "We're talking about billion-dollar rivers of money rolling through the Tarlow Company every year, for years to come. Billions of dollars and some very headstrong people."

"Family?" asks Mendez.

"Certainly not," says Norris, dismissively. "But someone close, outer circle. Someone with a lot at stake in Wildcoast, the many-billion-dollar city he wanted to build."

"Like who?" asks Mendez.

"No, don't be crude. I have no idea who. I hope you weren't expecting any."

"An investigation like this is never that easy," Gale says.

"What on earth do you mean by that?"

"The opposite of crude."

"Okay, but I can't see the Tarlows opening up to you about their company or their golden boy."

Gale, from the start, has seen this as a killing for money or revenge. Which might very easily involve a gun for hire. The gun being a .22-caliber semiautomatic pistol, easily concealed from Tarlow and fired point-blank, twice, into the back of his head. The barrel of which will have left unique tool marks on the bullets they've recovered. If they can find the gun, that is. Not likely, if the shooter is a pro, or even just reasonably careful.

Norris Kennedy casts a glance at the nearest diners, then leans forward and speaks softly, her West Texan accent drifting through the voices and the clinking of dishes.

"There are secrets, Mr. Gale."

"Such as?" asks Mendez.

"Bennet's stepmother, Camile, seduced him as a boy. He was seventeen. She groomed him. One time, one night. On an Amazon birdwatching trip she planned for them. It scarred him terribly."

"In what ways?" asks Mendez.

"He grew up emotionally remote. Almost hidden. Sweet and doting, like the boy she destroyed. He surrounded himself with women not so much for love, or even company, but for protection. He couldn't get close to us. He didn't trust us because he didn't trust her."

Camile Tarlow, thinks Gale. From his boyhood he has only scattered and dim memories of her, a blond bombshell who had exploded and disappeared.

Once a fixture in the Southern California media, now reclusive, seldom photographed, never interviewed.

Norris glances at arriving customers, who are choosing a table adjacent.

She stands and asks them, "Would you mind sitting over there? We need privacy and it's a better table anyhow."

The dad is a young surfer still in his half-john wet suit and flip-flops. His wife is clad likewise, as are two children, a boy and a girl, twins by the look of them.

"Sure," says the dad. "Cool."

The mom stares at Norris.

"Thank you! You're a prince," Norris says, sitting back down. "Where was I?"

"Tarlow hid behind women but didn't trust them," says Gale.

"I didn't feel hidden behind at first," says Norris. "He was sweet and attentive and deferential. Eager to please. Always in touch when one of us was out of town. Thoughtful gifts. Wonderful travel, though I always paid my own way. We chased beautiful birds all over the world, all so Benny could photograph them. I'm sure you saw the pictures in his Laguna home. But . . . over time, we didn't go further. He couldn't. He was guilty about what he'd done. The more he tried to bury his guilt with abstinence and gifts, the more angry and depressed he became. We broke up a year ago. A mutual decision."

Norris sets her napkin on her chair and heads into the café proper, restroom-bound is Gale's guess.

Mendez shakes her head. "Maybe I believe this chick and maybe I don't. What's her motivation? Why wait until now? Hmmm. Why was she on Tarlow's calendar the week before he died, if they'd broken up a year before?"

Norris is back five minutes later. Lipstick fresh and hair brushed. She sits down, works her sunglasses from her purse and puts them on.

"No, Detectives, Benny didn't hide what happened, but it was pretty much the last thing we talked about before he moved on. He was emotionally and physically absent long before I learned that ugly truth. He said I was the first and only person he'd told. Said nobody else in the world knew, not even his father. I don't necessarily believe that, but I choose to. Out of respect for his beautiful nature and his scars."

"Why tell you the secret he couldn't tell anyone else?" asks Mendez.

"He loved and trusted me."

Norris Kennedy takes a sip of her bubbling water and nods. "And I'm telling it to you so you can more accurately understand your . . . victim."

"What was their relationship after?" asks Gale. "Camile and stepson Bennet?"

"Ben said very little about her. Mostly casual references and factoids. 'Camile's great. Haven't seen much of her lately. Dinner with Dad and maybe Cam on Saturday. She's always a maybe. Sorry I can't invite you but I'm protecting you, believe me. Maybe later.' Now I sound like her! What he actually sounded like was a twelve-year-old boy. Before the fall. He told me she'd went MIA from his life, after that fall. Liked to travel with friends. Liked buying European art. Not clothes, though, because as a newly minted recluse, she almost never went out. She day-traded on her computer, up in her private suite. Made and lost fortunes. Then off to buy more art. Opened a gallery for it in Newport Beach, but never even went in except on Sundays and Mondays when it was closed. It's still there."

"Why were you on Bennet's calendar the week before he died?" asks Mendez.

"You people are thorough," says Norris. "The truth is, since we'd parted ways, I occasionally chased him down and forced my way into his life for an hour. Lunch here or coffee or a walk on the beach."

Gale thinks of Tarlow's calendared date with Patti DiMeo, right here in this café, the morning after he died.

"Do you know Patti DiMeo?" Gale asks.

"No. Should I?"

"She's a real estate broker on Lido," says Gale. "Bennet had a coffee date with her, set for the morning after he died. Right here, where we sit."

Norris looks away from Gale, then quickly back.

"Pretty?"

"Yes," says Mendez.

"Well, maybe she was to be his next woman to hide behind. I met others when I was with him, and others since we broke up. And, of course, there were more, down the years before we met."

"I'm sorry to bring back unpleasant memories," says Gale.

"It's part of the job," says Mendez.

"I am a big girl now," says Norris. "Like the Dylan song."

"Did Tarlow bet on the Fury-Wilder rematch?" asks Gale.

"Of course."

Another absorbent quiet from the detectives.

"He had half a million on Deontay by knockout in the fourth," says Norris. "But Deontay got knocked out."

"Who did you have?" asks Gale.

She nods. "A hundred grand on Fury by knockout in the eleventh. It hit at eight to one. My treat for a week in Bali and some incredible birds of paradise. Beautiful place, beautiful birds, beautiful photographs. I remember he was almost happy then. Almost."

"Almost a million dollars for you," says Mendez.

"I bought treasury bills with the rest," says Norris.

Norris Kennedy sighs and stands.

Gale watches her walk down Forest, toward Coast Highway.

Coast Highway and Wildcoast, thinks Gale.

Wildcoast and Deontay Wilder, knocked out in the eleventh.

Putting eight hundred grand into Norris's bank account, enough to take her reluctant lover birding in Bali.

A prominent real estate developer wearing a silver pendant of a bird as he gets half eaten by a mountain lion in a county park near the future site of his own dream development.

Gale adds all that Norris has just told him about Camile Tarlow, and the Tarlow Company strife over Wildcoast, to what he's learned from spending a few hours in Tarlow's homes in Laguna Beach and Newport.

Considers the coincidences and contradictions, mysteries, deceptions, conspiracy theories, and half-truths that are nothing like those of any homicide he's ever worked.

Mendez's phone pings. It's flat on the table and she screens it with both hands, then lifts it.

"Fuck," she says softly.

And gives Gale a prohibitive look. "No," she says, fingers and thumbs flying.

An awkward moment later she's talking with Grant Hudson, making an appointment with Kevin Elder.

"Three good?" she asks Gale.

"Perfect."

18

The Acjacheme Nation Tribal Hall is an adobe brick building on crowded Paseo Ramon in San Juan Capistrano, two blocks west of the mission.

Gale and Tribal Councilman Roger Winderling sit on a bench outside in the shade of a large pepper tree, where the lunchtime air smells of tortillas and grilled meat.

They're class of '01 Capistrano Valley High School, both tackles on the Cougars football team.

Cougars, thinks Gale, adding the name of his team to the coincidences that keep popping up in his investigation of the murder of Bennet Tarlow.

Small talk now, some predictable reminiscences, and an odd air of displacement between two men descended from an Indigenous tribe that dates back ten thousand years to this very place. The displacement of subjugation, Gale thinks. Of "conversion," and the slow death of a culture unrecognized by the Bureau of Indian Affairs and the other authors of history.

"What's up, Lew?"

"I'm interested in the Tribal Mentor Program."

"You mean donating to it?"

"No, I mean being a mentor."

"Well, that's just terrific, Lew. What brought this on?"

Gale has been wondering how to explain it. "It" having come to him gradually, then suddenly.

"I want to help a kid," he says. "Be, like, a brother or a dad. Give them what I know and show them how to do the things I've learned. Basic stuff, like what you do and don't do as a grown-up. Just a few hours a week, you know."

"Do you want an Acjacheme?"

"Sure. Or mixed, like us."

"We match up boys with men and girls with women, of course."

"Yes, a boy."

Winderling gives Gale a long, thoughtful look. "There's no monetary compensation at all, not even for gas."

"Fine. My truck gets okay mileage."

"What kinds of activities do you propose for your . . . we call them Young Braves."

"I can show him how to catch a fish at the beach. How to throw a football and a baseball, make bows and arrows the old way. Shoot a gun. I can bring him to work and have lunch in the cafeteria. Introduce him to deputies, just, you know, show him the place. There's a crime lab and the jail, helicopters, patrol cars. Might be able to get him a ride-along. Maybe, you know, he might want to be a deputy someday. We're always hiring."

Winderling smiles. "Scare him straight!"

"There's that, too."

"Fantastic, Lew. This is great."

"I'm glad you think so."

"There's an Acjacheme boy signed up with us," says Winderling. "Rose Deming's boy, Dylan. He's ten. A big Indian. Easygoing. Handy with a football. Dad let the booze kill him."

Gale thinks of his own relationship with alcohol and his weakness for it.

"I can talk to him about that," he says.

"How long were you married, Lew?"

"Eight years."

"Do you have children?"

"No. Neither of us wanted to. Then."

"Now?"

"I'm not in that position."

Winderling purses his lips. "Meaning . . ."

"I'm single, not attached. I'm forty-three now. Can't just snap my fingers and have a child."

"Would you like that?"

"Yes, I would. The days seem to be going by. I don't want this murder job to be all I do."

"Gotcha. There's adoption."

"I wanted one of my own."

Winderling stands. "I understand. Remember how hard we used to hit those running backs?"

"Sure. But mostly I remember Marilyn."

"How is she?"

"We haven't talked in five years. She danced on Broadway. Her dream."

"I remember that homecoming dance and her dress. Thought you were the luckiest dude on the planet."

"I was!"

"Lew, let's go to the office, get the Young Braves paperwork."

Winderling's Tribal Hall office is a neat white box with one wall festooned with Acjacheme baskets, several of which Gale recognizes as his mother's creations. Two-hundred-year-old bows and arrows decorate another wall. Gale has always wondered how he hit anything with them. When he was ten, he tried out one of his grandmother's old bows and it was pretty hard to get those arrows to go where you wanted. They cut through the air in tangents rather than flying true. When he started making his own bows and arrows in the Indigenous way, the hardest part was getting the willow arrow straight.

Now Gale wonders if he was just too young.

Behind Winderling's desk hang old photographs of the mission and the Native huts outside its walls.

Roger takes a moment to browse a short stack of papers, then pushes them across his desk to Gale.

"Just read and sign them, bring them back when you're ready."

"Can I just sign them right now?"

Winderling smiles again. Gale thinks of him twenty-five years ago, number 78, grinning through the face cage and a bulbous black mouthpiece after crashing a hapless quarterback to the grass.

"Sure, Lew. No hurry, though. Or maybe there is?"

"Tell me about this boy."

Gale, with a lifelong hostility to forms, applications, and details, signs swiftly without reading them, instead listening to Roger's description of Dylan Deming, ten or eleven, great kid, quiet, big, doing okay in school, plays football and lacrosse. Two older sisters. Mom is Rose, works a day shift at the Cahuilla Casino way out in Aguanga, but they live right here in San Juan.

Hands over the forms.

"Well, that didn't take long," says Winderling, browsing through them. "Here, you didn't date this one."

Gale dates it and hands it back.

"Isn't that surprising about Bennet Tarlow?" asks Winderling. "Your mother told me you were working it."

"Good old Mom, always protecting my privacy."

"She's just proud of you. What I can't figure is what Tarlow was doing out there in a wilderness park alone at night."

"He wasn't alone. He was with a man. We're not sure who."

"The guy killed him?"

"It looks that way."

"Like a friend or something? Or did the guy maybe have the gun on him, like abducted him?"

"Can't say. Did you know Tarlow?"

"Never met him. Weird though, I met his stepmom, be about ten years ago, long after she kind of dropped out of sight. I was working at the Capistrano Trading Post at the time and she bursts in with two young men in dark suits and sunglasses. I'm sure you remember her—the flamboyant dresses and that gigantic blond bouffant? Camile Stanton Tarlow. She wanted California Native crafts. The older the better, not current day knockoff things. I showed her what we had and she bought it all. The men loaded it into a big white SUV. I told her the Native Museum here had a few of the good old Acjacheme pieces. Not any left in the world. Anyway she asked me to take her there and introduce her to the owner. Which I did. Remember old Richard Bear? He told her that none of the Native arts and crafts were for sale. He was firm about it, but polite. Should have seen the look on her face. Talk about cold. That was that, then two weeks later I hear that she had bought the entire museum and everything in it. The building, land, and all."

Camile Tarlow, thinks Gale.

There are secrets.

19

Fresh off Winderling, Gale drives his Explorer through the Caspers Wilderness Park entrance off Ortega Highway, just a few miles from San Juan Capistrano.

Parks again in an open Cottonwood Creek Campground space, gets his binoculars and puts on his straw Stetson against the bright October sun, locks up. Notes the campground restrooms, in which Vito Pesco had probably heard Bennet Tarlow and possibly Vernon Jeffs making their way from Tarlow's Last Supper to his final rendezvous with a very large owl feeding her young on a dark night.

He skirts the homeless encampment almost hidden in the dense cottonwoods, sees the glimmer of shopping carts and the blue of tarps within trees.

Gale climbs a hill that gives him a view east, raises his binoculars to where an OC Sheriff's Department Expedition raises a cloud of dust as it lumbers toward the massacre site of the three Laotian cannabis slaves. Still working the crime scene, Gale thinks.

He wonders again at the recent violence here, lobbed into this beautiful wilderness from the surrounding 3.17-million-people-strong Orange County. Land of the Acjacheme and the Juaneños and the Luiseños, he thinks. Land of deer and mountain lions. Later, land of the Spanish and the Mexicans. Much of it owned since the Civil War by the Tarlow Company. Land to someday become a utopian city, born in the eyes of Bennet Tarlow III. Land, too, of dope grows and murders. His friend Detective Peters is heading up that case, and Gale is not envious.

He comes to the kill site in the wash of the seasonal creek. Sees the hole the CSIs have left after digging soil samples heavy with Tarlow blood. Feels the hush he always feels, looking at a place fresh with the dead.

In his detective years, Gale has revisited crime scenes many times, sometimes more than once, hoping to shine new light on what had happened there, and why, and how. The light is, of course, his own. It's not always present. But once in a while he sees what he hasn't seen before, recognizes a bit of truth he's overlooked, makes a connection.

Kneeling now, he rakes his fingers through the loose soil of the hole and rubs the dirt between a thumb and a forefinger and lets his thoughts wander.

If Jeffs is a hired gun, who did the hiring?

A man or a woman with something valuable to lose, if Wildcoast gets built? A competitor. Another builder. Someone who is part of Tarlow's rarified world of the very rich, or at least adjacent to it, or maybe willing to kill to become a part of it.

Norris Kennedy thinks so.

Norris, a gently jilted lover, too. Strong and loyal and beautiful. What if she's wrong about motive? The fury of a woman scorned?

If Jeffs killed Tarlow on his own, why?

Revenge? Jealousy? Himself a jilted lover of Tarlow? Seems unlikely.

What was Jeffs to Tarlow?

Something more than a guy who could lead him to a large owl

not usually found within hundreds of miles from here, so the eccentric developer and utopian dreamer could photograph it?

Gale knows his search warrant request may well be turned down by Honorable Carl Schmidt.

The chance that a judge, even a law-and-order judge like Carl, would issue a warrant based on a statement from a woman who claims to have seen Jeffs—whom she does not know and has only seen a few times in her life—in Tarlow's Newport home the evening of the murder?

Slim, thinks Gale.

Unreasonable search and seizure.

Probable cause.

So Gale ponders his alternatives:

Knock on Jeffs's door and ask to come in and talk? Hope to see the .22 in plain sight?

Jeffs would punch me in the face before he'd do that, Gale thinks.

Gale stands, rubs the tacky soil off his thumb and forefinger, and heads back to his vehicle.

He drives the dirt road, leaving Caspers Park, heading east toward the Santa Ana Mountains. A rider on an e-bike behind him glides past. Gale thinks of the previous Orange County mountain lion killing here—twenty-one years ago—a fit bicyclist just like that guy, fixing a blown tire, kneeling, making him appear small to the lion who killed him and dragged him into the trees.

Gale shifts into four-wheel drive to climb a narrow, rocky two-track certainly used by deer and rabbits and mountain lions, motoring through country he'd biked and hiked and hunted as a boy.

At the top of a rise, standing on a big boulder and panting, Gale lifts his binoculars to the Wildcoast building site below. It's five square miles of hills and meadows. Wooden grade and survey stakes mark roads and buildings-to-be. Hot pink flags wave from elevation stakes.

He's surprised by the size of it. Half the size of the city of Laguna Beach, he thinks, according to the miniaturized Wildcoast model in Tarlow's home office.

Two white pickup trucks with Empire Excavators emblems on their doors are pulled off a wide dirt road that looks recently graded. Neat berms of earth packed down on either side to form gutters. Two men with jackhammers toil away in deep holes, the domes of their yellow hard hats just visible from here, the clatter of their hammer blades windblown and distant. Between them and the trucks, a man and a woman who look dressed for a safari watch them.

Gale arrives after a bumpy downslope ride, steps out.

The woman strides purposefully toward him, aviators on, her hands raised in a stop-right-there command; the man stays where he is.

Gale runs her stop sign, raises his badge, and introduces himself.

"Thank god, I thought you were another damned reporter," she says. She's tall and looks strong. "Kate Hicks, Empire Excavators."

"Detective Lew Gale, Orange County Sheriff's."

She gives him a long look. "So, how can I help?"

"I'm investigating the murder."

"He was killed way back there near the Cottonwood Creek Campground. You've overshot it by three miles."

"I came here to see how Wildcoast is coming along."

"Well, here she is," says Hicks. "Only about two hundred permits and fifty public hearings away from a county green light. I don't think they'll ever get it passed."

She smiles and nods. "Okay, you *do* look familiar. You're the sniper from Afghanistan. Took out the wrong guy and got blown up for your trouble. I read that article in the *Times*. Great piece. I was in Helmand, one tour."

"I'm glad you made it home."

"Came *this* close to tripping an IED." Hicks shows him her

thumb and finger, almost touching. "Hid in a pile of trash along the road."

Gale sees Private Guy Flatly, blown up on a morning patrol not twenty feet ahead of him. The *whop*, the chunks of flesh and bone blown into the air, the mist of the blood on Gale's sunglasses, the sudden fire in his own legs and groin. A flash. A moment that became eternal, that reshaped him, that warped his body and his mind and his marriage, and drew him to the bourbon and the painkillers and the antidepressants. Now, with the years, this eternal moment overwhelms him less frequently and with less clarity, and the pills are gone, and the bourbon is almost controlled, but a comment like Hicks's can be enough to bring the moment back to him.

He feels the pain again. Flatley's and his own. Then they are gone.

He looks over at the jackhammer men. "Why dig there?"

"Perc test. We're trying to see if septic is right for Wildcoast, or if we'll have to go full sewer. Big cost difference."

"Can I have a look?"

"Suit yourself, sir. Don't fall in. McNab's in charge and you'll have to leave if he says."

Gale walks toward the clattering electric jackhammers, trading nods with McNab, remembering that Velasquez mentioned him that night at the Grove. As he nears the pit he sees the shovel stuck upright in the ground, the sharp white bedrock fragments and freshly loosened soil thrown from the hole.

He stands over the first test pit, sees the Day-Glo-green-vested man in his yellow hard hat, his shoulders and arms throbbing as the rocks crack and the dirt flies. The pit is almost six feet deep. As if sensing Gale, the digger glances up at him, then turns back to his work and presses on.

The second pit is deeper. Gale stands back in the rubble of broken bedrock and loose soil. A red-handled shovel stands upright, its shadow on the ground reminding him of his three o'clock appointment with Supervisor Kevin Elder.

Then the clatter of the jackhammer stops, and the man looks up at Gale.

"Shovel."

Gale hands it down. "Hard work. What are you looking for?"

"Gold."

Gale smiles, remembering the legend of Spanish gold buried near the mission where he was baptized. His great-grandmother and -father were fountains of legend: Dana Point waves so big they blotted out the sun; a monstrous winged rattlesnake that could fly down from the clouds and carry you away; the white grizzly bear and her den of white cubs; the ancient lake that gave birth to the Acjacheme people and still lies just below the earth, where the souls of the Acjacheme rest.

The man, short and stocky, hurls a shovelful of broken rock and dirt over his shoulder.

Gale ducks it and moves to a safer place near the pit.

"Looks too hard to percolate," he says.

"No perc here."

The red shovel flashes and another load of rock and dirt clears the hole.

"So you'll have to go with a sewer system, right?"

The man stops, drives his shovel into the hard earth, and looks up at Gale.

"Sewer. Sí."

He picks up a shard of bedrock the size of a cantaloupe in his gloved hands and shot-puts it out.

Then another. The next one looks about the size of a truck battery and just as heavy. But the digger gets it up and out on his first try. Three more and his dirt-covered face is running with dark sweat.

He unties a red bandana from around his neck and wipes his brow. Hands the shovel up to Gale.

"Look for crystals."

"For what?"

"Big crystals. Mucho dinero."

Gale remembers a dramatic crystal-and-lapis pendant favored by Marilyn. "For jewelry and chandeliers?"

"I don't know."

"Is your company a good place to work?"

The worker shrugs, then stoops, choses another big piece of bedrock and heaves it out of his hole.

"Mucho trabajo, pero no mucho dinero."

"I'm a policeman investigating the murder of Bennet Tarlow."

Another shrug, then a grunt, and another boulder launched from the pit.

"I don't know."

He slaps his gloved hands together and takes up the jackhammer.

"Vaya con Dios," says Gale.

Checks his watch and hustles back to his plain-wrap.

20

At the wheel of her black Explorer, Daniela follows her son using the TeenShield app on her phone, which is propped up in a console cupholder beside a caffeine-and-sugar-loaded energy drink.

She has recently—and secretly—downloaded the TeenShield software onto Jesse's smartphone, allowing her to see his emails coming and going, read his texts, watch his social media interactions, and locate him in real time through GPS. It even has a geo-fencing feature that notifies her when Jesse enters a "Forbidden Zone"—an area where Daniela doesn't want him be.

She's still getting used to the bizarre power of this kid-protection app, of which Jesse is of course oblivious. And she's trying to get used to the idea that although she's protecting him, she's betraying him, too. She's terrified that he'll find out. If he did, it would drive him away, into the very things she's trying to protect him from.

She's four cars and a hundred yards behind him.

He's supposed to be in class right now, thinks Daniela.

Instead, he's in tart Lulu Vega's cobalt blue Subaru, eastbound on First Street, headed toward Barrio Dogtown.

Just half an hour ago, Daniela was sitting with Gale in the Moulin Café, having concluded her interview with the annoyingly cool and not-very-credible Norris Kennedy. Talk about a tart, thinks Daniela. A Tarlow tart.

As a strict Catholic, Daniela has a strong dislike of morally loose, privileged women. And respect and affection for the young victims she encountered in Vice, many of them innocent girls.

Virgins once, as she was, and of course was the Holy Mother.

Norris Kennedy, she thinks, to whom Lew Gale showed curiosity and respect and checked out with unsubtle interest.

She looks at Lulu's Subaru, remembering the look on Gale's face as Norris Kennedy walked down Forest toward Coast Highway in Laguna. While, according to TeenShield, Jesse was in Enrique's Liquor, the liquor store closest to her home, with a reputation for selling beer to minors with fake IDs. Definitely a Forbidden Zone.

Now Daniela follows the car south onto Edgar Place, then east on Colton, then right on Victor.

There's four cars between them now and she can see from her elevated SUV view that Jesse's driving.

The neighborhood is 1940s, stucco walls and wood-shake-roof one-stories. Twenty years newer than her bungalow a few miles west in Tustin. But the same leaf-strewn magnolias and avocado trees centered in sun-starved front lawns, same grape-stake fences surrounding backyards. Cars on the street and driveways and even lawns. A gleaming cherry red Chevelle lowrider under a blue tarp.

Graffiti on cinder-block walls and curbs, even on the metal phone-company switch boxes.

Varrio DT

Barrio Dogtown, alright.

Jesse pulls right into a driveway, and Daniela glides to a lucky spot three doors short.

She watches them park and get out, cuts her engine.

Jesse's got his standard black skinny jeans and a black *Death Games* T-shirt on and his clunky black Doc Martens. A case of Modelo dangles from a skinny arm; from the other his camo gaming duffel, most likely containing his two-part keypad, VR headsets, and a dozen games, all first-person shooter/fighter featuring spectacularly gory gun deaths, sword decapitations, machete dismemberments, grenade mayhem, etc.

She wonders if it contains some of the condoms she left in his room after he told her about this girl in his class, Lulu Vega.

In the side-view profile she has of Jesse just now, his face looks like Tim Malone's must have looked at eighteen.

Lulu is barrio chic in her sleeveless red plaid flannel blouse, a black miniskirt, and red ankle-high fashion boots. Her hair is up and her lollipop earrings sway in rhythm with her long-legged strides. She cuts an angle toward the front porch, leading Jesse under a sprawling magnolia whose big spent blossoms litter a threadbare lawn.

The door opens, and Daniela recognizes Flaco Benitez, the big guy from Bowl Me Over. Lulu walks into the house like she owns the place.

Jesse swings his beer through the open doorway, pulls the duffel in, and the door closes shut behind him.

Daniela Mendez leans her head back against the rest, feels the heavy thump of her heart.

Notion #1: Knock firmly on that front door, march in, and order him to come with her. Use her shield if she has to. Which of course could get her suspended. And worse, probably send Jesse packing.

Notion #2: Text him and tell him she's watching him. When he comes out, flash her headlights just to make sure he knows she's here.

Notion #3: Text him, say, *Hi, I'm working, just seeing how your day is going.* Be home regular time she hopes. Ask him casually about his day and see how he covers his visit to Barrio Dogtown.

Notion #4: *Cool off, bitch. Have a calm mom talk with your son* tonight. *Keep your ugly little TeenShield secret but try to put some sense into him. Get your own pathetic, fear-driven butt to the three o'clock interview with Supervisor Kevin Elder. You've got a decent chance of being on time if you leave right now.*

What it all boils down to is this, Daniela thinks. *The harder I try to protect him, the harder I'll push him away. I can stall and sneak and spy, but if he even suspects, he'll run from me. I know him. He came from me, and that's what I would do.*

Staring at the front door of the house, Daniela remembers herself at eighteen. She had graduated high school early, was working full-time as a secretary at Azusa Catholic College, part of her sprawling, beloved Church of the Holy Martyr, while she took criminal justice night classes at Citrus College in Glendora. She had applied to the Los Angeles County Sheriff's Department because she thought being a deputy would be a good career. You could start at a fat sixty-five thousand dollars a year back then, plus overtime, drive a fast car, arrest bad guys, and help innocent people defend themselves against criminals. Her dad had a friend in the Sheriff's Department, Albert Ybarra, who was a cool guy and said they were always hiring. He said the LASD got a bad name because of its racist gangs, but most of the deputies were good men and women. They backed each other up, both on the streets and off.

And Father Tim said she'd be a good policewoman because she genuinely cared about people, and wrote a letter of recommendation to the LASD Academy. It was the most positive endorsement of her "high character, spiritual strength, intelligence, and unlimited potential" that Daniela could have imagined. Coming from Tim Malone, it hit her like a judgment from the Lord himself.

She remembered crying when she read it, emailed by Father Timothy for her approval and any suggestions to make it better.

Now, using her binoculars to magnify a crack in a window curtain, Daniela sees darkness and the flicker of screen lights and a woman moving inside. As she considers the violent video games soon to be played inside the Barrio Dogtown house, Daniela thinks of her own attraction to guns when she was Jesse's age. Even before holding or firing a gun, she liked that they could make her equal to other human beings. Instantly. Could protect her. Make her powerful. Years later, after Jesse was born, when she fired her first handgun in training for the Orange County Sheriff's, she was surprised by its sudden explosive force and the recoil. What a machine, she remembers thinking. I'm *a machine with this thing in my hands. I am power.* But she never pictured the bloody results, was never enthralled by them like Jesse is at eighteen.

Her eighteenth birthday? A quiet dinner with Mom and Dad. Still the Virgin Dani. Still months away from storming Tim, and almost a year from giving birth to Jesse.

Looking out at the fallen blossoms of the magnolia tree, she remembers what it felt like when she first felt the living thing inside her. Thinking if he's a boy she could name him Jesus, but decided that would be melodramatic. You think things like that, Daniela knows, when you're eighteen and overwhelmed by a man you think is directly descended from God.

She wonders what Lulu thinks when she looks at her son. Is it possible that she sees—or thinks she sees—God in him?

Well, maybe.

But more likely she sees a handsome, shy young man who looks at her in a certain way. A young man who's a fun hang because he's smart. A really good smile. Still growing to full size, which, judging by his hands and feet, is going to be substantial.

And, as a bonus, she can easily boss him around. He has a desire to please. There's something guilty in him, too, giving Lulu the same target Daniela sights in on when she's trying to sway him.

Sometimes Daniela hates herself for exploiting that target. And right now, knowing that Jesse is inside a gangbanger's roost with a hot woman stronger than he is, she hates Lulu Vega, too.

What does Jesse see in her, Daniela wonders.

Easy. She's beautiful, confident, and proud. Actually gets good grades, according to Jesse's Tustin High School counselor, with whom Daniela some weeks ago had a long phone call. Jesse likes smart. Wants to be smart. And if smart is pretty in her short skirt, sleeveless blouse, and hot red side-zip boots, well, thinks Daniela, he definitely sees *that*. Get a few beers in him and he'd probably crawl through cut glass to impress her. Or do something really stupid like ask Lulu's older friends in Barrio Dogtown to jump him in.

With her eyes on the front door again, Daniela genuflects swiftly, asks God not to lead Jesse into temptation the way she led Timothy, careful not to suggest that God was in any way to blame for what she did.

Amen.

She starts the Explorer and tells her phone to take her to the Orange County Building in Santa Ana.

21

Supervisor Kevin Elder is not an elder at all.

More like a wolf of Wall Street, Gale thinks. Forty, a handsome face, and a head of wavy black hair with a silver widow's peak. His coat is off and a yellow tie loosened in the collar of a white shirt. Black suspenders. His teeth are perfect.

Mendez is thinking likewise, admitting he's easy on the eyes, but so what?

They sit in his spacious office in the County Building. Elder supervises the Seventh District, by far the wealthiest. Laguna Beach, Newport Beach, Laguna Niguel, Laguna Woods, San Juan Capistrano, Mission Viejo.

And more, thinks Gale.

He looks through the fourth-floor window at the Santa Ana Mountains to the southeast, beyond which lie Caspers Wilderness Park and Cottonwood Creek Campground, near where Bennet Tarlow took two shots to the head from behind and died in a swamp of his own blood. And, somewhere in those mountains, Gale knows there's an aged mountain lion that may or may not have acquired a taste for such blood.

All in Elder's Seventh District, thinks Gale.

Between him and the distant mountains sprawls the county, once home to citrus groves and small towns, now densely peopled and hectic, a thick carpet of suburbia.

OC small talk: Ohtani-less Angels flopping again this regular season, though Trout tried his best.

Drought threatening again after two great wet winters and La Niña on the march.

The median price of a home in Orange County, says Elder, according to this morning's *Wall Street Journal*, is $1.65 million.

"Do you have a person of interest, regarding Bennet?" Elder asks, his voice sharp and forceful.

"We do," says Gale. "He's got his wife's alibi for the night Tarlow died. But we have a witness who puts him with Tarlow that evening."

"She said, he said."

"She and she," says Mendez.

"Tell me about him."

"Vernon Jeffs," says Gale.

Elder nods but he doesn't blink and his expression doesn't change. No surprise or nerves, thinks Gale. But he waits to speak, familiar with the power of silence in an interview.

"Fifty years old, six-four, two hundred and sixty pounds of mostly muscle," says Mendez. "Red hair and sometimes a beard and mustache. Tan eyes. Scary. He tends bar in the Bear Cave in Huntington Beach."

"I've heard of it," says Elder. "Never been. This guy sounds like strange company for Ben Tarlow. A record?"

"A DUI five years back," Gale says. "A bar fight that got him six months, and a school-zone firearm charge ten years ago, dismissed."

"So he's a gun nut," says Elder. "Does he have one like the twenty-two caliber that killed Bennet?"

"He's not in the ATF, FBI, or state ownership registries."

"Can you get a search warrant?"

"Pending," says Gale.

Elder shakes his head, sits back.

"While we gather evidence, we're looking for a motive," says Gale. "It doesn't look like a crime of passion. Tarlow's wallet was still in his pants—plenty of cash and credit cards. Revenge? Maybe. But this looks like a hired hit. So who paid for it? Who gains by Tarlow's death?"

"No one I can imagine," says Elder. "He was a gentleman. Honest and generous. Huge on charities. The Catholic Diocese. The Tarlow Foundation for the Arts. Tarlow Charitable Trust. He wasn't just a visionary builder, he was a great man. I don't know who could profit by killing him."

"I keep coming back to Wildcoast," says Gale. "Billions of dollars in loans and options to finance it, but future billions to be made when the Tarlow Company sells the homes, the industrial buildings, the open parcels and acres—everything. It was Tarlow's baby, but the project has detractors at the Tarlow Company."

"It sounds to me like you should be talking to Tarlow II," says Elder.

"We will," says Mendez, giving Gale a look. "Norris Kennedy sends her regards," she says.

"Ah, Norris."

"She told us that Bennet was anxious and fearful over Wildcoast," says Mendez. "Late-night calls he wouldn't let her overhear. Anger. Evasion. Depression."

"Norris would know," says Elder.

"Do you trust her?" asks Mendez.

Elder looks at Mendez, taps his fingertips on his polished stainless-steel desk. "I have no reason not to. But I don't know her well. I think Bennet trusted her. He was in love with her for most of the time they spent together. I could say they were happy but I don't think Bennet was ever really happy. Should I not trust Norris Kennedy?"

"She's pushy and evasive," says Mendez. "Spilled some interesting dirt our way, about Bennet."

"Such as?"

"Can't discuss that now," says Mendez.

Kevin Elder, hands open. "Sure. I understand."

A long silence then, as the three humans consider each other and a jet angles down toward John Wayne Airport and supervisorial aide-de-camp Grant Hudson leans in.

"Sorry, sir, but you-know-who is on the line and he is royally pissed off."

"I'll call him back."

He smiles at the deputies. "Real-life detectives!"

"Get the hell out of here, Grant."

"Love your ponytail, Mendez. Adios."

The door closes and Elder sighs. "Sorry."

"I have a child, too," says Mendez.

Elder smiles, checking his watch.

"Five of seven supervisors oppose Wildcoast," says Gale. "Why don't you?"

"I have concerns, but I think overall it's good for the Seventh District. I talk to my citizens, and they talk back. Do they ever."

"Do you think Tarlow's death will kill Wildcoast, too?" asks Gale.

"Talk to the Tarlow Company about that," says the supervisor. "With Ben gone, the board could always nix it and do something else with those five square miles."

Gale goes to the window and looks out at Saddleback Mountain, the highest in the county. Sees the flat suburban blanket creeping up the mountain.

"I was out there earlier today," he says. "At Wildcoast. A crew from Empire Excavators was doing a percolation test."

"Oh? Seems premature," says Elder.

"They told me that creating an entire small-town sewer system is millions more than building it all on septic," says Gale. "And no perc means no septic tanks and leach lines."

"Yes and yes."

"A deal-breaker?" asks Mendez.

"Ask Tarlow the second."

"Do crystals out there mean anything to you?" Gale asks.

"Like quartz or something?" asks the supervisor. "Or for jewelry?"

"Big ones. High value," says Gale.

"You mean in the ground, under Wildcoast?"

"I don't know what I mean."

"Then I have to admit, Detective Gale, neither do I."

"Thank you for your time," says Gale.

He and Mendez take the elevator down in secure cop silence.

Outside the day has gone cool, flat-bottomed cirrus clouds coming in from the east.

"Something between him and Norris Kennedy," says Mendez.

"I heard it, too."

"I still don't trust her, and, by association, I don't trust Elder either. Politician slick. I doubt he's tied to Tarlow's death."

"No, not his style."

On their separate phones, Gale and Mendez watch a peaceful demonstration outside Tarlow Company headquarters in Newport Beach.

Gale on YouTube; Daniela on Google.

Gale's brother, Franklin, holds a sign saying WILDCOAST RIPS OFF THE ACJACHEME NATIVES, and a dozen or so of his UCI students—some dressed in mission-era Indigenous clothing—do likewise.

Frank reads from a list of species endangered by Wildcoast: the condor, the least tern, the sea otter, the monarch butterfly, the gnatcatcher, the mountain lion who was starved enough to eat Wildcoast's builder!

A striking young woman in a stiff-looking white dress and a seashell necklace dances to the beat of a young man's rattle.

Gale's phone throbs a notification through the demonstrators:

The Honorable Carl Schmidt has come through.

Warrant issued.

22

Two deputies in uniform—Rodriguez and Robinson—accompany the detectives to the front porch of Vernon Jeffs's home in Huntington Beach.

Late afternoon, cloudy but cooling.

The home is on Yorktown Avenue, in a fifties tract, inland from downtown and the pier. Its paint is peeling, and in a shabby open garage Gale sees two Harley choppers agleam—a black Softail and a Sportster in Mary Kay pink.

The rusted white van is parked in the driveway.

Mindy opens the door just enough for her face.

"Go away. He's asleep."

"We've got a search warrant."

"What for?"

"The house and the van. Any place where a handgun might reasonably be stored."

"What *specific* gun? A warrant has to say."

"A twenty-two-caliber semiautomatic pistol and ammunition. And anything in plain sight that could tie Vern to Bennet Tarlow."

"You people are dumb."

"Let us in and we'll get it over with," says Gale, holding up the warrant for her to see. "Shouldn't take long, Mindy."

"There's plenty of guns around but no pussy guns. Vern doesn't do pussy guns."

"I understand. We'd like to serve this out, now."

Inside, the house offers a fifty-fifty aroma of cigarette and weed. Mindy's got on red flannel pajama pants and a clashing orange snap-button blouse.

"The weed is legal now in California, in case you haven't heard," she says. "I'm going to get Vern. Don't you move one inch until we come back."

"We're going to get started, is what's going to happen," says Gale.

"Pigs."

He nods at Robinson, a large Black man, who follows Mindy down the hall.

From the foyer, the three deputies can see some of the small living room, dining room, and kitchen. Gale notes the old Royal typewriter on the dining room table and the thick stack of white paper with double-spaced writing on the top sheet.

He goes into the kitchen, checks the white countertops, the drawers. A pile of mail and flyers lie on the counter. The drawers hold flatware, kitchen implements, corkscrews, and bottle stoppers. A bag of ground coffee, a measuring spoon, paper filters.

A big revolver in an oiled leather holster.

"A long-barreled thirty-eight-caliber revolver," he says, shooting it with his phone.

Finds a snub-nosed cousin in a drawer half-hidden below a retractable cutting board. Shoots it, too.

"There's a 1911 in the pantry," says Mendez. "Protecting the cans and the Cap'n Crunch."

"My wife keeps her kitchen gun in the fridge," says Rodriguez.

"That's kind of pushing 'reasonable,'" she says, but swings open the door anyway.

"I think so, too," says the deputy.

Gale bangs through the pots and pans and lids in the cabinets but no guns.

Big Vernon Jeffs comes from the hallway in a bright tropical print robe and shearling slippers, followed by Mindy and the uniform. Gale has half forgotten how huge this man is.

His tan eyes are bloodshot and his face is stubbled red.

"I don't have a twenty-two pistol," he says. "I've got two thirty-eights, two forties, three forty-fives, two three-fifty-sevens, and a monster fifty-caliber Desert Eagle. Some ARs and tactical shotguns. You don't have to tear apart my house. I'll show you. Inherited some from Mom. Some were presents from friends. Bought the rest private party. Nothing stolen; nothing illegal. Some loaded, some not. Sorry, dipshits—Second Amendment."

"Were you with Tarlow the night he died?" asks Gale.

Jeffs stares at him, giving Gale a look of disgust. "I don't see how many times I have to say no. You can't prove anything. No lawyer, no talk."

"If we charge you, you'd have to talk," says Gale. "Then we lawyer up, too. I'll be honest, the DA's office is foaming at the mouth to file charges. Highest profile murder they've ever had. Murder weapon or not, they like you and your van out at Caspers that night. And your fingerprints at his Newport home. And the eyewitness who put you there not long before he died. They think after you did Tarlow, you went back to Newport and wiped your prints off of Tarlow's kitchen and the black countertops. The bourbon bottle. The plastic chopsticks. They think you have some explaining to do."

Jeffs hesitates. Seems to change his mind about what he's going to say.

"What horseshit," Jeffs says. "And I'm going to watch every second of this search. You won't find a twenty-two semi. I guarantee it."

"Because you dropped it off the pier here in Huntington?" asks Gale. "Along with Bennet Tarlow's phone? Or maybe in Irvine Lake. Or in the rocks off Laguna? We've got divers."

"We were together that night," says Mindy. "Here. You cannot change that."

"But our prosecutors will separate you and break down that alibi in less than an hour," says Mendez. "Welcome to Superior Court, against a state with deeper pockets than you, and a DA who runs for reelection every four years."

"We're trying to keep you two from going through all that," says Gale. "Help us help you."

"No weapon, no case."

"Don't bet on it," says Gale.

Jeffs turns in to the hallway, his left hand raised, waving the deputies forward. "I'll show you where they are."

Mendez and Mindy mad-dog each other from opposite sides of the dining room table.

"Nice old typewriter," says Mendez. "Who's the writer in the family?"

"I am," says Mindy. "Vern can't spell his own name."

"I want to write but never have the time."

"I just do it," says Mindy. "I got a story to tell."

She unsnaps the top two buttons on her blouse and folds the collar down to reveal the chemo port affixed beneath her clavicle.

Mendez nods. "I'm sorry. How is it going?"

"Not bad. A day or two of hell a week, then a good week after. I can still work a few days a month."

Mindy gives Daniela a steely look. "I use the typewriter because I'm mostly computer illiterate."

Mindy fingers the chemo port gently, then snaps the blouse back up.

"What did you and Vern do the night Tarlow died?" asks Daniela.

"Saying nothing to you about that. I know what you're trying, with Vern out of the room."

"If you lie, the DA will smash your alibi," says Mendez.

"It's shatterproof. Because it's true."

Mindy heads down the hall and Mendez follows her, then detours into the spare bedroom.

Where she sees the twin bed, made up with a soaring bald-eagle spread, and the drip trolley beside it, rigged with clear tubes and stop valves, but no bags or bottles.

Sees the syringes and needles on the nightstand and finds the chemo bottles and saline bags in the little black fridge under the desk that puffs the faint smell of isopropyl alcohol into her face when she opens it.

Sees the birds on the long cabinet: pheasants, a hen, and a rooster. Two band-tailed pigeons. Two wood ducks. A six-quail covey, four little ones following mom and dad.

They're frosted with dust and their eyes are dull.

No owl.

With Robinson alertly looking on, Gale lets Vern play tour guide in his bedroom:

A steel gun safe with a combination lock, containing eight AR-15s.

Another with six tactical, short-barreled shotguns and two regulation Remington Sportsman 12-gauge scatterguns.

"Number three lead shot in two-and-three-quarter-inch shells," says Vern. "Punch you right out."

A third safe is backed into a shallow closet and half hidden by

Mindy's skirts and Jeffs's mostly plaid shirts. It's taller and wider than the others.

Jeffs opens it to rows of handguns on pegs, small on the top, large at the bottom, and many gradients of size in between.

Single- and double-barreled derringers, both side-bys, and over-and-unders.

Revolvers, semiautomatics, even an enormous flintlock down on the bottom row just above the Golden Rod Dehumidifier.

"Where do you keep the twenty-twos, Vern?"

Jeffs smiles and slowly shakes his head.

"There's a couple more combat shotguns under the bed," he says. "One on my side and the other on Mindy's. Peace of mind, you know."

On his way out, Gale looks behind the open bedroom door. Sees the cobwebs, and a .50-caliber sniper rifle much like his own.

"That's where mine is," he says. "I got spiderwebs, too."

Back in the Explorer, Gale's phone throbs, and Sheriff Kersey's name appears on the screen.

"Lew, what's this about Vic Klavic?"

"We're interviewing him in half an hour. See what he knows about Vernon Jeffs. Daniela is on speaker."

A silent beat then, as Gale remembers the OC Sheriff's Department scandal centering on informants illegally planted in Men's Central Jail.

FBI got in on that one, much to the department's fury and embarrassment.

Kersey was undersheriff back then, but Gale watched him bear the weight of the investigation into his jail.

"We didn't put Klavic with Jeffs to spy on him."

"No, sir."

"He's a slimy little guy, though. Klavic. Parse him well. How good is Jeffs?"

"He's looking good but we need a gun. Or Tarlow's phone. Something smoking. None of which are available."

"I need results on this, Gale. We're getting bombed every day. Media. Tips. Advice. Fucking psychics. *The Wall Street Journal*."

"We're trying, sir. Nothing actionable. You know how it goes."

"Do I ever. Light a fire, Gale. The narrative I want here is, the OC Sheriff's has the best detectives in the world. And the headline I want is, Bennet Tarlow's killer is in jail."

"Working on it, Sheriff Kersey."

Kersey hangs up.

"Mindy's got cancer," says Daniela.

"Oh boy," Gale says softly, swinging the Explorer onto Coast Highway.

23

Gale and Mendez sit in a small interview room inside the Orange County jail. The table and seats are concrete, built into the floor. There's a small, steel, mesh-reinforced window in the door.

It's where lawyers, cops, and inmates have private talks, not one of the bigger interrogation rooms where detectives record interviews with suspects while more cops watch through a one-way mirror.

Mendez stands at the window, checking Jesse's whereabouts on TeenShield. He's home now, she sees. Probably gaming before his shift at Bowl Me Over.

She's still stewing about their fruitless search of the Jeffs home and van, which turned up a bounty of weapons of various type and caliber. A Desert Eagle .50-caliber handgun but no .22 semiautomatic.

Gale, seated across from a man in an orange jumpsuit, is surprised how old Vic Klavic looks. He's only sixty-one but he looks midseventies: hepatitis, end stage, according to his jailors.

Klavic was Vernon Jeffs's cellmate during Jeffs's six-month stint for battery. Now Klavic is in for a solid year for setting his car on fire to collect insurance money. The hepatitis means he'll die here. By trade, Gale knows, Klavic is a handyman and a career criminal who's spent almost thirty of his sixty-one years in work camps, jails, and prisons. Longest stretch was six years for armed robbery, starting when he was nineteen.

He's gray-haired and brown-eyed, pale in the face, and his tattooed right hand and forearm—burned in his insurance fraud attempt—swirl with ink-stained black scars.

"And so yeah, we were here for half a year together but I see no reason to tell you about it."

"Like the undersheriff told you, I might be able to get you out a little early," says Gale.

"'Might' is not a strong word."

"Sixty days," says Gale. "I'll try if you can give me what I need on Vernon."

"Which is?"

"Oh, come on, Vic. You know that's not how it works."

"I just rat him out until you stop me?"

"You know what we want," says Mendez.

"Oh sure, sure I do, honey. You want to know if Vern had ever told me he killed a man, in like fashion of how Bennet Tarlow got it."

"That would be helpful."

"Rat out a friend for sixty days?"

Gale leans back, taps his fingers on the cool concrete table.

"If Jeffs did what we think he did, you'd be doing the world a favor," says Mendez.

"Sixty days," says Gale. "Very sorry about your bad luck."

Klavic reacts not. Just stares at Daniela, standing by the window. Something in the way she leans against the door, Gale sees. Notes that Klavic has the passive eyes that so many lifelong, professional crooks have: distant, pleasant, and calculating.

"Daniela," says Gale. "Would you like to sit down?"

Gale and Mendez trade places.

Mendez takes the body-warmed seat across from Vic Klavic.

"You're nicer to look at," he says.

"But not much," says Mendez. "Must have been crummy, sharing a close-in jail cell with a six-foot-four bodybuilder."

"We got along just fine. We buddied up. In the mess nobody'd fool with me because of Vern. The black car, the brown car, the peckerwoods—nobody messed with us."

"What's he like?" asks Mendez.

"What are you like?"

"An average California-born Latina."

Klavic offers a small, dry smile. "Let me guess. Married once, divorced, four children."

"I've got a son."

"Name and age of?"

"Carlos," she lies. "Did Vern Jeffs brag a lot? About his badass crimes, his luck with the ladies, beating the shit out of people?"

"He bragged, sure. Not much else to do when you're in jail."

"Where would you place him on your bullshit meter?"

"Average plus."

"That's where he puts you," says Gale.

Klavic gives Gale a stony look. "Say hello."

"He says you offered him sex for protection," says Mendez.

Klavic inhales sharply, shaking his head. "A lie. I'm not that way, and they got cameras all over."

He gives Gale a hard stare, then Mendez another guarded smile.

"It's understandable, Vic," she says. "You have to protect yourself inside."

"Like I said, Vern's average plus on the bullshit."

"Well, that's what he said," says Gale.

"To get himself a better deal. Same as this."

"Did he ever talk about killing someone?" asks Mendez, leaning just slightly forward toward Klavic.

"Don't believe he said that about me, because, you know, we were jailhouse friends and it isn't true."

"I believe you," says Mendez. "And I don't care if it's true or not."

"Killing another person," says Gale.

"Fuck off, Tonto," says Klavic.

"You too, Kemosabe."

"Got that casino yet?"

"We're working on it."

Mendez looks to Gale, who shakes his head slowly at her: *Don't speak.*

Silence, stretching.

Klavic turns to Gale, then back to Mendez.

A uniformed deputy looks in, then continues past.

Klavic takes a deep breath, then lets it out slowly, like a hit from a cigarette or a joint.

"Jeffs told me he killed a woman for two thousand dollars once, and it wasn't worth the money."

"Who, how, when?" asks Mendez.

"Cheating wife, life insurance, too. Shot her in the head in a drugstore parking lot. Way back when."

"Not worth the money," says Mendez.

"He said two thousand for work that disgusting just isn't worth it. Wouldn't do it again."

Gale gets that nice bump of pulse that comes when you let things cook and it works.

Mendez the same, with a dash of her own disgust for a man having his own wife killed. More disgust than for the guy who pulled the trigger.

They watch as Klavic stands and, shackles on both wrists and ankles, clinks to the window and raps on it with his knuckles. A deputy appears.

Klavic turns to Mendez. "Get me those sixty days out of here. I don't have many left."

"We'll try, Vic," says Mendez. "Thanks for your help. You did the right thing."

It feels good to be outside the jail. Gale did his first year there, as do most new deputies. A sullen, poorly lit, and occasionally violent place.

Gale calls Jeffs, and it goes to voicemail.

Ditto the Bear Cave.

"I don't think he'll come downtown voluntarily," says Mendez. "But tonight's a work night for him."

24

"Thanks for meeting me on short notice, Daniela," says Kevin Elder. "I know you're very busy with Tarlow and other matters."

"Certainly. I sensed you had things to say that you didn't want Lew Gale to hear."

"Yes, that's true. Did you tell him we were meeting?"

"I did not. What didn't you want to say in front of him?"

"You cut to the chase."

"I live for the chase."

Elder smiles.

Mendez looks at the Grove Club dining room. Right before the dinner rush, quiet. Nods to bartender John Velasquez, who nods back.

"The Grove, right?" she asks. "Hudson told me you insiders never call it the Grove Club."

"I call it the Grub," says Elder. "Kind of a contraction, but kind of a description, too."

"As in grubbing—money and power?"

"You read my mind."

"What was it you wanted to say but not in front of Lew?"

"Two things, really. One is that Norris Kennedy showed what I think was an unhealthy zeal in helping Bennet pitch Wildcoast."

"Unhealthy."

"It was always Wildcoast. Here at the Grub. At my town halls and hearings. Laguna Beach city council forums. City of San Juan Capistrano. County chamber of commerce. Parties, galas, fundraisers. She didn't quite finish Bennet Tarlow's sentences, but close. I used to picture Norris with an arm up his shirt, moving his head left and right like a ventriloquist. Moving his jaws."

Mendez considers this odd image.

"Which, of itself, is not personally damning," says Elder. "Her interest in Wildcoast, I mean."

"Then why unhealthy?"

"The intensity of it. The relentlessness. During the year they were together, Bennet went from puppy-love happy to subdued to anxious to frightened to depressed. I saw him a fair amount. I finally asked him what was going on. This was just before they broke up. He told me he loved her but couldn't go on."

"Do you think she is in some way a part of his death?"

Mendez studies Kevin Elder's solemn expression.

"I didn't until I talked to Ben's father. Ben had written Norris into his will just weeks before he was killed. To the tune of five million dollars."

Mendez gets that wonderful pit-of-the-stomach, pieces-falling-into-place feeling. More like boulders dumped in a pile, she thinks. Gets her first glimpse of someone who would directly benefit—apart from the derailing of Wildcoast—from the physical death of Tarlow himself. A bedroom move lowered to street level. Low concept. Big dollars, plus a dash of revenge. Norris as architect, building her fortune on a lover washing his hands of her.

"Beyond interesting," she says.

"I thought you'd think so."

"Any of Tarlow's other women in the will?"

Elder shakes his head. "I didn't ask that, Daniela. Really, it seemed rude and gigantically none of my business. Tarlow II might tell you. *Might*."

Mendez thinks of Norris Kennedy at Moulin, when she ordered the young family to another table so she could talk in privacy to herself and Gale. Thinks of Norris making appointments with Bennet Tarlow, long after their breakup. Of her whisking Bennet off for a week of birdwatching in Bali, financed by her bet on Fury-Wilder III in Las Vegas.

"She has audacity," says Mendez.

"Indeed. Which raises questions."

"Have you seen her since the murder?"

"The burial at sea. It was sad. Funny sad, to see Norris and a bevy of Ben Tarlow's lovers grouped together on the deck in their black dresses, watching the ashes glitter down through the water. Tarlow had donated generously to Save the Whales, and guess what? A Titanic gray whale breached right off the stern, huge fluke waving as it went down, like it was saying bye to him. Or hello to us. So big it rocked the boat! I'm not a spiritual guy, but . . ."

Mendez hears a slight tremble in Kevin Elder's usually sharp, forceful voice.

"That must have been something," she says. "The whale breaching."

"The fluke looked thirty feet across, I swear."

Mendez takes a moment to imagine it. She's seen humpbacked whales breach, but never a big gray.

"Why not let Gale hear this?" she asks.

"I wanted you to know first. Like, a scoop for you."

"I don't quite believe that."

"I wanted an excuse to see you alone. As I would like to again, in the future."

Mendez is flummoxed by this. She really hasn't seen it coming. Wonders if Elder knows how superior, in-control, and staged he comes off to her.

His usual.

"What a nice surprise," she says.

"Oh?"

"I'm not sure what to say."

"Well, you haven't laughed at me. I take that as a positive."

Mendez studies Elder's handsome face, his eyes, the silver widow's peak in his head of black hair. The damned suspenders.

She looks away.

Then a long but oddly pleasant silence.

"I've got seventh-row Plácido Domingo tickets for tomorrow at Segerstrom. Il Fornaio is close. Be me and two good friends. High school crushes, now two sons and a daughter. You'd like them. I'll send a car for you at six thirty. Take you right to the restaurant."

Mendez shakes her head. "No."

She sees his disappointment.

"Why not?"

"I'm taken."

"By someone very lucky."

"Two of them, actually," she says. A true alibi.

Elder raises his eyebrows.

"Not like that," says Mendez.

"How about just friends? Coffee or a walk on the beach?"

"Not at this time, thank you."

Elder bores into her with clear, good-humored eyes.

Mendez feels a tear forming in her right eye, wills it away.

Elder watches without reaction.

"Changing your mind?"

"I need to go," she says.

Elder flags John Velasquez, who flags their waiter, who is at the booth forthwith.

At dusk, driving west fast for home on the Route 73 toll road, Mendez calls Tim.

With the call playing through the Explorer's speakers, she keeps her eyes on the road, and the golden fall foothills scroll past in her periphery.

"Bless me, Father Timothy, for I have sinned."

"This is not necessary, Daniela."

His beautiful, judgmental baritone.

"Then what is necessary, Tim?"

"I hear your anger."

"Yes, you do."

Daniela gooses the SUV up to eighty on the toll road. Lets a moment go by.

"Tim, I want to ask you again."

"What you've been asking for, all his life."

"Since before, even."

"I can't do that," says Father Malone. "It would damage him, and you, and destroy my standing in the Diocese. From before his birth I told you this, Dani, and you agreed with me because you knew it was right. And we proceeded together down this very difficult path. The three of us. Separate but bound together by God."

"I've asked you a thousand times to do it privately. Just us three. Not to the Church of the Holy Martyr. Not your career. Not the family or friends. We three will keep our secret."

"Daniela, I've always listened to your pain and told you what we need to do. For yourself, and Jesse, and for me."

"He needs you now."

"No, Daniela, he needs to return to the Church, as do you. Not to the Martyr, of course, but your parish in Orange—"

"They're drawing him in, Tim. Lulu and the Barrio Dogtown gang. I'm watching it happen. I'm losing him."

"Be firm, Daniela. Trust in God."

"He needs more than God and me and the web of lies I've spun for him. He needs his church. He'll need Azusa Catholic College next year. He needs to understand who he is and where he has come from. *He needs you.* Jesse is half you, Tim. Half yours. You are half responsible for creating him."

"Oh, more, Dani. More than that. The credit, and the blame, are more than half mine."

Daniela sees that she's gliding along at ninety miles an hour now, steps off the gas, and feels the vehicle sag. Like her heart.

"Can't you see how he needs you?" she asks. "It would be a new beginning of his life. To know you. Give him yourself, Tim. Become the man I loved and still love. He's your only son."

"Destroy my life's work?" he asks, his powerful voice gentle now. "My parish and college? My nomination to bishop? My whole self?"

"It would damage your temporary body. Not your eternal soul. As you teach."

She glances out at the hills and beyond to the mountains. Thinks of wildfires and the picture of Gomorrah in her childhood Bible companion, wonders if the Killer Cat is out there, wonders if Bennet Tarlow III had once loved his stepmother, then hated her for what she did to him. Both? Wonders how Jesse would feel about her, if she ever got Tim to accept her ancient request.

"I love you, Daniela," he says, his voice still soft.

"And I love you, Tim. Even more than when I was seven and I thought you were God. I love the man you are. Please open your arms to Jesse."

"My destruction."

"Your son. Jesus has already forgiven you. And the world will forgive you someday."

"My soul aches, as always," says Tim.

"It aches for Jesse."

"Yes. And selfishly, for what would be my destruction."

"Rebirth."

"Oh. Oh . . ."

In the rearview mirror Daniela sees the Highway Patrol SUV in her lane, coming up fast. Notes that she's doing thirty-five now on the sixty-five-mile-an-hour toll road.

The lights come and the siren whoops and she pulls over.

"Dani? A siren?"

"I'm muting you. Don't hang up."

"I will never hang up on you."

Daniela rolls to a stop and lowers her window. Beholds a highway patrolman from central casting: muscles in a tailored uniform, a brisk haircut, and Ray-Bans.

She hands the patrolman her badge and ID and he hands it back.

"Going a little fast back there, Deputy," he says. "And awful slow up here."

"I know."

"Everything okay?"

"Just talking to my boss on the speaker."

"Well then, drive carefully and have a good day."

"You, too."

Seconds later she's back in the right lane, setting sixty-five on the cruise control.

The patrolman blows by in the fast lane.

"I'm back, Tim," she says.

"Trouble?"

"Highway Patrol. It's cool."

"I have been thinking about what you're asking since before he was born," he says. "It is the central conflict of my life. It always has been. I will continue to think and pray. I will consult the Lord, as always."

"I wish you loved us as much as you love God," says Daniela. "And loved who you are to him. Let this cook."

"Cook?"

"You know, let things play out. My partner Gale always says that."

"Okay, Dani. I promise to let it cook."

25

Gale climbs vertiginous switchbacks on his way up to the Tarlow family villa above Crystal Cove, built by Bennet Evans Tarlow between 1949 and 1953. The buildings are late Roman in style, created with travertine from the quarry that supplied Rome's Colosseum and Michelangelo's dome ribs of St. Peter's Basilica.

The steepness of the road, and the way it seems to end in blue sky, stirs Gale's unease with heights. Three hundred feet below him, waves crash out of sight.

He briefly takes his eyes off the road to glimpse the two mansions high above him, clinging to a massive promontory shaped somewhat like Gibraltar, overlooking the vast Pacific.

He's never set foot on this property, but Gale knows that this compound is home to the patriarch Bennet Evans Tarlow and his wife, Jean—both in their nineties—and to their son Bennett Evans Tarlow II and his second wife, Camile, parents of the late Bennet Tarlow III.

A mansion for each Tarlow, into which Bennet would have moved upon the death of either couple.

To Gale's left is a wall of white oleander, to his right a rock wall beyond which the Pacific Ocean twinkles and the waves roll onto the pale sand of Crystal Cove State Park. The mansions wait above and beyond, high, eastern windows reflecting the morning sun.

Gale remembers that this dramatic bluff and the Romanesque extravagance before him were the Tarlow family's holdback for ceding Crystal Cove beach to the state. And that the Tarlow Company was given the state's incalculable gift to develop the pristine hills overlooking the surrounding coast. The adjoining palatial homes, retail, business centers, and restaurants are here, now a part of Newport Beach.

The road levels off and Gale pulls up to a gated guardhouse, from which steps a broad Latino in a black suit.

Gale rolls down his window and badges him, notes the security camera on the guardhouse wall, aimed his way.

"Lew Gale to see the Tarlows."

"Your partner is already here, Detective. Park beside her. You are meeting in the boss's and Jean's home—it will be on your right."

He goes back into the guardhouse and the gate rolls open and Gale watches the camera track him.

An elegant Black man in a black suit introduces himself as Davis and leads Gale up the steps and into Bennet and Jean Tarlow's limestone palace on the bluff. The marble foyer is large and filigreed with gold. Following Davis through a domed great room, Gale hears the sound of his heavy wingtips on stone. The room is bracingly cold.

An elevator lined in dark, stately oak brings them to the third floor, a spacious open-air piazza surrounded by chest-high limestone columns. Seagulls circle above in the blue, and between the columns Gale sees the ocean spangled and silver on this fall morning.

Five people are seated around a circular stone table in the center of the piazza.

Davis deposits Gale next to Daniela. Tarlow II and Camile stand briefly and sit without speaking or offering to shake hands.

Old Bennet and Jean sit back from the table, upright in motorized wheelchairs with steering columns and aggressive, off-road tires. The patriarch's is blue, his wife's is red. The couple is snug within tube jackets and both wear gloves and scarves. Their long gray hair lifts and shifts in the cold, incoming westerlies. They have smooth, pale skin. To Gale they look startlingly alike.

Daniela gives him an underfunded smile.

Gale, still standing, looks at each Tarlow in turn, then sits.

"I'm sorry for your—"

"We know that," says Bennet II. "But this is not a social call. It's an investigation into the murder of my son. Get to the point, if you have one in you."

Gale looks at Camile, and Camile continues to look at Gale. Her face is big and strong-jawed, her eyes green, as is her pantsuit. Her platinum hair is cut short. She looks like a contemporary statue of the glamorous, big-haired society maven that he remembers from *The Orange County Register* society pages of his childhood.

From this, Gale tries to extrapolate how she looked when she seduced her stepson at age seventeen, three decades ago. She would have been thirty-nine. This hearsay, courtesy of solitary witness Norris Kennedy, and as yet corroborated by no one.

If true, does Bennet II know?

If not?

Floating upon this dark current, Gale now recalls more hearsay from the Grove bartender John Velasquez.

"*. . . the basic plot is, Tarlow III loved the homes he built and doesn't cut corners. But his father prefers the office towers and warehouses—the monsters, the 'fulfillment centers'—out in the Inland Empire. Most of which—again, rumors—Bennet Tarlow II lowballs on cost and highballs on rents. The Tarlow Company owns those towers and commercial* centers outright. But the homes that III loved to build, Tarlow Company does not own. They get sold, right? Home ownership. American dream . . . These are rumors a bartender picks up, but from what I overhear in my bar, they're right on . . ."

"We're aware of the controversy within the Tarlow Company regarding Wildcoast," says Gale. "We know that enormous sums of money are involved and that your son's death may have a huge impact on Wildcoast and the Tarlow Company itself. We wonder how the powers within the company are reacting to Bennet's death."

"Killed him?" asks Camile. "My god."

"Maybe indirectly," says Gale. "Set the stage for his demise. Or did nothing to prevent it."

"Tarlow Company is family," says Tarlow II. "Ben was my son. You're fools to be accusing us of something so preposterous."

"No accusation at all, sir," says Gale. "But the Tarlow Company is not all family. What's preposterous about infighting in a powerful company? The egos. The competition. Are you denying such things exist in the Tarlow Company, in regard to Wildcoast?"

Camile swings one long leg over the other, leaning back in her chair. "We build homes for wealthy people. Good, sturdy, beautiful homes. We do commercial, industrial, and resorts, too. We build fulfillment and data centers."

"And we saw from the beginning, *twenty-five years ago*, that Wildcoast was risky," says Tarlow II. "My son was eighteen years old when he first dreamed it up. A boy's fantasy."

Again the bartender's words come to Gale.

"Grove gossip casts you, sir, as a high-profit, bottom-line commercial and industrial builder," says Gale. "The gossip is that you were contemptuous of your son, an American dreamer taking out huge construction loans, then selling Tarlow Company land and homes to pay them back."

"Mostly true," says Tarlow. "But 'contemptuous' is wrong. I loved my son. I love him now. I love so many things about him.

Things that transcend me and Camile. His soul. His mind. His energy. But his naivete was contemptuous to me. His misplaced idealism."

Tarlow stands. "Let me be clear. Wildcoast was doomed from the start, and still is. The Tarlow Company doesn't build *cities*. It cannot be done profitably. Working with government is not in our DNA. *Becoming* government will never be. Bennet Tarlow III for mayor. That was Ben's dream, not mine. Not the Tarlow Company's."

Tarlow II's eyes bore ferociously into Daniela.

Then into Gale. Ferocious grief, he sees.

"Sit down, you little bean counter," says the patriarch.

With this, Bennet Evans Tarlow suddenly reverses in his wheelchair and, hair bobbing, carves a semicircle around the big stone table and pulls up close beside his seated son.

"Tell them about Hal," he says. "And Rich."

"Rich has been dead for almost twenty years, Dad."

"Of course he has."

"And don't forget Tony Naster," says Jean, her voice high-pitched and frail in the breeze.

She cranks backward and steers around the table to flank her son.

"Right, Mom," he says.

Tarlow II gives Gale a flat stare. "Hal Teller is a managing partner. Sees the big picture and runs the show accordingly. A mentor to me and my boy. However, Hal has been a not-so-subtle enemy of Ben's Wildcoast from the very start. Ben wanted him fired but I wouldn't. It didn't quite get ugly, but almost."

Daniela gives Gale a look, then Tarlow II. "Will you arrange a meeting?"

"Of course. I'm always happy to help law enforcement waste its time."

"Very gracious of you," says Mendez. "So who's Rich?"

"Simpson," says Camile. "Resorts Division, long gone."

"I knew him some years ago," says Jean. "It's more important you know how I miss my grandson. I loved him."

Tarlow the patriarch nods, staring at his wife of seventy-plus years.

Gale notes the lovely smile blooming on Jean's pure white face.

"Camile, what do you think of Norris Kennedy?" Mendez asks.

"I don't think of her at all. I was pleased when Ben put her in her place."

"Apparently she loved him," says Gale.

"She's a climber is all."

"He put her in his will," says Mendez.

"Foolish."

"Did he write in any other friends, partners, lovers?"

"As far as I know he was foolish just that once," says Tarlow II.

"Camile?" asks Mendez. "Did something happen between you and Ben to make you hate him?"

"Not that I can conceive. Such as?"

"Enough of this nonsense," says Tarlow II.

"Wait," says Mendez, "did something happen between you and Ben that would make your husband hate him?"

"I loved that boy," Camile says. "So did his father."

"There's not enough love in the world," says Jean.

"Better than too much," says the patriarch, smiling at Camile. His face and teeth are white. "It can retard your progress."

"What do you say to that?" Mendez asks Tarlow II.

"To *what*?"

"Did something happen between your wife and son that could turn you against Ben? Maybe against them both?"

"I see we're dealing with ignorance here," says Camile.

Tarlow II, lips tight and face flushed, again stands. "Off the property," he says.

Camile pulls herself up by his coat sleeve.

Gale notes for the first time that she's taller than her husband.

"No sherbet?" asks Jean.

Tarlow II raises his hand toward the house. Davis and another man in black emerge from a shaded doorway.

Camile's face is a mask of offense taken, but her tone of voice is smooth and firm in the breeze.

"Detective Mendez, what did you do to make your son, Jesse, hate you?" she asks.

The silence is heavy.

"My turn to say preposterous," says Mendez. "How do you know of Jesse?"

Her hard face is flushed, and Gale catches the spite in her voice.

"I have sources, Detective," says Camile. "Quite good ones. In your department. Who led me to the Orange County Diocese. Which pointed me to the Los Angeles Diocese and Church of the Holy Martyr in Azusa. You are not as unknown as you think you are. You are a small island and I am the sea that you hear, way down there. I control everything."

"You have no facts and you have no power," says Mendez. "My son is off-limits to you. Stay away from him. I'm protective when it comes to Jesse."

"You know how it feels to have a son," Camile says. "And it's good to know we can communicate, woman to woman. Mother to mother. I feel that I'm coming to know you very well."

Mendez gives Camile a drop-dead stare, but says nothing.

"You are remembered fondly at the Church of the Holy Martyr in Azusa," says Camile.

"Good people," says Mendez with a rigid smile and, if Gale is reading her right, her stomach in a knot. "It's been decades."

"Two, actually," says Camile.

"The soldiers have arrived," says Tarlow the original.

"Deputies, get off the property," says his son.

"Mr. Tarlow," says Gale. "I was out at the Wildcoast property not long ago and I talked to one of the men digging the perc test. It seemed awfully soon in the process to be figuring septic or sewer. I mean, with neither the feds, the state, or the county having signed off on the development."

"Of course it's early," says Tarlow II. "You want to build a city, you start early."

"The shovel man said he was hoping to find crystals. Big crystals worth a lot of money."

"There are thousands of different crystals found in nature," says Tarlow.

"But what kind did he mean?"

Tarlow opens his hands in a palms-up, how-the-hell-would-I-know signal. "No idea, none at all. Again, Deputies, time for you to waddle off and write some tickets."

"I take it that Empire Excavators works for you?"

"And a hundred other subcontractors in California alone."

"Tell Hal Teller we need to talk to him," says Gale.

He sees Davis and his ally drawing near, and the elder Tarlow reversing in his wheelchair to watch them approach.

"Detective Gale," says Tarlow. "I want my son's killer on death row. Or laid out on a morgue slab, if he resists your arrest."

"We'd like to see that, too," says Mendez.

Gale and Mendez huddle at Bamboo restaurant on Coast Highway in Corona del Mar.

The waiter brings them menus and takes their drink orders.

"I get where you were going with Camile, but I don't see why," says Gale.

"Because I believe Norris Kennedy."

"But how does a thirty-nine-year-old stepmother lead us to the killer?" asks Gale.

"Your eyes are wide shut, Lew—Tarlow II."

"No. I don't think so."

"Why?" she asks.

"Because a father doesn't kill his son. Neither does a mother."

"But you saw his face when I asked if something had turned him against his wife and son. That hit him like an uppercut."

"I did see that. I also saw his expression when he talked about his boy. He's either grieving or a good actor."

"He knows what Camile did," says Daniela.

"Maybe," says Gale. "But he still wouldn't kill Ben. No more than you would kill Jesse. You'd *die* for him. I think you're jumping to wrong conclusions."

The waiter brings the iced teas, extra mint for Mendez.

"That's all for us," she says to him, handing back the menus.

"Listen to me, Lew. The father could have helped set the stage indirectly. Or simply did nothing to protect his son—exactly as you said back there. He finally snapped after thirty years. Allowed Camile's betrayal and the damage to his son finally carry him away. Folded them into a simple business disagreement. Looked the other way."

"I see Tarlow Company," says Gale. "Not the Tarlow family."

"Boardroom coconspirators?" asks Mendez.

"I like it. Why not?"

Mendez looks at him in differing silence, her phone suddenly throbbing on the tabletop. She takes it up and taps the screen with slender, black-polished fingernails.

Frowns, taps again, and sets it down.

"Sorry," she says.

"Jesse?"

"I track him through TeenShield."

"Mutual agreement or secret?"

"Secret Agent Dani. Good news: He's where he's supposed to be at this moment."

"How's the bossy girlfriend working out?"

"I wish she'd go away. Jesse doesn't."

"How does Camile know of him?" asks Gale.

"Her 'sources,' apparently."

"Did her knowing about Jesse surprise you?"

"God, yes. It pissed me off, then it kind of scared me."

"Contacts in our own department?"

"So she says."

"The Orange County Diocese?"

"I've never gone to Mass in Orange County."

"Azusa?"

Her eyes flicker with menace. "Long ago, Lew. We're partners, and I like you, but don't barge in."

He takes a sip of the tea. "I thought you handled it well. You were calm but you didn't back down or heat up. Whatever buttons Camile was trying to push, she didn't faze you."

"I draw a line at Jesse. And a line around him. He's safe there and nothing can touch him."

"That's good, Daniela. You should do that."

"I love him so much, Lew. He is so very alone."

"What does Camile want from you?" asks Gale.

"I don't know. It infuriates me to be investigated. Especially by an immoral billionaire who doesn't seem to be grieving the death of her stepson. Using people in our department."

"We've got four thousand eyes and ears," says Gale. "Some of them know you, or know of you. And Jesse. Tarlow Company's PAC helped elect Sheriff Kersey, so, favors done and returned."

The waiter brings the check, and Mendez takes it.

"I don't see Amanda Cho."

The waiter looks at Gale with placid suspicion.

"She doesn't work here anymore."

"Why not?"

"Didn't say. Just stopped coming in. Didn't return calls. People get better jobs and leave with no notice."

"When did this happen?"

A shrug.

Gale holds up a finger, gets out his phone, and finds Vernon Jeffs's recent State of California mug shot.

Holds it up to the waiter, who nods without hesitation.

"He was here three days ago."

"Was Amanda here when he came in?"

"She left through the kitchen door, and that was the last time we saw her."

"Did he follow her out?"

"He had lunch and left."

"Did you wait on him?"

"He had two lunches, three beers. Big man."

No answer on Amanda's phone, but Gale leaves a voicemail.

No answer on Jeffs's phone either, nor at the home number of the Huntington Beach home he shares with Mindy Jeffs.

Gale and Mendez wait for the Bear Cave to open at two, when the manager says Jeffs and Mindy are on a two-week ride on their bikes.

Don't ask me where, he says: no idea.

Now, parked in the quivering shade of the queen palms across the street from the Jeffs house—on a hunch that Vern and Mindy have gone to the mattresses and not on a well-earned vacation—Gale and Mendez lean against Gale's white SUV.

Gale takes in the warm, salty, oil-rich air of Surf City, watches the oil pump rise and fall, the oblong joint keeping time.

Wordless minutes pass.

Then, "This is when I wish I still smoked," says Mendez.

"Me, too."

"I do get the feeling we could be here a long time."

"I think they're still in town," says Gale. "They've either run off Amanda Cho, or reported her to ICE, or worse. Then there's the murder to consider. If they run, they attract attention. Better to hide in plain sight."

"I like your optimism, Lew."

"In the war I learned to wait. Hour after hour. Waiting is an art form. It messes up your sense of time, but then you learn to use it. Hours of boredom, then wham, there he is. All those hours brought him to you. Lured him in. He couldn't resist you."

"I know exactly what you're talking about," says Mendez. "I teach small arms at the LA Academy, Saturday mornings, once a week. And I'm always trying to get them to slow down, control your breath, control your *time*. Make it yours. Wyatt Earp was right: Fast is good but slow is deadly. In a gunfight, you need to take your time in a hurry."

"Sweet," says Gale.

Which is when the rumbling farts of Harleys come up the street, Vernon Jeffs chugging toward them on his chopped black Softail, Mindy abreast of him on her Mary Kay pink Sportster.

26

Black helmets, vests, and leather, their machines slapping wetly at low rpm until Jeffs makes the deputies and guns his machine into a wide U-turn.

Mindy follows him with a smoking roar.

Breaking for their vehicles, Gale and Mendez almost collide, then do a quick shuffle and get into their rides.

Gale is off first, running hard but cold—no lights or sirens on his detective take-home—and he sees Jeffs and Mindy out ahead, Jeffs sweeping south on Main, Mindy north.

In his rearview sees Mendez coming up on him fast, reaches through his open window and points her after the pink Sportster. Low-tech but Mendez gets it.

Signals early, gets a lucky green light, and follows Jeffs onto Main.

He's on the radio to Dispatch now, an all-units Huntington Beach alert for a black Harley southbound on Main Street from Yorktown Avenue and a pink Harley northbound on Main from the same. Vernon and Mindy Jeffs, white, fifties, presume armed.

Gale's Explorer is a Sport turbo that eats up Main Street like a shark, closing on Jeffs, who glides between lanes and charges fast ahead.

Gale can't follow, and the light turns red, so he gooses his SUV onto the shoulder and honks his way past the right-lane traffic, honking and yelling at *him*, and closes in on Jeffs again, who flips off Gale without looking back and swerves onto Coast Highway.

The southbound traffic is heavy, and Gale knows that they're miles from the nearest freeway.

Jeffs turns right off PCH and Gale knows it's a bad call: The farther Vern goes on side streets the better chance the sheriff will stop him.

But Jeffs seems to be thinking the same thing, carving a hard left onto Beach Boulevard, which Gale knows will take him to the San Diego Freeway, California 55, and Interstate 5—deep into the sprawling suburban thicket of Orange County, and beyond, as far as gas and adrenaline will take him.

Gale catches another lucky break, gunning it through the last of the yellow light and coming up hard on Jeffs and his caterwauling chopper.

He's close enough to hear the Harley's engine. And see Jeffs glance at his right-side mirror and clench his fists.

Then his brake lights flare and Gale thinks: *Don't do it.*

Jeffs cuts a hard right onto Atlanta hoping Gale will sail past, but his tires slide out from under him and his shining black bike goes down and Jeffs, on his backside, skitters across the asphalt, leathers rasping.

He rolls twice but clambers upright and takes off limping down the sidewalk.

Gale makes the turn, his turbocharger screaming.

Shoots past Jeffs, jumps the curb, and parks, cutting him off.

The big man angles away, stumbling.

Gale calls for backup and an ambulance, then joins the chase, fast catching up with the hobbled goliath.

"Police! Stop and drop! Stop and drop!"

Jeffs stops and turns and Gale launches into him hard, his shoulders weapons, his Capistrano Valley High School football skills on clear display.

The big man goes down and stays down, breathing fast and clutching his left knee through torn bloody leather.

Gale's got his gun in his right hand and plastic tie in the other.

"Roll over, Vern. Then get your hands behind your back. Don't even think of getting up."

Growls and profanities, Jeffs's voice electric with pain.

"A gun on your ankle and a knife in your boots, Vern?"

"I got a concealed carry permit, man."

"You're a felon."

Jeffs rolls over with a groan, and Gale cinches the tie around his thick wrists.

"I'll keep it loose until you mess with me," says Gale. "Next, I'm taking off your boots. You kick at me with those steel toes, you'll be very sorry."

"My knee is killing me," says Jeffs, his voice like wet gravel. "I need an ambulance."

Gale unzips Vernon's harness boots and pulls them off. Finds a pearl-grip derringer holstered on the inside of the big man's right ankle and a folding knife in a neoprene sheath glued inside the left boot.

"You get Mindy?"

"We'll get Mindy."

Gale zip-ties Jeffs's ankles together, the big man groaning again. "Fuck, that knee," he says.

Gale hears sirens, sees a Huntington Beach police cruiser swinging in next to his Explorer. And another on approach, lights flashing.

"You're under arrest for the murder of Bennet Tarlow," he says. "You have the right to remain silent. Anything you say can be used against you. You have the right to a lawyer before we ask you any questions. You know the drill, Vern."

"I didn't fuckin' kill him, man. And it's getting hard to breathe, face down like this. I weigh about half a ton. Keep your knees off my neck."

"I'll help you get on your side, it's going to hurt."

"Do it, pig."

With a sharp yelp, Jeffs tries to turn, and Gale pushes him all the way over. The big man is breathing harder. Gale sees the blood oozing through the left knee of his leathers.

"They hired me to kill him, but I changed my mind. I didn't, I swear."

Gale feels that sweet swelling of his soul that a confession brings. Even one that's probably at least half-false. His gut tells him Jeffs put two bullets in Bennet Tarlow's brain, and he almost certainly *was* hired: exactly what Gale had thought from the beginning.

Murder for hire.

Beautiful.

But Gale knows the DA can't charge Vernon Jeffs on the thin evidence he has. Amanda Cho seeing him in Bennet Tarlow's company the evening of his death is hardly enough. His van in the campground isn't enough. A cellmate snitch with a long-ago tale isn't enough, either. No murder weapon. No witnesses.

Vern will be free in forty-eight hours, Gale thinks.

But Jeffs doesn't know that.

"Who's they? Who hired you, Vern?"

"I don't know."

"Male, female, short, tall? Come on, Vern, you have to talk to me. Your jail cell awaits."

"Male! I never saw them. First time we talked was in a white Lincoln Navigator with a blackout glass between us in the Bear Cave parking lot. Two of 'em you know, a guy in the passenger seat and a driver. I only made out their shapes through the screen. They kept me in back. Tried to pay me half to kill Tarlow."

"Which was how much?"

"Thirty thousand."

"Why Caspers Park?"

"I wasn't there that night! I didn't do it! A lie can't stick to a truth. Here's the deal, Gale: You take me to a hospital and we'll trap 'em, those two guys, and *they'll* tell you who killed Tarlow. A hospital, man. No jail, no murder charge, no resisting arrest, no bullshit weapons charge, no reckless driving. When I'm a free man with a fixed-up knee, I'll tell you everything I know. Solid, hundred percent *truth*! I'll show you where they picked me up and where we drove to, three times, same white Lincoln Navigator and I know the plates. Weird plates. I'd recognize his voice anywhere. I'll tell you everything we said. I've got a photographic memory."

Gale follows Jeffs's pained smile to the paramedics van lumbering to a stop on Atlanta.

"You have a deal, Vern."

27

"Park right here," says Jeffs.

They've just rolled into the Bear Cave parking lot, where Jeffs claimed to have met the men who tried to hire him to kill Bennet Tarlow.

It's just after nine in the morning, twelve hours after Jeffs's release from Emergency at UCI Medical Center. The gravel has been removed from his knee and his bruised patella wrapped in a bandage that bulges under his baggy cargo shorts.

The mound of brown gauze contrasts with his big white, red-haired leg, which rests on his wadded-up denim vest on the black fabric of the Explorer's back seat.

Mendez drives, Gale riding shotgun, manning the video camera and a digital voice recorder propped up in a drink holder, its voracious mic aimed into the gap between the front seats.

Gale watches as Jeffs's head bobs and his lips move to some inner soundtrack, his Rx fentanyl, coffee, and two IHOP breakfasts making him painfully chipper and talkative.

They pull into a parking space behind the Bear Cave.

"A white Lincoln Navigator was right exactly there after work that night," says Jeffs, pointing. "Not far from my hog. About two o'clock. The back left door was open and the driver's window was down halfway. The driver had a Covid mask and a ball cap on. Angels. He said, 'Get in. We're friends of Vic Klavic and we have something for you. I knew Klavic from jail, years back.'"

"So you can't describe the driver?" asks Mendez.

"With a mask, cap, and no interior lights, could you?"

"His tone of voice, attitude?" asks Gale.

"Businesslike. No accent or nothing. By the sound of it I'd say young. A young white guy, probably."

"Where was the other guy?" asks Gale.

"Don't get ahead! I didn't see no other guy but I had this hunch he was there. Just black in there. So I went closer and looked in the open door. Nobody in the back and I couldn't see in front because of the privacy glass. Plexiglass probably. Full blackout, man. With a round grille on each side so you could hear and talk, like in a taxi.

"I got in the Navigator. Closed the door and rapped my knuckles on the glass. I said, 'I'm right here if you need me, you assholes.' And you know what the guy says back? The guy on the right, who I couldn't see? He says, 'Well, Vern, we do need a man like you. Someone brave, smart, honest, and dependable. We've got a job that will put fifty thousand dollars in your pocket. Half before, half after.' 'What's the job,' I ask him. And he says, 'We need some noise cancellation.' I said, 'Oh that's cute.' And he says, 'We want you to silence a guy. He's making bad decisions. Decisions that hurt our business, to the tune of many, many dollars.'"

Gale checks the voice recorder, sees the green light blinking. Consider Jeffs in the back seat, who blinks his tan, mountain-lion eyes at the detective.

"What?" says the big man. "Vern going too fast for you? Every word I say is a word that was actually said. On account of my photographic memory. You're getting perfect facts on that recorder."

"Keep talking," says Gale.

"The medicos said I get one of these every six hours, as needed," says Jeffs, twisting off the top of a round brown bottle. He chases out a gray pill with a fingertip that barely fits.

"That fent can hook you," says Mendez. "And kill you cold if you take too much."

"Vern's got self-control," he says.

"Don't forget to use it," says Mendez.

"Daniela," says Jeffs. "You're a pretty one but you've got a sharp tongue."

"I've heard that before."

"What did you take 'noise cancellation' to mean?" asks Gale.

"I wasn't sure at first. But when he said silence a guy that's making some bad decisions, I mean, 'silence' is a heavy word. Kind of final, like. I figure they wanted someone to give this guy the new look."

"Referring to Capstick, the hunter," says Gale.

"Right on," says Jeffs. "He was the greatest hunter ever. And a good writer, too. Wrote about killing animals the right way. The moral way. You give the animal the 'new look.' I wanted to be him and I hunted and fished some with Dad in Idaho before I joined up. After the Marines did some mercenary work in Congo. Ugly stuff but I was good with my Barrett. Came home, got a Harley, and hit the road. Did a lot of different shit, Montana to Louisiana to California. Colstrip coal mining, good pay. Fishing guide down on Bayou La Loutre, Saint Bernard Parish. Hard to find a swamp boat big enough to float me. Dope grows up in the Humboldt mountains, before the legalization. Best weed in the world, good pay. Now, thirty years later, I'm a bartender in Huntington Beach, California, and my wife rides a pink chopper. I got it boxed. Thanks for not making

Mindy crash her bike or throwing her in jail. Vern's had lots of girls and Mindy's the best."

"What made these two guys think you'd do something like that?" asks Mendez. "Give someone the new look."

"I figured Klavic, since they brought him up. Me and Klavic were in the same car in jail—the wood car. That's peckerwoods, white men, some with Aryan ideas. Being Idaho boys, we fit right in. So we kind of ran the car, bullshitted a lot. Cellmates. What else you going to do?"

"Bullshit about killing people for money?" asks Gale.

"Probably. Long time ago, man."

"You told Klavic you killed a woman for two thousand dollars," says Gale. "Shot her in the head in a dollar store parking lot. You said it was a disgusting thing to do for the two grand."

A beat. Gale points the video camera at Vernon's face.

"Just jailhouse bullshit."

Watching Jeffs's face now, point-blank through the eyepiece, Gale's back in Sangin, scoping the enemy with his Barrett .50 caliber. The old man with his bird gun and his opium stash in the abandoned granary. His worn-out Cheetahs. The new look for the wrong guy, thanks to Gale. Remembers shooting pictures and video of him. The young boy asking if he could come home with Gale when he left Sangin.

Point-blank like this, Jeffs briefly looks stymied and uncertain. Like he did that night at the Bear Cave, when he said he'd fought in Congo, a mercenary gig, no doubt.

Now with a deep breath, Vern's expression hardens, and he blinks, once and slowly, recovering something.

"If I said that, it was just bullshit from a long time ago."

"It didn't sound like bullshit to Klavic," says Mendez.

"I don't recall that specific story about the drugstore."

"So, your photographic memory wears out over time?" asks Gale.

"Doesn't everybody's?" asks Jeffs.

"Seems to me killing a person would be pretty hard to forget," says Mendez.

Gale lowers the camera. "Once you realized that they were trying to hire you to kill someone, what did you say?"

"I said no, I don't do that kind of shit."

"And?" asks Mendez.

"The guy on the right said, 'Have you ever made twenty-five grand in cash, off the books and tax-free?' I said sure, when I robbed a bank, put thirty-six thousand, five hundred dollars in a backpack, and got away on my Harley. Wore a helmet for the holdup and the getaway. Two blocks down I ran my ride up a ramp and into a U-Haul van. Mindy pulled the door down and drove us away. Cops passing us, sirens blazing, looking for a guy on a motorcycle. Fuck, it was great. Really a high point in my life. Don't worry that I'm just giving you detectives more work to do—fed and state statutes on bank robbery is only ten years. Long expired."

"Did you try it again?" asks Mendez.

"Never. I did a six-month bounce for battery, then got a job in Colstrip and went more or less straight for a while. Mindy thought it was a dumb thing to do, that we're better than that. Vern wasn't so sure."

"So what did the guy do when you told him no?" asks Gale.

"The driver got out of the car, cracked open the door, and dropped a Halliburton on my lap. That was when I saw his hair under the Angels cap was blond. Put that in your notebook. Blond hair. And the case was aluminum. Clean stacks of twenties inside, lined up perfectly straight, all the way to the edges. Smelled *good*. The guy in the passenger seat must have seen me. One-way window maybe, like when you cops interrogate. He said, 'Yes, Mr. Jeffs, that money on your lap can be yours. And the other twenty-five, when you're done.' He said, 'We think you should give this offer some serious thought.' I said I'll think about it, but tell me more about this guy. What did he do to deserve the new look? He said he's about to cost his partners billions of future dollars. Due to his bad decisions. 'What company is that?' I asked. 'Better you don't know,' he says. 'Better you don't know anything more about him.' I said I'd need to know where he works and lives, just for starters. He said, 'We'll make sure you have everything you need, Vernon. Call me Steve, by the way. This is Curtis up here driving.'

"Then I opened the door and got out and went to my bike. I stopped about halfway across the parking lot and looked back at the white Lincoln Navigator. Nice car. A power-punk operator's ride. I pictured a guy with soft smooth hands, perfect teeth, and a great haircut. I still couldn't see nothing inside. The plate was 9KYF334, trapped photographically in my brain. I assumed it was stolen or faked. End of chapter one."

"When and where did you see this car and these men again?" asks Mendez.

Gale's already on the radio, calling in the plates.

"Curtis called me the next day. Said they could sweeten the deal. Asked me to be waiting for them at the Nordstrom in South Coast Plaza. Ten thirty."

Mendez parks near the main South Coast Plaza Nordstrom entrance, elegantly sweeping granite steps leading up to glass doors that slide open and closed, flashing in the late-morning sun. Well-dressed shoppers climb and descend.

Gale mulls the stolen plates as he watches the gilded men and women on the granite steps. Thinks of Marilyn, who loved this place. She's been in his dreams again. He hears wisps of her voice, nodding off at night.

Fragments.

And fragments of fragments.

He notes the hard set of Daniela's jaw as she watches the shoppers, too.

"Where the beautiful people spend their money," she says.

"Don't see them types at the Bear Cave," says Jeffs.

South Coast Plaza is one of Orange County's premier shopping malls, Gale thinks, designed and expanded over the decades years by the Tarlow Company, led by the now ninety-five-year-old Bennet Tarlow.

He takes pictures of beautifully dressed shoppers, climbing up and down the steps.

Camile Tarlow's kind of place, he thinks.

And Norris Kennedy's and Patti DiMeo's and his own Marilyn's.

The kind of place that when he walks in, he feels alien—not only as an Acjacheme Native unrecognized by his own country, the country he was born in and almost died for, but as a human being.

"So just like the first time, I get in the Navigator," says Vern. "I was hoping that it being daytime would give a better look at them, but nothing doing. Windows that dark aren't even legal unless you're famous, or law enforcement, or a politician.

"And this time we don't just sit there and talk. They don't say more than hi Mr. Jeffs and we head through the lot to the freeway. Half an hour later we're in some park I've never even heard of. So, Detective Mendez, get back on the freeway and I'll show you where we went."

"Is this white Navigator a runaround?" asks Mendez. "Two guys you can't even describe. Just a bunch of make-believe to keep your butt free? It makes me wonder if you killed Tarlow and this is just a bunny trail you're showing us."

"No, ma'am, no. It's not. I'm just taking you where they took me, and telling you what they said. That's what we agreed to. You can make your own decisions from there."

Mendez sweeps past the sign for Aliso and Wood Canyons Wilderness Park, follows the entryway through dense green hills of coastal chapparal.

"Another county wilderness park," she says. "Maybe we'll get lucky again."

"What's lucky about that?" asks Jeffs.

"Bennet Tarlow III was murdered in a county wilderness park," says Gale. "After being seen with you the previous evening. As I'm sure you remember. Your photographic memory seems to be coming and going."

"I know that, just didn't put it together 'til now. The pain's back. Had to have myself a fent bump with my breakfast, so now the brain fog's setting in. By the way, why won't you tell me who this alleged witness is? The one who's lying about me being with Tarlow. Does he really exist or just more lame-ass cop game from you two?"

Gale gives him a long look, trying to pry his way past Jeffs's photographic memory bullshit and into the truth behind it, if any.

But all he gets are those Killer Cat eyes again, cool and unamused.

"There's a parking lot around the bend," Jeffs says. "I'll show you the exact spot we took."

Mendez parks on the far side of the lot, per instructions. There's only one other vehicle, and it's not far away, a tall putty gray Mercedes Sprinter with the side door open and a small man sitting on a narrow bed with a laptop across his thighs. Beside him is a small woman, engaged with a computer, too. A Chihuahua sits between them, its ears perked, barking intently on the invading Explorer.

"Second time you've seen these guys, then," says Gale. "Or at least one of them. Same white Lincoln Navigator. Walk us through it."

"Steve—the guy on the right—said he might have been wrong in presenting his offer. Wrong about the target. Wanted to know why I didn't kill the woman. I told him again I never did that. I don't *do* that. Not Vern. Something doesn't fit right inside, I don't do it."

"Why do you call yourself 'Vern' sometimes and 'I' the rest?" asks Mendez.

He glowers at her. "I look at myself from the outside and the inside. So it depends."

"On what?" she asks.

"Sometimes I'm me and sometimes I'm me looking at me."

"Which were you doing when you shot Tarlow?" asks Gale.

Jeffs's big head pivots, dragging the scowl with it. "We made a deal, piglets: You drop your fake charges and I lead you to Steve and Curt."

"Curtis?" says Mendez.

Jeffs leans forward, uses both hands to adjust his knee on the balled vest.

"Quit trying to confuse me," he says. "Police harassment is not part of our deal. Go ahead, bust me right now if you want. Watch your case collapse in court."

Both Gale and Mendez let the silence speak.

"So you told Steve you don't do that," says Gale. "Meaning murder for hire."

"He said he wouldn't have done it either," says Jeffs. "She didn't deserve it, says Steve. But our target richly deserves it. We mentioned that he's stealing away close to fourteen billion dollars from his own company? Fine. But he also rapes women. Women he knows and dates. Two of them for sure, maybe three. Quite likely, more. Our private eyes and lawyers are working up the big reveal for the media. They've got video. Graphic video. So, Steve says, Caesar—let's call him Caesar—is a multimillionaire businessman costing his company *billions* that will end up in his own pockets. And drugging and forcibly raping a series of women he's deceived into believing they mean something to him. Vern, he says, you'd be doing humanity a *favor* by taking him out.

"'How old a guy is he?' I ask. Steve says early forties. Movie star kind of face and hair. Makes you want to punch him. Top schools, comes from more money than I can even dream of. Which is what you want, is his money, I say. Only what's ours, Steve says. Only what we have worked very, very hard for, and Caesar wants to take from us. There are the women, too. They didn't do a thing to be defiled like that. The video would make you ill, Vern. You have a strong moral compass. That's why you disgusted yourself at the drugstore, whether you killed her or not. We want a man like you. I told them I'd think about it. And asked them about that pay raise they brought up.

"Steve says this offer won't last much longer. Says, we can increase the money. Thirty grand right here and now, and another thirty when it's done. You can keep the Halliburton. Two of them, actually. On us. Sooner, not later. Weeks, not months. We understand you need time to learn his habits and patterns. But it doesn't have to look like suicide or an accident. We just want him off the team."

Gale's disbelief of Jeffs's story crashes against the rocks of it. The rocks are winning right now.

"So I told them yes."

A long near-silence while the Chihuahua barks away.

"Two days later I changed my mind. Cancelled the deal when Steve called. They haven't contacted me. The thirty grand was under my bed in the Halliburton."

Another silence.

"And you haven't gotten more than a glimpse of Curtis," says Gale. "And not even that of Steve."

"They're just voices," says Jeffs. "I never forget a voice. Ask Mindy."

"Aren't you afraid they'll come after the money?" asks Gale. "Shoot you in the kneecap for their trouble, or worse?"

"Don't say kneecap! Let 'em try. They're not those kind of people. They're guys in suits. Lawyers, accountants, fixers. Slick and gutless. Not real people, like us."

Jeffs laughs quietly.

"They could hire it out," says Mendez. "Like they hired you."

"Tried to hire me. I have no fear, Daniela. They know I'll give the money back. I *want* to give it back."

"No," says Gale. "You're going to give it to us to process into evidence."

"Vern was afraid you'd pull that one on him."

"You just confessed to conspiring to murder Bennet Tarlow," says Gale. "Now you're under arrest for it."

Gale exits the Explorer, and Mendez hits the back door unlock. Jeffs glares at Gale but holds his hands out and together.

Jeffs smiles hugely as Gale applies the plastic. His red whiskers are growing out, and sweat rolls down his temples.

"Better tie my ankles, too," he says. "So I can't make a run for it. You still got nothing on me. The story about Steve and Curtis is pure bullshit, and I didn't kill that guy. Don't bother looking under my bed."

Mendez rolls out of the parking lot as Gale reads the big man his rights off a card he carries in his wallet.

"Yeah, man. *Yeah.* You still got nothing on me."

"How come you ate at Bamboo a few days ago?"

Jeffs's smile fades, and the sweat is still rolling down his temples.

"I was hungry, man."

28

After booking Vernon Jeffs into Orange County jail, Daniela fakes Gale with bogus doctor's appointment so she can surveil Jesse—who is supposed to be in class. She feels bad lying to her new partner, but not bad enough to let her son cut class and do god-knows-what with Lulu Vega.

She's parked down and across the street from El Jardin restaurant in Santa Ana in her black Explorer, slumped in the driver's seat, binoculars balanced on the lowered window.

For nearly three hours she's followed them through her Teen-Shield app, on a seemingly random tour of gang-infested barrios in Orange and Los Angeles Counties.

She's watched them go in and out of six dour little houses, returning from four of them with white plastic Ralphs bags and from the other two with brown bags from Vons. The bags look to be weighted by something heavy and small.

From the seventh house, way up in Long Beach, Lulu carried a large rectangular box with a picture of a drone on it, and the words

RAPTOR TX-395 CAMERA DRONE emblazoned on the side in red and black.

All of which, bags and box, Daniela watched Jesse and Lulu—not five minutes ago—set in the trunk of a portly man's gleaming 1955 aqua-on-white Chevy Bel Air lowrider, parked on the street in front of El Jardin.

Mendez knows this guy.

Oh, does she.

Before he closed the sleek aqua trunk lid, Daniela watched Jesse pull out one of the Ralphs bags and show him what looked—through Mendez's binoculars—to be a smartphone. Which drew an approving nod from the white-suited man, who snatched the re-bagged phone from Jesse, dropped it into the trunk, and carefully lowered the lid.

Now Daniela watches Jesse and Lulu being seated on the open-air deck of El Jardin along with the plump, white-suited man.

Now the hostess hands them menus and departs, leaving Daniela with a clear close-up of them, unimpeded by the blossoms of potted mandevilla vines lining the perimeter of the deck.

Jesse's wearing black shorts and calf-high white socks that look new and that Daniela has never seen. A red plaid short-sleeve shirt, collar open, silver chains.

Lulu's got on a black boob-tight singlet and a flowing beige skirt with a slit high up one thigh. Heels. Hair up, lollipop earrings, hummingbirds and vines tattoos on her shoulders.

Daniela has never seen this ink, either.

Uses the binoculars to study her son again, searching for new tats.

She wonders how she could have missed Jesse's high white socks and cholo shirt. He hid them from her, of course, but how could she have missed what he is becoming? Missed? Missed my ass—she thinks—it's called denial. Of what's happening to the thing you love most in this world.

Her heart pounds harder as she focuses in on the man, his clean-shaven, cherubic face and short, gleaming, pomaded hair. He wears his signature getup: a white suit and white shirt, shiny black shoes, and a priestly purple stole.

He's Alfredo Buendia of Santa Ana, a once-feared, former La eMe kingpin nicknamed "The Bishop" for his primitive, violent Christianity—a Pelican Bay prisoner, pardoned ten years ago by the governor.

Convicted of narcotics trafficking amounting to tens of millions of dollars, and mayhem—sliced open a rival's face with a knife.

Suspected of ordering thirteen murders, four committed personally, but witnesses kept disappearing or wouldn't talk.

Founder, years ago, of Camp Refuge for troubled boys right here in Santa Ana.

Camp Refuge for troubled boys.

Of fucking course, thinks Daniela.

Buendia is in perfect company here with her own and only begotten son.

A perfectly troubled boy.

The kind he can help, if you believe what he says.

But some people don't.

Such as those that Daniela—in her fifteen years with the Sheriff's Department—seven in Vice, has talked to about Buendia. Deputies. Social workers. Prosecutors. Her own informants. Her eyes and ears on the street.

Not a single one of which believes that Alfredo Buendia is even close to clean.

But the Orange County Catholic Diocese lavishly sponsors Camp Refuge and proclaims that Buendia is a modern-day saint, saved by Christ.

The media love his rise from the ashes, his gang-to-God story. Call him warmhearted, a homie hero. And Daniela's department treats Buendia as they would any law-abiding citizen, under the laws that she has sworn to uphold.

Innocent until proven guilty.

Happy pink mandevilla flowers flutter around the edges of her lenses, framing his divinity.

Mendez lowers her field glasses. A waitress arrives. Daniela watches as Alfredo Buendia stands, embraces her politely, and pecks her offered cheek.

Her heart is still thumping, and her stomach grumbles. Hot in here, even with the windows down. She wipes her brow with one of the Jack in the Box napkins she keeps in the Explorer for such occasions. Keeping a low profile, she rummages through the Explorer console and finds beef jerky and an apple.

Daniela watches another young couple being led across the patio by the hostess, menus in hand. She seats them at Jesse's table.

More troubled youth, thinks Daniela. They're dressed cholo and chola, like Jesse and Lulu. Swagger and style. Look like teenagers. Daniela thinks of the seedy neon motels on Beach Boulevard, and the young prostitutes and pimps she busted in Vice. Pretty, most of them. The johns older, shamed and pathetic.

And now asks herself the million-dollar question: Will Jesse move in to Camp Refuge?

More accurately, will Jesse move in to Camp Refuge if Lulu wants him to? Camp Refuge is for boys, of course, but Daniela once worked a sting near the camp, where two girls working Harbor Boulevard flopped at a dingy Airbnb, an easy walk to Camp Refuge, where they hung when they weren't hooking. Not enough reason for Vice to go after the church-backed camp or its suspect founder, although Daniela's Vice squad partner—a dolled-up Deputy Bonny Lilly—tried to tempt Buendia at the Grove, where he was a frequent guest of, supplicant to, and a parasite upon, the rich and powerful.

No luck. On the several occasions that Deputy Lilly dangled herself at him in the Grove, Buendia barely talked to her.

Well, Mendez thinks: If I ask Jesse about mystery plastic bags, and certainly the Raptor camera drone, he'll know he's been surveilled and would swiftly abandon ship. Absolutely. As had Daniela, abandoning *her* entire ship, with a secret that was just beginning to show.

Like mother like son: Jesse would go.

So, why not head for Camp Refuge? Free room and board, and plenty lax enough that pretty Lulu could come and go as she pleased. He wouldn't even have to change high schools. Could keep his job.

Mendez feels the frustration heating her up in the hot cockpit of the black Explorer.

Almost frustrated enough to go across the street and order Bishop Buendia to open the trunk of his lowrider.

And take Jesse by the collar of his red plaid cholo shirt, march him back here, and . . .

Ridiculous, she thinks. Stupid, destructive, and dangerous. She cracks a smile, self-disgusted and bitter as it is.

Daniela watches the two new arrivals order their food, and a few minutes later the waitress arrives with a tray of five platters and a stand. She remembers doing that at Applebee's in her Citrus College days, how those platters would slide around the tray when she tried to lower it to the stand.

She eats the jerky and the apple, looking in on Jesse at work on some big grilled shrimp.

Sees the beauty of the child still in him and the strength of the man he's becoming.

Hard to take her eyes off him but she finally does; starts up the SUV, cranks the air, and slowly drives away.

On her way to the Tarlow Company building in Newport Center, Daniela takes a call from Orange County Seventh District Supervisor Kevin Elder.

"Yes," she says.

"I apologize for calling you out of the blue. I was wondering if we might take a walk on the beach at Crystal Cove."

"Why?"

A pause, then: "For the reasons we discussed at the Grub."

"Norris Kennedy or the personal ones?"

"Not Norris Kennedy," he says quietly.

"Really I can't. I wasn't kidding about being taken."

"By two lucky men! Is one of them Jesse?"

"Yes."

"Well, are you happy with the other one? Does he treat you with respect and care about your happiness? Does he have any clue how singular and special and bitchin' you are?"

"You're laying it on pretty thick, Kevin."

"I'm serious, Daniela. Isn't there one thing I can do to get your company for a while? To see that pretty face of yours break into a smile? *Anything?*"

"I'm sorry. I'm taken and happy to be."

"You are single. A widow. Pardon me if you find my curiosity offensive."

"Single and happy enough."

"Woman, woman. I admire you and what you've been through. I am trying to offer you friendship. Okay, Daniela, I won't call you again. But you—if you ever need me for anything—please reach out. I'm always here and you know how I feel about you."

Daniela punches off.

Single and happy enough.

Happy as hell.

29

That evening Gale takes the barstool next to Geronima Mills in the Swallows Inn bar in downtown San Juan Capistrano.

She's got thick black hair, dark eyes, a pronounced Acjacheme brow, and a seashell necklace against a red, snap-button blouse.

He recognizes her from the YouTube Wildcoast protest, one of Franklin's comrades-in-arms.

To Gale, a handsome young woman.

"I didn't think you'd call," she says.

"Why?"

"Just my doubtful nature."

She waves the barwoman over, orders a shot of bourbon and a beer.

Gale does likewise. Reminds himself to go slow.

"How goes the case?"

"Plodding forward," says Gale, worried about his arrest, if the DA will choose to charge and arraign.

"A suspect?"

Gale nods, watching the barkeep set down the drinks. "Vern Jeffs. We took him in this morning."

"What's he do?"

"Tends bar. I can't tell you any more, Ms. Mills. Open investigation, all that."

"Salud."

They touch beer glass rims. Geronima Mills's thick black hair is held back in a comb that looks fashioned from bone. Her eyes are alert and prying. Gale notes the intimacy implied when Acjacheme women wear decorative bone, checks his vanity.

"How old are you, Lew?"

"Forty-three."

"I'm twenty-seven. Why do you live with your mother?"

Oh boy, he thinks. What he often thinks when asked a question he doesn't want to answer. "It's temporary."

"How long has it been?"

"Couple of years. Why?"

"I just think it's interesting," says Mills. "I love her baskets. Frank brought some to Native Studies one day and some of the old ones, too. Made way back when by our ancestors. I started making baskets last year, but they're atrocious."

"Mom told me she started at twelve and didn't get one she liked until she was sixteen."

"A four-year degree in basket making," Mills says with a humored smile. "Ever try it?"

Gale feels his candor slipping. "No. I made bows and arrows when I was a boy. I still do some of that. Helps me relax, get to sleep."

She lifts her shot glass. "To baskets, bows, and arrows."

Gale tastes the bourbon going down, feels its promise.

"I got a weakness for this stuff," she says. "You, too?"

Gale nods.

"Are you sad to let go of me as a person of interest in the murder of Bennet Tarlow?"

"Burn him at the stake and eat his face?" asks Gale. "Killer dot-com? Kill Wildcoast? You're still a very interesting person, Ms. Mills."

"That's just the way young people get things done now, Detective. It's called branding. The power of drama. Becoming a virus. Killing Wildcoast isn't killing Bennet Tarlow! It's just self-promoting theater."

"I understand that. So you're old enough to know better."

To Gale's surprise, Geronima Mills laughs.

"Lew, I asked you to buy me a drink so I could ask *you* to come on my *Kill Wildcoast* podcast. I want you to introduce you as the detective who considered me a person of interest in the murder of Bennet Tarlow III."

Gale flashes on his disastrous *Times* interview. "That's a firm no."

"I took it as honor, being a person of interest in the killing of a powerful man in a historically evil family. It made me a part of what happened, even though I had nothing to do with his death."

"No offense, Ms. Mills," says Gale. "Your violence-prone videos and online chatter are asinine and inflammatory. Violence-prone people listen to you. You feed the flames. You accelerate them."

"No, Detective. My followers see my words for what they are: exaggeration and self-promotion."

"Tell the Proud Boys that."

"Oh, Jesus. That's not who I'm talking to."

"But they're listening," says Gale. "Maybe not answering, but listening. You may not be capable of shooting Bennet Tarlow dead, but some of your followers might be."

Mills takes a sip of beer, gives Gale another prying, dark-eyed look.

"Actually, Lew, I've thought about that," she says. "I vet my audience and my followers by what they post and say. But . . . there are the silent ones. Out there. You are right."

"Well, maybe one of them pulled that trigger."

"You said Vernon Jeffs."

"He could testify as a silent follower."

"Which would make me an accessory to murder? An accomplice or even a coconspirator?"

"I'm not sure what a jury would decide."

"What have you decided?"

"I think you should tone down the violence, Ms. Mills. I don't want blood on your hands. You have beautiful, innocent hands."

She gives him a surprised look.

"I meant nothing flirtatious or suggestive by that."

"Oh, okay."

With a small smile, she sips bourbon and chases it with the beer.

"I still want you on my podcast," she says. "But the other reason I wanted to meet you was something Frank's wife, Cathy, said to me one night over drinks. She said Lew Gale is the gentlest person on earth, and she thought we would like each other. Opposites, you know. She told me to find the *Los Angeles Times* feature on you. It was a great piece. And your face in the picture broke my heart. An Acjacheme brave. Beautiful and innocent, like how you see my hands."

One of which she sets on one of Gale's, pats it twice, and takes it off.

"So, why *did* you call me today?" she asks.

"I want to talk to King Bear of the Grizzly Braves. He posts calls to violence."

Geronima gives Gale a long look, some disappointment undisguised within.

"Why bother, if you've arrested Jeffs?"

"He claims he was hired."

"By King Bear?"

"That's why I need to talk to him."

Mills studies Gale again, long and cautiously.

"King Bear is Tony Rueda," she says. "He plays puffed up and violent, but he's really just a petulant child. A braided pony tail and cool bolo ties, but he's a pretendian. He has one hundred percent no native blood that he can prove. So far as murder for hire, Tony doesn't have two nickels to rub together. None of us do. You're much more afraid of us than we deserve."

"What does he do when he's not posting or in class?"

"He works weekends at an indoor shooting range in Oceanside. Iron Sights."

"Good with a handgun, then," he says.

"He's good. I've shot with him."

"Twenty-twos?"

"Yes. He sold me one not long ago. An aluminum twenty-two, semiautomatic. Light as a feather, purse-sized and rose-finished. I wanted it for self-defense. Eight shots. He said it was inaccurate outside of six feet. But a good carry for a chick. Sold me a gun purse made especially for it, too, in matching rose leather with white rose petals embossed. It opens easy, and the gun grip is right there and you can draw it fast. Separate compartment from your lip gloss and credit cards."

Gale smiles at Geronima Mills's humor.

"I liked his post a couple of days back," she says. "On the website killwildcoast.org. The one about Wildcoast being a white fascist utopia and the mountain lion that tore apart Bennet Tarlow getting a golden statue at the mission."

Gale shrugs. "Okay, King Bear is a poser. But what about the Brunette Bombshell?"

"That's Tammy Tarango," says Geronima. "She runs a gator park outside Orlando. Has some Seminole, but she's far, far away from hiring Vernon Jeffs."

"Hatchet Man?"

"Bill Custer, doomsday prepper in Missouri."

"Hmmm."

Gale sips his bourbon and beer. Feels that little shiver, that hint of luck, of power coming on. Things he's felt before with bourbon and beer and Marilyn before the war.

"And, to be honest," says Geronima, "I called you because Frank told me you were a genuine warrior, and that we would like each other."

Her eyes light a little. "Old-fashioned tribal matchmakers," says Geronima. "So Frank and Cathy."

"Mom said that about you, too," says Gale.

Geronima looks out a window and Gale notes the long evening sunlight waning on her face in profile, the orange rays illuminating one eye, her catlike smile.

A smile that vanishes when she turns to Gale.

"I saw some strange things out at the Wildcoast site two nights ago," she says. "Big excavators and dozers, heavy-duty augurs, high-power water hose engines like the fire departments have. Nine total monster machines, not counting the generators. Gigantic floodlights beaming down—those white-hot towers of lights they use for freeway work at night."

"What time?"

"Four in the morning."

"What were you doing way out there?"

"I go out to the streams and the hills sometimes. For first light. Where the three o'clock ghosts can't follow. You get those?"

"They're pretty punctual."

Gale thinks of the Empire Excavators vehicles, of Kate Hicks, the supervisor who recognized him, the shovel laborer hand-digging a percolation test pit, joking about gold and big valuable crystals.

"Were there company logos on the equipment?"

"Too dark to say. Before dawn they killed the lights. Streamed away in their pickups and vans. Like vampires running for home. The night shift, I assume. Left all the flatbeds and the heavy machinery in place. Lights and all. I hunkered down in a stand of cottonwoods down by the creek. Wrapped in my coat. Dozed off and woke up two hours later to a bright, sunny morning. Looked out at the destruction and all the equipment. All shut down. Resting. No men. Odd."

Gale checks his watch.

"I need to see it," he says. "Come with me if you'd like."

Geronima finishes the bourbon and beer and gets off her stool. "I'll get the tip."

Gale lays some bills on the bar top, and they step from the dark bar into the evening.

Gale beholds the broad grassy swale where the alleged percolation test was being conducted.

Approaching in the golden light, he sees big mounds of loose dirt and a wall of unearthed boulders strewn in a wide circle. Looks like some prehistoric ruin, or maybe a fallen temple, he thinks.

Cranes and booms rise against the darkening sky, anchored by their tonnage. Two white pickup trucks, with PacWest Mining emblems: snowcapped mountains and a blue lake. The unlit floodlight towers lean and glimmer dully.

Gales notes that the surrounding earth has been leveled by bulldozers, flayed and flattened by their steel treads.

Climbing and pulling their ways up the pile of rock, Gale and Mills reach the lip of a deep pit. Gale feels that light-headed vertigo as he looks down.

What had been a six-by-four-foot pit dug by one man is now roughly fifty feet in diameter and thirty feet deep. He sees the shine of water down there, just before the last sunlight is snuffed out.

"What do you make of this?" asks Mills.

"Maybe it really is a perc test," says Gale. "They hit the groundwater. Now the hydrologists have to decide if there's enough room to drain an entire city or build sewers."

Gale remembers the miniature model of Wildcoast in Bennet Tarlow's home office in Laguna. One of the hundreds of many pins indexed to the notebook was stuck in the middle of Lake Wildcoast. Something about filling the lake with natural groundwater, if necessary.

"Tarlow anticipated this," says Gale. "He was going to make a lake with it."

"I still hate Wildcoast, lake or not," says Geronima Mills. "You know the ancient Acjacheme believed there was an ocean under the ground here? It was created by the god Chinigchinich as a resting place for spirits on their way to the afterlife. Isn't that a beautiful? Grandma told me. Gale, have you read Pablo Tac?"

"Some," says Gale.

"He was Luiseño, but they spoke a dialect of our Acjacheme language," says Mills. "You should read all of Tac. He's *us*, you know. Our racial ancestor. Father Peyri took him away from Mission San Luis Rey when he was eleven. Eleven! Peyri knew Tac had something special. They sailed all the way to Rome. Pablo became a scholar at the College of the Propaganda, a Catholic outfit there. Studied Latin and Spanish and wrote a Luiseño dictionary and translated it into Spanish. Wrote about hunting and fishing and living off acorns and rabbits and fish. Drank the rabbit blood fresh. Ate the rest raw. Deer, too. Didn't cook anything until the Spanish made them. Played lacrosse against us Juaneños. War, too, against other Indians, like us! Unbelievable stuff. His is the only book about native life in California before the Europeans, written by a native. He loved Father Peyri, you know. So I guess that little Franciscan devil must have had some good in him."

"I remember about the hunting and the wars."

"You talked about it in the *Times* article," says Mills. "Becoming a warrior. *Your* grandma's stories. You making bows and arrows the old way. Baskets, too."

Gale senses Mills looking at him.

"Sorry," she says. "I lecture people just to prove I'm still alive. Pablo Tac died in Rome, age nineteen."

Gale looks down into the cavernous pit again. Sees just a flicker of light on the water.

"Tell me more about the underground ocean," he says.

"The ancients believed it was put under the earth by Chinigchinich before the great ocean was formed. Our Pacific, I would assume. It was very deep and its crystals grew up from the ocean floor, very large ones, and they contained a magic substance that was heavy and produced light. I'm sure they had a word for it but it's not in Tac's dictionary."

"Heavy? Gold, silver?"

"I don't know. Technically, no one does."

"Did the ancient Acjacheme consider the crystals valuable?" Gale asks. "Something to be dug out and traded, maybe. Or worshipped?"

"They believed the crystals formed gigantic caverns," says Mills. "And these were where the spirits waited. There were fish with lamps growing on their heads so they could see in the underground dark. This is according to Father Boscana and the three aged Acjacheme wise men, who Boscana believed were sent by God to help him write a scientific account of the Acjacheme. Boscana believed that we natives were savages in need of conversion. He wrote of sanctioned whippings and forced labor. Breaking up families. Taking our names away, outlawing our dances and our language and our gods."

Gale's great-grandmother Anna had bitterly recounted to Gale the mission days of *her* grandmother Gabriella. Gabriella had been a good basket maker and storyteller, and her accounts had fired Gale's imagination. At first, she had welcomed the Spanish God into her life, just as her elders had welcomed the Friars and soldiers onto their land. But when her father was whipped in front of her family—for dancing—she was no longer able to believe in their Jesus and his miracles and his love. She told Gale that she had become fierce as the white mountain lion that prowled the creeks hunting deer.

"The guy digging the hole with the shovel that day," says Gale, "talked about looking for gold and crystals. I figured he was just being funny."

"Maybe he was just being Acjacheme."

In the darkness overhead a jetliner descends toward John Wayne Airport.

Gale and Geronima Mills climb down from their rock lookout and walk in silence amid the cranes, excavators, earthmovers, and drilling rigs. The racks of floodlights. The generators.

"Why work at night but not in daylight?" asks Mills.

Gale had been wondering the same. "Maybe they've found what they're looking for."

"All I saw in that pit was groundwater."

"A simple perc test," says Gale.

"I don't believe that. Too early. Not necessary."

"I don't either. Whatever they're looking for, maybe they'll have to go deeper."

"What do you think Bennet Tarlow was doing out here the night he was murdered?" asks Mills.

"I ask myself that question a hundred times a day. I need to answer it."

They walk the dirt road toward Gale's truck.

The moon is full and low, and the truck is pale in its light.

He watches as Geronima Mills steps toward the passenger-side door but she stops, turns, and considers him.

"They almost killed our dances, but not quite," she says. "Pablo Tac made some wonderful drawings. We didn't dance to music. We danced to rattles and drums."

With this, she raises her arms and sways her hips, writhing and stomping in rhythm to her clapping hands.

Gale recognizes her motion from one of Tac's sketches, a movement he and Frank tried to re-create as boys.

He steps closer and claps the rhythm and tries to get his shrapnel-shot legs and graceless feet to keep the beat. But they won't or can't, so Gale backs away watching Tac's dancer whirling in the moonlight.

Later that night Gale stays up with his mom, restringing one of his willow bows with fresh nettle-fiber, a beauty he'd made just weeks ago.

Sally is working on a medium-sized basket, which Gale recognizes as a vessel for transporting and storing water from the creeks long before the age of pumps and plumbing. The coils of deer grass wound tightly enough to be waterproof. He sees that she's about halfway done with it, the coils climbing ever so slowly upon the rush frame in the traditional clockwise fashion.

Sally is pensive tonight and Gale utterly distracted by Geronima Mills and the feelings she set loose in him.

He pours a second bourbon and gets a look from his mother.

"Your father came by today," says Sally. "Wanted some family pictures. He's making some kind of history of his families."

All three of them, thinks Gale. As always, mention of Edward Gallego stirs his sense of diminished value.

"I told him you'd love to see him."

"I'm reading Luis Verdad again," he says.

She gives him a smile. "The boy who gave me your name."

"I'm still trying to figure out what he made up and what really happened," he says.

"*Blood & Heart* is all true," she says. "Magdalena and El Diablo and Bernardo and Water Dog. Chinigchinich. The dancing and the battles. The marriage of Luis. All true. All corroborated by your great-grandmother, and her mother, and hers."

The stubborn detective Gale still doubts that all of Verdad's story is true.

"I wonder why the fathers and grandfathers don't tell the stories," Gale says.

"Oh, they do. We're just better at it."

"Night, Mom."

"Night, son. Say hello to Luis from me."

30

Gale sips and reads.

We wrapped Magdalena in my sleeping blanket and took her to San Juan Creek and washed what was left of her. When she was clean we wrapped her in the blanket.

Bernardo wailed and I was not able to control my tears or the awful pounding of my heart that I thought might explode.

We carried Magdalena back home and there was a two-day fast and the dance of the dead, for which we paint our bodies in red and white pigments. Then the ceremony of fire.

When it was over, Father Serra allowed us to pour her ashes from a raft into the Pacific Ocean, five kilometers away. This is not how the Franciscans treat their dead.

I became sick for two days, with fever and pain and vomiting. I slept many hours and felt better.

Late one evening Father Serra brought me into his office at the mission and he prayed for me and for the eternal soul of my sister, whom, like me, Father Serra had baptized.

There was a wooden box on his desk. It was shaped as a coffin is shaped, but smaller. It was shiny in the candlelight.

He asked me to open it. Inside was a blunderbuss, which is a flintlock gun shorter than a musket. It has a flared muzzle for easier loading of balls or shot. *Blunderbuss* is taken from Dutch words meaning "thunder" and "container."

Father Serra asked me to bring it to my shoulder.

"This is for El Diablo," he said. "You need more than your bow and arrow against him."

It was shorter than the soldiers' muskets but very heavy. I raised it toward the office door and it was difficult to hold steady.

"Good, good," said the father. "There is a fork rest in the box. It makes the gun accurate. This gun takes fifteen seconds to load, even if you are an expert. It is thunderously loud. It creates a white cloud with a strong smell. If you believe, God will help guide your ball."

I set the gun back in the box, alongside the fork rest, which was polished oak and lustrous.

"You will only get one shot at El Diablo," said Father Serra. "You must be close. Ten meters or less. You will kill him or he will kill you. He will only run at you, not away. The devil never runs away."

In the candlelight Father Junípero Serra was small in his brown robe, and his tonsure shined and its frame of hair was soft, and his white face had the glow of an angel or a god.

"Thank you, Father."

"The soldiers will give you instruction on loading and shooting tomorrow morning after Mass. I know you are considered a good warrior. And want to be a warrior-priest someday. God will be with you, Luis."

Two days later, Bernardo and Water Dog and I were back in the mountains where we found Magdalena. We brought two more dogs, Brown Dog and Kajitca, which in Acjacheme means to attack or bite.

I felt no fear, only grief and a cold anger directed at El Diablo.

We lived in the mountains for six days, eating and thanking the deer that Bernardo killed with his silent arrows, and we left carcasses in a pile, to attract El Diablo. We hid in the bushes quietly, with sage rubbed on us to disguise our scent, Bernardo with his bow and arrows, I with the blunderbuss that I named Thunder Girl, and the fork rest erected for accurate shooting.

I imagined my one-shot kill. I prayed to God, Jesus, Mary, and to forbidden Chinigchinich.

I dreamed of the shot, and in the dream Magdalena, whole and living and beautiful again, steadied the fork rest.

Lions came on the first five evenings, but none carried away a deer. I believe one lion came twice, by the pattern of his coat. How many lions matters not, because none of them were as enormous as El Diablo had been described.

Looking down the barrel and using the sight, I aimed Thunder Girl at them, and she was steady on the rest.

Grizzlies watched us, following their powerful noses to the pile of deer but keeping their distance because of our dogs' snarling attacks. Bears and dogs are mortal enemies. A large bear pursued Water Dog but Brown Dog and Kajitca pursued *her*, and she whirled upon them and chased them until she was tired and stood in the grass for a long while, then turned and crashed back into a stand of sycamores.

On the seventh morning El Diablo stood high on a ridge above us, approximately one-half kilometer away. Even at that distance his enormity was clear. And, just as the descriptions of him had claimed, he was lighter in color than other lions but his facial mask was very dark. When he yawned in the new sunlight, his fangs were white within the dark mask and very much bigger than I had foreseen.

The dogs were unaware.

He watched us with what appeared to be boredom and absolute calm. As if measuring us and our intents.

Then he vanished in the blink of an eye, only to reemerge a few minutes later, lower on the ridge, drawn by the odor of the deer, blending with the boulders, but closer to us by half.

And later again by half of that, as the sun continued to rise.

At noon he revealed himself again, closer, but still well above us, perhaps two hundred meters away. Much too far for Thunder Girl, even with the fork rest and Father Serra's blessing.

The dogs caught El Diablo's scent and scrambled up the steep hillside, frenzied but slowed by the boulders, only to return with dragging tongues and a visible sense of penance.

That evening we built another fire and lit candles in the darkness. El Diablo screamed down on us with the sound of a woman. I had heard this many times in my life but never this close. Our shamans and ritual specialists say this is the sound of tribesmen and women and children the lion has killed. This may be true but it sounded as if he was trying to say something to me. It was hard to identify what. Was he taunting me? Was he building his courage? Was he warning me? Or calling out to a mate? Or was this screeching, pitiful sound truly the voices of the dead? Magdalena?

The dogs curled near the fire and snarled at each other and looked ashamed of their fear.

Bernardo and I took turns sleeping but neither of us slept well. While one tried to sleep, the other sat on a big fallen oak branch that together we dragged near the fire, Thunder Girl primed and loaded and resting on the polished oak fork, pointed toward the ridge and the occasional hideous screams of El Diablo.

Things are often more true at first light.

I was on duty at sunrise, my body cold and buttocks numbly falling asleep on the log, Thunder Girl trained on the ridge.

The fire was almost gone and Bernardo and two of the dogs were snoring.

When I heard a sound in the dry leaves behind me, I realized I had made a foolish and terrible mistake.

I heard El Diablo snarl behind me and the dogs, too, and I sprung to the opposite side of the fork rest, lifted and reversed Thunder Girl, and got the flint ready to light the powder.

I saw El Diablo through the high tan grass that was his own color, well-hidden, his dark-tipped tail flipping left then right through the blades of grass. Then all three snarling dogs charged but stopped well short of the lion crouched in the brush, and Bernardo pulled up beside me with his bow drawn and his arms quivering and I waited for the lion to charge.

I did not wait long.

He launched high into the sky, front legs apart and out, his back legs trailing together, tail up, claws and teeth flashing, swiftly covering the distance.

Neither snarling nor roaring, he reached his greatest height, then dropped toward me with strange silence through the growling of the dogs, and I sparked the flint to the powder, hoisted Thunder Girl off the fork rest, and brought her to my shoulder.

It happened fast. His shadow fell upon me, and his great sprawled body descended, and I saw his face, past the muzzle of the blunderbuss, his eyes and the great open mouth framing his knives of teeth.

And with my front sight on that open mouth, I pulled the trigger.

The sound was truly thunderous.

Suddenly I was blinded by a thick white smoke from the burned gunpowder and its sulfurous smell.

El Diablo landed on me, but I broke his weight with my strong warrior legs, abandoned the gun, and with my hands hurled him off me to the ground.

I felt his claws slash my chest and arms.

He landed on his side but then righted himself and his legs shook and found no strength or coordination and his mouth was open still and with his tan eyes tearing into me I could see, from my now standing position, the great empty hole in the back of his head, a gaping, brainless cave.

He whirled in circles in the dirt like a drunken dancer, three circles one direction; three the other.

Then he stopped.

Bernardo jumped in and placed an arrow in the lion's heart.

El Diablo's tail tapped once and a spasm quaked his body and he went still.

31

Forty-eight hours after his intake at Orange County jail, Vernon Jeffs is released.

Undersheriff Elke Meyer calls Gale.

"Lew, what kind of an arrest was *that*?"

"Jeffs played Knox like a fool."

"Sounds like he played you and Mendez like fools. Button down, Lew. I need an arrest clean and fast. Not dirty and weak. Kersey needs it."

After seventeen hours of questioning, District Attorney Chris Knox has decided the people can't arraign on conspiracy and murder for hire based on Jeffs's recanted and comically flimsy story involving two men he's barely seen and can't identify.

Jurors won't believe it and neither should you, Knox told Gale and Mendez.

Whom—much to their disappointment but no real surprise—have found exactly no money and no Halliburton on the Jeffs's property, or the Bear Cave, or a small storage unit up on Bolsa, just two miles from his Huntington Beach home. The DA seems surprised that the detectives arrested Jeffs in the first place. He says all he can do is order Jeffs to keep his fat ass in Orange County or risk a flight charge. Maybe he'll produce Steve and Curtis, he says, on the off chance they do exist.

Now, very late on this Saturday night, Gale and Mendez stake out the parking lot of the Bear Cave from across the street.

This is the first time they've been here since recording Act I of Jeffs's conspiracy confession, days ago, when the white Lincoln Navigator allegedly appeared here in this lot.

And the first night the big, limping red-haired man Vern and his small skinny wife have been back to work.

Gale and Mendez have good views of Jeffs's white Econoline and the rear kitchen door, closed in the cool night. A coastal fogbank has locked in above them, smudging the streetlamps and the blue neon Bear Cave sign.

Just minutes ago, Gale surreptitiously affixed a magnetized tracking device on the rear chassis of the white van and synched it to his smartphone, propped up and facing him in a console cupholder.

"Glad we get overtime for this," says Mendez. "I could be home with my son."

"Put the money in Jesse's college fund."

She looks at Gale as if he's just said something absurd.

She continues staring at him, the silence long and uncomfortable for both.

"Jesse is surrounded," she says. "I don't know what to do. I don't want to talk about it. No, second thought, I want to talk about it. I want to talk about it."

So Mendez unloads, her voice soft and fast: Jesse is under Lulu's sway; Lulu's tight with the Barrio Dogtown Vatos; both Jesse and Lulu are consorting with Bishop Alfredo Buendia, a reformed La eMe kingpin now running Camp Refuge for troubled boys.

"Like there's such a thing as reformed eMe," she says. "God knows what he's putting his camp boys up to."

She tells Gale about the drone and the phones that Jesse and Lulu collected from various gangland haunts and stashed in the trunk of Buendia's sweet 1955 aqua-on-white Bel Air.

"The hell do you think of that?" she asks.

"I'm pondering."

"Maybe the phones and drones are just plunder, and they're fencing it off to the bishop?"

"That comes to mind," says Gale, thinking back to the drones they used in Sangin. Not the big armed ones hurling missiles to earth, flown remotely from Texas or California, but the smaller, quieter ones for surveillance and target acquisition. The kind that helped him kill the old opium user with the hunting gun and the Cheetah athletic shoes.

"Always a market for phones," he says. "Drones, I guess if you know the right people."

"Yeah," says Mendez. "Reformed eMe, they know all the right people. Hopefully they didn't steal the swag. What can I do, Lew? Confront Jesse? Show him I know some things? Play dumb and hope he makes good choices?"

"I could talk to him," says Gale. "That way he'll think it's the Sheriff's Department shadowing him as part of an investigation of Buendia. That way you're not blown. Right department, wrong deputy."

Silence then, as Daniela consults her phone. "At least he's home now," she says. "Hopefully alone. Lulu's last text is two hours old. I know what you're thinking, Gale. And yes, I do feel like a scumbag, spying on my own son."

"I might do the same," he says, getting that sense of wonder—grown fainter by the years—of what it would be like to have a child or two, be a dad, have a family.

"Mom from hell?" she asks.

"Not at all."

"I lied to him about his dad," she says. "I've lied to everyone about his dad since before Jesse was born. His dad didn't die. His father is still very much alive. I can't tell you more than that, regarding his, Jesse's . . . nativity."

Gale tries to solve this mystery, fails.

"Then that's who should be talking to Jesse," he says.

"That is impossible for reasons you will never know."

"Oh boy."

"Yeah," says Mendez.

"Have to let this one cook."

"I've been cooking it for nineteen years, Lew."

"I'll talk to him if you want me to."

"You are a kind and generous man," says Mendez. "I wish you were his father. No, sorry. I don't mean it that way, literally, I mean. Just, you know, like as a theory. Shut up, Dani, shut your mouth and cut your losses. Do your job and earn your overtime. For your son's college fund."

They watch Jeffs throw open the kitchen door and limp toward a dumpster with a bulging white bag. He's got on the same baggy shorts from days ago, and his knee bandage is noticeably smaller.

He throws open the lid with one hand and slings in the trash, the heavy lid clanging down.

"Do you still think he did Tarlow?" asks Mendez.

"Yes, you?"

Mendez shrugs. "I can't figure out if he's dumb as he looks, or if he's a crafty pro and a great liar. The more I think about the white Lincoln and Steve and Curtis, the less I believe them. Photographic memory, especially for voices? Come on."

"We didn't find the money because he put it somewhere else," says Gale. "Steve and Curtis aside, I think he took the job from somebody, got paid, and killed Tarlow as contracted."

"Then why implicate himself in murder for hire?"

"He's just sending us after phantoms."

"Well, he sure played that one cool. Cool enough to convince our district attorney that a jury won't convict."

Gale watches Vernon Jeffs swing open the kitchen door, take a long look at the parking area, and go back inside.

An hour later, at the Bear Cave closing time, Jeffs and Mindy cross the lot hand in hand, Jeffs with a stylish wooden cane. He climbs into the passenger seat.

Gale at the helm gives them a two-minute head start, then pulls onto fog-shrouded Yorktown Avenue.

To Main, headed away from the coast, the old Econoline blending with the fog.

Not the way home.

Mindy takes the 405 north to the 22 east, into Garden Grove. Pulls into Store 'N Save, punches something into an intercom keypad on a stanchion outside the office.

Gale glides past in the fog, U-turns, and heads back. The Econoline has already disappeared into the rows of brightly lit concrete bunkers, each with a roll-up door.

The woman answering the intercom asks for Gale's passcode, and he IDs himself as a sheriff's deputy. He can see her through the window.

"Is there a crime in progress here?" she asks.

"You better hope not," says Gale, holding out his badge.

"You'll need a warrant if there isn't."

"This is a murder investigation," Gale says. "An innocent man has died. Open the gate. Now."

A beat, then: "Yeah, sure."

The gate rolls open on small black tires, and Gale hits his fog lights. Then noses his SUV up and down the wide drive, marked with big red arrows for a one-way flow of traffic. There's a surprising number of vehicles here this late on a Saturday night.

Lights spill from the opened storage units, people move in and out, some taking away, others loading in. Like ghosts, Gale thinks.

Gale goes very slowly, knowing he'll be on top of the van before he sees it if he goes faster than a crawl.

Rounds a corner and sees the Econoline a few hundred feet ahead, on his right, and strong light coming from inside the unit.

Hulking Vern, cane-free now, sets what looks very much like a rifle case through the van's side door, Mindy not visible to Gale, perhaps still behind the wheel. The case is relatively short, Gale notes, for a carbine or an AR-style gun, or a cut-down combat shotgun.

Mendez already has her night-vision binoculars up, and Gale worries the darkened lenses will reflect the yellow caution lights illuminating the unit numbers on the walls.

"Steady with the glasses," he says.

"Got it."

Jeffs goes back inside his storage box and comes out with a small, thick pistol case in each big hand, puts them in the van one at a time, and closes the door.

Reaches high and pulls down the door by its rope, then leans down to close the padlock.

Before getting into the van, Jeffs looks through the fog at Gale's Explorer, then awkwardly climbs in, using a hand to hoist in his wounded leg.

A minute later Gale tracks them back onto the Garden Grove Freeway, westbound now.

The fog has lightened and the traffic is light and Mindy holds the Econoline steady in the third lane.

Gale holds three cars back and one lane over.

"Looked like cases for a short assault rifle and handguns," says Mendez.

"Maybe a cut-down shotgun."

"That's a vicious thing. Kept one under my bed until Jesse was born. Now I've got a locked 1911 Gold Cup he can't open."

"I've got one, too. Sweetest shooting handgun there is."

"Stop a tractor, too."

Mindy merges with the 405 south, retracing her route from the Bear Cave and, perhaps, home.

"Okay, Gale, are we going to pull them over and rattle their cage? We've got no warrant, no cause for a search, not even a broken brake light. No authority to open those cases."

"And no reason to spook them for nothing."

"I hate it when people get away with shit," says Mendez. "And you watch them get away with it. You just sit there like a dumbass with your hands tied."

In the periphery of his vision, Gale sees that Mendez is looking at him. Sees her sharp dark eyes catching the dashboard lights.

"Thanks for talking to Jesse," she says. "Best if he thinks I've got nothing to do with it. Tell him you're after Bishop Buendia, which is how you know about their lunch at El Jardin, and the drone and cell phones. He'll be suspicious of you, but maybe a little scared, too. He also might respect you."

"I'll scare him straight."

In his periphery again, Gale sees a slight smile on her hard, pretty face.

Ahead of them the white van lumbers past the turnoff for the Bear Cave and the Jeffs home.

"Well, well," says Mendez.

Gale follows.

Forty minutes later he's headed east/northeast on Ortega Highway, passing the entrance to Caspers Wilderness Park.

"Interesting," says Mendez. "Tarlow and the Killer Cat and Jeffs's Econoline, all right here just a few nights ago."

"I see the cat in my dreams," Gale says. "I catch him looking at me. Stalking and studying."

"What about Tarlow and Vern?"

"More the cat."

"Oh boy." They climb the steep, fogless mountains of Cleveland National Forest, the sky above them black and alive with stars.

Half an hour later Gale brakes through the Ortega's treacherous downslope turns, morning's first light climbing in the east ahead of them.

A sign comes at them in the headlights: LAKE ELSINORE 5 MILES.

The white Econoline pokes in and out of view on the curvy grade and, ten minutes later, Mindy slows and makes a right.

Gale passes the PACWEST MINING sign—a painting of snow-capped mountains and a lake set into a river-rock monument and lit from above.

Makes a U-turn.

"Kyle McNab of PacWest Mining had dinner with Tarlow and Kevin Elder at the Grove, the week before he was murdered," says Gale. "Velasquez the bartender said McNab was pissed."

"What's a biker outlaw like Jeffs have to do with PacWest Mining?" asks Mendez. "And what's he doing here at five-fifteen in the morning with a van full of guns?"

"Floating them down the iron river," says Gale. "Our enormous, invisible black market."

Gale makes the left at the PacWest sign, takes another quick look at the snowy mountains and the blue lake.

"I don't like this," says Mendez. "Vern Jeffs and his crazy-ass wife with a van full of guns, out in the middle of nowhere. Calling on a Tarlow Company subcontractor, who, last we heard, was pissed off about something at the Grove. We're out of jurisdiction here, so if something goes froggy, it's Riverside Sheriff's for backup, which of course they may not provide in a timely manner."

"It's just a knock and talk. We're here about McNab's dinner with Tarlow, and Jeffs came up in the net."

"No one will believe *that* at six in the morning."

"Trust me."

"I do but I still don't like it."

Gale parks on the shoulder, lets his SUV idle. A PacWest pickup truck dims its brights and swooshes past.

Then another.

Followed less than a minute later by a tractor trailer loaded with an immense drilling rig doing less than ten miles an hour up the grade, Gale's guess. The augur sways and rattles loudly. The Peterbilt engine groans.

"Daniela," says Gale. "We need to go in now."

"You're the boss, boss. Let's let the sun come up. I want to see what I'm doing. Sorry, just a little nervy about this."

Ten minutes later Gale pulls into a large gravel parking lot in front of a wooden, Swiss chalet–style building, brown with scalloped white trim. Red geraniums bloom in barrels and flower beds.

The Econoline and three PacWest pickup trucks are parked in front of the office. One of the trucks backs out as Gale and Mendez crunch across the lot.

In a meadow adjacent to the chalet office, Gale notes the battalion of excavators, backhoes, earth-diggers, loaders, boom trucks, and drill platforms, all surrounded by a ten-foot chain-link fence topped with razor wire.

The office porch light is on and the door is open.

32

The young woman behind the counter eyes the detectives skeptically. Brunette, a black suit. Her countertop nameplate says BELLA.

"Help you?"

Gale introduces himself and Mendez, who holds up her badge.

Bella squints at it. "Orange County."

"We're here to see Kyle McNab," says Gale.

"We don't actually open for another hour. Mr. McNab came in early but is in a conference right now. Have a seat if you'd like. Coffee there, at the end of the counter. Is this about Bennet Tarlow?"

"Very much so," says Gale. "Did you know him?"

"Not really, but he was here a few times. His father and mother have been here, too. And Hal Teller, the projects director."

Behind the counter is a glass wall etched with the PacWest logo—snowcapped mountains and a broad lake—through which Gale sees Vernon, Mindy, and a husky man seated around a table in a spacious, low-walled cubicle.

Jeffs laughs, a muted bray from beyond the glass. Then stands and brandishes his cane in one hand, like a very long-barreled pistol.

Mindy stands and raises an AR-15 to her shoulder and swings it like she's tracking a bird.

Gale studies the husky man, still seated. He's got a red leather moto jacket and a black T-shirt. He's smiling and handling a matte stainless-steel semiautomatic pistol. Gale recognizes Kyle McNab from the PacWest website. A black aluminum briefcase lies on the table. Gale sees the rifle and handgun cases resting on the carpet next to Mindy's harness boots.

Gale and Mendez pour coffee and sit in the lobby. The walls are cedar plank, hung with vintage skis, snowshoes, and ski posters. Gale knows from the PacWest Mining website that owner Kyle McNab is a Colorado native and an avid big-game hunter. Has a Boone and Crockett elk. His warrants check—which Gale ran the same day that McNab's name came up twice on Bennet Tarlow's home-office calendar—had come up clean. No criminal record.

Gale had found it interesting that Kyle McNab is a skilled hunter. Big game no less and obviously handy with a gun.

Now, based on Tarlow's and Jeffs's shared relationships with McNab, Gale adds McNab's hunting and gun skills to the strange brew of coincidences, connections, conspiracies, deceptions, and seductions that underlie the life and death of Bennet Tarlow.

Through the glass, Gale sees Mindy putting the AR back into its case.

The men shake hands, and Mindy hugs McNab.

Bella strides across the lobby, fashion boots on hardwood, followed by Jeffs, who stops when he sees the detectives, sets his cane.

"Not you losers," he says. "What did I do now?"

"We don't care what you did, Vern," says Gale. "You're a free man. We came here to see Mr. McNab."

"I didn't see you behind me in all that fog."

Mindy rounds big Vern, carrying the black briefcase, long-legged and skinny as an egret in the harness boots, followed by McNab.

"Damn you cops," she says. "Vern, we have a police harassment lawsuit on our plate now."

McNab looks wider and older than in his pictures, and unimpressed.

"What do you want?" he asks Gale.

"We want to talk about Bennet Tarlow. But since we saw you back there buying and selling guns, maybe you should start with that."

"I'm a federally licensed dealer," says Mindy. "I do the background checks, make 'em wait the ten days, deliver the goods, and collect the money. ATF loves me. Legal and fun!"

Which explains why none of Vernon Jeffs's guns made the ATF radar, thinks Gale. They're *hers*.

"Perfectly legal," says McNab. "Unless the guns are stolen, the numbers filed or modified. Mindy can show you the ATF forms if you want. I just bought a used AR-15 and four handguns, great condition. I hunt. I collect. This is not a straw purchase that's going to end up in Mexico. Occasionally I sell, which is not a crime. I use the same ATF forms every gun store does."

"But no twenty-two-caliber semiautos," says Mindy. "Just in case you're curious."

"Open the briefcase," says Gale.

"You'll need a warrant," says Mindy.

"Open the damned case, honey," says Jeffs. "We got nothing to hide."

She lifts the case to a lobby coffee table, clicks open the spring-driven latches, and raises the lid.

Gale sees the bundles of cash.

Mindy closes the case and heads for the door.

"All ours and all legal," says Jeffs, pointing his cane at Gale. "See you around, shit birds."

Mindy turns and flips off the detectives.

"It's all in my book," she says, headed for the exit.

"I've only got a few minutes," says McNab. "I'm sorry what happened to Bennet Tarlow. But I'm still mad at him for taking us off the project. Come on back. I'll explain."

McNab leads Gale and Mendez past the warren of low-walled cubicles where the gun buy had taken place. The overhead lighting is fluorescent and nervy.

Through a window Gale watches the white Econoline lumber out of the lot.

And sees the first employees climbing out of a luxury tour bus with the PacWest Mining logo across the side.

Kyle McNab's office is upstairs, with expansive views over the city of Lake Elsinore.

Kyle hangs his moto jacket on a hatstand and sits behind a large desk made of a single marble slab. Gale notes the white and silver marbling in the black rock, as the morning sun hits it through a window.

"Why are you here? For Jeffs or for me?"

"Jeffs is a suspect," says Mendez. "Our DA declined to charge him, so he walked. I'm sure he filled you in on all that."

"He sure did."

"He spun us a murder-for-hire story about some guys he never really saw," says Gale. "Steve and Curtis, propositioning him in a white Lincoln Navigator with a blackout screen between them."

"Sounds weak," says McNab.

"Vern put some good spin on it though," says Gale.

"He's good at that. I've only known him a few weeks."

"How did you meet?"

"At Muldoon's in Newport. Tarlow introduced us. We hit it off—Vern and me—gun people, you know?"

An odd trio in a swank Newport Beach restaurant, Gale thinks.

"What did Tarlow introduce Vern Jeffs *as*?" asks Mendez.

"Well, a bartender, I guess," says McNab. "We drank a bit. Stayed late. Vern and I have both fished and hunted Saint Bernard Parish in Louisiana. Vern had some funny stories about growing dope up in the mountains in Humboldt. Bennet—he's a bird photographer, you know—somehow got Vern going on this big owl Vern said he'd seen up in Humboldt, biggest owl on the whole continent, the great gray owl, I think it's called. Vern said the biggest one he'd ever seen was just a week ago, out at the Wildcoast site. Bennet didn't believe him. Said Wildcoast is four hundred miles out of its range. Said it was a great horned owl. Vern bet Tarlow a thousand dollars it was a great gray, out of its range or not. More drinks. More Vern Jeffs tales."

Gale thinks of the blood-encrusted Canon EOS mirrorless camera near Tarlow's kill site. A birder's camera to be sure.

Connecting it with Jeffs puts it in a much different light. His heart thumps and he gets that adrenaline-clear vision he got in Sangin when he had a kill in his scope.

"When was this?" asks Gale. "Be exact, if you can. It's important."

"Late September."

McNab looks at his watch, which Gale sees is a big Rolex with lots of gold.

"Did you know him well, Bennet?" asks Mendez.

Kyle McNab shakes his head resignedly. "Not well. But it's terrible. Tarlow was a good guy. A little eccentric, but whip-smart and bighearted. In a nutshell, the Tarlow Company picked us to do some exploratory excavation at the Wildcoast site. Months ago. They wanted a percolation test for the development, to see if they had to go with sewers, or build the whole thing on septic."

"Why?"

"Cost. He said they were rethinking Wildcoast. Big hurdles with the County of Orange and the Cities of Laguna Beach and San Juan Capistrano. We had a handshake deal with the Tarlow Company, but Bennet unshook my hand. We had estimated the perc testing on a five-square-mile parcel would take six months and run about six million dollars. So, PacWest was very disappointed. No discussion, no negotiation, just out of the blue. Bennet pulled our plug. The not-so-funny thing is that I liked him and he liked me. I felt that he dropped my company under pressure. From who I can't say. No idea."

"And gave Wildcoast to Empire Excavators," says Gale.

"Which finally broke ground on it just last week. Or so my soldiers tell me."

"They've done a lot more than break ground," says Gale.

"How deep are they?"

"Twenty, thirty feet. How deep until they hit groundwater?"

"In decomposed granite, fifty feet down," says McNab. "If there is groundwater. But if they hit bedrock, then no septic, because the effluent can't percolate down into the aquifer. So you add scores of millions of dollars to build a sewer system to accommodate a city of fifty thousand people. Raises the price of the homes, dramatically."

"Bennet wanted to build affordable, Tarlow-subsidized homes for a full quarter of the Wildcoast population," says Gale.

"That's why sewer is a terrible idea," says McNab. "Goodbye, affordable. Maybe even goodbye, Wildcoast, if you're Bennet's asshole father, Tarlow II. He wanted to put a *fulfillment hub* on that land. Warehouse space in the hundreds of millions of square feet. Sky-high leases. Smart development, high profit."

"So sewer costs would be a nonissue, in a metropolis of warehouses," says Gale. "There wouldn't be anyone living there. Cheap septic would do it."

Gale considers something that's been bugging him since he first talked to the Empire Excavators guy digging the test pit.

"What if it's not a perc test?" asks Gale. "What if they're looking for something else?"

"Like what?"

"Gold? Crystals? What else is down there?"

McNab laughs. "They wish. But there's nothing but trace gold in those mountains. So far as crystals, what kind? There's worthless quartz to gem-quality tourmaline—pink to deep green—beautiful stuff. My wife's got some."

"Silver?" asks Mendez. "Oil?"

"Standard and Texaco perforated that whole area after World War II," McNab says. "But nothing doing. The oil was north of there, from Huntington Beach up into LA County. Deputies, I have a seven o'clock."

"Thank you for your time," says Gale, rising.

"I hope you catch this guy."

"Do you remember the night Tarlow died?" asks Mendez.

"Of course I do," says McNab. "NLDS, Padres and Dodgers. Jennifer and I saw it at Petco Park in San Diego. She'd tell you the same thing, if that's what you're getting at. Because, yeah, Bennet Tarlow dangled a lot of money at me, then took it away. Cost us millions, if you want to look at it that way. But I sure wouldn't kill him."

"We have to follow up on this kind of thing," says Mendez. "Just procedure."

"Jennifer runs accounting here," says McNab. "Gets in at nine, extension fourteen. Ohtani went three for four, but it wasn't enough. Ask Jen. Pads won it, three-two."

Gale and Mendez are halfway to the Explorer when Gale's phone rings.

Amanda Cho:

"I'm returning your calls. Sorry to be not available."

"Have you talked to Jeffs?"

"I saw him at Bamboo but he didn't see me. I fear him. I'm with relatives now, in Chinatown."

"Be alert. Pay attention. Stay around people."

"I'm used to hiding," she says, and hangs up.

33

Hal Teller wears a chocolate brown suit tailored in the loose British mode, a white spread-collar shirt, and a shimmering lavender necktie.

Gale considers Teller's short gray hair brushed back from a dome of a forehead, his light blue eyes, a face lined and tanned from ocean fishing, some of those hours documented by colorful mounts on his office walls.

They're on the seventh floor of the Tarlow Company in Newport Center, windows south and west for views of the Pacific Ocean, which glimmers silver in the morning light.

Gale has his notebook on a crossed knee, Daniela Mendez a cup of coffee.

"So yes," says Teller, "Tarlow Company brought me on as an engineer when I was young. I mentored Tarlows II and III on the building arts as well as which projects to take and which to leave. Twenty years later I was the showrunner: residential, commercial, industrial. Now, at eighty, I'm captaining the ship with Bennet II.

When I heard about Benny, I sat down in this chair and cried. Four hours later I was still here."

A respectful silence from Gale and Mendez.

"I understand you were opposed to Wildcoast from the start," says Gale.

"Opposed? No. But I was aware of the long-term financial realities and said so."

"You were pulling for warehouses, weren't you?" asks Mendez. "An enormous fulfillment center not far from Caspers Wilderness Park."

"Still am. The county, the state, the country needs it. More goods on more doorsteps. Warehousing and distribution from a perfect location—proximity to the big ports for the trucks, and a freeway system that ties the whole nation together. And, because we own the land, we own the warehouses. Benny hated that idea. But, to be honest, I never hated Wildcoast. I just see a better use of our time and capital."

"Where was Bennet's father on all this?"

"Torn, I'd say. But you should ask him yourselves."

"Is the Tarlow Company done with Wildcoast?" asks Gale.

Hal Teller's blue gaze goes from Gale to Mendez, then he sits back.

"Far from. With Bennet's sudden death, we're taking a strategic pause, to consider. In the last few months we've seen rising antagonism toward Wildcoast. From the cities of San Juan Capistrano and Laguna Beach. The governor. The Juaneño Indians. The Orange County Board of Supervisors, with the exception of Kevin Elder's Seventh District, which is bullish on a dream utopia adjacent to county land. Which was ceded by Tarlow Company to the county in 1953 for a wilderness park. In return for Newport Coast development rights."

"Quite a trade for the Tarlow Company," says Gale.

Teller nods.

"Especially considering that you bought that land out from under the Acjacheme natives for pennies on the dollar."

"Pennies on the millions of dollars," says Teller. "I realize, Mr. Gale, you are a member of that nation. The land grab was shameful, but legal. And let's not forget that the Spanish taught farming and ranching and building skills to the heathens. Brought them muskets for hunting. And Spanish soldiers for husbands. Sent them away better than they found them is one way to look at it."

"And trimmed the Natives down from three thousand, nine hundred to eight hundred and sixty-one," says Gale.

"Shameful. Again. Yes."

Teller purses his lips and looks down at his immense, curving, glass-top desk.

Trying for penance, thinks Gale.

Penance 101.

"Do you have a suspect in Benny's murder?" Teller asks.

"We had a suspect that our DA declined to charge. Vernon Jeffs."

"What was Benny doing way out there in Caspers?"

"We believe he was in the company of Jeffs," says Mendez.

"Doing what?"

"Possibly to photograph a giant owl not even found in Southern California. We don't know," says Gale.

"Do you know him, Jeffs?" asks Mendez.

"Kind of. Benny introduced us at the Bear Cave biker joint one evening. A dive, and I only went because Benny asked me. This was a couple of weeks ago. Jeffs was tending bar. As you know, he's big, loud, and crude. Benny liked larger-than-life characters. Enjoyed their antics, their stories I guess. Benny told me they hit it off over birds. Benny was an insane birder, if you didn't know. A great photographer, too. Of birds, all over the world."

"Hard to think of Jeffs as a birder," says Mendez. "Doesn't fit with a motorcycle outlaw."

"Not at all," says Teller. "They were talking about some rare owl that Jeffs saw out at Caspers when he was with his wife. Said it's enormous, and way out of range. Hunts by night, which is when Jeffs allegedly saw it. Benny wanted to photograph it. You know all about his bird travels and photography, I'm sure."

A beat.

"It might have been all bullshit from Jeffs," says Teller. "That seemed to be what he's made of. He tried to tell me the secret to catching ocean fish is Jack in the Box hot sauce, directly applied to the fly or lure. Can't be Taco Bell or McDonald's. Says he guided in Louisiana, but I doubt that. Can't picture a guy that big in a flats boat."

Gale remembers this hot sauce theory from his days just back from Sangin, when he would relive his fishing memories on YouTube from his bed at the Naval Hospital Camp Pendleton, wondering if he would fish again, wondering if he wanted to remain alive.

"It looks like you've fished all over the world," says Mendez.

Teller surveys his radiant mounts, points to a large fish jumping through acrylic spray. The fish is iridescent yellow with green and blue splatters as if thrown on with a paintbrush. "That's a dorado down in Baja," he says. "East Cape. Costa Rica, Brazil, Christmas Island, Fiji, Mauritius, Australia, South Africa, all over."

"How come you don't have any pictures of yourself with a fish?" asks Mendez.

"The fish are prettier than me."

"A modest man."

"I'm rarely accused of that."

Gale remembers a dorado he caught in Baja. The thing is, they shimmered brilliantly when alive, their colors flashing and traveling up and down their bodies, but if you killed one for the grill that night it went dull and one-dimensional in seconds.

Light is life, he thinks.

He wrestles his mind back from the Naval Hospital, certainly among the darkest hours of his life.

Light is life.

"Mr. Teller," he says, "I was out at the Wildcoast site just a few days ago, and there's quite a bit of excavating and drilling going on. If Wildcoast is under a strategic pause, as you say, why?"

"We've already paid our subs for the first phase," says Teller. "The new people are just finishing it out. And if we decide to go ahead with Wildcoast, we'll need the perc tests after all."

"Are you looking for something besides groundwater?" asks Gale.

"Such as?"

"Gold?" asks Mendez.

A humored smile. "Not much in those mountains."

"Crystals?" asks Gale.

"Quartz, for sure, which is essentially worthless. Tourmaline, maybe. There's probably rhyolite in there. No, we'll be happy when we hit fifty feet and either hit the aquifer or not. See what we're up against."

A pause.

Gale again remembers Geronima Mills's words about the Acjacheme creation myth—"*. . . an ocean with rooms of gigantic crystals beneath the earth . . . a resting place for spirits on their way to the afterlife.*"

Wonders what if Hal Teller has heard of it.

Wonders if Hal Teller wants to find a resting place on his way to the afterlife.

"Why did you replace PacWest with Empire Excavators?" asks Mendez.

"Proprietary," says Teller. "But things in this world always come to dollars and cents."

"Does the future of the Tarlow Company change, with the death of Bennet?" asks Gale. "Big picture?"

"Certainly."

"For better or worse?" asks Mendez, leaning forward to set her coffee mug on Teller's crystal-clear desktop.

"No one knows," he says. "Different. TC is one of the great Western developers, and for the last twenty years it's been Benny's company. His vision. Who can see the future? I can't."

"What makes you a good businessman?" asks Mendez.

A shrug and a somber assessment of her.

"I'll tell you a story," says Teller. "After a few years of working for the Tarlows, I realized that their company was not created to make homes. It was created to make money. When I graduated from high school, my father told me that's what *all* businesses were for. I thought it was cynical and crass until old Tarlow told me the same thing. The founder, that is—Bennet Evans Tarlow. He used the exact same words. Bennet III and I had been arguing that idea for decades."

A beat then, as Teller gazes down at his clear glass desktop. "I miss Benny."

34

Late that night, after the floodlights have been turned off and the equipment operators have padlocked the gates and left, Gale, Mendez, and Geronima Mills climb the chain-link fence surrounding the alleged perc test pit on the building site of the proposed city of Wildcoast.

The cranes loom against the sky in the moonlight, and the drilling rigs and earthmovers and backhoes cast faint shadows.

They come to the mouth of the pit.

"Look at this monster," says Mills.

Gale sees that the pit has grown to three, maybe four times the circumference it was just a few days ago.

The grading around it is now level and cleared of boulders.

And a steel-stepped stairway disappears into the cavernous dark, its railings lined with day-glow green safety tape that reflects the beam from Gale's flashlight.

From the top of the steps, he trains his light down, sees no water as before, just the steel stairway, anchored to darkness.

Mendez runs her flashlight beam along the far wall but it's far enough away that Gale can't make out much more than blurred, dark sandstone.

"I'll stay here in case Tarlow security shows up," says Geronima. "If they do, I'll holler."

The stairway is too steep to take into the dark, so Gale slides his flashlight into his belt, takes the railings in his hands and backs down.

Mendez follows.

Metal scrapes on stone as the stairway wobbles with their descent.

Gale sets his feet patiently.

"You have to catch me if I fall," Mendez calls down to him.

"Gotcha, Daniela."

Every four steps down, Gale feels the temperature drop. He counts the steps as he used to count steps on patrol in Sangin.

"Hold up, Mendez!"

"I'm holding up."

"I mean stop."

"I'm stopped, I'm stopped."

Gale works his flashlight free and feels his vertigo as he turns, holding on to the railing with one hand.

The floor looks to be another fifty feet down. The walls shine in his beam, but he neither sees nor hears dripping water. There's a dank, metallic smell—something between mold and blood.

Gale holds his light beam on a cavern, lined with enormous crystals.

The largest crystals he's ever seen, or heard of.

Some of them fifty feet high. Some calved away like icebergs to lie on the cavern floor.

Gale circles his flashlight, in disbelieving awe.

Eighty enormous crystals, he guesses. A hundred?

They're silver-white, softly luminescent in his flashlight beam.

Some are as big around as telephone poles, he sees, with tops tapered into neat points and bottoms thickly rooted into the beach-sand-colored cavern floor.

"What are they?" asks Mendez.

"I've never heard of crystals this big."

"They shimmer. Who would know?"

"A geologist or hydrologist, maybe."

Hal Teller or Kyle McNab, he thinks. Or the digger with the shovel, with his cracks about gold and big crystals worth a lot of money?

"I'm amazed," says Mendez. "And I don't amaze easily."

The cavern floor is wet but firm under Gale's boots. In the flashlight beam it looks like beach sand. He estimates they're two hundred feet down. The darkness is complete and tangible.

They circle the cavern slowly, Gale in the lead, Mendez with her phone light, both reaching out to touch the crystal trunks. This close, in Gale's flashlight beam, the crystals glow faintly with white particles, like dust motes.

Beam aimed down, Gale sees an angled white protrusion and, kneeling, picks it up. It looks like a bone shard, small and sharp.

Rakes his fingers through the pale mud, unearthing another, and, just a few inches away, another.

"I'm finding bones," says Mendez.

"Me, too."

"Bachstein the coroner knows his bones," she says.

Gale rises, slips a handful of shards into his pants pocket.

They photograph the cavern walls with their phones, the flashes bright and sudden in the deep dark.

"Enough amazement for me," says Mendez. "Kind of claustrophobic down here. I'm heading up."

"I'll be there."

Gale uses his pocketknife to pry a miniature crystal from its larger sponsor, then another.

Puts those with the bone shards, then pushes his flashlight into a rear pocket and, heart pounding, follows Mendez up through the black.

Aboveground now, the night seems almost bright compared with the blackness below.

Gale gets waters from the Explorer, hands one to Mendez and one to Geronima, then guzzles his.

Mendez consults her phone, stepping away.

"I need to go," she says.

"Do you need help?" asks Gale.

"Everything's fine. Everything is going to be fine."

Mendez boards her SUV and heads out, throwing road dirt.

"A cavern of crystals fifty feet high," Gale tells Geronima. "They glow. Bones in the sand, possibly human. I've never seen anything like it."

"I didn't bring this flashlight just to look at excavators and backhoes," says Geronima.

Gale considers the risks and rewards.

"Are you prone to panic?" he asks.

"I am not."

"You'll need two hands," he says. "Keep the light in your pocket until we hit the floor. It's a couple of hundred feet down and the steps are steep. Face the stairway, back down. It's dark and damned scary."

"I can do it. Lead the way."

A few stairs down, Gale stops and watches Geronima lower herself, both hands on the railing as she descends.

Gale stands behind her as Geronima unlocks her front door and orders her yapping dog to shut up.

"Don't mind Hulk," she says. "He's all bark."

She lives in one of the small adobes on the east side of the mission that were built in the late 1800s. It's on Acjacheme Court, huddled between 1920s cottages and bungalows.

Gale follows her into a small living room with a hardwood floor, adobe brick walls, and oak ceiling beams. Plein air landscapes, shelves of books, a framed Robbie Robertson poster, bold red-and-black Navajo print drapes. A red fabric couch and a steamer trunk for a table.

She gestures to the couch and Gale sits at one end. Hulk—a small terrier mix—launches onto his lap with a plush white shark in his mouth.

Geronima sets a whiskey glass on the steamer trunk near Gale and one for herself. Pours two fingers each and leaves the bottle midway between them, then sits opposite him on the couch.

"Oh, boy," he says.

"How do I interpret that?"

Gale catches her scent mixed with bourbon as she passes. As soon as she's seated, Hulk bolts onto her lap, with his shark.

"I say it when I'm presented with a choice that has an upside and a downside," he says. "And I'm not sure how I'll choose."

"The bourbon."

"Yes. Anyway, this is a nice place."

"Thank you. I love it. Rent's high, but worth it. My God, Lew—those crystals down there are huge. I'm still trying to process what my eyes saw."

"Fifty, maybe sixty feet," he says, hearing himself exaggerate like the fisherman he used to be. "Fifty, anyway."

"The billion-dollar question—what are they?"

"No clue."

Gale stands and fishes the bone shards and crystals from his pocket; leans across the couch and sets them on the steamer trunk near her glass.

"I got a few, too," says Geronima. "Human?"

"My lab can tell."

"The rounded ones look like the edge of a vertebrae," she says. "Human size."

"I thought that, too, or the tail end of a big dolphin or a young whale."

Geronima shoos Hulk off her lap and picks from Gale's collection a short, tubular bone about the diameter of a human phalange or a turkey leg. Smells it.

"This could be one of our distant relatives," says Geronima.

"The ancient Acjacheme cremated their dead," says Gale.

"Maybe the char got polished off by the sand and the centuries."

"The cavern reminded me of the legend," Gale says. "The room where the spirits waited."

She sets down the hollow shard and smiles at Gale. "I have goose bumps all up and down my back right now, Lew."

"Me, too."

"What if the legends weren't legends at all," she says. "And the bones were purposely put there. The ancients talked about the crystal room because they'd *seen* it."

"A cavern of light in an underground sea," he says, hearing Luis Verdad's words in his head.

They lean in, touch glasses, and drink.

Geronima dims the lights with a remote, and they sit in silence, each lost to the immense crystal cavern, the bones.

Gales catches her studying him from behind a half wall of thick black hair.

Geronima orders Alexa to play Robbie Robertson's *Music for The Native Americans*.

Gale loves this music. Listened to it incessantly as he languished in the Naval Hospital Camp Pendleton, his manhood and his desire to live both undecided.

Now his worse angels try to take him back to that vast citadel of pain and mutilation, of awful sights and sounds, but Gale wills himself back from it, focusing on Geronima Mills and Hulk in order to stay in the here and now.

"Ghost Dance" comes on.

They listen to the song in silence, sipping the bourbon. Then "Skinwalker."

Gale feels as if the music is pulling him into some faintly luminous place, somewhere much like the crystal cavern.

Music and silence now, except for Hulk tearing apart the shark.

"My heart wants to fly back to where we just were," says Geronima.

She gets her phone off the trunk and swipes through the pictures.

Gale watches the light frame her downturned face. Her black hair shines. She hauls a handful of it over her shoulder, eyes still on the screen, then swipes to the next picture.

"Can I be blunt?" she says. "I get blunt when something interests me."

"Blunt away."

"Are you single?"

"Divorced, no one steady since."

She's still not looking at him. "Do you like it that way?"

"The divorce was the right thing. My bad, though. Well, our bad, really."

She sets down her phone and looks at him now, eyes reflecting light from the kitchen. "Are you happy?"

Gale considers. "Enough."

"How do you know what enough happiness is?"

"I wonder about it," he says. "Sometimes I feel good, but sometimes bad. Same day, sometimes the same hour. Even though nothing has changed. Does that make sense?"

"Totally," says Geronima. "My Indian half thinks the right to the pursuit of happiness is a strange right. Strange as in, get out of my way so I can be happy—I'll need your land, your daughters, your things. My non-Indian half says I should be happy enough to just survive."

"That's what I meant about feeling good. Just being here, surviving is enough."

She pours them each another drink, picks her glass off the trunk, and takes a sip.

Gale drinks.

"Until it isn't," Gale says. "Just surviving, I mean. And I doubt it's all worth it."

She studies him. "That sounds serious."

"I'm not impulsive enough to do anything final."

"You seem about impulsive as a tortoise, Lew," says Geronima. "I like that."

"Thank you. I'm not good playing the room for laughs."

"I've had plenty enough entertainers," she says. "You and your ex get along?"

"Pretty distant," Gale says. "When it was over, it was over. We talk now and then."

"And what part of it was your bad?"

Gale feels the old black thoughts coiling around inside.

The fragments, and the fragments of fragments.

Always ready for another round.

"I brought back some wounds from the war, post-trauma stress for sure. Killed a man who turned out to be a noncombatant. Took him out thinking I was God himself. Other stuff. Lots of painkillers and mood stabilizers. Too much of this," he says, tilting his glass. "Things just got darker and darker."

"Until?"

"A breakdown. Almost pulled the plug. Had all the stuff ready. But I talked to a great doctor at Pendleton instead. He was a sniper in Vietnam. Let him keep me a month in the ding wing. Stopped the pills cold turkey. Back home I cut the drinking way back. Started putting one foot in front of the other."

Geronima considers this, twirling her whiskey glass gently. "I remember that phrase from the *Times* profile on you—'one foot in front of the other.' You look different now than in that picture."

"I'd just gotten back when that picture was taken. Wouldn't have let them run it, if I'd known they were going to."

"Dress blues and a thousand-yard stare and your hair long and messed up," says Geronima. "Chills up my spine, warrior-soldier. Am I making you nervous?"

"I think you're bright and beautiful," he says. "So, yes. Do I make you nervous?"

"Sure, Lew, but more just happy you're still here. In this world and in my house. And that we got to see the crystal cathedral in an ocean of light. Souls in transit, you and me. I'd really like it if you said my full name. For the first time."

"Geronima Mills."

She looks at him in the dim light with a hopeful expression.

A long silence now, Gale staring through a serape-print curtain. A distant mission-bell streetlight spreads a cone of light on the empty street.

"I've lived my whole life in this town," he says. "My ancestors helped build the mission."

"Mine, too," says Geronima. "They must have known each other, two and a half centuries ago. Maybe that's why you seem so familiar to me. Like I've known you for a long time. I recognize you."

"Those are nice words. I think I recognize you, too, Geronima Mills."

Another silence.

"I don't take this lightly," she says. "And I invite you to share my bed tonight."

"Oh boy."

"I expected that!"

Gale again faces the stark future that the explosion gave him. The quick, sharp moment that reshaped him forever.

"I can't do that," he says. "Some of me didn't make it back."

"From the war," she says.

"The war."

"I'm so sorry, Lew."

Gale watches a matte gray pickup truck glide by on Acjacheme Court, an electric one, nearly silent. Rivian, he thinks, very cool.

Hulk, perched on a chairback, watches through a window but doesn't bark. Looks back at Gale like he can't figure why this truck doesn't make noise.

"I'm so very sorry," she says.

Gale sips the bourbon. "Don't be. It's contagious. I don't feel bad or empty, Geronima. I believe that my work is valuable. My life, too—and Mom and Frank and even Dad."

"Oh, Lew, you are more than valuable. *In*valuable. Incalculable. Priceless. I wore my shells and bone comb for you, to make you love me."

To Gale, the long silence is a roar.

"I still can't honor that bed of yours like a man should."

"I want you there, anyway."

"Thank you very much, but no. You made my day. A lot more than my day. It's hard to explain. What you said was important to me."

"I meant it. Every word."

"I should go."

"Need an Uber?"

"I'll walk. I'm down off Rios, so not far."

"Nightcap first?"

"Sure."

35

Gale walks toward home. The streetlights are soft but the stars are bright in the partial moonlight. He's solidly drunk and he knows it, the bourbon fueling his confidence and his stride, the old groin and upper leg scars taut and itchy. It took him almost a year to walk without pain so now there's some pleasure in this locomotion, prickly surgical scars or not.

He walks fast, trying to get far away from Geronima Mills and her innocent but humiliating proposition, her crushing beauty, his impossible desire. He's made that soul-wrenching confession before—to Marilyn—but tonight, for some reason, it's worse.

Tonight, he felt like he was saying hello to a friend he'd made a thousand years before he was even born.

A sister.

A mate.

He cuts across La Calera to carless Acjachema Street, walks past the up-lighted ruins of the Great Stone Church destroyed in the 1812 earthquake during Mass—leaving forty of his ancestors dead and now buried just a few hundred feet from here.

He follows the broad sidewalk of Old Mission Road.

Gale has always loved this little city in the early morning, loved the high mission walls with the bright violet bougainvillea spilling over the top, the smell of the gardens from within, especially at night like now, no tourists and most of the townspeople tucked in and sleeping, an occasional coyote trotting small-footed down the middle of Camino Capistrano with no apparent care in the world.

But what Gale sees now stops him in his tracks.

Halfway across Old Mission Road, a big mountain lion lopes along with a coyote dangling limply from his mouth.

The cat gives Gale a bored inspection without breaking stride, cheeks bright red, eyes tan in the streetlight, the coyote's thin legs and bushy tail flopping along on the asphalt.

Gale crouches and sidles to the curb, his vision locked on the big lion as he continues down Old Mission, his long, black-tipped tail flicking left then right, testes shifting, shoulder muscles bunched and swaying beneath his tawny fur.

Spooked, the cat heads away from the mission, galloping onto Arguello Way and disappearing into an abundant flower garden that separates two ancient adobes, the tall hollyhocks parting, then shivering, then not.

A moment later, Gale sees the tan smudge of the lion emerge from the garden and disappear down the alley that intersects Trabuco Creek. Which, he knows, will lead the cat out of the town and into the rough hills, dense with oak and toyon.

His heart still thumping with the adrenaline, Gale listens for cars behind him but sees only a gray pickup parked curbside and apparently unoccupied.

He starts across Ramos in the near-silence of early morning, headed home. Wonders if it was the bourbon that saw that cat, but knows he was real just like El Diablo was real, and Luis Verdad and Magdalena.

Suddenly, bright light flares and tires squeal on asphalt behind him and Gale looks back over his shoulder and breaks into a run, the gray pickup coming at him fast.

He scrambles onto the sidewalk, the nearly silent truck missing him by inches. Hurdles a four-foot wall, hits the grass, and rolls, banging face-first into a massive oak tree.

Stands and finds his balance, draws his gun. The gray truck is already out of sight, its electric engine offering no noise to follow.

Gale clambers back over the wall and charges up the sidewalk.

The truck is so quiet that Gale has to guess where the damned thing went. His gut tells him it's the same gray Rivian he'd seen from Geronima's darkened living room.

Which means that whoever's in the truck followed him here from Geronima's place.

Which means they could be heading there right now, figuring on Gale's return.

By the time he makes it to Acjacheme Court, Gale is breathing hard and his war scars are burning and he's tasting blood, but he's relieved that the Rivian is nowhere to be seen.

He hunkers in a hedge of white oleander. Holsters his gun, then rests his hands on his knees, breathing in and breathing out, eyes on Geronima's house.

He looks out through the hedge, also relieved to see no lights on and knowing that high-strung Hulk will go ballistic if he hears anything unordinary out here.

Calls in an APB for a gray pickup truck, a Rivian, California plates, last seen on Ramos Street in San Juan Capistrano, *fucker tried to kill me.*

Uses his phone light to inspect the rear undercarriage of his Explorer; removes the magnetized Vigilant tracker, its red indicator light blipping, clamped to the steel chassis. Careful not to deactivate it, he slides it into his coat pocket.

Gale feels tricked and stupid and angry with himself.

Back in the driver's seat he sets his gun in one cupholder and the tracker in the other. Looks out at the Mills residence in the first, salt-and-pepper light of morning.

Text message to Mendez:

> They tried to kill me here in San Juan a few minutes ago. A Rivian pickup truck, quiet and fast. I jumped a wall and off it went. Your APB alerts are probably going off by now, so know I'm alive and well.

Daniela calls immediately.

"You see the driver?"

"Just reflection."

"Jeffs?"

"Only a guess."

"Hired by Steve and Curtis again?"

"Jeffs doesn't profit from me dead any other way that I can see."

"You stay up late drinking with Geronima?"

"Moderately."

"Did you make it home?"

"I'm outside Geronima's house. Found a tracker on my Explorer, so he saw I was here. I'm thinking he might circle back for another shot."

"I'm on my way."

"No. I'm getting her out of here now. The adrenaline and bourbon have worn off and I'm clear in the head. Got my trusty Colt, nine in the magazine, one in the chamber."

"Squeeze, don't pull."

"Yes, ma'am."

"I worry about you."

"I'll be fine."

He knocks on Geronima's front door, Hulk shrieking inside.

Through the door's side window, Gale sees a light come on and the dog stops barking.

Geronima, Hulk in her arms, opens the door.

"They tried to kill me at the mission. You're not safe here and neither am I. I'll tell you about it on the road. We need to go."

"You've got blood on your face and clothes."

"Just got skinned up a little. Get dressed, get ready, and we'll go."

"Hulk, too?"

"Bring the dog."

"Bring him where?"

"I've got an idea."

A moment later they're on their way to the Hilton Garden Inn in Dana Point.

Gale checks in using one of his Vice squad undercover IDs and a Navy Federal Credit Union credit card bearing the name Luis Verdad.

36

Two hours of restless sleep later, Daniela Mendez is following Jesse's old but spiffy-clean silver Corolla from a safe distance, her TeenShield app stuck inside his phone like a virus, secretly tracking him from home, through Tustin, then into Barrio Dogtown in Santa Ana.

Jesse's first stop is the little stucco house on Edgar Place, where he went inside with Lulu and his gaming duffel and a case of Modelo and didn't come out for an hour.

Daniela pulls up well short of the house, turns off the engine, and waits. Sees the candy apple red Chevelle lowrider, the magnolia tree surrounded by fallen blossoms, the brown lawns, the graffiti on the walls and curbs.

Jesse gets out, dressed in his new cholo finest: white singlet, black Dickies work shorts, knee-high white socks, and black high-top Converse All Stars. She'd found it all on the floor of his cluttered closet, still in the Walmart bags and boxes, no real attempt to hide them.

Worst of all, notes Daniela—Jesse has shaved his beautiful hair sometime after she kissed him good night and the time his alarm woke her up just over an hour ago. He must have been quiet about that, sneaking the electric shaver she got him for his fifteenth birthday out to their little garage so as not to wake her.

Now, skinny and tall with his bald, dark-whiskered head, Jesse looks like a cartoon character in cholo clothes, dressed up for a show on TV.

How can he not see this?

How can he cut off all that beautiful, black, wavy hair?

How can he try to show off those attempted muscles in his cute, spindly arms?

Although, to be honest, they are growing some, the muscles. Also in the back of his closet: Muscle Milk protein drinks guaranteed to pump him up.

Lulu's got on lavender short shorts and a tight T-shirt the same brown as her skin and a white straw fedora with pink Day of the Dead skulls painted on. She leads the way to the front door, which opens well before they get there.

Through her binoculars Daniela recognizes fat Flaco Benitez from Bowl Me Over, smiling at them.

Less than five minutes later, the three of them come back out, Flaco carrying the boxed Raptor TX-395 camera drone, smiling again and chattering away.

He puts the drone in the trunk, then gets into the car, his weight rocking it as he drops into the passenger seat. Lulu sits in back.

Then down Civic Center Drive toward the Sheriff's Department, just a short drive from Flaco's place.

Daniela watches from three cars back as Jesse passes the Corner Market on Raitt Street, where Cesar Chavez and Ted Kennedy spoke about civil rights and labor.

Then Jesse swings into the El Salvador Park parking lot and they get out. Daniela remembers Father Malone telling her first-grade class about the famous gang truce that took place at El Salvador Park in the early nineties. She was six. Tall, handsome young Tim Malone—active in reaching out to gang-culture youth—said this truce was made with the help of God in heaven. Tim had helped bring some of the combatants together to hash out the truce.

Daniela thinks of Father Tim—so idealistic and full of saintly spirit back then—now unwilling to even make eye contact with their own son.

Which would be the first he's looked into his son's eyes since Jesse was seven days old.

God, she loves them.

Swallows so hard it hurts.

She finds a good place along the street, gets out her binoculars. Glasses Jesse leaning over his car trunk for the drone and, as he does this, Flaco rubs Lulu's butt. She swats his hand and hops flirtatiously away.

Two more cars arrive and park on either side of the Corolla. A Chevy Malibu and an old Dodge Magnum. Three young men and a hefty chola get out and head straight for their homies, all fist bumps and signs, no smiles except Flaco and Jesse, just tough salutes before getting down to serious business here, whatever that might be.

They set off across the lot for the grassy slopes of the park, the chola carrying a plastic Vons grocery bag that looks heavy. Cell phones, Daniela reasons, based on her El Jardin restaurant stakeout.

Which of course makes her wonder if Bishop Buendia is going to show, or if he's too busy rescuing the troubled boys of Camp Refuge.

And lo, she thinks, as if on cue, here comes Buendia's '55 aqua-on-white Bel Air, lowered and gleaming, the chrome moons bright as mirrors, fuzzy fucking dice dangling from the rearview. To Daniela it's funny but gorgeous. She's always known that whatever it is in Mexican-American blood that so adores old American cars altered to scrape the asphalt, grumble and hop and raise and lower—well, she's got it, too.

Bishop Buendia, portly and white-suited and cherub-faced, his hair pomaded and his priestly purple stole proclaiming his favor in the eyes of Christ, exits the Bel Air with an air of untroubled authority.

Through her field glasses, Daniela watches him follow the seven youngsters across the broad grassy park. Then he veers away from them, takes a few long swallows from a drinking fountain, and sits on a green bench in the shade of a white gazebo.

The magnificent seven now huddle in the grass, gathered in a loose circle around the drone. Only Lulu remains standing, probably to keep the grass off her legs.

The chola hands Jesse what looks like a cell phone from her bag. Jesse flips the drone onto its back in the grass and it looks to Daniela that he's attaching the phone to a gimbal.

To use as a camera, she thinks. Seven little spies, with Bishop Buendia in supervision. Shooting pictures of who? What?

You can probably buy a setup like that for three hundred bucks, camera included.

Then the spies take off, leaving Jesse standing alone in the middle of the park with the drone resting upright on the grass and the controller in his hands. He seems to be toggling and adjusting the settings; hard to tell from here.

Bishop Buendia observes from the shade of his gazebo.

Daniela watches the young spies split up and head around the park's structures—an auditorium, an amphitheater nestled in the trees, the staff and security buildings.

They're out of her sight now, and Daniela checks in on Buendia again, then lowers her binoculars. The sun is low still and casts a soft orange light.

Daniela watches the drone wobble into the air, gets her binoculars up fast, and sees the spindly thing climbing and heading toward the buildings. No sound, and its four propellers and landing legs are hard to make out against the background of trees.

A moment later it's above and beyond the trees, and Daniela

thinks she wouldn't be able to describe it if she didn't already know what it was, the Raptor TX-395 camera drone, red and black just like the box it came in. And she thinks: Come on, baby, do your job. Shoot that video, send it back to base camp by satellite or internet. Pinpoint where the bad guys are. Show the target house is empty and safe for entry. Or maybe, if gunmen are standing by.

Checks her watch and three minutes later, here comes the Raptor back her way, already over the amphitheater, the six merry spies running hard to catch it, looking up and laughing.

Jesse stands in the green grass, a rail of a boy with a newly shaved scalp and a smile on his face, and Daniela tells herself she can never, never lose him.

As the drone lowers toward Jesse, Daniela sees that the phone is no longer attached. Accidentally dropped in flight? Dropped on purpose by Jesse like a bomb? Pried off by one of the spies?

Suddenly the Raptor slows, hovers, and climbs away, headed toward Bishop Buendia.

Jesse pivots with little steps, still smiling, working the controls, piloting the Raptor toward Buendia, who stands, looking up as the drone hovers not ten feet above him.

Buendia softly claps.

The hell is going on, Daniela thinks. What is this, like, a jamboree for wannabe bangers?

The six spies converge on Jesse, with Lulu in the lead, brandishing a cell phone that she hands over to Jesse. They circle him, shadow-jabbing and feinting kicks like UFC fighters warming up, some of them shooting the action on their phones, Jesse watching them from the center of things, a man in charge.

He holds up the phone that Lulu brought from beyond the amphitheater buildings, which Daniela decides is the same one that the Raptor took off with.

Not a spy drone at all, thinks Daniela, returning her magnified gaze to her proud-looking son.

A delivery drone, just like Amazon.

He raises it high, turning in Bishop Buendia's direction.

Daniela glasses the portly, white-suited Bishop Buendia, who remains seated in the gazebo, facing his neophytes with an approving smile.

37

Gale takes the bone shards from his pocket and lays them on Bachstein's stainless-steel examination table. It's got a basin on one end, faucets with hand-held sprayers on the other, a swing-out magnifier and strong LED lights overhead.

Mendez upends an evidence bag and adds more pieces of bone to the table.

"What happened to you?" asks the coroner, eyeing Gale's bandaged nose.

"Hit a tree. It hit back."

Gale pictures Geronima, nursing his ragged little wound in the bright light of her bathroom.

Bachstein is tall, slender, and pale, with a domed forehead, thinning brown hair, and heavy glasses. A UCLA PhD in chemistry. He spreads the bones with an index finger, taking his time. Finally picks one with a round edge, rinses it off, and sets it on the table.

"Where'd you get this?"

"Out at the Wildcoast site."

"Underground?"

"Two hundred feet down," says Gale. "In a beach-sand slurry of some kind, in a cavern full of gigantic crystals."

Bachstein gives him a skeptical look.

"You must have felt like Indiana Jones."

"No snakes or monkeys."

"Adventurous, attractive women?"

"Two, actually."

Eyes bugging behind thick lenses, Bachstein looks to Mendez, waits for clarification, gets none, then swings the magnifier, turns on the circular light, and lowers his big forehead.

"Definitely a bone," he says. "Mammal, probably vertebral. Maybe human. Maybe deer or cow. Given the depth underground and undersea seismic activity, maybe a very young whale. Although, as they say, the contents may have shifted. Maybe a dog or coyote or a big cat. Were these pieces near each other or spread out?"

"I saw them in the beachy-looking sand," says Gale. "I kneeled down and picked up two or three, then ran my fingers through and came up with a couple more. So, yeah, near each other."

"A possible burial site. I'll carbon-date this, but to the eye, I'd say five hundred to seven hundred years old, maybe more. That liquid slurry has smoothed it. Buffed out the venous grooves and the superficial pores, which has helped preserve it. Cleaned off the burn marks, if any. Animal bones are less porous and greater density than ours. Here, take a look."

Gale steps up to the magnifier, peers down at the brightly lit shard.

"Lunar," he says.

"Let's run it through the electron scope. See if we can humanize this thing."

In the crime lab, Bachstein greets the techs with a wave of his hand, introduces Gale to them.

"We're going to get this Tarlow guy," says one of the coroner assistants, a petite Chinese woman. "I looked at what the lion did to his face and almost fainted. I've never fainted in my life."

"That was a rough scene," says Gale.

"Here's an open scope," says Bachstein.

He puts the specimen in the glass tray and turns on the microscope. Gale and Bachstein both watch the magnified image appear on the monitor.

"Oh, yes," says Bachstein. "Trabecular microstructure, not cortical. Osteons scattered and evenly placed. Not so in nonhuman animals. I'd say we have a human vertebrae here, based on that and its shape. Eyeballing the wear and tear, micro and macro, I'd put this partial vertebrae at roughly a thousand years old. I can radiocarbon-date it, but it'll take some hours."

Gale stares at the scattered osteons, evenly placed.

Has no idea what an "osteon" is, but they confirm what he has suspected, that this cavern of light in an underground sea is a resting place for spirits on their way to the afterlife.

What Chinigchinich created, and Luis Verdad wrote about.

What else could it be?

"Let me know as soon as you do," he says. "What's this?"

Gale fishes his pocket collection for the small crystal he was able to cleave off from its gigantic parent.

In the good LED light of the crime lab, it has that faint, white, almost powdery glow.

"The crystals luminesce in direct light and smell kind of like mildew and metal," says Gale.

Bachstein holds it up like a prospector assaying a sample, then places it in the electron microscope.

A strangely abstract image blips to the monitor. Gale considers the perfectly joined parallelograms, stacked layer after layer after layer. A wall of them.

"Lithium," says Bachstein.

"As in batteries?" asks Gale.

Bachstein gives him a sorrowful look.

"Yes, Detective, one of the most valuable chemical elements on the planet now. Every bit as precious as water. It's going to power the future. Businessmen and politicians call it white gold. Every electric car from now to forever is going to run on it. Every energy sold by every utility—renewable or not—is going to store their energy in lithium. It's very expensive to find and mine it."

Mendez shows the coroner her pictures of the crystalline cavern. Two of them are selfies for comparison, with the fifty-foot crystals behind her.

"Holy smokes," says Bachstein. "Most large lithium crystals are one *one-hundredth* that size. The whole cavern is lined with them?"

"Scroll," says Mendez.

The coroner holds the phone close and waves a finger across the screen.

"I'm not qualified to assess this economically," he says. "But even a lowly coroner can tell you that the lithium in these crystals is extremely valuable when isolated electrolytically into lithium chloride. The 'beach-sand slurry' you were walking on will be dense-packed with lithium chloride. This is the future of energy storage here, Detectives. This cavern and its crystals and walls and brine slurry will be worth billions of dollars over the years. Many billions."

On what was once Acjacheme land, thinks Gale. And much better than a casino.

"More valuable than a city?" he asks.

"Well, in terms of dollars, I would think many times," says Bachstein. "I'm no futurist but we need lithium in large amounts. Another city? Well, who's to say if we need one or not?"

"Who owns the mineral rights under Wildcoast?" asks Gale.

"I would assume the Tarlow Company," says the coroner. "Kevin Elder would certainly know."

* * *

Gale and Mendez wait an hour to see Kevin Elder, who has been in a meeting since noon and not returned their calls. The Orange County magazines on the lobby tables glossily promote the "OC lifestyle." Gale notes the holy trinity of high-end real estate in golden beach towns, luxury electric vehicles, and plastic surgery.

Elder, navy suited and vested, white shirt rolled up to his elbows and red necktie askew, stands and gestures to the two handsome leather chairs in front of his desk.

He shakes their hands across the table, sits, and links his hands behind his head. "Sorry," he says. "One crazy day here. What's with your nose?"

"I ran into a tree."

"Poor tree."

He gives Gale a doubtful look and Mendez an underpowered smile. Gale notes that the dashing silver widow's peak in the supervisor's otherwise black hair has been freshly trimmed.

"Good news?" asks the supervisor.

"Who owns the mineral rights to Wildcoast?" says Mendez.

To Gale, she seems curt and uncomfortable in her chair.

Elder unlinks his fingers and leans forward.

"Tarlow Company," he says. "But it depends on what minerals you're talking about."

"Lithium," says Gale.

Elder nods and purses his lips. "White gold. Let's find out."

The supervisor taps his desktop keyboard, sits back.

"We'll go straight to the tax assessor for this," he says. "Cassie Staples runs the place, great lady. Ancient and wise. Don't tell her I said ancient."

An awkward moment later, as he stares at Daniela Mendez, his phone rings.

Elder puts it on speaker: "Cass, thanks for being quick. Hey, who owns the mineral rights to the Wildcoast property?"

"Why, of course the Tarlow Company, Mr. Elder."

An aging voice, thinks Gale, thin and crackling, like old paper.

"Cass, do those rights include lithium? I've got some detectives here, need to know."

"Give me just a second."

Gale can hear Cassie's fingers on her keyboard. "Okay . . . back in 1915, when the TC gave us the land for Caspers, the surrounding Wildcoast parcel was reassessed—of course—minus Caspers. The mineral rights beneath the Wildcoast parcel include lithium. This is interesting: Tarlow Company retained all mineral rights under Caspers, too. You know, that is not a surprise. Back then, lithium was being mined and synthesized into the antidepressant lithium. The one they took off the market because it had so many bad side effects. No one was thinking of batteries then, not that I remember."

"Ms. Staples, I'm Detective Lew Gale. I'm here in Mr. Elder's office with my partner, Daniela Mendez. We're investigating the murder of Bennet Tarlow III."

"I am pleased to meet you," she says, with a trace of warmth in her voice. "Mr. Tarlow was a gracious and generous man. A kind man. I sincerely hope you arrest the killer."

"There's no doubt we will," says Mendez. "Ms. Staples, did the Tarlow Company ever mine lithium under the Wildcoast parcel or the section of Wildcoast that became the park?"

"One moment, please. Hall of Records for that."

Again, the sound of Cass Staples's fingers on her keyboard. They sound fast and strong.

Kevin Elder looks intently at Mendez as Cass Staples's voice comes through his phone speaker.

"No, Ms. Mendez, there is no record of lithium exploration or extraction from the Wildcoast parcel. Why, have you found some?"

"Yes, but only a trace," says Gale.

"Well, we're all aware of how valuable it has become, with all these Teslas and electric everythings. I bought one myself."

"White gold," Elder says again, this time with a laugh. "Thank you, Cass. Detectives, anything else for our wonderful county assessor?"

"Thank you, Ms. Staples," says Daniela.

"Very much," says Gale.

Elder punches off and leans forward, elbows on his desktop. "Talk to me. You found lithium at Wildcoast?"

"Just the trace Daniela mentioned."

"Why is trace lithium important to your investigation?"

"Mr. Elder," says Gale. "I'll be honest with you, there's more than trace lithium under Wildcoast and Caspers. A lot more. The Tarlow Company knows it. Apparently, it was discovered during a perc test commissioned for Wildcoast."

Gale sees an odd loss on Elder's face. "Wildcoast is my district. My people. Bennet Tarlow III was my friend. I've been shepherding Wildcoast through since it was a dream of his. I don't believe he knew anything at all about lithium. He would have told me."

"I'm only speculating," says Gale.

"How much lithium, would you guess?"

"Have you been down in that pit, Mr. Elder?" asks Mendez. "It's really something."

"No, Daniela, I certainly . . . *what* pit?"

"The so-called percolation test pit," says Gale. "Now it's two hundred feet deep and a hundred feet across."

"Courtesy of Empire Excavators and Kyle McNab of PacWest Mining," says Mendez. "You probably remember him from the Grove."

Gale notes again the solemnity on Elder's face as he considers Daniela. Wonders if something has transpired between them that he has not seen.

"Sure, I know Kyle," Elder says softly. "But I can't see why Benny would know that a metal this valuable is under Wildcoast and not tell me. I'm kind of in shock right now."

Elder's young aide-de-camp, Grant Hudson, comes through the door. "Detectives!" he says. "Great to see you guys. Love the nose job, Gale. Boss, we're on with Mayor Petrie in ten at Il Fornaio. I'll bring the car around. Detectives, please—do you have a believable suspect by now?"

Mendez rises and slings her bag over her shoulder, turns to Hudson. "Not you again," she says, then back to the supervisor. "Thanks for your time, Mr. Elder."

"Anytime, Detective Mendez. And you know I mean that."

Gale and Mendez sit in the shade outside the county building, watch the employees heading out for lunch.

"What's between you and Elder?" asks Gale.

"He hit on me and I turned him down. Twice. He was insistent, which leaves me kind of edgy around him."

"Sorry to pry."

"I'm not great at hiding things."

"Me neither," says Gale. "Marilyn read me like a book, like, the smallest thoughts. She heard them, somehow."

"Lew, I've decided to talk to Jesse myself. He's pulling some stuff I don't even understand. With bad people, though. So, thanks for offering to be my proxy. I may take you up on that later but I need to get some things straight with him pretty much right now."

"I'll be ready when you need me."

Gale sees the quiver of a smile on Daniela's hard, pretty face.

Then the black Lincoln Navigator with government plates pulls into the long concrete porte cochere alongside the county building entrance.

Watches Elder get into the front passenger seat.

When the Navigator swings past them, the driver's-side window closes, erasing Grant Hudson's profile on its way up.

Gale feels that funny, lucky bump he gets when something impossible seems to fit.

Or almost fit.

But probably not fit at all.

"Slick and gutless," says Mendez. "Not real people like us. Although, Steve and Curtis probably don't exist outside Vern Jeffs's colorful imagination and his photographic memory."

"We can't not see what happens next," says Gale. Ten minutes later Gale and Mendez sit in Gale's Explorer near Il Fornaio restaurant. The black Lincoln is parked along a LOADING ONLY curb, a valet ticket on the windshield.

No old white Econoline van in sight.

No black Harley.

But there is a beautiful Harley, in Mary Kay pink, in the DISABLED ONLY space up front.

Looking at the pink bike, Mendez shakes her head.

An hour and a half later, Kevin Elder, Grant Hudson, and skinny, leather-bound Mindy Jeffs step out of the shaded restaurant entrance and into the crisp Orange County sunshine.

"No Vern," says Mendez. "Maybe he's home, catching up on his sleep after trying to kill you last night."

"Letting Mindy negotiate his fee with the big boys."

Mindy tips a valet at the booth, then climbs aboard her machine. Pulls onto the street and Gale follows, three cars back. Traffic is steady and brisk.

"We can try all we want to put Elder in that white Navigator," says Mendez. "But I don't think he's got the balls to kill his friend and political ally. And he has the brains not to."

"Agreed," says Gale.

"Then who?"

"With Bennet Tarlow dead," says Gale, "Wildcoast can die, too. And the Tarlow Company trades a risky utopian city for billions in lithium."

"Hal Teller as Steve?" asks Mendez.

"Absolutely," says Gale. "Or at least the bank."

A pause as they follow Mindy onto Harbor, headed in the direction of home.

"No, Lew," says Mendez. "Teller's too old and rich to kill a business partner he once mentored. Or to bankroll a hit. Bennet was a guy who looked up to him. How much richer does Hal Teller need to be? I'm not seeing Teller in this."

"He's the one who said the Tarlow Company is about making money, not homes and buildings," says Gale. "Imagine how mineral rights to a cache of lithium would light his fire?"

"No, I'm sorry but it's not adding up, Lew. I still believe Vern was hired to kill Tarlow, and—based on last night—you, too. Who did the hiring? Let's let this cook."

Gale nods and smiles; Mendez gives him a prying look.

"My disbelief that Keven Elder isn't involved has nothing to do with him trying to date me," she says.

"I'm sure of that," says Gale. "Just shows he's got good taste."

A small smile then from Mendez. "Stop. Enough."

They follow Mindy onto Yorktown and park down the street from Jeffs's house. Looks the same as last time, but Gale notes the mail bulging from the curbside box.

Gale watches Mindy rumble onto the driveway on her pink bike, and the garage door rises.

No white Econoline out front.

"No black Harley," says Mendez.

"No Rivian," says Gale.

"The mail," says Gale. "They're pretending nobody's home."

"A staycation," says Mendez.

The garage door closes.

No Vern at the Bear Cave or the Metro Gym, either.

38

Early that evening his father's yellow Challenger is parked in his mother's driveway, so Gale finds a place on Los Rios Street.

He and Geronima walk the alley toward Gale's boyhood home, Hulk on a leash, lunging at the butterflies that thrive in the profuse gardens of sage and lion's-tail and milkweed.

Gale's alert to the cars and pedestrians on busy Los Rios, his Colt holstered high on his hip under a light sport coat, his ankle cannon secure and uncomfortable.

Gale has activated the Vigilant tracker and left it in a big terracotta pot of flowering ice pink hibiscus on Geronima's front porch, and the matte gray Rivian is nowhere to be seen.

He's got the Capistrano Sheriff's patrol units on a hot surveillance of Geronima's neighborhood on Acjacheme Court.

Now sundown casts a warm orange tone on the world, and Geronima sweeps Hulk into her arms.

"I like this street," she says. "Had a friend in school who lived near the end."

"Our house has been in Mom's family for a hundred and fourteen years," says Gale.

"Acjacheme all the way," says Geronima.

"My dad's here. Mom didn't tell me. He's a challenge. Haven't seen him in a year."

Inside, the smell of stewed rabbit fills the tiny house.

"Thanks for this, Mom," Gale says to Sally as she looks at his nose. "You know Geronima. Dad, Geronima Mills."

"My genuine pleasure," says his father, with his killer smile. "What a cute little brute you've got there!"

Hulk growls at Edward Gallego from the safety of Geronima's arms. When she sets him down, he stops growling to smell this stranger's running shoes.

Edward Gallego's bear hug of his son is powerful, in keeping with his San Diego State University wrestling prowess. His grip on Gale's cheeks just short of painful.

Sally looks fresh from the salon, her thick, gray-black hair trimmed, wearing a long white dress under a black tunic into which she has woven small seashells.

"I won't be able to stay long," Edward announces, sitting down at the table.

Gale sees the forbearance on his mother's face as she serves Edward a bowl of stew, then one for Geronima and another for him.

"It's been a while, Ed," Gale says. "Almost a year."

"I miss your mom. And you and Frank. Maybe not so much Frank."

"Does Isabelle know you're here?" Gale asks.

"We have our arrangement and a good marriage. So let that one go."

"Tell Geronima about her."

Edward gives Gale a sharp look and Geronima another smile.

He explains that Isabelle is his third wife, very young and beautiful, a recognized Cahuilla native. They live out in Aguanga—not much more than a general store, a modest sized casino, and a gas station on Highway 371. It's a bit of a commute, says Edward, because he teaches and coaches football at the high school here in Capistrano.

Which makes Gale think of the native boy, handy with a football, whom Tribal Councilman Roger Winderling is supposed to introduce him to. Apparently, the boy's mother isn't so sure about that.

"Well," says Geronima. "You're a lucky man to get a woman like her."

"It's not all luck," he says.

Sally sets her bowl on the table and elegantly raises her long white dress to sit.

"You look great tonight, Mom," Gale says. "You got all beautified for this conquistador?"

His father gives Gale a steely glance. Same flat gray eyes as his son. "Watch it, son."

"Come on, you two," says Sally. "Here, let's drink a toast."

"To families," says Edward.

Gale notes the calm detachment on Geronima's face as she considers his father. She's wearing what she left home in with Gale early this morning—black jeans, red canvas sneakers, and a red Western shirt with pearl snap buttons.

They raise the bottles of beer.

"Tell us about that nose, son."

Gale loosely synopsizes his and Daniela's inspection of the Wildcoast test pit, courtesy of the student activist Geronima, the mountain lion with the dead coyote in its mouth, the nearly silent pickup that tried to run him down. Geronima cleaning him up. Nothing about lithium crystals.

"Geronima," says Edward Gallego. "You've got a lot of Facebook followers, don't you?"

"Not really. Ten, twelve thousand. More on X."

"You're an attractive warrior, but you do say some ugly things."

"I'm honest about what I see. I'm sorry if you're offended."

"Not in the least. Do you and Lew have a thing?"

"We just met."

"Another dead end for you, son?" he asks, turning to Gale.

"Ed, please," says Sally.

"I didn't mean to hurt his feelings," says Ed, looking at Sally, then Geronima.

"My feelings are just fine," Gale says.

Ed looks at his son with disappointment, something that Gale has tried to avoid his entire life. His father's disappointment, that is. There's also a vein of sadness in it, which eats at Gale even more. He's never been square with his dad about the war. And Sally has honored her promise of silence, so far as Gale knows.

"I want what's best for you, son," says Ed. "The love of your life. A family. Sons and daughters. All the things your mother and I have. And more. I was hoping that Geronima might prove to be part of that grand scheme."

The goddamned killer smile again, Gale notes.

"I'll get what I deserve," says Gale.

"I wish you held yourself in higher esteem, son," says Edward. "I feel like something has been beaten out of you, but I know it wasn't me that did it. I gave you the best I had, until it was time to leave. I've forgiven myself for that, as you know."

"It's harder to stay than to go," Gale says.

"I couldn't disagree more."

"Seconds on that stew, Ed?"

Silence while she serves him, then Gale.

Geronima declines seconds, sipping the stew thoughtfully, thinks Gale. Knows her well enough to suspect she's furious but constrained. She gives him an analytical look, then reaches down and pets Hulk.

"Lew, do you know who was driving that truck?" asks his mother.

"I never saw him. I was trying to get away, jump that wall along Camino Capistrano."

"But why him, not her?" asks Edward. "You know how some women text and drive—she might not have even seen you."

"That's pretty far-fetched, Edward," says Sally. "Lew, do you think it's tied to the Tarlow case?"

"I do."

"Not so fast," says Edward. "No skeletons in the closet from past cases? No released felons who might want revenge on the cop who busted them? You, as a sheriff's detective can easily get that kind of information."

"No skeletons, Ed," says Gale.

"I like that you're political, Geronima," says Edward. No smile now, just his gaze boring into her. "That you are passionate about all things native. Big into the social media, very political, always bad-mouthing the European and American oppressors, as you call them. I teach history. I thought you might like that. But you know, the history I teach isn't the progressive nonsense you espouse. The Franciscan friars who founded the mission here, and converted and taught the natives, were not genocidal oppressors. They were godly and selfless. And don't forget, Father Serra sailed all the way here from Spain *on a wooden boat with no motor and no lights*. It took a year and a half. He arrived here with three Franciscan helpers and eight soldiers. That was the invading army you all talk about. Upon first meeting the Acjacheme here, there was a moment when thirty Indian braves placed arrows in their bows. Father Serra, a tiny man, couldn't speak their language, and the Indians couldn't understand his. But he knelt before them and looked them in their eyes while he said a prayer. And when he rose, the native chief ordered his braves to disarm their bows. Later, the Spanish set up camp and the natives— mostly naked people—brought them food and water. The food was uncooked, as was the custom. Raw rabbit and deer and quail. Here was their place to build a mission. For naked primitives with blood dripping down their chins."

Sally says, "That was somewhat moving, Ed, but don't forget that those Spaniards killed thousands of us—two-thirds—with their diseases in a few short years, replaced our language with their own. Changed our names. Choked our customs and beliefs as they baptized us into their church, then married the young women and made families."

"They made you into God-fearing, tax-paying citizens of New Spain," says Ed.

"Using whips and chains."

"The Franciscans saw in you what I saw two centuries later, Sally. Native beauty and strength. Unlimited potential."

"Edward, we've been having this conversation since the day we met. I don't blame you for what your ancestors did to mine. I loved you as well I knew how, but our marriage was a brief moment. I don't blame you. I forgive you."

Edward swallows the last of his beer.

"My kingdom for a toothpick," he says.

Sally moves the shot glass of wooden toothpicks to him.

Edward takes one, sets it deep between his teeth and stands.

"I love coming over here," he says. "I miss you both. And Lew? I'm sorry we don't get along and your anger does hurt me. Again, for the thousandth time, I am sorry for what happened to you, though I have no idea what it is. All I know for sure is that I am not responsible."

"You're off the hook, Dad," says Gale. "Except for abandoning your wife and sons."

"A genuine pleasure to meet you, Geronima Mills. You are native strength and beauty at its finest. I wish you all the best. Don't bite the hand that feeds you."

Edward heads out the door, Hulk growling along behind him.

Minutes later, Gale parks a few houses down from Geronima's driveway. The early night sky is moonlit and salted with stars. With his infrared binoculars, he glasses the 'hood—a jumble of old houses built close together. Notes the ice pink hibiscus on Geronima's porch. Sees the lights in the windows, the cars in driveways and along the street, a young couple getting into a sedan. Hears the doors clunk shut.

Then the rooftops, always the rooftops.

Watching for the shooters watching you.

He's systematic about it, a left-to-right one-eighty, then back the other way. Notes the air conditioners, the sagging telephone lines and ceramic insulators, the occasional solar panels, the exhaust vents, the skylights, the satellite dishes and coaxial TV cable, the bougainvillea and rocktrumpet climbing the tiles.

"It's not too late to change your stubborn mind on this, Geronima."

"I'm not going to a hotel when some giant badass is trying to kill you. He's not after me. You might need backup. Consider me your Mendez. Who I happen to like and respect but why isn't she here with her partner?"

"She's staking out Jeffs's home and workplace."

"I understand. I'm all in with you, Lew."

Gale pulls on to, then off the street, and turns in to Geronima's driveway.

A Sheriff's Department radio car glides past in Gale's rearview.

"Keep Hulk on the leash and both of you moving along," says Gale. "Have your key ready and don't touch the tracker. Leave the lights off. I'll be a few steps behind you."

"Got it, sarge."

"I was a private."

On the porch, he pockets the GPS tracker and slips it into his coat.

Inside, Geronima locks the security screen door and the windowed main door.

Gale cracks the bright serape-print drapes, turns on and mutes the TV. Wants the place to look occupied.

They sit at opposite ends of the couch, facing the living room windows. Geronima sets her tiny rose-colored .22-caliber handgun on the steamer trunk.

Hulk between them sitting upright, button-eared and alert.

"Is he always like this?" asks Gale.

"When he's not tearing his toys apart. He's a natural-born guard dog."

"Perfect."

"He knows that we're on the lookout for trouble," she says.

Hulk turns to look at each of them, knows they're talking about him, too.

"I took in a street dog when I was ten and he was like that," Gale says. "Sparky. Mom and Dad didn't like him much. But I fed him and cleaned up after him and housebroke him. Taught him basic obedience, and he won them over. He was about half-feral when I got him, but he grew out of it. Took years, though. He was like Hulk, always on guard. Always looking for the enemy."

"Good for you. Good for Sparky."

Silence as an old VW hippie van putts down Via Acjacheme. Gale likes the yellow-on-white paint job, visible in the mission-bell-shaped streetlights.

Then another sheriff's cruiser going the other way.

Eat that Rivian alive, thinks Gale.

"Very cool of Sally to harbor us gunslingers," says Geronima. "But I really wanted out of there."

"I knew your hair was on fire."

"I didn't want to embarrass you."

"He's clueless and mean-spirited," says Gale. "Sexist and vain."

"Make America Great Again."

"That's him. He's trying."

The hippie van backfires and suddenly, Gale's in Sangin on that steep, rocky path leading from the FOB down into the river valley, Guy Flatly on point.

Then, just as suddenly, he's back in Geronima's darkened living room.

"You okay, Gale? You flinched."

"I used to a lot. Now, not much."

The hippie van has made a U-turn and is now coming back toward them, one headlight canted up, the other down.

"Doesn't seem like Vernon Jeffs to drive a car like that," says Geronima. "From what you've told me about him."

"I doubt it. They put out about forty horsepower. It's a good disguise though."

The van crawls down the road toward the mission and Ortega Highway.

"Do you think he'll come tonight?" she asks.

"The tracker is broadcasting to his phone right now," says Gale. "He'll come here when he's ready."

"So it's a question of when."

"He's got choices. He might not try the pickup truck again because we'd see it coming. He could come up on foot."

"Use the twenty-two he used on Tarlow?"

"Maybe, but it's hard to get up close to a target who's watching and ready. A rifle is best. Jeffs sniped in Bosnia. Hush-hush CIA stuff. Claims ten kills. He has a Barrett, like mine. Keeps it behind the bedroom door."

"Are you afraid of him?"

"Yes. I'm afraid of rattlesnakes and killer mountain lions, too."

"I remember you talking about it in the interview, how with a rifle in your hands time speeds up, your heart slows down, and you can sit still for hours, all night or all day sometimes. Take your finger off the trigger and fall asleep right where you're lying. Then wake up and do it again. Eat from your pack. A bucket for a pot.

"I'm really sad you shot the wrong guy, Gale. But you shot a lot of the right ones, too. So maybe if they tally up the good things and the bad things at the end, maybe you'll come out ahead. I'll never forget that picture of you in your dress blues. Absent. Broken down."

Gale nods, watching through cracked blinds as moths tap against the porch lights. "I don't like to remember any of that."

"Shitcan the bad memories," says Geronima. "Play the good ones, over and over."

Gale pinches the bandage, his nose bruised but the swelling down a little.

"I remember, before the war, when I got married to Marilyn I thought I was going to die because I was so happy. Die of a heart attack or a stroke or an aneurysm. Something launched from inside me, not a car wreck or a bullet. But something my happiness had caused. Death by happiness."

Those were the happiest days of my life, he thinks, that old Pretenders song drifting through his brainpan.

Silence then, as Gale sees a big pale owl winging by above them through a skylight. One of Tarlow's obsessions? He wonders. Very rare, so what are the chances?

Conspiracies, coincidences, connections, he thinks.

"Gale, I'm brain dead."

"Get some sleep. Hulk and I are on watch."

She stands, picks up her gun. "I'll leave my door open so the dog can get in. That goes for you, too."

Gale considers. Contemplates the dull eternity of not being able to be a man in that way.

"Just sayin', Lew."

"Thank you. I brought Verdad to keep me company," he says.

"I love Luis Verdad."

Gale makes coffee and turns the lights off except for the slender, flexible reading light on the end table next to him.

A few minutes later Geronima comes from her room, still in her jeans and Western shirt, but she's traded her red sneakers for shearling moccasins.

She sits at the opposite end of the couch again, sets her rose-colored pistol on the trunk, leans back, and crosses her feet next to the gun.

"Read to me," she says. "Mom read *Arabian Nights* to me every night for a year. Over and over. I miss that."

39

So Gale reads aloud:

The claws of El Diablo tore my flesh and Bernardo washed me in the creek while the dogs played in the water.

The cuts to me were six in all, and they were not very deep but deep enough to bleed and be moderately painful.

Bernardo then made a paste of sage blossoms, prickly-pear cactus meat, and sand from the creek, and applied it to my cuts to stop the bleeding. With this accomplished, he wrapped deer grass around my body and left arm to keep the healing paste in place.

We dragged El Diablo to the creek and let his blood run into the water. Bears watched us from far back in the cottonwoods. Bears often steal kills from lions, and these bears would almost certainly attempt to steal the lion from us.

Bernardo and I disagreed about what to do with the body of El Diablo. Bernardo said to leave him here by the creek for the bears, and we could safely return to Mission San Juan Capistrano.

But I wanted to display his body to my family, such that we could all heal our grief over Magdalena by burning him and releasing his eternal spirit into the sky. My people believe that all living things wait for the afterlife in the cavern of light in the underground sea. And when they are ready, they ascend to the place where the sky and the earth overlap. Father Serra calls this place heaven.

So we made a sled from the cattail canes growing around the spring, lashing them tightly with deer grass, and weaving a strong rope to pull El Diablo through the mountains and valleys to Acjacheme Village.

When the boulders were too big and steep or the trail too narrow, we took turns carrying El Diablo across our shoulders while the other pulled the empty sled. My wounds soon were bleeding again and we stopped along a creek to clean them and renew the healing paste and wrap them in the grass. Each time we stopped we saw a bear following us, a female with two cubs, the most dangerous of bears. The dogs' hackles rose and they began pursuit, but I called them back to protect us.

In the late afternoon we were startled to see the mother bear and her cubs that had circled around and gotten ahead of us on the trail. They were approximately three hundred meters away. She had that posture of stillness that grizzly bears have before they charge, a look of determination as she stared at us with her small eyes. Mother bears teach their cubs how to kill.

You cannot run faster than a hungry or hateful grizzly. You stand your ground and if you have a weapon you prepare to use it. Or you back away slowly. Bernardo advised me to leave the dead lion on the trail and back away, but I was as determined to bring El Diablo to the tribal fire as was the bear to eat him, and perhaps we men and dogs also.

I primed and powdered the blunderbuss and readied the flint. Then Bernardo, with El Diablo upon his shoulders, and I, with

Thunder Girl heavy against the magnificent pain in my arms and chest, began to walk toward her, bellowing together a tribal battle chant.

The three dogs snarled viciously but stayed close.

When we were one hundred meters away, the sow bear rose to her hind legs and bellowed back at us. With this, the dogs lost control and charged up the trail, baying and yelping like tortured souls.

The bear bellowed again and fell to all fours and charged us.

I arranged the fork rest and steadied the flint. I forgot the pain and my hands were not shaking. I was too distracted to pray.

Eighty meters between us, then fifty, and the dogs closing in.

Then the sow turned away in a wide half circle, and the two cubs turned and followed her into the big oaks, where they vanished in the direction of the creek, where we had first seen her, stalking us, the dogs in furious pursuit.

The dogs, barking, disappeared in the trees. I knew it was useless to call them back, and my chest hurt too much to tighten the muscles into a loud voice.

Late in the night we climbed the last hill and saw the pale mission walls in the light of a half-moon, and the village of Acjacheme nearby, its small adobe casitas with candlelight in their windows, the wickiups casting gray shadows on the ground.

We went to the village and I lowered El Diablo to the dirt, then went inside and awakened my parents, sister, and brothers.

"That's one brave Brave," says Geronima.

"I like the way he writes," says Gale. "Not too much drama. *Blood & Heart* reads like a police report. He makes all of it seem true."

Hulk bolts from the red couch and skids to a stop at the screen door, bunching up the rug and growling.

Through the screen, Gale watches a Tesla silently gliding by. Hulk gives Geronima the same look he gave Gale when the Rivian truck went past last night, almost silent.

"That part about a cavern of light in an underground sea makes me think of the crystal cathedral," says Geronima. "The bones of our ancestors and prehistoric crystals powering the twenty-first century."

"And creating a fortune for the Tarlow Company," says Gale.

Hulk leaps back onto the couch and sits upright, midway between Gale and his master, ears perked and still looking through the screen.

"He's got good hearing," says Gale.

"He hears the mail truck turning onto the street five minutes before I do. Full conniption. Hates that thing, and our mail lady is so nice. She tried to give him treats and he just growled."

"Little dogs," says Gale. "We had Labs for birds and rabbits."

Geronima makes another pot of coffee and sets the mugs on the steamer trunk.

Gale reads:

The Fire Ceremony for El Diablo lasted two days.

First we removed his feet and tail to cure in the sun. We sprinkled his body with gunpowder. Then we burned his body in a large fire of oak branches stoked with dried grass and Arundo reeds.

The next day when the burned bones had cooled, we cast them on the ground where El Diablo had taken Magdalena, and the village danced upon the bones from sunrise until moonrise.

The women painted their faces black and red, and the elders wore feather headdresses of the sacred great horned owl, four kinds of hawks, bald eagles, crows, and doves. And many shells from the ocean. The warriors, elders, and our ritual specialists swallowed the peyote cactus and, after vomiting, had visions they communicated in dance. The women took peyote also, and drank the very strong wine made in large iron vats deep within the mission.

Acjacheme dancing begins slowly then builds into a frenzy. The dancers make the rhythm with sound sticks, drums, and rattles. Most of the movements have been created by the ritual specialists, then taught to the people. Some of the movements have meanings that only the specialists and elders know. The children were forbidden to dance but they fought mock battles in the trees away from the fire, and some of them stole wine, which the Franciscans believe is the blood of Jesus, using metal cups "borrowed" from the mission that were intended to hold the blood.

We ate while we danced, in the Acjacheme custom for the fresh, raw meat of rabbit, deer, mission cattle, birds, fish, and dried lizards, the blood and fat of which ran down our chins and elbows and fell into the soil and the scorched bones of El Diablo.

I danced with Dulce Agua, which means "sweet water" in Spanish. Before Father Serra took it away, her name was Shongwa'ala Mo'yla, which means "moon woman."

She was very beautiful, painted, and rhythmic, and my peyote visions said I would marry her within thirty days, which came true.

She told me she had the same vision.

We danced until the moon came up then I went to my adobe brick home and slept until late the next day.

Hulk bounds from the couch again and scampers down the hall, screeching. Gale checks the street, but no cars, bikes, or pedestrians.

Geronima picks up her tiny gun and follows Hulk into a bedroom, flicking on the hall lights.

Gale moves to the security screen door and leans into the wall, gun drawn and at his side. He's invisible from outdoors, except to someone perched on a rooftop or in a tree, with a view through the western window, as he would have been perched in Sangin or Vernon Jeffs in Bosnia.

Snorting loudly now, Hulk blasts back into the living room and jumps onto the leather chair, framed by the western window, hind legs extended from the seat, front legs braced on the chair's back, tail straight up, stiff and still.

In his mind's eye Gale envisions Jeffs on the rooftop across the street, putting the Barrett's crosshairs on vigilant Hulk, just a bouncing silhouette beyond the serape blinds.

Gale smells the opium poppy scent of Sangin Valley, not the sage-and-savanna aroma of San Juan Capistrano.

Eardrums pounding, he may as well be into a twenty-hour speed-and-energy-drink jag in the rocky hills of Sangin Valley, waiting for the old man in the Cheetahs to come out from the granary.

Geronima comes back down the hall now, flicking off the lights.

"Lew . . . what is happening?"

"Freeze, Geronima! Down!"

Gale defaults to training, clambering on hands and knees toward Hulk, his fingers pinched hard between the gun and the floor.

He stands and with one hand hauls the growling dog to his chest, then pivots toward Geronima, ducking away from the window and into the hallway.

Gale guides Geronima with his gun hand, prodding her into the little bathroom, Hulk tight to his ribs like a football.

Closes the door and sets Hulk down, kneels, then gently pulls Geronima to her knees in front of him on the black-and-white floor tile.

He speaks in the glow of a night-light.

"He can't see us here."

"Who? Did you see him?"

"No, but Hulk might have. I think he might have."

"Your nose is bleeding."

"Hulk caught me when I picked him up."

"Is there someone out there or not?"

Gale sees doubt and fear in Geronima's dark eyes. A wordless interrogation.

"They could be everywhere. I don't think so, Geronima. I really don't know. I need to just kneel here a minute."

She sets her gun on the floor, then Gale's.

Holds his hands to her cheeks.

Gale feels his thighs trembling and the patches of old scar tissue tight and hot.

Hulk squeezes in close and licks his master's ear.

Gale's phone, Mendez on speaker:

"Jeffs just parked his Harley in the back lot of the Bear Cave," she says. "He's limping a little, but moving pretty damned well. On the lookout, aware. Past the dumpster now, headed for the kitchen door. The fog is back."

"On my way."

"Go," says Geronima.

40

Gale circles Geronima's neighborhood slowly, twice, attaching the suction gumball light and siren to his roof, then calls Dispatch again to get a tighter patrol around her home. He guns the Explorer onto Camino Capistrano, headed for Interstate 5 to the San Diego Freeway to Huntington Beach and the Bear Cave.

His nerves are settling and his adrenaline runs strong as he sails through the thin two A.M. traffic at ninety miles per hour, exiting onto Bolsa just as Daniela calls.

Daniela:

"He's back on his hog now, heading toward Yorktown and home. Funny how that knee healed up so fast."

"I'll park close."

Gale drives carefully up Bolsa to the traffic light.

Weaves his way through the Jeffs neighborhood on Yorktown and parks close to the house. He can barely see it through the fog. Garage closed, porch light on but no lights inside.

Daniela:

"If Vern's heading home, he's taking the scenic route."

"Think he's onto you?"

"He's pulling into the Jack in the Box drive-through. You spend the night with Geronima again?"

"Some of it."

"She looks at you with pride of ownership. I understand and like her. Be careful. Vern's ordering. Good thing he's got the saddlebag. Stand by."

Gale to Geronima:

"You okay?"

"Everything's fine."

"What's that sound?"

"My neighbor, Neal. Bringing in his Peterbilt from a two-week haul."

"Why isn't Hulk screeching?"

"Asleep."

"Where are you?"

"Bedroom. Lights out, doors locked, Hulk on his pillow, the rose-colored semiauto under mine. Itching to kill a bad guy, Gale. Reading *Blood & Heart*. I will not fall asleep."

"Careful the dog doesn't blast off and step on the trigger. That's happened, you know."

"It's under my pillow, Lew. I'm not worried about it. I'm worried about you."

"I'm better. It's over. I'm worried about you, too, Geronima. I like you very much and I want you to live forever."

A pause then:

"Sweet of you, Lew. Sweet Lew Gale."

"Signing off."

The fog lightens. Gale contemplates the Jeffs residence, one of thousands of 1950s stucco tract homes in what was then booming postwar Orange County. By the time Gale was born, the citrus orchards and packinghouses were mostly gone, replaced by tract homes and shopping centers. Sleepy San Juan Capistrano was booming. So was the Tarlow Company. Orange County had become the OC.

Mendez again:

"White bag into the saddlebag, Lew. Looks heavy. Okay, now he's back on the road. I have to stay way back on these neighborhood streets. Wish me luck or off he'll go."

"I've got the house, Daniela."

"Vern has your dinner. Over and out."

Through Gale's windshield, pockets of fog roll across the darkness from the sea. The oil pump churns.

Down Yorktown comes a Mustang e-car.

A moment later, a lumbering 1980s Suburban.

Gale watches them closely, but his thoughts are of Geronima, and he's trying to forget his confusion and uncertainty at her house, trying to forgive himself for it.

Who are you?

Lewis Gallego—half Acjacheme, half Anglo.

Since Sangin, half a man.

Or is it more like a quarter?

A second-class Native, unrecognized.

Unrecognizable?

Fragments of the past whirl inside him.

Fragments of fragments.

You're dangerous, he thinks. A man sworn to protect and serve. But tonight, barely competent. Barely there. Humiliating. Hulk was better.

Vern's black Harley Softail emerges from a ball of fog moving across Yorktown like a big tumbleweed.

He's not moving fast but the Harley pops and growls loudly as he passes his house, then powers past Gale, slouched down in his seat.

And disappears down Yorktown.

Mendez's black Explorer glides to a stop along the curb, facing Gale a hundred yards away from the opposite side of the street, headlights going off, and the sound of Vern's Softail diminishing through Gale's open window.

He flashes once; Mendez answers.

Three minutes later Vern is back, approaching his house with more velocity this time before he decelerates and turns in to his driveway.

He gloves the handlebar remote, and the garage door opens. The lights go on. He pulls in, kills the engine, and kickstands the heavy bike, swinging his right foot over and down, his left leg a little wobbly.

Then movement from the hedge of oleander on the side of the garage: something upright, taller than a monkey and thinner than a bear.

With a handgun and a ski mask over its face—the gun silenced and the ski mask red.

Gale jumps out, nudges the door closed, draws his sidearm.

Ski Mask sidles into the garage behind Vern, who now turns and pulls off his right glove, reaching for the revolver holstered low on his leg like a gunslinger's.

Even from here Gale sees his big face and wide eyes, blanched by the fluorescent lights overhead.

Daniela closes fast, from up the street.

Gale, too, yelling, *"Freeze!"*

Stops at a hundred feet and takes a Weaver stance.

Vern looks at him but Ski Mask does not; instead, he points his handgun at Vern, unsteadily, barrel wobbling like he's going to drop it.

"Drop the gun and down!" yells Daniela. "Drop and *DOWN!*"

Ski Mask spits a round into Jeffs.

Gale shoots twice, moves in as Ski Mask drops to his knees, and Daniela puts three more bullets into him.

Gunsmoke hangs in the jittery fluorescence, metallic and strong.

Beyond his sights, Gale watches Ski Mask, on his back now, arms out and gun fallen from his right hand, chest rising and falling.

Gale hears his gasps, catches a glimpse of Mendez out in the perimeter of the garage lights.

Vern, huge and motionless, lies on his back beside his gleaming black Harley.

Mindy bursts from the house into the garage in a baby blue robe, sees Vern and screams, throwing herself on her husband.

Mendez stands over Ski Mask in his widening blood, his chest no longer rising and falling, his stillness absolute.

She squats and pulls off the mask to reveal Kevin Elder's handsome face, his aquiline nose and the streak of gray in his widow's peak.

His eyes mostly pupils.

Mendez looks at Gale with dull surprise.

A gray Rivian pickup truck comes slowly toward them on Yorktown, hesitates near the driveway, then U-turns and speeds away.

Their shots puncture the eerie silence, and the Rivian's rear tires burst, and the sleek machine veers suddenly, jumps the curb, and runs through the oil pumper fence, bashing to a stop against the great arm of the thing, which is still rising and falling when the truck's lithium battery catches fire and the flames ripple up through the seams of the hood.

Grant Hudson throws open the door, sees the fence surrounding him, then turns and faces the detectives, hands up.

Gale squeezes through the pierced chain link as Mendez covers him and Mindy wails beyond the fog.

"My favorite detective!" says Grant Hudson. "I have broken no laws and will not talk without a lawyer."

"On the ground, cockroach. Face down."

"It was all Kevin and Hal Teller. I was just following orders. Swear to God."

"Hands together," says Gale, cinching the tie snugly, then yanking him to his feet.

Back to the garage behind Mendez, pushing Hudson along in front of him, Gale sees that Mindy is still sprawled over Vern, but now silent.

She rolls off him and plops cross-legged on the bloody concrete, her nightgown soaked with blood.

Looks with dazed eyes at the players surrounding her, settling on Mendez.

"You people don't know shit," Mindy says.

"Tell us what we don't know," says Mendez.

"We needed the money for the cancer. These pukes hired Vern, then turned on him when he started talking to you two. When you found the crystal cavern, they wanted you both dead. Vern said fuck that—Gale's okay, a jarhead sniper like me."

"Vern got Tarlow out to Caspers for the owl," says Gale.

"The great gray owl," says Mindy. "They're sacred. They don't exist here."

Gale holsters his gun, orders Grant Hudson to sit and stay, watches Mindy Jeffs contemplating the blood on her blue robe.

Mendez stares down, first at Vernon Jeffs, then at Kevin Elder, in their mingled pools of blood, with an air of dazed wonder.

The neighbors have gathered on the sidewalk across the street. Gale sees robes and flannels, long tees and shearling boots and cell screens held high, aglow in the night.

41

Just hours later, at first light in her humble Tustin home, Daniela showers off the dried sweat and blood, puts on jeans and her OC Sheriff's windbreaker for the October chill, and looks in on her sleeping son again.

Look at him, she thinks. Just look.

She takes a mug of coffee to the table in her small living room, watches the local news. Nothing about the fatal shootout in Huntington Beach yet, but two men with ties to the Aryan Brotherhood have been arrested for the murder of three Laotians out in the mountains near Wildcoast.

People with guns, thinks Mendez.

Fuck them all, but not us. Defund us not.

She's too weary to sleep, her mind scrolling through the last hours over and over but in random order:

Grant Hudson's Rivian crashing into the oil pump.

Fog and gunsmoke.

OCSD Internal Affairs Form 1-C Deputy-Involved Shootings.

Mindy's blood-smeared robe.

The suppressed bullet tearing through the heart of large Vernon Jeffs.

That smacking sound.

Kevin Elder's blue eyes and his gray widow's peak.

The jump of her pistol in her hands and the flicker of blood in the fluorescent lights as her and Gale's bullets went through him.

We needed the money for the cancer . . . these pukes hired Vern . . .

Wiping the blood off the soles of her Adidas on the thin brown lawn of the Jeffs's front yard.

"Morning, Mom."

"Jesse. You're up early."

"School. Remember?"

"Sit down. I want to talk to you."

Jesse gets a cup of coffee, loads it with creamer, and sits across from his mother. He's in his black-and-white flannel PJs, his shiny scalp recently shaven, his eyes fastened on hers.

"I know about the drone," she says. "I know about you and Bishop Buendia. I know you and Lulu have been running with Barrio Dogtown and I know from the counselor you've been cutting most of the few classes you have."

"How do you think you know all this?"

"Friends. People at work. Buendia's under surveillance by the gang squad, and you came up. Lunch at El Jardin. Drones and phones at El Salvador Park. You were observed to be a talented pilot."

Jesse blushes with what Daniela can only surmise is pride. "Your friends are all cops, Mom."

"A cop is what I am, Jesse. And your friends are all gangsters and wannabes. Such as yourself."

He swallows, his Adam's apple thickly bobbing.

"Well, about all that," he says. "So what?"

"What does Buendia want you to do with them, the drones and phones?"

"They're for rescue work in disaster zones. One of the things the bishop's Camp Refuge does is disaster relief in California. You know, like wildfires and floods and the fentanyl epidemic."

"So you shoot video and pictures from the sky?"

A smile and a nod. "Absolutely we will. The phones and drones are donated."

"Not stolen?"

"See, Mom? You imagine the worst in me, so that's what you see. All you *can* see. We'll be delivering food and survival blankets—the lightweight, silver ones."

"I see a lot of good in you, Jesse," says Mendez. "Intelligence. Light. Bigheartedness. Love."

"You hate Lulu."

"I hate what she wants you to become."

"You don't know anything about her or what we want together. Do you want me to move out?"

Daniela chokes back the painful lump in her throat. "Absolutely I do not. I love you more than life, Jesse, and I want you to be here as long as you want to be."

"Mom, either way that's not going to be long."

"Either way?"

"Whether I go now or later."

"Go where?" asks Daniela.

"Lulu's got family and friends in LA."

"Have you spent a single day in LA?"

Another blush, fueled not by pride, but by being exposed.

Jesse shrugs. "Maybe get away from Dogtown."

"Oh?" Daniela reaches across the scarred wooden table and sets her hand on her son's. She's surprised again by how much she doesn't know about him. *Maybe he's right*, she thinks. *Maybe I only imagine the worst and that is all I can see.* "That would be a good thing, Jesse."

"Even with Lulu?"

"Even," says Daniela.

"She's better than you think. Maybe even as good as you."

During her next few heartbeats, Daniela Mendez considers her life, her passion and seduction, her lies, her failing to protect her own son.

The story of my life, she thinks: circles and lines and knots.

I've got nothing on Lulu.

"Jesse, you said maybe move to LA. So, remember that college I've been telling you about? Azusa Catholic, run by Holy Martyr—my old parish, when I was your age. It's in LA County, Jess."

"I never liked my first Catholic school."

"Holy Martyr is different," says Daniela.

Is it ever.

He eyes her suspiciously. "Maybe. But I'd rather work and game than study."

"There's money to help pay for it."

And your father can get it, she thinks.

"I can live at Camp Refuge for free, Mom."

"While you run with Barrio Dogtown? No. I'm talking about a real school. Private. Nice dorms. Good faculty."

"Priests and nuns, Mom. Hell."

Jesse slides his hand out from under his mother's, stands. As does Daniela. Who looks across the table eye to eye with him, wondering how he's managed to grow four inches in one night.

All the things I do not see, she thinks, while I'm imagining the worst.

He heads down the hall.

"I love you, Jesse."

"Early auto shop, Mom. Muffler repair."

"Work tonight?"

"Oh yeah."

Daniela sleeps until five that afternoon, dreaming of shooting a man she knows but doesn't know, who gets up and tells her it's okay, I'm alright, just want to be your friend.

Again and again.

Until her phone vibrates on her nightstand.

TeenShield notifies her that Jesse has entered the forbidden Barrio Dogtown 'hood to which her son has become a frequent flyer.

Work tonight, my ass, she thinks.

Jumps into her Explorer and heads out.

Halfway to Dogtown, Daniela sees that Jesse is back on the move, southbound on Victor Street.

To Colton to Edgar.

Picking up Flaco Benitez and his drone and cell phone team?

Is Lulu with him?

Jesse heads onto First Street, then Santa Ana Boulevard.

Daniela follows the TeenShield GPU car icon, which enters her own stomping grounds: headquarters of the Orange County Sheriff's Department and Forensic Services buildings; the federal building and courts; Orange County courthouse; the county supervisors; the hulking, concrete Orange County jail.

When she pulls close to the blipping icon, she spots Jesse's shiny silver Corolla just four car lengths ahead, listing to starboard, probably, from the immense weight of Flaco "Skinny" Benitez in the front passenger seat.

Jesse stops at the parking structure across from the jail, punches in, takes a ticket, and waits for the arm to lift.

Daniela gives him two minutes to change his mind but the silver Corolla doesn't reappear.

A red Tesla sweeps past the rising arm and Daniela pulls up, pushes the button, and waits.

This is the hairy part: Jesse's going to make her black take-home Explorer if she doesn't spot him first.

Spying, distrusting Mom.

Busted.

TeenShield shows his car a hundred yards ahead, which seems

longer than the parking structure is wide, so Daniela figures part of that distance is *up*, not out.

The roof?

She plods along slowly, like someone looking for just the right space, some privacy, maybe, or to prevent door dings.

This late, the open parking places are many.

The higher she goes, the less cars.

Level four, spotty. Level five, nearly vacant.

She taps her brakes for a dusty silver Corolla, clearly not Jesse's.

Then: ROOF, and an arrow pointing up and right.

Daniela takes a level-five space, puts the ticket on the dash and a wide-brimmed sun hat on her head, locks up.

Through the open-air railing near the elevator, she sees two young men and Lulu on the roof, huddled with exaggerated casualness around Jesse, almost totally blocked by Flaco Benitez, blue sky and white clouds above them.

She recognizes the two men from the recent drone-and-phone mission at El Salvador Park.

Looks around for Bishop Buendia, sensing that he's hanging back, letting his foot soldiers do their thing, whatever that is. And, of course, letting them take the risk.

Her inner cop knows this is wrong: She's not close enough to note details, and she's not high up enough to see what a drone—once in flight and depending on its direction—might be flying toward.

She takes the elevator up one floor to the roof, exits quietly, her back to the boys and Lulu, sticking close to the safety railing, looking out and up as if enjoying this nice rooftop view, protected from the stunning sunset by her stylish hat. Pushes her thick black hair up under it.

Hears laughter from the gang, Lulu's soprano and Flaco's deep baritone.

Takes cover behind a security light stanchion and watches.

The others step away from Jesse, who lifts the drone for inspection. Daniela recognizes the red-and-black Raptor TX-395, fitted with what looks from here to be a smartphone, as before.

Lulu pulls Jesse's arm her way, adjusting the phone, then clapping her hands and jumping up and down in her little skirt. She pecks Jesse's lips and Flaco puts a hand on her back.

Daniela looks past the happy drone squad, recognizing the slot-windowed, forbidding jail buildings—Men's Central Jail to the south, and Women's Central Jail to the north. From her sixth-floor rooftop perch here, she's looking down on the largely barren rooftops—enormous air conditioners sprouting thick hoses and pipes, electrical junction boxes, structures that look like backyard tool sheds but she knows to be exits. The roof panels are gray and rain stained.

Then Flaco takes the drone and holds it out over the railing like offering a sacrifice. The propellors blur and the Raptor TX-395 lifts off from Flaco's big hands and, with the spindly lightness of a mosquito, rises into the sky.

Daniela watches her son, balancing the controller on the railing, and the drone, climbing toward the Men's Jail.

High over the jail now, the Raptor begins its descent.

Movement on the jail roof, then Daniela sees a man, clad in an orange jumpsuit, slip from one of the exits, drop to the gray, stained panels, and scuttle into the shade of a huge air conditioner.

Lulu turns and looks at her.

Daniela moves in tighter to the big stanchion.

And sees the drone circling lazily down, Jesse sidling along the railing to keep the visual, controller held out, his fingers assured on the buttons and the toggles and the tiny joystick.

Lulu has turned back to the action.

Mendez watches the drone settle onto the Men's Jail rooftop, not far from the inmate hidden in the AC's shadow. Its rotors slow to a stop.

The orange-clad man hops from the shade, kneels, and removes the smartphone from the Raptor gimbal suspender and slips it into a black waist pack.

Then dodges back into the shade of the air conditioner.

The Raptor lifts off and climbs again, rising from the rooftop in a loose spiral and leaning toward Jesse and his team.

Daniela is pretty sure she gets it now.

There will be another smartphone and another.

Smartphones being even more valuable in prisons and jails than good dope, strong liquor, breakout saws, or weapons.

Phones are how inmates who haven't seen the streets in years command them.

Such as Buendia's Mexican Mafia royalty in Pelican Bay.

The Bloods and Crips in prisons and jails up and down the state, the nation.

The Aryan Brotherhood.

The Asian gangs in Los Angeles and Orange Counties.

Smartphones, often smuggled into correction centers by enterprising guards, crooked lawyers, crafty family and friends.

In this case, however, smuggled in by wannabe banger Jesse and his idiot friends, in the employ of Bishop Buendia.

Free phones to important gangsters.

Or for sale to anyone at two thousand a pop.

Felonies both.

Mendez smiles. It's a bitter smile in her hard face but there's mirth in it, too.

Over the next fifteen minutes, she watches her son pilot four more smartphones to the inmate slipping in and out of the shadows of the Men's Central Jail roof.

"Jesse forgive me," she whispers. "But maybe I can trade Buendia for you and your bonehead friends."

She calls for backup, code red, no weapons on scene, tells Dispatch to run them in cold, no lights and sirens or we'll lose them.

Flashes of botched arrests and excess force shoot through Daniela with the adrenaline. "God, he's my son. Don't hurt him."

"The jail rooftop? Holy *shit*."

Lulu turns in Daniela's direction again, then she says something to Jesse, who ignores her, bringing the empty drone back from the jail.

Two minutes later, four Sheriff's Department cruisers come up the ramp and onto the roof, running silent.

She waves them toward the Corolla even though it's one of only three cars this high up, this late in the day.

Lulu pulls Jesse by the arm but he's still got the Raptor in the air.

The radio cars sweep across the parking slots, spreading out and slowing as they near Jesse's car.

Daniela strides toward Jesse with all of her considerable purpose and authority.

"Jesse! Lulu! *Freeze!*"

Flaco lumbers toward the stairs.

Six uniforms pile out, guns drawn.

Then two more, veering after Flaco.

Jesse faces the rushing deputies and lands the drone halfway between himself and them.

Sets down the controller and raises his hands.

As do the Dogtown boys.

Not Lulu, who raises something small and black and shiny, holding it away from her body.

Daniela sees that whether phone or gun, it really doesn't matter, it's enough to get her killed.

Jesse jumps and yanks the thing from Lulu's hand, and in this moment Daniela knows he's about to die. But Jesse stoops to backhand it across the concrete toward the closing deputies, the flat black phone skipping like a rock on a lake.

Flaco's gigantic white Nikes plop loudly on the concrete as his right hand burrows into the pocket of his hoodie.

"*Stop and down, big boy!*" one yells. "*Stop and get the fuck down!*"

Flaco stumbles but doesn't fall. Doesn't stop as ordered, either. Can't quite get his feet under him. Given his modest speed, he's still a long way from the stairway.

"*Freeze!*"

He pulls the gun from his pocket and points it at the deputies, who unleash a roaring storm of bullets.

He backpedals and collapses. Butt-flops, then backslaps to the floor, arms and legs spread wide.

42

Grant Hudson sings like a mockingbird to Gale and Mendez in the interview room at Men's Central Jail. They keep the donuts and Red Bulls coming, and Hudson will not shut up.

"Kevin tried to commission an exploratory dig years ago," he says. "Based on some Juaneño legend of gigantic crystals underground, with magical light and powers. Some shit he read in fourth grade, studying the missions. Had no idea what it was. No dice from Tarlow Company on that nonsense, but Kevin still thought there might be something to it."

Hudson then claims that once Elder learned what was down there—just a few weeks ago—he hired Vernon Jeffs to kill Tarlow. But he, Grant Hudson, had "absolutely nothing do with that," except driving the car in which Elder and Jeffs negotiated the terms of a sixty-thousand-dollar hit.

Hudson says Elder hired a lawyer to write the mineral rights agreement signed by Tarlow Company's managing partner, Hal Teller, and Elder Fund LLC, a shell company registered in Grand Cayman.

Hudson is happy to give them the executed document, signed by Hal Teller and Elder.

"Anything, for my favorite detectives," he says. "And, you know, for helping me plead down these hysterical and very untrue charges."

"Shouldn't be a problem," Mendez says, with a deadpan glance at Gale.

Hudson tells them the mineral rights agreement is in his personal safe-deposit box at Wells Fargo, and what it says is the Elder Fund will be paid 1 percent of Tarlow Company pretax revenue on the sale of lithium ore, crystals, and related materials for the remainder of Kevin Elder's life.

"Tarlow Company agreed to a ten-million-dollar minimum per year," says Hudson. "Once the mine is up and running. Paid quarterly. Hal Teller told us it would run a lot higher than that. Direct deposit."

"Did Hal Teller green-light Elder to kill Bennet?" asks Gale.

"No," says Hudson. "It was never discussed in that way. I could make something up if you want. But all Kevin and Teller talked about was that Wildcoast was Bennet's baby, and Kevin would have to find a way to convince him that a huge lithium mine would be more profitable and less risky than a utopia for millionaires."

"Enter Vern Jeffs and his great gray owl tale," says Gale.

"Yeah," says Hudson, pursing his lips. "Bennet was so smart but so naive."

Two days later Hudson pleads not guilty on charges ranging from conspiracy to commit murder to destruction of private property—the fence around the oil pump—makes bail on Seventh District funds and returns to work just an hour later, where he is placed on paid administrative leave.

Gale and Mendez climb down the courthouse steps and into the dazzling Orange County sunlight.

"He's dreaming," says Mendez. "Knox won't make a deal with him."

"No, Knox would rather eat him alive at trial," says Gale. "Great publicity in an election year."

Gale walks Mendez to her car in the sheriff's lot.

"How's Jesse?"

"He's talking to us about Bishop Buendia and the drones and phones."

Gale nods, pondering this.

"Brave, but risky, fingering Buendia," he says.

"Grand jury," Mendez says. "Sealed testimony. No public disclosure."

"We're talking eMe and hundreds of street soldiers."

"I know, I know. Big picture though, Jesse's good, Lew. I've got a plan. I'll fill you in later."

"And how are you holding up, Daniela?"

"I'm exhausted."

"Take a trip," he says.

"I've got one planned."

"You've earned it."

"And how about you, Lew?"

"I have a trip planned, too."

She smiles and climbs into the black Explorer SUV.

43

Jesse buries himself in his phone as Daniela heads up the freeway for Orange.

She holds her red Corvette to five mph over the speed limit, feels that lovely powerful rumbling in her gut.

For the first time in her adult life, she feels happiness is coming to get her, just around the corner.

Almost literally.

Jesse hasn't said much to her for three days now, since his arrest in the parking structure and bailing out. He's been gaming in his room, texting with Lulu and three friends from school, according to TeenShield, which she monitors studiously, even when her son is in his room.

She feels his emotions strongly. His numbness and detachment and isolation. But he carries no rage that she detects. She expects him to disappear from home suddenly and completely, but quietly.

Just as she did when it became obvious that the almost Virgin Dani would be giving birth.

Simply a matter of moving from one world to another, enlarging her four dimensions into five.

Reconstituted, reconfigured, reborn.

Is there a ray of light in all his numbness and isolation? she wonders.

Yes, Jesse's willingness to appear before a grand jury to answer questions about Bishop Buendia has taken Daniela by surprise. She thought that his fear of Buendia and the Mexican Mafia, and his apparent loyalty to the Barrio Dogtown Vatos might blunt his instinct for self-preservation.

Not so, she thinks.

Is Jesse finally learning to think for himself?

How can you think for yourself if you don't know who you are?

But it would be a miracle, she thinks, one of the many that she has prayed for, regarding her only begotten son.

She pulls into the driveway of Father Tim's tract home in Orange, stops at the gate. Notes that the high wall of white oleander is freshly trimmed.

The gate rolls open and Daniela parks in front of the closed two-car garage.

Jesse looks up from his phone, studies the neat fifties ranch-style house.

"What's this? Why are we here?"

"There's someone who wants to meet you. Come with me, Jesse."

He sighs, sweeps his phone, searches for the Corvette door pull, which is inset and hard to see.

When he gets the door open, Daniela is waiting. She takes his hand and helps him unfold from the low, sleek cabin.

"What's that smell?"

"Orange blossoms. The world used to smell this way."

"Hmm."

Jesse sees the tall man waiting on the porch, the front door open behind him.

Jesse steps onto the porch with his mother.

Studies the man's somehow familiar blue eyes, his thick black hair brushed back and peppered with gray, his blue jeans and running shoes, his dumb-looking pink tennis shirt with the crocodile on it.

"Jesse," says Daniela. "Meet Timothy Malone, your father."

44

Gale and Dylan Deming throw the football back and forth on the Capistrano Valley High School field on a breezy Saturday morning in November.

He's a chunky ten-year-old, straight black hair to his shoulders, five-feet two-inches tall already, a hundred and fifteen pounds. Baggy yellow shorts, a Cougars tee, red running shoes.

Gale's impressed by his balance and sure feet, and his strong delivery of a regulation PACWest college football, which was Gale's introductory gift to him just three weeks ago.

Handy with a football, indeed.

Nice spirals, occasionally.

"Put it out in front of me!" calls Gale, cutting across the deep green turf to snag the boy's wobbling pass.

Gale pulls up and lofts the ball back to Dylan, who barrels forward and smothers it and hurls it back in a high, beautiful spiral.

Gale turns and runs under it, looking back over his shoulder, watching the brown ball descend through the blue autumn sky. He ignores the tug of his old scars, the fragments still there inside him long overgrown by his flesh, a part of him now.

Makes the grab.

They sit in the bleachers and swill athletic drinks.

"Next Sunday I can take you on patrol," Gale says. "Show you my old beat, when I first got on with the sheriff's."

"Good."

"Maybe get lunch after. Santa Ana's got top-notch taquerias."

Dylan Deming, a stout boy of few words, nods.

Gale, not much of a chatterbox himself, watches a silver jet climbing from John Wayne Airport, its white tail dissolving.

What is there to say?

"I like hanging with you."

Dylan nods again, looking up at the jet.

Gale drives him home, watches the big boy lumber toward his apartment, on the porch of which his mother waits.

Dylan stops and turns and holds up his ball up for Gale.

A trophy, he thinks.

Gale sits on a hilltop boulder out near Caspers Wilderness Park, looking down at what was once to be the city of Wildcoast and is now a gaping cavity brimming with orange-vested, hard-hatted miners with battery-powered jackhammers.

They swarm in and out of the mine on four different staircases rather than the single one that Gale, Mendez, and Geronima used just a few short weeks ago.

From this distance they look like ants, excavating the earth one grain of sand at a time.

Beyond the huge pit, at the base of the mountains where Gale had looked into the tan eyes of the Killer Cat, enormous earthmovers and backhoes now rip the mine wider and deeper. Gale hears the distant roar of their diesels and the violent shear of iron on rock. Sees the black exhaust rising and disappearing into the gray sky.

He lowers his binoculars and pictures the cathedral of lithium crystals. He remembers the strange, almost silver light down there, the bone-littered beach of an underground ocean under his feet. It's hard for Gale to convince himself he actually saw it. He wonders how far and deep it will prove to be, with the help of these industrious, well-equipped ants.

All the way to the Pacific, then under?

The cavern of crystals below the earth that is a resting place for spirits on their way to the afterlife.

Legend is truth, and truth is legend.

Sacred places, thinks Gale.

Full of fortune beyond measure, that will give us ants the energy to devour the world that gives us life.

A sleek silver helicopter lowers from the sky into the rising diesel exhaust of the excavators.

Through his binoculars Gale recognizes the Tarlow Company logo, a stout green oak tree standing alone on a plain of yellow earth.

The chopper circles and lands, and old Hal Teller hunches under the blades as he trots through the swirling dust.

Gale notes the wobble in Teller's eighty-year-old body, pant legs flapping.

He glasses the boulder-strewn mountains surrounding the pit and sees the Killer Cat lying high in a patch of sun, not far from where he saw him that first day.

The age-bleached face and chewed ear, the tan eyes.

The big cat looks down at the excavators, then yawns and rolls slowly onto his back, wriggling his rump on the warm ground, tail flicking.

45

Later, Gale and Geronima walk the beach at Crystal Cove up in Newport. The afternoon is cool and gray, and the offshore wind blows crowns of spray off the waves.

Geronima ignores the NO DOGS ON STATE BEACH sign. Hulk streaks, shrieking, his leash splashing the sand behind him as the gulls reluctantly lift off and relocate.

Gale looks south to the great cliff on which the Tarlow mansions tower over the ocean below. Pictures happy Tarlow and beautiful Norris Kennedy in Vegas for that fight. Pictures them in exotic parts of the world, chasing their spectacular birds. Pictures Tarlow trying to get a good flash shot of the great gray owl and her young in the nest that night, as behind him new bird buddy Vernon Jeffs brings a gun to his head.

They walk the mile north to a restaurant and by the time they start back after dinner the sun is low in the west.

Orange sunlight hits mansion windows. And hits the sand on which they walk, as their ancients walked.

Geronima beside him, wind in her shiny black hair, tired Hulk at heel beside her.

This is what you get, Gale thinks.

This is what you need.

ACKNOWLEDGMENTS

I'd like to thank Mark Owen Gottlieb, Trident Media Group senior vice president and agent, for his insightful early read of this novel.

And Kristin Sevick, Minotaur Books editor, for her perspicacious editing, enthusiasm, and general good humor.

Also, my thanks to Evan T. Pritchard, founder of the Center for Algonquin Culture, for his detailed and very helpful notes on the Indigenous Acjacheme people of California, who inspired, inhabit, and haunt this novel.

Last, but always first, thanks to Rita Parker, who always sees what I am trying to see, and finds a way to explain it to me.

AUTHOR'S NOTE

The spirit and history of the Acjacheme people of Southern California helped inspire this book.

Often called "Juaneños" because of their eighteenth-century relationship with Mission San Juan Capistrano in Orange County, California, the Acjacheme rarely refer to themselves in that way. They have for centuries ignored the Juaneño label.

Most of my research for this novel is from the books and articles about the Mission Indians, of which the Acjacheme are one tribe. They are not recognized by the federal government, and the State of California has no official "recognition" laws or policies for native Californians.

The best book I found is Stephen O'Neil's *The Acjachemen (Juaneño) Indians of Coastal Southern California*. Wonderful stuff.

I used the writings of Pablo Tac, who was a Luiseño native (associated with Mission San Luis Rey; just as the Acjacheme are associated with nearby Mission San Juan Capistrano). These two tribes played each other in lacrosse-like games, and made war upon each other, and intermarried. The friars of San Luis Rey took the fiercely intelligent Pablo Tac to Italy as a fourteen-year-old, where he studied at the College of the Propogation of the Faith in Rome, writing in both Luiseño and Spanish about his life in and around the mission in the early nineteenth century. His writings, later translated into English, are illuminating. Pablo died in Italy at the age of nineteen.

Also, I used *Chinigchinich*, a booklet written in the early 1800s by Friar Geronimo Boscana, focusing on both Acjacheme and Luiseño peoples. It's an odd and contradictory book, vivid and passionate but condescending, and very clear on the idea that Spaniards like himself created the missions of California to convert the natives to Christianity and recruit them into enlightened lives as citizens and subjects of Spain.

In order to give a voice to the Acjacheme—whose existence in California can be traced back some five thousand years—I created a character in *Wild Instinct* who tells his story about helping to build Mission San Juan Capistrano. His name is Luis Verdad, and he relates a harrowing hunt for a mountain lion that has carried off his little sister.

I've wandered around these missions for hours. Restored, they are old and beautiful places, alive with history and art and the Catholic Church. They are also the stately reminders guarding the sometimes dark and shameful collision between the California natives and their European, American, and Mexican "masters."

ABOUT THE AUTHOR

Rita Parker

T. Jefferson Parker is the author of numerous novels and short stories, the winner of three Edgar Awards (for *Silent Joe*, *California Girl*, and the short story "Skinhead Central"), and the recipient of a Los Angeles Times Book Prize for best mystery (*Silent Joe*). Before becoming a full-time novelist, he was an award-winning reporter. He lives in Fallbrook, California.